Copyright 2024 Cal Clement

All Rights Reserved

With the exception of certain historical events and notable figures, the characters and events portrayed within are fictitious. Any similarities to real persons, alive or dead, are coincidental and not intended by the author.

No part of this book may be reproduced or stored in a retrieval system or transmitted in any form or by any means, electronic, mechanical, photocopying, recording or otherwise without express written permission of the author.

ISBN-978-1-7376655-7-1

Cover Artist: Juan Padron

This book is dedicated to my Great-Grandfather, who I was named after.

Calvin Clement

He was a man of love, honor, resilience, hard work, and duty. His example serves as a shining beacon that persists through generations.

A Bloody Beginning
By Cal Clement

"I have not yet begun to fight."
 -John Paul Jones

A Bloody Beginning

Part One

A Bloody Beginning

CHAPTER 1

4th March 1770
Boston Harbor

Columns of late afternoon sun broke through hazy overhead clouds and lit the waters of Boston's harbor as a ship angled her way in from the open ocean. As the ship turned southwest, its sails fluttered briefly while sailors rushed to adjust them in the rigging. A heartbeat later the canvas snapped taut, and the ship made her way further into the harbor.

"She's a whaler, Tom. In from the North Atlantic to sell her oil before heading back out again." Jack Horner said to his friend as they both sat with their feet dangling from the edge of Long Wharf.

Tom, the son of a shipwright, shook his head. "She's a tender, Jack. Whalers have a high bow for breaking waves and low railing and gunwales to aid in harvesting oil from the whale's blubber. The whalers don't bring in the oil themselves, they offload it to tenders so that they can keep on the hunt."

Jack smirked at his friend and lifted himself up to stand on the pier. His legs were stiff from the cold and from sitting on the hard planks for most of the afternoon. "You are an insufferable know it all, Tom. It's no wonder I am your only friend."

Tom laughed and hoisted himself up from his seat on the pier. "I don't know everything. Just a fair amount about ships. It goes with growing up in a shipyard. I'm sure if I came to your father's shop and started blurting out nonsense, you would become an insufferable know it all too."

Jack rolled his eyes at his friend before turning to start his long walk back to his father's shop. "Why would anyone want to pass the time sitting in a blacksmith's shop?"

"It's warm, at least," Tom offered with a playful punch at Jack's shoulder.

Jack nodded as the two young men plodded along toward the shore end of the pier. "Warm, it is. Stifling is more like it, stifling and smoky. But, if it is a tender ship, like you say, I imagine my father will want to bring down a few of the harpoons he has been turning. They fetch decent coin, and it has been a while since he has sold any."

"He might want to hurry, Jack. Those tenders don't linger in port long, especially when the whalers are on a good streak. She'll be making sail

A Bloody Beginning

by tomorrow evening, if not turning with the morning tide."

Jack narrowed his eyes and looked over his shoulder at the ship sailing its way toward the pier they were walking on. "That soon?"

"The captain makes his coin by hauling in the harvested oil and selling needed goods picked up in port. Once he unloads the whale oil and takes on fresh dry goods and water, every hour spent in port is an hour wasted. Your father would do well not to waste any time," Tom said with a sigh as the two friends reached the end of the pier and crossed onto a cobble paved street.

"I'll be sure to let him know," Jack replied over his shoulder as he turned up Anne's Street. He cast a long glance over his shoulder at the long row of masts protruding high above their respective ships. His heart was filled with joy from the afternoon spent visiting with his friend and watching the seagoing vessels move in and out of the harbor. The idea of a sailor's life excited him with adventure. He marveled at all the different vessels and their various rigging. He took every opportunity he could to watch ships as they traversed the harbor or listen to the sailors on their forays into town. It drove his father mad.

"They are stepping a new main mast on that Brit man of war in the yard tomorrow, you should come by and see," Tom called as the two friends parted company.

A Bloody Beginning

Jack's inside fluttered with excitement. He had never seen the yard crews step a mast before. "I'll be by. First thing?"

"No," Tom answered, "it will take them most of the morning to get her in position before they step it. I'd say around noon they will start rigging to lift."

"I'll be by if I can," Jack called back. "I may be busy running errands for my father."

He turned up Anne's Street and pulled at the lapels of his wool coat. It had belonged to his father at one point, so there were a couple of holes in the right sleeve and one just under the arm along the side seam. His mother had mended it as best she could, but the stitching that held the hole under the arm was coming loose. Evening was setting in, and the skies were growing darker. It wouldn't be long before his father doused the forge fire and hung up his hammer for the night. Jack decided he would take the long way back and meet his mother as she finished her labor for the day. He knew if he walked his mother back to his father's shop and thus shortened his walk home at the end of the day it would please him.

He took a left on King Street and walked to the intersection of Shrimpton Lane, where his mother worked in a tailor's shop near the corner. The smell of wood smoke and cooking food lingered in the evening as the air grew colder. Jack came to a halt outside of the shop and peeked into the window. Warm yellow light from an oil lamp in the front room spilled through the large pane of

A Bloody Beginning

glass out into the street. Jack could see his mother in her plain gray woolen dress with her dark hair tied up into a messy knot. She was holding up a bright red coat trimmed in blue piping with brass buttons on the lapels and the shoulders. Jack hunched his shoulders against the cold and watched his mother hang the garment onto a wooden frame. The tailor, Mr. Albright, came into the front room from a dimly lit corridor that led back to a pair of sewing rooms, a small office and an even smaller storage room. Jack despised the tailor his mother had to endure for her wages. He was a tight-faced old Brit who had come to the colonies to inflict them with his condescending tone. Or, that was what Jack's father had said. Not only was Mr. Albright a tailor, but he was also a landowner. He owned the shop Jack's mother worked in, as well as a tavern up the street. In addition, Mr. Albright also owned more than half a dozen homes in the Boston area, one of which Jack and his parents had the misfortune of being tenants in. Jack's father often lamented that his blacksmith shop was better insulated against the wind than their drafty one room home, and when it rained, as it often did in Boston, the roof kept out only a fraction of the downpour. Mr. Albright stood in the shadowy corridor entrance as rigid as the garment frame that held the Royal Army officer's uniform coat. It appeared there was an exchange between him and Jack's mother as the boy looked in through the window, thus unnoticed by either party inside the tailor shop.

A Bloody Beginning

Jack's mother dipped her head for a moment as Mr. Albright said something and gestured toward a stack of red uniform coats piled on a table. Then, just as Jack was surrendering to a long wait in the cold while his mother worked late, he saw his mother's figure go rigid through the glass. Mr. Albright had stepped close to her. He raised one hand and ran it over his jaw before shaking his head and walking out of the room and back into the darkened corridor.

"You beat me to it, boy," Jack heard the voice of his father over his shoulder. He glanced back and noticed the strained expression of exhaustion and coldness.

"Yes, sir," Jack answered, "I thought if I could walk mother over to your shop it would save you the trip over here."

Jack's father smiled, and he plopped a hand on Jack's shoulder. "I appreciate it boy, but the walk to pick her up from work doesn't grieve me, even when the wind bites bitterly. I take joy in it, but not near as much joy as it gives me to see you looking out for her as well." He grimaced and looked through the pane of the shop's front window. "Does it look like she will be done soon? Or is that stuffy old bastard going to make us wait around in the cold all night?"

Jack cupped his hands together and blew into them to ward off the bite of the cold on his fingers. "No. I think she will be out soon, though Mr. Albright does seem to be rather upset about something."

A Bloody Beginning

Jack's father pulled the collar of his coat high and folded his arms together. He rubbed his hands and blew into them in the same fashion Jack had. "He is always upset about one thing or another, son. Some men are just that way. They have no joy in this life and so they feel they must rob others of it as well. It is not a path to aspire to."

Inside the glass window of the tailor shop, Jack watched as his mother pulled on her wool coat and made for the door. A bell rang as she opened the door and came outside before carefully closing it behind herself.

"How lovely to have such fine-looking men to escort me home," Jack's mother said with a broad, bright smile. "I apologize for the wait. Mr. Albright wanted me to stay late and work on the officer coats he took in today. There has been quite the influx the last few days. Navy officers, Army officers and regular soldiers, there must be three dozen uniform coats in there."

"I'm sure they will still be there in the morning," Jack's father said with a devilish grin. "Mr. Albright should consider his backlog before taking in more work. This isn't the first time he has put himself in this predicament."

Jack's mother gave her husband a resigned look. "It isn't, but I feel like he has gotten weary of me refusing to stay late. The other ladies do so without hesitation."

"Or extra pay," Jack muttered before he could stop himself.

"Jack!" His mother scolded.

A Bloody Beginning

"Colleen," Jack's father said as he wrapped an arm around her shoulders. "The boy is right. He demands extra labor but offers no extra pay. It isn't fitting for him to get something for nothing when the rest of us toil and pay extra at every turn. He accounts the crown's extra taxes for his raising our rent this past winter, but he offers no raise in wages in his own shop. He can't take both ways."

Jack's mother rolled her head onto his father's shoulder. "Try telling him that, dear. He acts as if our wages are a charity as it is."

"If he offered an extra wage, I would understand," Jack's father said with a bit of grumble in his voice. "But, he is doing us no favors at any rate. I'm sure there will be some more demand for my work soon." He turned toward Jack and furrowed his brow into a frown. "Maybe your friend's father has need of a good smith. The shipwright?"

Jack nodded. He knew what was coming next. "Tom's father? He may. I can ask him. They employ their own smith in the shipyard though."

Jack's father grinned and nodded. "Of course they do. And, how is your friend faring? Did you see him today while you were loitering down on the pier?"

Jack felt his chest tighten. "You knew I was down on the pier?"

Jack's father shook his head and looked down at the ground as they walked up Shrimpton Lane toward the market square. "I didn't. But, I do

A Bloody Beginning

now," His father paused and Jack knew he was searching for patience. "If you continue to evade school, you will fall behind in your lessons. Schooling may not seem as important or exciting as watching ships in and out of the harbor, but I promise you it is. Grammar and figures, son, and a touch of history and literature. You are robbing yourself and nobody else. The harbor will be there when you finish your studies, as will the ships sailing in and out of it. Would you rather be the carpenter, or the shipwright?"

Jack shrugged and kicked at a small stone. "I'm not sure. I think I would like to be a sailor."

"Better an officer than a deck hand, Jack," His mother chimed. "Their wages, and their comforts are a stretch better. Education is what separates them."

"I think the seafaring professions are good, honorable, honest ones, Jack. I really do. But, whether you sail for the navy, or on a merchant ship, or a whaler, either as an officer or a regular sailor, it is a hard life, for sure."

Jack's heart nearly seized at the mention of whaling ships. "Father, I forgot to mention. One of the ships we saw come into the harbor today was a tender ship for the whaling fleet. I thought you might be able to sell the harpoons you made."

The trio made a few paces in silence and Jack's father shifted his gaze from the street in front of them to his son. "A tender, you say?"

A Bloody Beginning

"According to Tom, yes," Jack replied. "He did say that it would most likely sail soon, possibly even with the morning tide."

Jack's father remained silent as they continued from Shrimpton's Lane across an open market square toward the intersection of Union Street and St. Anne Street. Their breath left plumes of vapor in the cold as the last rays of daylight faded from the sky. The yellow glow of oil streetlamps lit the way and the smell of wood smoke grew ever thicker in the night air.

"I have a dozen of those harpoons," Jack's father said to no one in particular, "and the last time I sold them, they netted us nearly four pounds apiece. I can't let an opportunity like that pass us by, we dearly need the coin."

Jack's mother drew a deep breath and released it in a sigh. "Dear. Does this mean that you won't be joining us for dinner?"

Jack's father shook his head. "Not at all, my love," He paused and looked over toward the darkened harbor. "In fact, I think we may be able to serve two needs with one trip this evening. How would the two of you like to have a tavern supper down by the pier tonight?"

"Killian, we can hardly afford it," Jack's mother protested.

"Not if I sell those harpoons, my love. I could pay our inflated rent for two months and have enough for us to enjoy a nice hot meal prepared by someone else. That is, if you don't mind parting from your escorts for an hour or so." Jack's father

A Bloody Beginning

offered a smile and a wink as he tried to soothe his wife's objections.

"Which tavern were you thinking?"

"Where else? The New Englander. They always have a hot stew on and good dark ale besides, or if you prefer, my dear, you could get a seafood dish," Jack's father said in a voice laden with excitement. "Jack and I will fetch up the wares from the shop. I think between the two of us, we should be able to carry them. We will take them down to that tender ship and bring back a haul of wages. What do you say, my dear?"

Jack looked his mother over. The soft angles of her face betrayed an edge of excitement as well. "I will go to The New Englander and get us a table. Meet me there when you are finished, and we can enjoy our supper together."

"Splendid," Jack's father exclaimed. He turned to Jack with widened eyes. "Now, boy. We must hurry. We can't be keeping your mother waiting on us all night."

"Yes, sir," Jack replied as his father turned and shot up the street in a hurried rush that bordered between a fast walk and a near run.

"Do you think you can carry six of those harpoons, boy?" Jack's father asked as his shoes ground into the cold stone of the street.

Jack nodded, even though his father's stare was locked straight ahead. "Yes, sir. I can."

Jack's father increased his pace and leaned forward at the waist into long strides that seemed to stretch further with every step. "We'll see.

A Bloody Beginning

Whatever you can't carry, I will take myself. Though if we can each carry six, we'll manage to haul the load in just one trip."

"We can do it, father. Last time you sold eight, and I carried four. I can carry two more." Jack said between forced breaths that plumed vapor into the night.

"Last time," Jack's father replied, "I sold eight. In that you are correct. But, I remember relieving you of one of your share before we reached the wharf." He turned and shot Jack a wry smile. "But, that was near a year ago. Let's see if time and toil has lent any additional strength to your arm, boy."

Jack shook his head. His father forgot nothing. Especially when it came to labor. He tried to keep pace with the long strides as they crossed St. Anne's Street again and turned up a narrow alley where his father's shop sat nestled in between a storage warehouse and a cooper's workshop. The stone street turned to hard, frozen mud beneath their feet as they made their way up the alley. They passed a livery and a saddle maker's shop, a butcher shop, and the workshop of a weaver who specialized in nets and net pots for catching lobster. A rattle of iron keys echoed through the narrow alley as Jack and his father finally approached the blacksmith shop.

"If I had more time, and iron, I would try to turn a few more," Jack's father said through a ragged breath.

"How long does each one take?" Jack asked.

A Bloody Beginning

Jack's father shook his head as he clicked his key in the thick padlock that held together a heavy chain threaded through a hole in the weathered timbers of the double doors. "Hours too long, and I wouldn't want to keep your mother waiting at the New Englander. She would skin me alive."

Jack smiled as his father disappeared into the depths of the blacksmith shop. He tried to imagine his mother being that cross with his father. Sitting in the New Englander for hours only to have them not arrive would certainly do the trick. His smile faded as his father reappeared with an armload of cold iron rods with barbed spear points on their ends.

"Here is your share, boy," Jack's father said in a throaty breath before disappearing back into the shop. Jack took the bundle and hefted them onto one shoulder. The ends were heavy. Never before had he carried six of the deadly instruments at one time. Their weight dug into his shoulder, and he could feel the hard iron digging into his flesh even through his winter layers. He regretted his previous bravado. The wharf was a long walk, and his hands were already cold from holding the bundle of iron rods balanced on his shoulder. He dared not complain. Something inside of him burned to make it to the wharf without having to ask for his father's aid. But the heavy iron weighing on his shoulder taunted him, and it seemed so far from where he stood.

With a clanging rattle, Jack's father materialized from the darkness within his shop. He carried a

A Bloody Beginning

stack of six harpoons over one shoulder as if he had hoisted a half empty laundry sack. Jack noted no strain on his father's face, only a cheerful grin and a wide-eyed look of determination.

"Let me lock up and we'll be off," his father said. "Which pier did the tender ship make berth at?"

"Long Wharf, near the end opposite the shipyards," Jack answered while adjusting the stack of iron on his shoulder. It was a long walk, and he had already tried to shift the haul twice because of the concentrated load digging at his collarbone.

Jack's father clamped the thick padlock shut while simultaneously balancing his own load of harpoons across one shoulder. He turned and faced Jack with a grin. "Alright, boy. Let's sell this lot and reap our wages. Keep up, now. I don't want to keep your mother waiting."

Crunches of leather soles pattering on frozen mud echoed between the vacated shops lining the alleyway. The cold night air bit at Jack's nose and burned his throat as he stretched his legs in strides to match his father's. At first, he kept up with the hurried pace. Down the alley they went, bent forward and lunging each stride to cover as much ground as possible. After the first block, Jack pulled the knitted wool cap from his head. The cold bit at his ears but his exertion had caused a thin layer of sweat to form around his brow and at the collar of his shirt. The iron dug at his shoulder and pressed the flesh so hard that he felt like it would leave a permanent indentation. He

A Bloody Beginning

imagined himself deformed from the heavy load with a permanent hunch in his back and a deep depression in his shoulder.

"Keep up, boy, those sailors could shove off at any time," Jack's father chided over one shoulder as he crossed St. Anne's Street at a near run. "If we miss them on your account, you will pay the rent for the next two months, and explain to your mother why we aren't eating at The New Englander tonight."

A fire rose in Jack's gut. He remembered what Tom had said. The tender ship could set sail as early as the morning tide. He had mentioned nothing about them leaving the same night they had arrived. But, there would be no reasoning or negotiating with his father. Once the stubborn Irish blacksmith had his mind set on something, he set his course and pushed with reckless abandon. If the tender ship was moored in hell, Jack's father would plow right through fiery gates and over the top of the devil himself to get to it. His legs burned. Sweat rolled from his brow and chilled as it ran down the skin of his face and neck. His lungs ached from the cold air. The tinny taste of blood rose in the back of his throat as he beat forward step after step. His father drew further ahead so Jack redoubled his efforts to keep pace. The iron harpoons seemed to increase in weight.

St. Anne's Street ended, and Jack's father made a left turn just before reaching Shrimpton Lane. They followed the edge of the market square before turning onto Merchant's Lane. Long Wharf

A Bloody Beginning

lay just half a block ahead. Jack shifted the harpoons on his shoulder. The smell of the sea invaded his nose as Jack's shoes finally clattered onto the timber planks of Long Wharf. His chest felt like it would explode with pride. He only had a few hundred more feet to go, and he would prove that his claim of being able to carry the load hadn't just been boastful bravado.

Sailors milled about the long wooden boardwalk. Some were passing from ship-to-ship trading goods or gossip while others made their way into town to enjoy a night ashore in a comfortable bed with a decent meal in their belly. Jack couldn't take the time he normally would have to marvel at each vessel as he and his father made their trek toward the tender ship near the end of the wharf. The chatter of sailors and bells mixed in his ears, whistles piped, timbers creaked and groaned, orders were called out and repeated. Under the weight of the iron harpoons, he lifted his head to look forward. She was still moored right where he had seen her as he had left the pier. Her masts jutted up proudly into the night sky. The pier next to her was a buzzing frenzy of activity. Sailors had formed a line and were handing heavy canvas sacks from one man to another up a gangplank while a load of barrels were being swung over the ship's gunwales in a web of netted rope suspended from a yardarm.

"Keep hold, you swine," a graveled voice called out, "those barrels hold your damned wages and mine."

A Bloody Beginning

Jack's father finally relented his pace as they drew close to the large tender ship. He hefted the load of harpoons down from his shoulder and set their blunt ends on the frosted timbers of the pier and gave Jack a nod of approval that filled him with a burst of pride so potent, the harpoons on his shoulder seemed to lose their cumbersome weight. Jack lowered his own load of harpoons to the decking at his feet in the same manner his father had and stood in stark amazement at the bustle of activity on the ship and pier.

"Excuse me, sir," Jack's father called over the din of activity. "But, I have some wares you may be interested in before you put out to sea."

The sailor who had been shouting about barrels and wages looked over the tender ship's railing and cocked an eyebrow at Jack and his father. He was a stout man, taller than Jack's father and broader in the shoulders. He wore a close-cropped beard and sported thick chops that protruded from beneath his knit cap. His face was weathered from too many days in the sun and wind, but he flashed a smile that Jack judged to be friendly.

"Harpoons?" the sailor asked in a shout.

"Yes, I have a dozen of them," Jack's father called back.

The sailor nodded his head and pursed his lips together. "A dozen. Is that all?"

A roll of laughter carried across the deck of the tender ship and Jack instantly felt a flush of embarrassment on behalf of his father. His fists clenched around the cold iron of the harpoons.

A Bloody Beginning

"Well, the last time I sold these, the sailor who paid me asked if I had more. I thought I would come better prepared this time," Jack's father said with a shrug. "How many will you take?"

"I'm sure the captain will want all of those and more to boot," the sailor replied with a broad grin of stained teeth. "Say, are you the smith who turns them with a bladed double barb?"

"I am, sir," Jack's father answered. Jack felt the tension of his rising anger subside as he realized the sailor's jab was meant in good humor.

"Aye, those will do. The whalers were asking about your harpoons. I believe the captain was going to send a search party into town to try and track down who made the last set." The sailor looked up at the suspended web of ropes while a pair of men eased the load they were carrying over the pier with a guide line. "We have a few dozen more barrels to unload. But I suppose I could fetch up the captain from his cabin. Wait there. I'll be right back."

Jack's father turned to him. A broad smile covered his face. "Perhaps it is not such a bad thing that you spent your afternoon at the wharf, son. This stroke of fortune may well tide us through the hardest part of the spring."

Jack grinned back at his father. "Does this mean I can forgo my afternoon lessons?"

Jack's father playfully jabbed him on the shoulder. "Not a chance, boy."

CHAPTER 2

4th March 1770
Boston

    "There are foul winds blowing, and if we aren't careful, we will all be caught in the storm," said a man huddled over his table in the corner of The New Englander. With one hand, he clenched onto a plain wooden tankard while with the other he picked at the food on his plate. His companions seemed to be largely ignoring his rantings, but the tone of his voice had caught Jack's attention from where he sat with his parents. "Taxes upon taxes from the crown, all to refill the coffers of a king who got where he is by stealing and killing. And what does he do when his unjust grab for money causes unrest amongst the populace? He sends his soldiers over in droves to march through our streets and further disrupt our lives! I say enough is enough. A man cannot make himself a living under these conditions." His pudgy, unshaven face was red from consumption and the fervor he had worked himself into during the course of his conversation with his dinner companions. One of the man's friends touched at his arm and whispered something. They both looked over at Jack who realized he had been caught staring.

"Jack?" The voice of his mother caught his attention.

"Yes, mother. I am sorry, I couldn't help overhearing that man and got distracted," Jack said shifting his attention back to his parents and the bowl of stew in front of him.

"Your father said that you carried half of the harpoons all the way from the shop to the wharf. That is quite a feat for a boy your age," Jack's mother said with a smile. "You should be proud."

"That was a man's work, and he did his share without a stitch of complaint," Jack's father said, while lifting his tankard to praise him. "I couldn't be prouder."

Jack felt his chest swell with pride. He felt a little taller sitting next to his mother and father over a shared meal of hot stew and freshly baked bread. The New Englander seemed to grow a little smaller as a group of British soldiers filtered their way in and took up seats at a table near the door.

"God damned red coated swine…" said the man who had been complaining earlier. "We ought to club them over the head and toss them into the

A Bloody Beginning

harbor. King's men, huh? We'll see how loyal they are when musket balls are flying."

Jack couldn't help but look over as the man's words grew angrier and louder. A silent tension fell over the lamplit dining room and Jack noticed he wasn't the only person staring at the disgruntled diner.

"Finish your meal, boy," Jack's father muttered. "We need to be leaving."

Jack took a spoonful of his stew and chased it with a large bite of the warm bread. The meal was a far cut richer than he was used to. Not for a lack of culinary skill on his mother's part, more so that his parents often could not afford more than a few ingredients at a time. And the cost of spices and seasoning had gotten so high in the last couple of years, they were oft seen as a luxury that his father was hesitant to part with any coin on them. The stew was thick with tender bits of beef that were no doubt from a far choicer cut than his parents could normally afford, and laden with an assortment of vegetables cooked to perfection. The bread, slathered with butter sweetened by honey, was soft and warm with a sweetness all of its own. Jack wolfed hungrily at his food as he sensed the confrontation was going to escalate and prompt his father to cut the rare meal short.

One of the redcoats seemed to be paying close attention to the table next to Jack and his parents. He looked over several times as he and his fellow soldiers waited for their meal and ales. Tension washed through the room while the whispers of

A Bloody Beginning

the disgruntled man's dinner companions became more audible as he grew angrier at the sight of the soldiers.

"I spoke with a fisherman up in Salem the other day. He said that not only are they quartering soldiers with families in their homes, he told me there are rumors of press gangs," the disgruntled man seethed over his tankard.

"Soldiers quartered in homes that aren't yours and secondhand rumors are not grounds to start a fight here tonight. You have had enough to drink, Todd. Let's go, before something happens," said one of the disgruntled man's companions.

Jack looked to the table of soldiers and then back at the fuming man in between bites of his stew, all while sensing that his father wanted to finish eating and leave as soon as possible. The chatter of conversations from the other tables had died away, and an awkward silent tension had fallen over the entire establishment. Dim yellow lantern light left details of the soldiers soft and hazy across the open dining area, but Jack could see that they had stacked their muskets into the corner behind their table.

Todd, the angry man who kept muttering his dissatisfaction louder and louder, slammed his empty tankard onto the table and abruptly stood up as the chair he was sitting on clattered to the floor. "You are right. I have had enough. Let's go."

The eyes of the entire establishment, including Jack's, locked onto the angry man and his friends as he stumbled his way past their tables towards

A Bloody Beginning

the door. He was a stout built fellow, and dressed in the plain, sturdy clothes of a tradesman. His forearms told the tale of countless hours of hard labor and his weathered hands looked as strong to Jack as his father's.

"Bad enough we're taxed until the price of goods prohibits working families from their necessities. I won't suffer the insult of dining with them on top of it," the man slurred as he passed the table of British soldiers in their crimson coats.

"Perhaps you should take your friend's advice and just leave," said the soldier who had been staring earlier. "Or we will add injury to your insult." He scarcely looked over his shoulder as he uttered the threat.

As quickly as the words were spoken, the irritated man lashed out. He grabbed a full tankard from the soldier's table and slammed it across the back of the nearest head he could reach while spilling dark brown ale all over the redcoats that were still seated. His first swing was so furious the tankard fell from his grasp and he continued the assault with a flurry of bare fisted punches.

"We need to go. Now," Jack's father said before wiping his mouth with his sleeve. "Jacky, up. Let's go. Stay close to your mother." He bolted from his chair and lent his arm to Jack's mother as she stood from her seat. The front of The New Englander had become a brawl scene as the soldiers retaliated against their attacker. At first glance, Jack thought the fray would end quickly as

A Bloody Beginning

the redcoats soon overpowered the irate man and had him pinned to the floor. But in the very next instant, the attacker's friends joined the fight. The quiet pub had turned into a wild melee as the redcoats were soon defending themselves against three men. One of the soldiers was knocked into an adjacent table and spilled full tankards onto laps and chests, which rallied another pair of men into the brawl.

Jack followed his father and mother while chaos erupted all around them. Tables were overturned. Chairs and bottles were wielded as weapons. One soldier was dragged from his feet and pummeled by a pair of thick forearms that belonged to the man who had started the incident. Shouts echoed through the room. A woman screamed. Jack's father reached out for the front door just as a single gunshot tore into the thick timber frame just inches from his fingers.

"Aghhh!" Jack's father recoiled his arm. Blood dripped from the back of his hand where a set of wooden splinters had dug in like pins in a cushion.

"Nobody move!" The shout came from a soldier standing in the pub's corner. He dropped the spent musket onto the table where he had been sitting with his cohorts and hefted another from the small stack in the corner behind him. He cocked the weapon and swung it wide across the room. "The next one who charges against us will meet his maker tonight! Now, all of you, sit down." His face looked wild as blood dripped

A Bloody Beginning

from his nose and his brow. He looked to one of his companions before swinging his musket barrel back across the room. "Dillard, run to the garrison and fetch us the watch officer. Tell him we need a dozen armed men down here to quell a riot."

"It's a pub brawl, nothing more," one participant objected.

"An assault on the king's soldiers is the same as an assault on the king himself!" the musket wielding soldier shrieked. He jabbed the weapon forward, his hands trembled so hard Jack feared he would discharge it unintentionally. "You lot will be arrested and tried. Every one of you!" He nodded to the soldier he had called Dillard. "Go. Alert the watch officer and tell him to bring down a dozen men with him."

Jack looked over at the soldier named Dillard. He seemed to be around the same age as Jack, perhaps a year or two older. Dillard shuffled his feet before heading for the door.

Todd, the angry man who had started the entire altercation, shouted, "Don't let him leave!"

A pair of men lunged for the young soldier. A shot erupted and filled The New Englander with its thunderous report and a plume of acrid gun smoke. Jack's father heaved open the splintered front door and pulled Jack and his mother out into the street. "This will not end well for anyone. We should have left the minute those soldiers came in." Shouts and the sound of breaking glass carried on inside the pub as Jack hurried behind his parents while they rushed down the street. All at

A Bloody Beginning

once, the cold seemed to bite at Jack's face again. He had grown used to the potent warmth within the walls of The New Englander. More shouts spilled from the pub as Jack and his parents rounded the corner and turned up King Street. Plumes of vapor rose from their mouths and noses while Jack's father set a pace nearly as rushed as he had on his way to deliver the harpoons from his shop down to the pier. A shrill scream rose in the distance behind them, followed immediately by the barking report of a single gunshot. Jack felt his blood run cold for a heartbeat. He wondered who had fired the shot and why the man in the pub had been so hostile to the soldiers.

"I can't say I blame a fellow for being cross about the taxes levied against us of late," Jack's father grunted as he continued his stretching pace up King Street toward the intersection with Shrimpton's Lane. "But to strike a man while his back is turned is abhorrent. There was no honor in it, none at all."

"What do you think will happen, Killian?" Jack's mother asked between strained breaths, "Will those soldiers come looking for us?"

In the night's darkness, Jack's father continued for several paces in silence before answering. "No, my dear. From the look of how things were going when we left, there will be a handful of missing soldiers come morning. They will look for their own, not us."

Jack piped in, "That shot-"

A Bloody Beginning

"My bet is that shot landed in one of those redcoats, boy," Jack's father interrupted. "One of them slipped away to go raise the alarm and bring more men. Our fellows in the pub decided they didn't much want the company of more soldiers. That is my wager." He paused for a few more paces and drew a long breath. "We will speak of this to no one. We were not in that pub. There isn't a man or woman in there that would name us to a magistrate. So, we carry on tomorrow as if nothing happened." He turned and looked Jack dead in the eye with a cold seriousness plastered on his face. "Do you understand, boy? You don't discuss this with anyone. Not your friends at school, or the shipwright's son. Nobody."

"Yes, sir," Jack replied. The warmth of pride he had felt at his father's compliment earlier faded. He resented being scolded for something he hadn't done yet, and he searched for the words to express to his father that he needn't worry about him blabbing to half the town about what they had seen in The New Englander. But the words didn't come. He lowered his face and marched on behind his parents as they made their flight across town. From Shrimpton's Lane, they crossed the open market square. By that hour at night, it was long abandoned. Vendors and market stalls were shuttered, the streets were vacant.

Jack continued to follow his parents and his father's urgent pace finally relented as they crossed from the open market square onto St. Anne's Street. It was late, much later than Jack was

A Bloody Beginning

accustomed to being out in town. He had never seen the streets so devoid of activity, especially this close to the harbor.

"I can feel it in the air," Jack's father said with a sigh. "There is a storm coming, just as the man in The New Englander said. Foul winds blowing or some such. I haven't seen tensions like this for a long time. Probably since I was a boy in Ireland. People are fed up with the crown."

"But, what can we do about it, Killian? It's not our lot to keep the peace," Jack's mother said as they rounded the corner from St. Anne's onto Paddy's Alley. The house Jack's family lived in was only a few hundred yards further. The smell of wood smoke and spring chill was thick in the air. Jack relished the smell as the night bit his cheeks and chin. His legs ached from their strenuous exertion earlier and he longed for sleep.

"I think it's best if we just keep to our own business, my dear. There is sure to be strife, getting involved will only bring trouble and heartache. I'm as opposed to the heavy-handed measures of late as anyone. But violence and bloodshed will bring more of the same." Jack's father extended an arm and ushered Jack and his mother up the walk to their home in front of him. Jack paced ahead, anxious to open the door and stoke a fire to ward away the chill that had sunk its teeth into his skin. He stopped cold in his steps when he saw a note of paper tacked to the front door of their home.

A Bloody Beginning

"Father?" Jack reached up and pulled the note off the iron tack. Jack's father pulled the paper from his hand and squinted at a single line of scrawled ink.

"That bastard," he growled from somewhere deep in his chest.

"Killian," Jack's mother scolded. "Cursing? What has come over you?"

Jack's father crumpled the note and shoved it into his coat pocket. "From our landlord and your employer. It seems that he is raising our rent. He must have caught wind that we made a few coins." Jack's father opened the front door to their home and gestured for Jack and his mother to go ahead.

"But, how could he have known?" Jack's mother said with a frown as she made her way inside and motioned for Jack to mind a fire in the hearth.

"That is just frustration talking, love. It is more likely that he wants me to protest the increase with him so he can leverage you into working longer each day. It's maddening. I have half a mind to march down and slug him in the mouth, tell him to bugger off with his damned drafty shack. I swear Colleen, some days I don't feel the wind until we are indoors!" Jack's father pulled the crumpled note out of his coat pocket and handed it to him. "Here, boy. Use it for tinder. That's about all you can count on from Mr. Albright. In fact, he may bill me for the cost of that too. Damn the luck."

"Yes, sir." Jack took the note and wadded it with a handful of wood shavings. He piled some small

35

A Bloody Beginning

sticks and gingerly placed his tinder bundle in the center before pulling a flint and striker from the mantle of the hearth. Despite being inside, his hands were still rigid from the cold and he desperately yearned for the warmth of a fire. With a well-practiced motion, he struck the flint with the steel striker several times until he landed a spark in the small bundle of tinder. It glowed orange for a second, and Jack gently blew into the bundle. The little orange speck spread as it caught the surrounding material. Jack inhaled quickly and blew another lungful of air as gently and steadily as he could onto the growing brightness until a small flame sprung to life. A smile spread across his face and Jack grabbed the wood and leather bellows. He aimed the device into the hearth and pumped it a few times until the small fire breathed and spread to the rest of the kindling. Warmth reached out and chased away the icy grip winter had placed on his face and hands. He added a pair of split logs to the growing fire and stood to remove his coat.

"How much is he raising our rent, Killian?" Jack's mother asked as she lowered herself to sit in a ladder backed rocking chair.

Jack's father shook his head. "An unreasonable amount, dearest. He and I will discuss it tomorrow. He can't truly believe I will pay double next month what we just paid for this."

Jack felt his stomach tighten. The subject of rent was a monthly conversation in the Horner home. Mr. Albright had raised their rate once already

A Bloody Beginning

that year, and Jack knew it was a source of significant stress for his father. He made his way to the washbasin, knowing that if he didn't, it would be the next thing he heard from his mother.

"Killian, maybe we should move. I doubt he will change his mind, and you work too hard-" Jack's mother stopped abruptly as her husband squatted onto one knee in front of her.

"I will discuss this with him tomorrow, dear. Don't trouble yourself with it. Whatever needs be done, I will take care of it." He looked over his wife's shoulder at Jack. "Let's all get some rest, eh? We have work to do tomorrow, all of us." He slapped Jack on the shoulder. "And you have your studies to attend to. Maybe another windfall awaits us soon. Let's not let it ruin our night."

The morning greeted Jack with a chill kiss on his forehead and cheeks. He rolled to one side and rubbed the sleep from his eyes before looking up into the rafters of the single room home. The first hints of dawn were showing through the lone window by the front door. Jack craned his neck to look at the hearth. The fire had gone out. With a heave of effort, he pulled himself up from his thin straw mattress and wrapped himself in his blanket. He padded over to the hearth and inspected the remnants of last night's fire, hoping to find live coals. An iron skewer aided him in

A Bloody Beginning

rolling the last remaining log. He was greeted by the welcome sight of three glowing red spots. Jack scooped a handful of bark and wood shavings from the neat stack of split firewood next to the hearth. He placed the tinder next to the coals and worked the bellows until tongues of bright, warm flame licked upward. He added a pair of logs to the growing flame and pulled the blanket up over his shoulders. Wind whistled as the morning blustered outside. Jack could hear his father's complaints from the previous night. Their house was as drafty as an open-faced market stall on calm days. When the wind was blowing outside, it was almost intolerable.

The house was empty but for him. His parents had already departed to begin their labors for the day. Jack settled into his mother's ladder-back rocking chair and let the warmth of the fire drown away the chill that had gathered within the house. He thought of Tom and the shipyard. They would step a mainmast on a warship this afternoon. Jack wanted to watch the process but remembered his father's scolding from the day before. School seemed like an impossibly high wall blocking his path toward a future of adventure and conquest on the high seas. But he didn't want to disappoint his mother, or provoke his father to anger. He surrendered his morning to the droll affair of sitting through lessons in history and English, math, and science. If only he could learn about more practical things of the world, like how a

A Bloody Beginning

shipyard crew managed to step a mainmast that is more than two feet thick.

A breakfast of cold biscuits with the last remnants of a jar of apple preserves served to fuel Jack as he bundled into his coat and forced himself out the door and into the world. A blast of cold air greeted him and gripped his face in its icy clutches. The smell of impending snow was on the air and a thick layer of frost covered everything in sight, from tree branches and fence posts to roof thatching and the rutted surface of the frozen alleyway where his family's home was situated. The sun had made its initial appearance on the eastern horizon and just as quickly tucked behind a thick blanket of heavy cloud cover. Jack longed for the warm days of summer that lay ahead when he could spend his time freely watching ships enter and leave the harbor. He turned and faced the alleyway leading west. Wind whistled through the bare branches of trees thickened by the appearance of clinging frost. He inhaled deep through his nose and felt the burn of the freezing air as it was forced through his nose and into his lungs without warming. He should go to school, he knew. But, he wasn't going to. Not today. Not when the shipwright and all his skilled workers and sailors were taking on such a monumental effort. Jack performed a rigid about face and stepped his way eastward. While the schoolhouse would be warm, he found the shipyard to be far more interesting, and his foray to the pier yesterday had proved far more fruitful than sitting

A Bloody Beginning

in the stuffy schoolhouse would have. Perhaps he would find another boon for his father's business.

With a pip in his step, aided by the prospect of skipping school to watch men ply their various trades in the shipyard, Jack hurried up Paddy's Alley. The rutted mud was frozen and little puddles from the last thaw had gathered to form patches of ice here and there. Jack avoided the ice easily enough, though it made his progress haphazard as he rushed forward headlong with visions of sailors hoisting a tall mast in his mind. He wondered what the process was like and how many men it would take. Surely, they couldn't just heave the old timber straight up. They would have to rig it off of another mast, or use some form of dockside leverage. Jack bristled as his foot found a patch of ice and he nearly slipped. With a quick extension of his arms and a bend at both knees, he recovered his balance quickly enough to avert a fall. He grumbled over the ice for a moment before continuing down the alley toward St. Anne's Street.

"I'll bet it takes a hundred men. As big as that warship is and of course, it is her mainmast! The timber itself must be near three feet around, maybe more. They will have men up in the rigging, and men on the deck, and dockside," he muttered to himself. "Maybe there will even be officers present." He pondered for a moment on the thought, his eyes locked downward on the frozen mud and ice. "Maybe even the ship's captain." His head spun with possibilities.

A Bloody Beginning

"Wouldn't that be something? To see a captain dressed in his finest uniform, inspecting the work being done to his sh-"

Jack's head blundered into something. He had been watching his footing to avoid another patch of ice and allowed his thoughts to stray into the activity awaiting him in the afternoon. A clatter and a curse followed as Jack toppled over onto his side and landed with a painful thump on his ribs and right elbow.

"Bloody fool! Watch where you are going," a voice scolded.

Jack pushed himself off the frozen mud and found himself staring at the perturbed faces of four soldiers in their crimson coats. One of them was recovering from his own fall. His musket and hat lying next to him in the frozen mud.

"Terribly sorry, it was my fault, sir," Jack said as he fought his way up to his feet.

The soldier laying on the ground snatched his hat and sat upright with a jerk. "Of course it was your fault. What are you, a dullard? Watch where you are going!"

Jack nodded, and brushed bits of snow from the sleeve of his coat. "My apologies, sir. I will take more care."

The soldier grabbed up his musket. His face glowered almost as red as his uniform coat. "I should hope so. I have half a mind to flog you right here in the open. That would teach you a lesson. Or, maybe we should have a talk with your parents. I could flog your old man for raising an

A Bloody Beginning

empty-headed whelp. How would you like that, eh, boy?"

Jack felt a rush of rage build within his chest. His face flushed red, and he could feel the muscles in his arms and legs tense. He narrowed his eyes at the group of soldiers as they helped their fallen friend up from the cold ground.

"Where are you off to in such a hurry, anyway?" One soldier asked, "Shouldn't you be in school?"

For a moment, Jack froze. He couldn't think. Words refused to form on his tongue. His eyes darted over the soldiers, who were now all staring at him.

"Maybe he is a dullard," another of the soldiers remarked. "There you have it Trenton. Not only did you threaten to flog the poor stupid boy, you threatened his father too. Perhaps we should keep from making any more remarks, eh?"

"I am not a dullard," Jack cut back, his voice dripping with anger. "My father is a blacksmith. I am on my way to the pier to see if there are any ships that need his wares. I was in a hurry, and I apologize for blundering into you."

The last soldier to speak, a freckled face young man that Jack judged to be barely three years older than he, reached out and patted Jack's knit hat. "That's a boy. Now, run along to your father's errands."

Jack had to bite his tongue behind lips pulled tight. The soldier's condescension was not lost on him, but he turned and started up St. Anne's Street. He tried to shift his thoughts to the excitement in store that afternoon, but the soldier's comments had taken up residence in his mind and refused to let go. He looked over his shoulder and saw that the group of four had turned and headed back towards the north. Jack eased his mind and uttered a silent curse at them for their threats and insults. No sooner had he seen the last of the four soldiers, than he turned around to find two more groups with four soldiers each patrolling the market square.

"The city is thick with redcoats," he grumbled, "nothing better to do, I suppose." He grinned to himself when he thought of the sailors busying themselves with the work of refitting their ship. They had better things to do than harass citizens minding their own business.

Boston's market square was showing signs of life as Jack crossed from St. Anne's Street toward the row of piers. He decided it would be better to avoid King Street and Shrimpton's Lane, lest he be seen by his mother and suffer a scolding before being redirected back toward the schoolhouse. Stalls and shops were opening their windows and putting wares on display for the day while sailors and townsfolk made their way through the lively square. A thinning bank of fog hung over the harbor, its tendril fingers extended inland as far as the timber piers and rocky shore. Jack could hear the peal of a bell from a ship navigating its way out to sea and he scanned the dockyards to see if the whaling tender was still in port. Tall masts were framed in a misty shroud. They stood stark

A Bloody Beginning

against the gray skies and Jack looked at the base of the tallest ones to find their vessels. The tender ship stood proudly at the end of the pier, her masts unmoved by the slight chop rolling in from the greater part of the harbor.

Chatter from the market, gulls cawing and squawking, ship's bells, and the gentle lap of waves rolling into the rocky shore all mixed in Jack's ears. The salty sea smell cut through the cold and wood smoke and filled his nose and throat. His smile grew. He could make out the silhouette of the big warship through the dissipating cold fog and his heart seemed to beat a little faster when he realized the mainmast had not been stepped yet. With a deep breath, he continued toward the shipyard and all but forgot his run in with the soldiers.

CHAPTER 3

5th March 1770
Boston

 "Hands to the capstan, hands to the brace lines! Prepare to haul," a coarse voice echoed through the shipyard and sent a score of men scrambling across the deck of the big warship. Repeats of the order followed, and after a lull in activity, the beat of a drum struck up. "Haul away!"

Jack watched with intense scrutiny from his seat on an adjacent pier as the process unfolded. The morning had seen a steady increase of activity on the decks of the warship and the dock it rested next to. Rigging had been configured for the task, and then reconfigured after the appearance of a smartly dressed officer in a fine-looking bicorne hat. Over two score lines, blocks and tackles had

A Bloody Beginning

been rigged and re-rigged to prepare for this one monumental task. Sailors moved gracefully through the rigging, along the yards, and up and down the shrouds. Orders floated through the air and echoed off of the calm surface of the water between the wooden docks. Straining lines creaked and groaned, pawls from the capstan clattered as men heaved against the crossbars. The hulking timber trunk that would soon be the warship's main mast rose from the deck in a slow procession while deck hands and top men fretted over every phase of the lift. To Jack, the shouted order seemed like another language entirely. Petty officers were snapping for men to pay off certain lines while hauling away at others. Every line seemed to have its own name, and each new name he heard sounded stranger than the last.

"Slow your haul on those main clew lines and let the main head lines catch up!" a rough voice shouted, "you there, pay off on the damned braces, will you? We shouldn't have to fight her weight and your stupidity at the same time!"

Jack's eyes were as wide as he could open them as he tried to absorb everything. The orders and activity, the vernacular, and the sailors' easy swagger as they worked to accomplish something that made his head swim. Officers that appeared on deck seemed calm and reserved, almost as if they weren't even paying attention to what was unfolding before them. Jack scanned over the small group huddled together on the warship's quarterdeck, they looked to be chatting while a

A Bloody Beginning

steward appeared on deck from a cabin door and distributed cups of some type of warm beverage. The petty officers roamed the deck freely, each one paying close attention to a certain area and bellowing out orders from time to time. The sailors were what truly caught Jack's attention. Whether on deck or up into the tops, they carried themselves with an almost casual countenance. It seemed impossible to Jack. Here they were doing something that had been the highlight of his week, maybe even month, and the sailors on deck and in the rigging carried on like it was just another Tuesday.

"Hold your haul! It's too much strain on the mizzen head blocks, something is going to give!" a sailor called down from the higher positions over the rear of the ship.

"Hell you say, sailor? I will tell you when we will hold our haul!" a red faced man shouted from the deck just forward from the base of the new main mast. He turned toward the front of the ship and raised a brass speaking trumpet to his mouth. "Haul on those lines for all you are worth, you dogs! We'll be seating her in place before the glass turns or there will be hell to pay!"

Groans of exertion floated up from the warship's deck as men threw all their strength into pulling. Jack watched, his heartbeat radiating into his throat, as the massive wooden beam tipped further and further toward the upright position. It was at an angle almost halfway to upright, and progress seemed to slow to a crawl.

A Bloody Beginning

"Heave damn you! Put your back into it!" the red-faced petty officer boomed over the forward decks. "I'll have every last one of you with a holystone in your hand until you wretch, if you don't get this hefted!"

Suddenly, a flurry of movement erupted in the rigging. Jack saw sailors moving quickly on the deck and in the tops. A loud twang sliced through the air. Voices rose in alarm and a general sense of panic seemed to grip everyone on board. Even the officers moved in a rush from the center of the quarterdeck to the side closest to the dock.

"Look out! We've lost a mizzen head block, and the rest can't bear her weight," a shout sounded. All across the deck men raced into action. Some grabbed hold to shore up the remaining lines bearing the mast's weight while others raced to recover the lines that had been lost to the fouled head block.

"You there, run us another loop from the foremast as high as we can get it. Clew blocks, head blocks, doesn't matter. Just do it smartly," the red-faced man shouted toward the forward decks.

Jack felt his mouth go dry. His heart threatened to leap out of his chest as it drummed harder with each beat. His hands clamped into fists within the pockets of his coat. He could feel the tension from across the shipyard as sailors and apprentice shipwrights fought to salvage their efforts. His face flushed warm despite the frosty bite of cold wind that nipped at his chin and cheeks.

A Bloody Beginning

Near the front of the ship, two men raced along the sides of the vessel with heavy ropes strung over one shoulder. Jack watched as the men ran along the deck, one trailing the other's movement from across the ship, and then steadily catching up before lagging back again. The two runners pulled their respective lines all the way to the quarterdeck before looping around and heaving them over large deck cleats to be pulled taut.

A loud cry boomed over the deck, "Alright, now, all together, heave!"

For a long moment, the thick mast seemed frozen in place as the crew battled against its weight. But as they collectively strained, and their shouts and groans wafted up from the deck to mix with the sounds of bell peals and washing waves, the mast resumed its travel into the upright position. Jack's heart raced faster as they drew closer to success. Soon the mast was as close to upright as it could be and a crew of deckhands lumbered forth to leverage the mass of timber into its place. Mallet strikes clattered. The officers gathered on the quarterdeck made their way collectively to the forward railing in order to witness completion of the task.

Another voice shouted, "One last heave and we'll have her in place, put everything you have into it boys!"

Jack watched as the mast finally reached the fully upright position. The clattering mallets stopped, and a cheer erupted throughout the entire crew. Even the stony reserve of the

A Bloody Beginning

clustered group of officers seemed to thaw momentarily, and Jack witness as one man in a dark blue uniform coat clapped his hand onto the shoulder of another.

A Coarse shout brought the cheers to an end. "Alright, you lugs, brace lines fore and aft. We haven't the luxury of lounging about, now get to it!"

The clunk of footfalls on wood announced Jack's friend Tom as he approached. A slight afternoon wind had brought with it gently falling snowflakes that were melting on contact with the ground. Jack brushed his trousers and pulled himself up from the dock to greet his friend.

"Did you see?" Tom asked. "They nearly lost it at one point. I thought my father was going to tip off for a while there. He kept telling the captain that they needed more leverage from the bow, but those damned Brits think they know everything when it comes to ships."

Jack nodded and let a smile break through the icy cold saturating his face. "I watched the whole thing. What a sight! I thought that mast was going to come toppling back down! That would have been a catastrophe."

Tom shoved his hands into his pockets and rocked back on his heels. "It would have crushed the taff rail and probably half of the quarterdeck

A Bloody Beginning

planking for sure, maybe even some of the brace beams for the captain's cabin. Lucky thing they got it when they did. Father says they are refitting her for a cruise to the Caribbean. Can you imagine? I've heard sailors say the sea down there is sapphire blue and there are shallows where a man standing on the bow of a ship can see straight to the bottom in near eight fathoms! Can you believe that?"

Jack shook his head. "Well, no. Actually, I don't. The oceans aren't that clear."

"Down there they are!" Tom said with a chuckle. "We should stow away and escape this infernal cold. What do you say, Jack?"

A cold gust of wind bit Jack's face. He could feel its icy fingers reaching through his wool coat and sinking into his arms and chest. Tropical heat sounded nice. But stowing away on a Royal Navy ship? His parents would be crushed, his mother heartbroken. Jack tried to imagine their reaction. "I don't think stowing away is how I would like to see the world. What happens when they find us?"

Tom clapped one hand onto Jack's shoulder and the two started walking up the dock. "Well, then they would make us part of the crew, of course. I'm sure they would take some wages because we weren't signed up proper in port, but they would make us sailors. I'm sure of it."

Jack shook his head. "I don't know, Tom. I don't think things would happen that way. My father has talked to sailors from up north. They say the Royal Navy is pressing men into service with no

A Bloody Beginning

wages for the first six months. I don't think they would pay wages to a couple of stowaways, and with no experience-"

"Speak for yourself, Jack. I know a fair bit of what happens aboard a ship at sea. I listen to sailors and officers talk all the time in the shipyard," Tom interrupted.

"But that is talk, Tom. That's a far cry short of experience at sea. No. I won't be stowing away on anything, much less a Royal Navy warship. No thank you, Tom. You have fun," Jack replied, and then smiled, "be sure to write me when you get to Barbados." They both laughed.

At the end of the dock their steps met the cobblestones of Crab Street. Jack stopped and looked back at the towering masts of the warship where the crew had already begun raising the maintop and hanging the yard.

"They still won't be ready to sail for days. Will they?" Jack asked.

Tom shrugged his shoulders. "It's hard to say. Sometimes these Royal Navy crews expect to be in port for weeks or months, until a packet from Portsmouth arrives with new orders, and then they will work day and night to set sail in a few days' time." He paused for a moment as they both looked over the warship's high mast tops and rigging. "Did your father sell any wares to that whale fleet tender?"

Jack remembered the mad dash he had made with his father the night before; his legs were still sore and the tenderness in his shoulder had yet to

A Bloody Beginning

fade away. "He did. We carried a dozen harpoons from his shop all the way down to the wharf. They bought them up and asked for more."

"That's a fair bit of business, Jack. I'm sure your father was pleased." Tom replied.

"He was, though I think he wishes he had more on hand," Jack said, deciding he didn't want to continue the line of conversation lest it lead to matters Tom would not understand. "But he was happy with the deal."

"That is good, Jack, I am glad your father could strike up a bit of business with them," Tom said. "I feared they would make sail before he got to them."

Jack shook his head and flexed the sore muscles in his legs. His hand drifted to the spot on his shoulder that had been rubbed raw by the weight of the harpoons. "He would not let that happen. I thought I was going to die trying to keep up with him. I honestly think I saw bits of smoke coming from the heels of his shoes when we arrived."

Tom laughed, and Jack joined him. Together, the two young men turned and looked out over the calm water as the press of falling snowflakes intensified. A bell pealed. Through the falling snow, the outline of a ship could be seen making its turn to approach the harbor.

Jack furrowed his brow and narrowed his eyes at the new arrival. "What do you make of her?" He asked.

"Two masted," Tom replied casually, "a brig, probably a merchant ship. Nothing extraordinary."

A Bloody Beginning

Jack fought the urge to roll his eyes at his friend. Tom was forever playing up his constant proximity to the more impressive vessels that made port in Boston. His father was a renowned shipwright, both in the colonies and abroad. So much so that even British captains sought him out for his expertise in refitting or repairing their vessels.

"I wonder where she is in from," Jack wondered out loud. "Maybe somewhere in Europe, or the Mediterranean."

Tom remained quiet for a spell before clapping Jack on the shoulder and turning on one heel. "I have to go. There are chores I put off watching that mast being stepped and I better get to them before my father notices."

Jack thought of his own parents, and that he had shunned going to school for the same reason. "Likewise. Once my parents find out I didn't go to school again, I am going to get it twice over."

The two friends parted company at the intersection of Crab Street and Mirk Street as scores of sailors made their way from the shipyard into town to make the most of their remaining time ashore. Jack wondered how much longer the warship would be before she set back to sea. The task they had completed in an afternoon seemed so large to him, but the sailors who casually strode their way past him seemed nonplussed, as if stepping a mast was as modest a chore as splitting firewood. The parade of sailors enveloped the

A Bloody Beginning

street and Jack could not help himself but to listen in to their conversations as they passed.

"What was the tavern?" one sailor asked.

"The New Englander," another answered. "And, no, I'm not going. The captain said any man caught there will be flogged for disobeying orders. A pair of soldiers went missing after a dust-up there last night. Best give her a wide berth. Let's wet our whistle at that spot over on King Street. What was the name of that one?"

"Brass Whale, I think it was," the first voice replied.

Jack felt a flush spread through his face as he continued walking while throngs of sailors made their way around him. He had known all along that the sailors he had been watching were king's men, British sailors of the Royal Navy loyal to crown and country. The thought hadn't crossed his mind that they would have been aware of the disturbance that occurred the night before.

A third sailor chimed in, "Let one of these bumpkins try their hand with me! They'll find more than they bargained for, let me tell you!"

"Only if they smell you first," the first sailor quipped.

Jack slowed his pace and let more of the sailors pass. His stomach tightened. He thought of what his father had said about keeping what they had seen to themselves and what the angry man in the tavern had said before he started the fight that had cut their special supper short. He knew there was a growing population in Boston that despised the

A Bloody Beginning

crown, what it represented, and its representatives. For himself, Jack wasn't sure exactly where he stood. He had heard his father complain about the taxes levied on the colonies, but he had also heard his father speak of maintaining peace and keeping to their own affairs. "Don't go looking for trouble, there's plenty out there to be found and surely some looking for all of us." Jack could almost hear his father's voice as the words rang through his head. He continued up Mirk Street to the intersection of Leveres Lane, where he turned north. In his mind, he had already submitted to the inevitable conclusion that his parents would discover his willful dereliction of studies for another day of larking at the harbor. He decided that if he waited to walk his mother home from work, it may soften his father's temperament.

Ahead of Jack, there was a perceptible shift in the crowd of sailors. Someone shouted back through the crowd. Jack couldn't understand what was said, but at hearing it many of the sailors broke into a run. Jack narrowed his gaze, confused about the excitement and wondering what he missed while he had been wrapped in his thoughts.

"There's trouble up ahead. A group of locals are causing a fit, and they have some soldiers cornered. Let's go help those boys out!" A sailor's voice carried through the crowd. Shouts of approval echoed, and a few more of the sailors broke into a run. Despite the soreness in his legs,

A Bloody Beginning

Jack quickened his pace along with the sailors around him. He hurried to a quick shuffle, but finally broke into a run as he heard more of the sailors shouting about the disturbance up ahead of them.

"Hurry, lads. There is a crowd of these bastards and they have our boys cornered!" A voice from the far end of the lane shouted over the running crowd. "They broke out a window and there is glass everywhere, there's more'n thirty of them!"

A burst of cold wind came from the east as Jack and the running sailors crossed from Leveres Lane onto King Street. He looked in both directions and found nothing but a press of backs and shoulders. The street was packed with sailors, Jack couldn't see over the thick of the crowd. He tried to move across the street by threading his way through gaps in the crowd. All around him sailors muttered curses and oaths or complained about the waste of their precious time ashore. The sound of a shattering pane of glass cut through the din of chatter and Jack could hear shouted threats from the opposite side of King Street. Progress of the crowd of sailors had halted. All at once the gaps Jack had been squeezing his way through were narrowed until the sailors were standing shoulder to shoulder. The scream and cry of a woman sliced through the air and a waft of smoke filtered its way into Jack's nose.

A voice thundered, "Make way, damn it all. What is this commotion?"

A Bloody Beginning

Jack turned and found a tall, uniformed navy officer with broad shoulders emblazoned by gold epaulets and a row of medals on his chest. His bicorne hat was similarly adorned with gold piping along the crest. Like the parting of the Red Sea for Moses, sailors formed an opening for the officer. Brows and hat brims were knuckled as the officer made his way through the crowd of sailors while the chatter died away. Jack took advantage of the opening and followed the uniformed officer as close as he dared.

Shouts continued from somewhere on the other side of the crowd and Jack followed the officer across the width of King Street and to the intersection of Shrimpton's Lane. He watched the officer closely. Every step was sure and steady, as if he owned the very ground he was walking on. All around them, his presence seemed to bring a hush to the crowd of sailors while they lifted their hands to knuckle their foreheads or touch the brim of their caps. It awed Jack that the sole presence of this man seemed to create order out of bedlam all around him. He followed the officer as the crowd continued parting until they had crossed onto Shrimpton's Lane and reached the edge of the press. Jack looked beyond the finely dressed officer and could see a line of four soldiers in their crimson red coats. They looked disheveled as they held their muskets at the ready. Across from the soldiers was a scene of chaos as men disbursed in flight from the growing confrontation. Jack's heart sank as he laid eyes on Mr. Albright's Tailor Shop.

A Bloody Beginning

The windows had all been smashed to bits of shattered glass that lay strewn on the cobbled street before it. Red uniform coats, the same kind that Jack had seen his mother working on the evening before, were scattered on the ground amid the fragments of glass and splintered window framing. A stream of smoke curled out of the shop and filtered into the cold afternoon.

"You there," the officer's voice boomed as he extended one hand to point at a nearby sailor. "Take two men and get that fire out, smartly." His voice exuded calm and confidence, while Jack felt nothing but fear and panic. He searched the dispersing crowd for any sign of his mother but found nothing.

The naval officer stepped in front of one soldier and looked the man over with a demanding stare as if he were conducting an inspection. "What was the cause of all of this? Where is the watch officer?"

The soldier blundered his speech for a moment before lowering his musket. "We saw a group of about six men, sir, they had already broken out the window and were throwing the uniform coats onto the street. One of them broke a lantern and spilled the lamp oil onto the coats. I believe he intended to light them on fire. We ordered them to halt, but they began throwing bricks and rocks at us. It is a lucky stroke that your men arrived when they did, sir. I am not sure we could have ended that without firing into the crowd."

A Bloody Beginning

The officer nodded, the point of his bicorne hat emphasizing the gesture. "God help us all if that ever comes to pass. Now, report this to you watch officer at once. He will need to increase patrols to keep the king's peace. Off with you."

Jack's eyes locked on the front of the tailor shop as a pair of sailors barreled headlong into the building. He stepped away from the edge of the crowd, fixated on the front of the shop as the smoke billowing outward turned thicker and darker. He searched the street again for any sign of his mother and found none. She had to still be in there. Fear laced his blood. He felt it wrap its fingers around his chest and threaten to squeeze the air from his lungs. Without thinking, Jack bolted toward the tailor shop. His legs complained with each stride, but he ignored them. His thoughts centered on his mother and extracting her from danger.

"You there, stop!" The officer's voice shouted. Jack ignored it. He crossed the vacant portion of cobbled street until glass was crunching under his shoes and smoke choked his breath. With a lunging jump, he cleared the bottom edge of the shattered window and hurled himself into the depths of the ravaged shop. Heat stung his face where only a few heartbeats ago he had felt the icy kiss of winter. His vision blurred as his eyes watered from the stinging smoke. A feeling of disorientation seized him, and he turned back and forth several times to gather his bearings. Jack stepped forward and his head ran into the hard

A Bloody Beginning

corner of a tall cabinet. He recoiled and brought a hand to his brow as a bolt of pain pulsed through his forehead and across his scalp. His lungs burned from the smoke and despite his best efforts to control his breathing, he broke into a fit of coughs. The walls of the shop seemed to close in around him. Savage heat choked the few breaths he was able to pull in between his coughs. Footfalls sounded on the wood planks of the floor. The feeling of sticky liquid ran down the side of his face. Jack touched his hand to his face and inspected his fingers, he found they were covered in dark red blood. The room he was in seemed to spin and Jack was forced to his knees by an unseen hand that gripped the thick wool of his coat. Consciousness became a struggle. He felt strength slipping from him.

"Below the smoke, laddy, else it will choke you to death," a rough voice growled. Jack felt the hand tug on his coat. "Follow me, boy. We're leavin' this death trap."

Jack pulled against the hand with little success. "My mother, I'm not leaving without her!"

"Jacky?"

Jack recognized the voice of his mother through the smoke and heat. Fear melted from his veins. "Mother!"

"Come on, Jack. Come with us. These men are taking us out of here!" Jack's mother said. He felt her hand reach out through the smoke and touch his face. "Come on Jack." Jack tried to crawl. He willed his muscles to obey through their failing

A Bloody Beginning

strength. The floor rushed up beneath him and he felt himself dropping through it into an abyss like he had been swallowed by the sea.

"You don't lack for courage, lad," the officer's deep voice reached into Jack's consciousness. "But a might short in the reasoning division, I would say."

Jack opened his eyes and found the face of his mother. Blurry, at first. But, after he blinked his eyes a few times he found her comforting features smiling down at him. "You rushed in to save your mother? Just wait until your father hears this. He will burst with pride, Jack. You are your father's son, every bit of him and then some."

"Heroic, indeed." The officer's face appeared in Jack's vision. He was standing behind Jack's mother as she cradled his head. "I'll say, you would make for a fine sailor. If you were interested in that sort of endeavor."

Jack's mother turned and looked at the officer over her shoulder. "Please, sir. Give my thanks to your men. They saved both of us."

The officer offered only a brisk nod of his hat, exaggerated by his large hat. "I am happy we could be of assistance, ma'am. But, see this young man to a doctor at once, that brow won't mend without a few stitches, judging by my experience, that is." He paused and looked over toward the

A Bloody Beginning

tailor shop, which was by now completely engulfed in flames. A band of townsmen and sailors alike had taken up the battle and were slopping pails of water into the fire with little success. The officer turned back toward Jack and his mother. "I could have my ship's doctor have a look at that nasty little wound you have there, son. Free of charge, of course." He paused again and offered a tight grin to Jack's mother. "I didn't think to consider your means before recommending you seek a physician, ma'am. Quite thoughtless of me, and I apologize. Let's have him over to the ship, and my doctor will get the brow stitched up without fail."

Jack could feel the cold creeping in through the fibers of his wool coat. His head swooned from the smoke and the throbbing gash he had opened on that infernal cabinet. The naval officer broke his stony reserve and smiled down at him before extending a hand to help Jack to his feet.

"Come on, lad," he said, "let's get you over before the good doctor gets into his cups for the evening."

"Jack? Colleen?" the voice of Jack's father interrupted before Jack could offer his thanks to the naval officer. "What happened?" Jack's father looked him over before turning to his mother and wrapping her in a tight embrace. "What in God's name? Are you two alright?"

Jack's mother replied, "Killian, oh my dear, it was horrible. A mob of men were outside the shop. They were shouting curses and threats, so I

A Bloody Beginning

went into the back storeroom. They broke out the window and threw all the garments I was working on out onto the street. One of them poured lamp oil all over them and another started a fire in the front room of the shop. Mr. Albright bolted the back door when he left and I was trapped. If it wasn't for those brave sailors, and our heroic young man, I believe I wouldn't have made it out of there alive."

Jack watched his father's face flush red with anger. "Mr. Albright wasn't here?"

"No," Jack's mother answered in a hushed tone. "He left late in the afternoon, but I'm not sure exactly why. He didn't offer an explanation, and I didn't care to ask."

Jack noted a change in his father's demeanor when his eyes settled on him. "Jacky. You do me right proud, son. I only regret that I wasn't here with you."

The naval officer cleared his throat in a not-so-subtle gesture to move things along. "Let's get this young hero off to the doctor, shall we? That wound on his brow needs to be cleaned up and stitched to heal properly, and I fear if we delay any further, the ship's doctor will prove incapable. We are ashore, after all. Sailors do tend to excess while on land."

Jack's father nodded emphatically. "Yes, kind sir. I thank you for your kindness and the bravery of your men. I should like to buy them all a round of ale."

A Bloody Beginning

"I will convey your thanks, but that is wholly unnecessary. My men were doing their duty. Protecting the king's peace," the officer replied with casual dismissal. "The uniform coat I was on my way to retrieve is lost to me. I will have to seek compensation from the tailor."

"Best of luck with that," Jack's father offered in a sarcastic growl. "Mr. Albright doesn't know the meaning of fair play, sir."

CHAPTER 4

'H.M.S Raven'
5th March 1770
Boston Shipyard

The smell of the ship was one of the first things Jack noticed as he descended below the weather deck behind the officer who had offered his doctor's services. Where Jack had been accustomed to the smell of the sea, and imagined a ship to smell entirely the same, his notions evaporated as his senses were drowned by the odd combination of smells. Not all of them were pleasant, but not all of them were offensive. At first, Jack could smell the pungent aroma of freshly tarred lumber. This he had expected. But there were also notes of stale tobacco, spiced rum, leather, and cooking food. They made their way

A Bloody Beginning

down a set of stairs that were steeper than any Jack had ever seen and crossed the length of the stairs to another set that led deeper into the belly of the ship. Before descending the second flight, Jack stole a look across the open deck and found that both sides of the ship were lined with sleek looking blackened cannon barrels sitting on sturdy timber frames. The guns gleamed in the dim yellow lantern light and cast long shadows that stretched out toward Jack like menacing fingers. As he followed the naval officer to the deck below, the sharp smell of turpentine invaded his nose and was just as quickly replaced by the lingering odor of a space where many men shared cramped living quarters. Jack kept close as the officer made his way past a pair of marine sentries standing watch outside a door. Both men snapped to attention as the officer approached and one of them opened the door, revealing a narrow corridor leading toward the rear of the ship. The officer stopped next to the first door in the corridor and rapped his knuckles on its polished wooden surface.

"Doctor Woodworth, I have a patient for you to see, if you are able," the officer announced.

A long silence elapsed before a voice replied. "Shore leave does come with a cost, captain. Send him in."

At the mention of the title captain, Jack felt a bolt of lightning run through his blood. He had not considered that this officer would be the

A Bloody Beginning

commander of the warship. He had assumed that a ship's captain would be older.

As he opened the doctor's cabin door, the officer corrected, "He is not one of ours, doctor. A local boy, young man, rather, who ran into a burning building to rescue his mother. He came away with a nasty gash on his forehead. Would you have a look and get him cleaned and sewn up?"

Jack peered into the recesses of the cabin and found that the cramped space was little more than a dimly lit broom closet with shelves stocked full of medical supplies, implements and books. The doctor, an aging, spindly thin man with thick black eyebrows and deep recessed eyes, looked to have an almost permanent scowl of disapproval on his face.

"A local boy? Well, this is irregular," the doctor growled before offering the officer a half smile of stained, crooked teeth. "Have you gone soft, captain?"

"Not in the slightest, doctor," the captain returned the doctor's smile with a deep frown. "Is that gin I smell?"

The doctor's eyebrows shot upward, and his demeanor took on a defensive tone. "Medicinal spirits, captain. Medicinal spirits only. I have a bit of a cough that just refuses to let go, damn this cold climate."

The captain nodded. "I am sure. See to the boy and send him ashore when you are finished. His parents are waiting dockside."

A Bloody Beginning

"Aye, sir. I will have him mended up in no time," the doctor answered before shifting his focus from the captain onto Jack. "I say, that is a nasty bit of business there. Step in here young man, we'll get that fixed up and have you on your way in no time." He waved Jack to come in with a set of bony fingers.

Jack stepped into the doctor's cabin and was instantly assaulted by the potent aroma of alcohol. It was so strong that Jack felt a shudder crawl up his spine and through his neck. The doctor reached out and gently pulled his head close for inspection. He muttered something inaudible to Jack before reaching for a bottle that rested on one of the shelves at the back of the cabin. With a swift pull from his bony fingers, the doctor uncorked the bottle and used the contents to wet a cloth bandage the size of Jack's palm.

"This is going to burn a bit, but nothing that a young man who charges into burning buildings cannot handle. Stitches may be more than you are used to, but necessary, yes, that nasty cut on your brow just won't heal right without a little helping hand." The doctor patted his hand onto a squat wooden stool. "Have a seat, I'll have you fit for service before you know it."

Jack sat on the stool. His head spun from the sights and smells; all the activity he had witnessed over the last two days felt like it was closing in around him. Here he was, aboard a real warship at the captain's invitation, no less. The doctor held the liquid-soaked bandage onto Jack's wound. It

A Bloody Beginning

felt like tingling fire for a moment, but the sensation passed.

"Do you make a habit of running into burning buildings? Or was this your first?" The doctor muttered in an almost absent voice as he fished a curved needle already threaded with a thin string.

"This is a first for me, doctor," Jack answered as a pang of pain pulsed through his scalp. He felt a tugging as the doctor threaded the string through his wound and another bite of pain as he started the next stitch.

"Brought on board as the captain's guest as well. That is rare indeed. You must have really impressed him. Captain Fullard hasn't made an invitation aboard to a civilian in my memory, but then again, my memory is not all that good either. He is a hard man, but the men love and respect him. I guess that is all that a commanding captain could hope for, anyway." He sat upright and inspected his work for a moment before looping the string around his fingers. Jack felt another tug and the doctor fished out a small pair of scissors from a pocket in his vest. "Alright, lad. That will do the trick. Now, you keep that clean and washed. Have your mother snip the line with some sharp sewing scissors in a fortnight." He paused and leaned away from Jack while giving him a scornful frown. "You have got a mother, haven't you? You aren't an orphan boy, are you?"

Jack nodded. "Yes, sir. I have a mother; she is waiting dockside with my father. And she has sewing scissors."

A Bloody Beginning

"Good, good. Well, you watch your head on your way out of here, some of those beams ride awfully low for a tall lad like yourself."

Jack stood and offered the doctor his hand. "Thank you, sir. It was a pleasure to have met you."

The doctor's permanent scowl melted and Jack saw the same crooked smile full of stained teeth that had flashed before the captain earlier. "The pleasure was mine, son. Now, off with you. Don't keep your parents waiting."

Jack ducked his way out of the cabin and looked around for a moment to gather his bearings. Everything seemed tight, the walls, the doors, the images he had imagined of sprawling warships and spacious cabins had evaporated within the close quarters and suffocating smells. He made his way out of the door where the two sentries remained on watch and up a steep set of stairs to the next deck. Another steep stairwell led him up to the weather deck and into the fresh evening air. Snow was still falling and the cold bit at his exposed skin. He looked around the deck of the warship before finding his way to the gangplank that led down to the pier where his parents stood visiting with Captain Fullard.

"I can't thank you enough, sir. You have done me two true kindnesses this day," Jack's father said to the captain as Jack came within hearing.

"It is no trouble, you have raised a brave lad, he would do well in the king's service," Captain Fullard said. "If he has ambitions of that nature."

A Bloody Beginning

Jack's father smiled as he saw him coming down the gangplank. He wrapped an arm around his shoulders and pulled him tight. "Well, he may have a future seafaring someday, but I would be satisfied if we could just get him to attend his lessons."

"Education is important," the captain replied and looked Jack over with narrowed eyes. "I was just talking with your father. It seems you have a penchant for shirking your schoolwork to lark at ships here in the harbor."

Jack nodded, feeling his face flush red with embarrassment. "Yes, sir. Yes, I do."

The captain shook his head and pursed his lips. "That won't do lad, dereliction of duty. No, we cannot have that. I will say, I was struck by your spirit today. There are grown men who would not have done what you did, regardless of who was in that shop. But, don't cheat yourself, young man. The sea isn't going anywhere, and mathematics are critical for navigation." He offered Jack's father a parting handshake and nodded to both Jack and his mother. "Do be safe, Boston has become a different place since I last made port here."

Jack and his family departed the shipyard in silence. Daylight was already dwindling, and snow was falling with a renewed vigor. Jack winced as he drew his knitted hat over his head. He tried to pull the front of the hat over his stitches without touching them, but when the wool touched his stitched wound, it started a throbbing that pulsed through his scalp and down

A Bloody Beginning

into his neck. He felt as if someone had stabbed him with a dagger just above his eye. With his hat in place, Jack tugged at the collar of his coat and tried to shield his neck from the blowing cold. Snowflakes were sticking to the ground and collected on the windward east side of brick and mortar buildings. He noted that his mother, who had lost her winter coat in Mr. Albright's shop, was now wearing his father's coat. The sleeves were dirty from being worn in his blacksmith shop and there were holes in the sleeves where sparks had caught in the wool fibers.

Cobblestones were becoming slick with gathered snow as the family of three crossed from the rough plank boardwalk of the shipyard onto Mirk Street. They stopped before crossing the road to let a formation of six soldiers in crimson red coats pass by.

"There has been enough trouble in town, I think we ought to keep our distance from Shrimpton's Lane this evening. Mirk Street leads us right by the garrison. We can cut across Tanner's Lane and Water Street to get home a little faster, but I think it would be smart for us to avoid the waterfront and the marketplace as much as possible," Jack's father said with a deep sigh. "I fear these troubles will get worse before they get better."

"I am worn thin, Killian," Jack's mother said. "I care not how we get home, just that we get there as directly as we can. I am sure Jacky is tired too."

A Bloody Beginning

Jack's father paced on in silence for a moment. "I'm sure he is. We will get there, my love, without delay."

"Our brave young hero needs to rest, and I'll be wanting to have a look at that stitching on his brow," Jack's mother said while giving his shoulder a squeeze.

Her words were meant kindly, but Jack felt a pang of guilt along with the throbbing pain in his forehead and scalp. He didn't feel heroic. He had run into the shop to save his mother and only became another burden for the sailors who completed the task. His face flushed red as he thought of the defeat, and the kind words he kept hearing to placate his pride. Fifteen years old and he couldn't even save his mother without the aid of better men. His face drooped low to face the cobbled road at his feet. Bitter cold wind gusts drove him further into his thoughts while he trailed along behind his parents. His shoes were soaked through from the snow and his head was pounding miserably. He shifted his thoughts to the afternoon, and his pleasant time talking with Tom and watching the great mainmast being stepped into position. But, eventually, his line of thought drifted back to the crowd of sailors and their chatter about what had occurred in The New Englander the night before. He hardly noticed when his parents turned up Tanner's Lane other than the slight direction change of the footsteps he was following. Their low chatter was lost to him, except between the frigid bursts of gusting wind.

A Bloody Beginning

Jack heard just enough to pick up they were discussing what had happened at Mr. Albright's shop.

Jack's father said something inaudible before Jack heard, "... tensions about taxation."

"But, violence will only make matters..." His mother's reply was lost to a blast of icy wind.

Jack buried his chin in the collar of his coat and continued to follow his parents, but he stopped trying to listen to their conversation. His mind drifted back to the doctor's cabin aboard the warship. The strong smells and the close quarters hadn't matched the image his mind had conjured for most of his youth, but it hadn't dismayed him either. If anything, seeing the inside of such a ship had only served to stoke his curiosity. His thoughts drifted to the powerful cannons that lined the sides of the ship, and he tried to imagine how loud they must report when fired.

"Killian, something seems off," Jack's mother said in a hushed voice he could barely hear over the wind. "The streets are vacant. Even in the cold, there are normally still people about town."

Jack looked around and found that his mother was right. They were alone on Water Street, not a soul could be seen. It gave Jack an eerie feeling, like someone was watching them.

"Word has gotten around about the trouble in town of late, I'm sure. We can only hope it brings some peace," Jack's father replied.

The family reached the end of Water Street and turned northward onto Cornhill Street. Jack

A Bloody Beginning

looked up the lamp lit lane and found barren cobblestones collecting snow. Again, not a soul to be seen. He hoped his father was correct in his judgment, he hoped there would be no more trouble. In just the last day he had seen a brawl, been stopped and questioned sharply by soldiers, and very nearly lost his mother. A piece of him craved the dull monotony of school. He vowed to himself that in the morning he would turn west when he left the house, he would attend his studies and mind the words Captain Fullard had said. Mathematics are important for navigation, if he kept that in mind, perhaps school wouldn't seem so dreary.

The winds didn't seem to blow as hard on Cornhill Street. Most of the way was blocked to the east by tall brick and mortar buildings. But, Jack braced himself for the crossing of King Street. King Street ran east to west and opened to the broad part of the harbor where Long Wharf adjoined the shore. The winds would be strongest there, bitter cold blowing in off of the Atlantic and carrying snow with it. It gave Jack a shudder that he could feel in his soul.

"Killian, what is going on up there?" Jack's mother said. Alarm was creeping on the edges of her tone.

Jack looked around his father's shoulder and found that the intersection of Cornhill and King Streets was packed with a crowd. Torches and lanterns dotted the gathering and served to illuminate the size of the group. Jack felt a knot

A Bloody Beginning

form in his stomach. He could hear shouts drifting through the cold winter wind.

"I'm not sure, my dear. But, we will be alright if we just keep to ourselves and stay on our course," Jack's father growled while rubbing his hands over his upper arms in furious motion to ward off the cold. "Whatever their grievance, it has nothing to do with us." They continued walking while shouts from the crowd grew more audible. "Hurry now, let's be past them as quick as we can."

As Jack and his parents came closer to the gathered crowd, there was a sort of tension Jack could feel wriggle into his blood and take hold over his muscles. It was the same feeling he had experienced when the group of sailors had gone running to the shouts for help earlier that day. He felt as if there were something of magnitude hanging in the air, just about to drop.

A shout cut above the noise of the crowd, "Go back to England!"

Jack looked over the gathering. There were men holding heavy looking wooden clubs scattered throughout the crowd. More shouts cut into the night's cold wind, each growing more hostile than the last. Jack felt a tug at the collar of his coat and looked to find his father staring at him with wide eyes.

"Let's go Jacky, there is trouble brewing here," he said with a pull on Jack's collar.

Jack quickened his pace as his parents wound their way through the crowd. The press seemed impossible to navigate. Men cut their way in

A Bloody Beginning

between Jack and his parents, one of them bumped into him and nearly knocked him off his feet.

"On your toes, son," the man said as he quickly disappeared into the thick of the crowd. Jack noted that the man wore a red band tied around his right arm and as the stranger slipped between bystanders he caught a glimpse that made his blood run cold. A flintlock pistol was in the man's hand. Jack felt himself being pushed. A shift had come over the crowd and around him men were making their way forward. He looked desperately to find his parents, searching for his father's face or his mother's hair.

"Mother?" he called out while stretching onto his toes in search of any sign she was nearby.

More men hurried through the crowd. Jack felt a rush as a pair hurried past him. They too were wearing scarlet red armbands. One of them held a brick in one hand while the other carried a low held pistol. Their tricorne hats were pulled low, and they were moving with purpose. Jack felt it in his bones. Something was about to happen here.

"Let's drag them away and tar the bastards!" a shout erupted.

"I say we gut them and send their carcasses back to their damned king!"

The sound of breaking glass brought a wave of quiet over the crowd. Jack froze in his tracks. He looked in the direction of the sound. The crowd had come to a halt and bodies were pressed close to one another. Jack searched desperately for any

A Bloody Beginning

sign of his parents only to find stern looking faces returning his glare.

"In the name of the king, I order you all gathered here to disperse immediately," an authoritative voice rose from the head of the crowd.

Jack slipped in between two men and ducked beneath the raised arm of another man who was shaking his fist high in the air. He worked his way forward, slipping between gaps in shoulders, chests and backs. Occasionally, he spotted another red armband. Few at first, but as he worked his way through the crowd in search of the other side, he saw more and more until he was surrounded in men wearing the blood red bands.

"Piss on your king!" an angry voice cried. The insult brought on a storm of shouts and cheers. It was impossible to move through this part of the crowd, all around him men were pressed shoulder to shoulder with their focus locked straight ahead.

"Here, send him this!" a shout rose above the crowd.

Jack heard the clatter of something fall, like a brick hitting stone. Shouts echoed through King Street. The crowd erupted with a frenzy of insults and threats.

"Jacky boy, where are you?"

Jack heard the voice of his father shouting.

"Jack? Jack?" His mother's voice wavered from somewhere up ahead of him.

Jack tried to press through the crowd. Two men wearing red armbands stood ahead of him. He

A Bloody Beginning

moved to cut in between them, but stopped cold when he saw one of the men lift his arm to hurl a brick through the air. He followed the projectile by cupping his hands around his mouth and screaming, "Back to England! Go back to England you bastards!"

A voice shouted from the head of the crowd. "Make ready!"

"Jack! Where are you?" his mother screamed. Her voice was plagued by a panicked urgency.

Jack lifted his head and cupped his hands around the sides of his mouth. He drew a breath and began to shout back to his mother, the words barely formed on his lips when a tremor ripped through the air. A single shot erupted, its boom was as loud as thunder between the tall brick buildings of King Street. Silence followed the shot, while the crowd dropped low to the street. Jack remained standing, his eyes searched for his parents in the chaos ensuing all around him. A hand grabbed the sleeve of his wool coat, followed by a voice warning, "Get down you blundering idiot!"

"Fire!"

A wave of deafening reports thundered. Jack felt the concussion of the shots press the air above him. Screams followed. A moan drifted up into the night air, carried by a cold wind that ceased for nothing. Jack lifted his head. Everywhere around him the crowd had flattened themselves to the cobbled street surface. A group of redcoats stood at the head of the gathering, their muskets still

A Bloody Beginning

shouldered, thin ribbons of smoke curled from their muzzles.

Jack fought himself up to his feet. His knees felt shaky and unsteady. His mouth was dry, and his head pounded with throbbing waves of pain that started at his stitched wound and radiated back to the base of his skull. "Mother? Father?" He said in a trembling voice that barely seemed to break the threshold of a whisper. Cold air stung his eyes and bit at the skin on his face. He felt separated from himself as he stepped over men who were still sprawled on the street.

"Murderers!" An angry shout sounded from somewhere in the street.

One of the redcoats drew out a sword. "Fix bayonets!" he shouted as he wielded his blade around to a defensive posture.

Another angry voice shouted, "Cowards! You shot into a crowd of unarmed civilians!"

With every step, Jack's heart slowed. He felt a crushing weight press down on him as his eyes scanned the mass of sprawled men covering the street. Another voice lifted to send a curse toward the British soldiers. Some of them moved gingerly in their prone positions, unwilling to stand after the onslaught sent forth by the line of British muskets. Jack stepped over arms and legs, torsos, shoulders. He searched out places for his feet to land where he wouldn't be stepping on a hand or an ankle. At first it was difficult to work his way through the crowd, it became easier as he made his way forward toward the line of soldiers. He

A Bloody Beginning

had heard his mother's shouts, and they had come from the front of the frenzy.

He found them both at the head of the group. His mouth opened, but no words would come. It only took one look for him to realize that both of his parents had fallen victim to the volley. Jack stood over his mother, her face was frozen in a distorted grimace of pain and worry. Jack's eye blurred as a rush of tears welled before streaming down his cheeks. The form of his mother became a hazy blur of shape and color under the wavering yellow light of oil streetlamps. He blinked away his tears and dropped to his knees. The cold cobblestones were hard, but the discomfort hardly registered. Jack's lungs felt as though they had seized. He took one of his mother's hands in both of his own and pulled it to his chest.

"Mother?" he whispered while squeezing her hand. Tears flowed faster. He could not keep his eyes clear no matter how fast he blinked. Breath finally came to him. He gripped his mother's hand tight, feeling her fingers and palm going cold even as he held firm. A pool of blood was spreading through the street where she lay, it collected in between cobblestones and flowed outward in a twisting spread like a river carrying away everything Jack held dear. His gaze followed the blood until it touched a familiar looking pair of shoes. With terror in his heart, Jack lifted his gaze from the unassuming leather shoes. He found worn, wool trousers with burn marks and a blood-soaked linen shirt. Jack rose from his knees and

A Bloody Beginning

stepped over the pooled blood. He found his father laying on the cold street, breathing in ragged rasps and lifting one blood-stained hand up toward him.

"B-b-boy, come here..." his father's voice was weak and strained. Jack dropped to his knees and took his father's hand.

Jack tried to draw breath, but it seized in his throat. Tears streamed from his eyes and ran down his cheeks and chin. He felt his father's grip. It was strong. As strong as it had ever been. There was life in him yet.

"Jacky boy, you go, get home. Get out of here." Jack's father wheezed before drawing a labored half breath. "Your mother..."

Jack shook his head. He closed his eyes, as if he could shut out what had happened and begin anew.

"You be good, Jacky boy. You have to be a man now..." His father's voice trailed away while the strength of his grip on Jack's hand faded. Jack stared at his father, paralyzed by grief and shock. He squeezed his grip on his father's hand. There was no life left in him, it was going cold just as his mother's had.

A shout came from the line of British soldiers, "In the name of the king, I order all subjects to immediately disperse! Anyone defiant of this command will be placed under arrest and stand trial for unlawful assembly and assault against a representative of the king!"

A Bloody Beginning

Jack's eyes cleared. His heart started to beat harder in his chest. The breath he had been unable to draw earlier seemed to flow without resistance. He felt a rush of warmth spread through his face. The throbbing pain he had felt pulsing through his forehead and scalp disappeared. The agony of grief was overpowered by a wave of unrestrained rage. Lowered his father's hand to the cold ground and noted bloodstains on his own fingers. For a moment, Jack stared at the stillness of his father's face, until he noticed an object laying on the cobblestones just beyond him. There was another man laying on the street, his blood mixed with that of Jack's father and mother. Jack saw the red armband tied around the fallen man's upper arm. It puzzled him for a moment. He reached for the object that lay on the snow caked cobblestones near his father's head. It was a flintlock pistol, its brass fixtures stained by the blood of the strange man with the armband.

"Disperse immediately!" the voice of the British officer was beginning to waver.

Jack held the pistol in his right hand. He knew next to nothing about the weapon. But he knew that to fire it all he needed to do was cock the hammer and squeeze the trigger. He rose to his feet, pistol held low at his side. The British officer who had brandished his sword before the volley fired now stood behind the line of soldiers. It had been his voice bellowing commands over King Street. Jack turned to survey the remnants of the crowd. Dozens of men were fleeing while nearly

A Bloody Beginning

half a dozen bodies lay motionless on the cold ground. In the midst of the fleeing crowd, like stubborn outcrops of rock refusing to surrender to the current of a rushing river, a group of nearly twenty men stood their ground. Their faces wore the stony complexion of resolute defiance in the face of intimidation. On their right arms, they wore scarlet red armbands. The closest of the men to Jack faced the line of British soldiers with his tricorne hat pulled low. He lifted one hand just above his shoulder and opened his palm toward the scattered group of men standing their ground behind him.

"I think it would be prudent for you and your men to leave with all haste. What you have done here will be answered, in one way or another."

The officer stepped in line with his men and narrowed his eyes at the defiant speaker. "Who are you to be giving me orders? Did you not hear me? I commanded everyone to disperse!"

Jack looked back to the man who had warned the soldiers lowered his hand to his side. His head cocked slightly, emphasized by the point of his hat. "My name is Samuel Adams, founder and leader of the Sons of Liberty. I am telling you, sir. If you do not take your men and leave, there will be more bloodshed this night." He paused for a moment and looked over at Jack briefly before turning back to the soldiers. "Let us tend to our fallen with dignity, or I promise you, there will be no place of safety for you. Here, or in England."

A Bloody Beginning

A hesitation fell over the soldiers on King Street. Jack looked at Samuel with awe while the rest of his Sons of Liberty stood firm behind him. The expressions on their face spoke volumes of their intent. They were not leaving. Snowflakes fluttered from the dark night sky and swirled as the bitter wind drove them in turbulent patterns through the Boston street. Jack felt as if his heart would beat out of his chest as he waited for the soldiers to respond to Samuel's threat. The cold brass of the trigger bit at his finger while he felt like his thumb would be frozen to the hammer forever.

"Detail," the officer in charge of the line of soldiers snapped, "stand down. Back to the garrison, lads. We will allow these, gentlemen, to dispose of their dead undisturbed."

CHAPTER 5

6th March 1770
Boston

Boston felt a little colder than it ever had. Cold and somehow empty despite the throngs of pedestrians making their way through the streets. Jack watched through a glass pane while snow continued to circle ever downward onto the already thick layer covering Boston's streets.

"Damn it, Sam. There is enough chatter about you still circulating from the riots that followed the Stamp Act. Are you determined that our family name must live in infamy until the second coming? Or are you just trying to get yourself shot, or marched to a gallows and hung?" Sam's cousin, John, scolded in a voice riddled by exasperation. He was shorter than Samuel, and stouter around the middle. But, his rounded

A Bloody Beginning

cheeks had given Jack an easy smile when he had greeted him along with his cousin Sam. Jack felt endeared to both men, even though they were in the middle of a heated debate. "We share a last name, Sam, and I would prefer to live my life peaceably and without these controversies and scandals. I have a law practice that I would like to continue, but that will only happen if I am able to find clients willing to pay for my services. People don't often seek out an attorney who is rumored to be inciting anarchy and stirring up trouble."

Sam rose from the chair he had been sitting in and let one hand come to rest on Jack's shoulder. "John, they opened fire on a crowd last night and murdered at least five, including both of this young man's parents. What is he to do now that he is orphaned? Who will hold these soldiers accountable? They must be brought to justice."

John sat behind his desk, a storm of conflict in his eyes as he shifted his gaze in between his cousin and Jack. "I know what it is that you want, Sam. I know. And I will tell you here and now that I will have no part in it! Justice means a fair trial, an unbiased jury, and a proportional sentence. Marching those soldiers out into the market square and hanging them from the nearest tree does not constitute justice."

Sam shook his head and squeezed Jack's shoulder. "I suggested no such course of action. My only point is that a trial should be commenced before those soldiers find their way back to England, which will guarantee them partiality in their favor. They deserve a fair trial, John, not one with all the odds stacked in their favor. I can only see more fervor and discontent coming from such."

John stood behind his desk and slammed an open palm on the hardwood top. "How are we to combat the endless occupation of the British army if you continue to stir unrest? If you were a Baker or a Smith it would not matter to me, but you are not. You are an Adams! And it is my name you sully alongside your own, damn you!"

"There is a time for appeasement, John. There was a time for reasonable disagreement, when we could debate these issues as policies, whether just or unjust. But, that time has passed, John. Blood has been spilled. There is only one response for that," Sam said. His voice was even and measured, as if he had planned his response while John had been speaking.

John rubbed his forehead. His face had gone red despite the pervasive chill in the law office. "I am no more for the policies of the crown of late than you are, Sam. But I do not believe further agitation is the path forward. We need to look for every available opportunity to compromise with the crown. Gain ground where we can, Sam."

Jack felt as awkward as he ever had in his life. Both of these men wore clothes that cost more than his family's entire wardrobe. The panes of glass in the office where he sat were nearly free of distortion, and the brass lamp sitting on John's desk was fueled by whale oil, something his

A Bloody Beginning

mother had only dreamed of. He lowered his gaze to the tight knit of plank flooring beneath John's desk. Despite the fervent argument taking place, he could not shake the images from his mind. His mother's twisted expression of pain, his father's blood-soaked shirt. The red ooze that had flowed in between cobblestones on the street as snowflakes melted into the warm liquid. Pale linen draped over their bodies. Their limp limbs when the undertaker and his apprentice had piled them onto a cart with the others. He felt tears welling in his eyes all over again. The seams of the floor became blurred.

"Jack. Do you have any family in Boston? Someone who can take you in until you can establish yourself?" The voice belonged to John. Jack looked up, only to find John a blurred mess of skin and red in his teary eyes.

"No, sir. No family nearby," Jack replied.

John pressed the line of questions. "Where is your extended family, if any?"

Jack wiped his eyes with the sleeve of his coat and thought for a moment. "Ireland, I suppose. I'm not sure exactly whereabouts though, but I know my mother had a cousin still in Ireland."

"And your father's family? What of them?" Sam asked in a friendly voice.

Jack shook his head and tried not to picture his father's face. "He never spoke of any family. Not even his parents." His stare lowered back to the floor under John's desk. "My father's blacksmith shop still has his tools, and his forge and anvil are

A Bloody Beginning

in good repair. I can work them both well enough, and sleep in the loft if I must. But, I had intended to make my life as a sailor."

Sam stepped in front of Jack and squatted down to look him in the eye. "In that respect, I may be able to help. I have a good friend, a gentleman of some repute here in Boston. He owns several merchant vessels, among other things. I believe we could make arrangements for your occupation of choice."

"He is a boy, Samuel," John objected. "He ought to be in school, at least for another year or two."

Sam turned to his cousin with a sharp frown. "Is that your offer to take him into your home, John?"

Flustered, John crossed his arms in front of his portly chest. "I have sons of my own, Sam, you know that."

"Then a job aboard one of Mr. Hancock's vessels is probably the best we can do for him. He will have a bed, or a hammock as it were, and meals in his belly. Mr. Hancock pays a fair wage for honest work…"

"Honest is a stretch if the rumors are to be believed," John sneered.

"Loyalist slanders don't concern our young friend," Sam retorted. "As it happens, I believe that one of Mr. Hancock's more profitable vessels is still in port. Though I am not sure how much longer it will remain." He reached to a coat rack and withdrew his finely made wool coat and tricorne hat. He waved his hat in a gesture for Jack to head for the door. "We will go call on John

A Bloody Beginning

Hancock, Jack. I am sure he will be able to find you suitable employment."

Jack felt a hot streak run through his blood, like he had been struck by lightning. He was about to become part of a ship's company. A sailor. He would become a sailor. Deep down, the sorrow and angst he felt for losing his parents assuaged slightly under the promise of seeing distant horizons. He stepped through the door as Samuel opened it and out into the cold Boston morning.

"Unprovoked, eh Sam?" John's challenge rang loud out into the street.

Jack turned back to the law office to find John and Sam facing each other, John's thumb and forefinger pinching at Sam's red armband.

"As I said, John. They fired into a crowd of civilians. Their actions will be answered, and if it be left to the Sons of Liberty to do so, then so be it. We will answer the call." Sam pulled his arm free from his cousin and closed the door with enough force that Jack feared the glass window panes might shatter. He paced into the street and offered Jack a firm nod. "With me, young man. Let's not let my cousin's sullen mood foul our day. You already have enough woes to last you a lifetime over. Let us seek out a better situation for you, eh?"

Jack searched for what to say. His head was awash in a storm of emotions. He felt the sharp edge of grief, still fresh from the night before, he felt shock from the whirlwind of events that seemed to be accelerating his life down a path he

A Bloody Beginning

had imagined years into his future. The new prospective future excited him, but it also brought the bitter taste of guilt to his mouth. His mother and father would have wanted him to finish school. His mind bounced and reeled from one state to the next in an unrelenting storm that had him so unsettled he was struggling to find words. He managed a feeble sigh and a nod of his head.

Sam clasped one hand onto Jack's shoulder. "I feel for your loss, young man. I really do. But, you cannot let the pain of your losses rule your life. You have to take opportunity when it presents itself. Seize the day. An hour lost is an hour wasted, and we have a limited number, as you well know, young man. Seafaring is a noble trade, and a merchant fleet will have you positioned to do well in life. Don't look at this as becoming a sailor, look at it as becoming a sailor with the possibility of someday becoming a captain in command of a ship, or better, owning the ship a captain sails in your name. Such are the opportunities that lay before you."

Jack followed Sam through the icy Boston air. Hardly a minute elapsed that he was not greeted by someone on the street. A woman waved and called out as she opened a second floor window. A man tipped his hat and offered both Sam and Jack a pleasant greeting as he passed in the opposite direction. A pair of stony faced men working in a rope yard offered nods and smiles as Jack and Sam approached the waterfront. It seemed that half of Boston knew Sam. Moreover, those who knew

A Bloody Beginning

him were eager to offer their greetings. He was well liked in a city known for its rough edged defiance and hostility.

"Sam!" a young man called from across the market square. "Is it true? Are the British withdrawing their regiments to the fort?"

Sam shook his head as he continued through the crowded market space. He answered the young man, "In due time, young man. All in due course and time, though it probably won't happen for a while, I imagine the events of last night must weigh heavy on the governor's mind."

Jack's mind drifted back to the scene on King's Street, the snow caked cobblestones and the dark outline of two story buildings towering around him. He could still smell the acrid gun smoke and see the blood as it oozed in between his parent's bodies. Jack flexed his right hand, feeling the morning's icy chill on his skin as he recalled his father's grip and his final words. He mumbled to himself, "I have to be a man now."

The peal of a ship's bell cut through the morning air and brought Jack back into his present surroundings. Boston's harbor lay sprawled out before them with tendrils of cold fog rising from the water's surface. The tang of salty air flooded Jack's nose while the chill of the wind coming in off of the Atlantic bit at his chin and cheeks.

"Come, now, young man. Only a little further and we will have you on your way in life," Sam said in a brisk tone. "It appears that the British warship is making ready to set sail, how prudent of them." He nodded to a passerby before crossing the last of the market square onto Merchant Lane. His pace seemed to quicken as they passed several shop fronts before he came to an abrupt halt in front of a brick building with large glass paned windows overlooking the harbor. He faced jack and cocked his chin upward. "Jack, Mr. Hancock is a distinguished gentleman and a wildly successful businessman. He has been a dear friend to me for many years, he is both an honest man and a staunch supporter of independence for the colonies. You would do well to mind your first impression. He is a friend you want to have."

Jack nodded as he tried to swallow the lump of apprehension that had formed in his throat as Sam opened the polished wooden door. A rush of warmth greeted him as he stepped into the front office, Sam followed Jack and promptly closed the door behind them both.

"Mr. Adams, how pleasant for you to come calling," said a dark haired young man sitting behind a desk just a few paces from the front door. "Mr. Hancock is eager to see you, in fact, I believe he was about to send me to fetch you here. It is fortunate for me that you decided to drop in, I was dreading the weather."

"It is cold, Matthew, painfully cold," Sam answered with a grin as he removed his hat and coat. "But, I can always count on Mr. Hancock to have a piping hot stove to drive away the shivers. I assume he is about?"

A Bloody Beginning

"He is," Matthew said with a nod toward his shoulder, "back in his office, sir. He is meeting with a captain as of this minute, but you may wait out here. He is quite anxious to speak with you."

"Very well then, we shall take in the warmth while he is occupied," Sam replied before turning toward Jack and helping him remove his coat.

"Would either of you care for some coffee? It is fresh in off a brig from South America," Matthew asked with a flourish of the quill in his hand.

Sam looked at Jack with raised eyebrows before turning back to Matthew. "I think we should both like that very much, sir, and I thank you for your generosity."

Matthew placed his quill on the desk in front of him and stood. "Mr. Hancock insists that his guests are all well received. With the exception of those in red coats, I should say." He moved to the corner of the front room and took up a kettle to place on top of the stove. "We have a ship that is due in from France, overdue actually, but winter weather on the Atlantic, these things can be expected. Mr. Hancock is expecting several dozen casks of genuine French wine, among some other things, I am sure he will fill you in on the details, Mr. Adams."

"French wine, that does sound delightful, now, doesn't it?" Sam nodded and offered a slight grin in return of Matthew's. "There are other matters of import I would be more interested to hear of from France. I don't suppose you have any knowledge of the sort?"

A Bloody Beginning

Matthew had taken up a tall cylindrical grinder and was winding a crank wheel attached to the top. He paused at Sam's question and peered over his shoulder. "As I said, Mr. Adams, French wine, among some other things. I am sure Mr. Hancock will discuss the matter with you, he knows how important these matters are, and I would rather not discuss his business in mixed company."

Sam leaned back at the comment and then shot a look toward Jack through the corner of his eye. "Right then, well, we will enjoy some coffee while we wait. How much longer do you think he will be?"

"Only a few more minutes, Mr. Adams. His affairs with the tender captain were mostly settled last night. I believe they are discussing the shortcoming of their crew. It has been very difficult to maintain crewmen, especially with the press gangs operating so vigorously up north. I have heard that the fishing fleets up by Salem have been utterly decimated, hardly an experienced hand to be found any more," Matthew finished his grinding and returned the cylinder to a shelf on the wall. He lightly tapped the side of the kettle and shook his fingers from the heat it had built. "A minute or two more. If Mr. Hancock becomes available before it is ready I will bring you both a cup in his office."

"Delightful," Sam replied before easing himself onto a wooden bench alongside the front office's side wall. "Press gangs are but another example of the crown's long list of abuses. The people have grown weary of them, and I foresee things getting worse before they improve." He patted one hand next to him on the bench in a gesture for Jack to take a seat. "It sounds as though you may be in luck, young man. If Mr.Hancock is short handed aboard his vessels, he will surely take you on."

Matthew looked over his shoulder while he continued preparing the coffee. "Oh. You are interested in coming aboard one of Mr. Hancock's vessels, eh? Well, have you any seafaring experience?"

Jack shook his head while he lowered himself onto the wooden bench next to Samuel. "No, sir. None at all."

Matthew shrugged. "Unfortunate. But, I should say it won't bar you from employment. We are in desperate need of capable hands, but capable hands only get that way through experience. Work hard and learn quickly, they'll have you up in the tops before you know it. Then when you get a voyage or two under your belt, your captain will rate you an able hand and you will earn yourself a half share in addition to your wages. It can be lucrative, if you apply yourself."

A creaking door interrupted the conversation, followed by the sound of footsteps on hardwood floor. The footfalls preceded a pair of men that could not have looked more dissimilar. The first to appear into the front office was a short man, thick around the middle to the point that the buttons on his vest appeared in danger of losing their hold at any moment. He had a balding head and plump, rosy complexion under a set of eyes that appeared to be in a perpetual smile. Following him was a much taller man with a slender build and a rigid disposition. His clothes looked immaculate, dark blue trousers over white hose with a dark blue jacket over a flourishing white blouse that Jack thought looked like silk.

"With your provisions loaded, I expect you should set sail as soon as practical. If you are unable to recruit crewmen here in Boston, I will permit your free hand in making port before your voyage back out to the whaling fleet. But, do not delay excessively. Every day in port is a costly, and we run further risk of having our sailors pressed by the damned crown," the tall man said in a flat tone. "Spring is upon us, though we would be hard pressed to know it by the weather. The whalers will be on the move soon to follow the migration. If we miss them, every day spent searching for the fleet will be money out of my pocket, and yours." His eyes scanned the room and landed on Jack and then shifted to Sam. "I've been expecting you," he said. "Come, we have much to discuss."

With hardly an acknowledgment the tall man turned and proceeded back through the doorway and into the recesses of his office. Sam nudged Jack with an elbow before standing in an abrupt motion. "Come now, young man. Here lies your chance. Be sure your handshake is firm and you make eye contact."

A Bloody Beginning

Jack followed Sam into the back office. At first, his eyes had to adjust to the darker room that seemed almost cavernous compared to the front office. Tall bookshelves loaded with volumes lined the walls, they varied in height to accommodate several paintings featuring tall masted sailing ships navigating storms or engaging in battle. On the far end of the room sat a large wooden desk with intricate carving on the front, on the wall to either side of the desk hung paintings of world maps, one that showed Europe and the other the new world. A fireplace sat in between two tall cases filled with books and scrolled papers. Jack wondered at the wisdom of their placement as the hearth contained a fire crackling away and spreading a penetrating warmth into the room.

"I hear the king's soldiers were kept rather busy last night, Sam. How did this happen? The tall man asked in a demanding tone.

Sam removed his hat and held it in both hands in front of his waist. "The people of Boston are sick of the king and his heavy handed methods of control, his taxes, his soldiers. From what I understand, it started with a few boys throwing snowballs."

The tall man turned back toward Sam and Jack with a snap and a look of disgust. "Snowballs? They fired on a crowd over snowballs?"

"The crowd grew in size after a patrol reinforced the lone sentry. What started with snowballs may have escalated to stones, though I did not see that with my own eyes," Sam replied with a sober look.

A Bloody Beginning

"They fired on the crowd, seven were killed, including this young man's parents." He gestured toward Jack with his hat. "Several more are wounded. Time will tell if their wounds will be too much to overcome." Sam paused and exchanged his glance between Jack and the tall man. "Excuse me, Mr. Hancock. I am remiss. My companion here is Jack Horner, and as I said, his parents were both slain in the volley on the crowd last night." He turned to Jack and offered a half grin. "Jack, this is Mr. John Hancock."

"I am pleased to meet you, sir," Jack offered in a quaking voice that he immediately chided himself for.

Mr. Hancock's face softened as he looked Jack over. "My deepest sympathies, young man. What a terrible thing to endure. If there is anything I can do to ensure that justice finds them, I am at your disposal."

"Jack is looking for employment, Mr. Hancock. He aspires to be a maritime man. I thought that perhaps you would be able to find something for him, given his recent tragedies, it would be good for him to get out of Boston for a while." Sam said with a gentle hand on Jack's shoulder.

Mr. Hancock swapped his gaze from Jack to Sam and then back again. "I see," he said. "Have you any sailing experience, young man?"

Jack shook his head. "No, sir."

Mr. Hancock nodded and ran a hand over his chin. "Right, well, that ought not to prevent you from employment. Though I will warn you, a life

A Bloody Beginning

at sea is one devoid of many of the luxuries ashore. There is no personal space to be had aboard a ship, and your first three months may see you plagued by seasickness among other plights. Boys and young men oft romanticize a life at sea without knowing of its inherent hardships. I would not have you aboard one of my vessels unwarned." He paused and gestured toward the map of Europe. "In addition, while we remain uninvolved in the greater European conflicts, that does not mean we are not affected by them. The Royal Navy continues its practice of impressment. You could sign up as a merchant sailor and find yourself forced into months or years of service to the crown as a sailor, imperiled against your will."

"I understand, sir, but there is little left here for me. I do not have the skill to continue my father's trade as a blacksmith, or the coin to continue living in my family's home," Jack replied. He did his best to maintain eye contact with the wealthy businessman, but found it impossible as his eyes glazed over at the mention of his father and his former home.

"Very well, then," Mr. Hancock relented, "consider yourself warned." He paused and seated himself behind the desk in an overstuffed chair. "I have several vessels in need of fresh crewmen. But, only one currently in port. We could keep you here in employ as a longshoreman, loading and unloading cargoes. I will leave the decision to you, young man."

A Bloody Beginning

Jack chewed at his lower lips with his front teeth for a long moment. "There is no choice for me, at the moment, sir. I have no place to live, and I cannot afford to continue the rental agreement my parents had with Mr. Albright."

A wry smile crossed Mr. Hancock's face. He shook his head. "I know Mr. Albright, and I extend by condolences for the heartache your family has been through on his account. He is a miserable, stuffy old Brit if there ever was one. From what I understand his tailor shop was vandalized yesterday. I can't say I didn't smile when I heard the news, though it is unfortunate for those under his employ, I cannot think of a better man to misfortune. He is truly a pig headed money monger. Boston would be better without him."

"I can agree on that count, sir," Jack said, his voice finding its strength again.

"Well, if it is to be the sea for you, son, then let us get you to it without delay," Mr. Hancock said. He stood from behind his desk and paced around the side to stand in front of Jack and Sam. "You will make for a fine deck hand on my tender ship, the Salem Tide."

Jack felt a tinge of excitement trace through his blood. He was about to become a sailor and embark on the journey of which he had only ever dreamed of. His excitement was followed shortly by a hard edge of guilt and the sudden onset of shame. He longed to hold his mother's hand or tell his father of the new endeavor. He grappled with the conflicting emotions.

A Bloody Beginning

"Thank you, sir," Jack muttered, as his head spun with the events that seemed to transpire faster than he could process.

Mr. Hancock nodded to both of them. "We do need to make haste, however. I just scorned my captain for lingering in port for too long. I imagine he will be putting to sea in short order."

At that moment, Matthew appeared at the office door with a tray of steaming cups. "The coffee is ready, gentlemen. Mr. Hancock, I took the liberty of preparing you some as well."

"Unfortunately, Matthew, we cannot partake. Though I am sure my guests appreciate the gesture, we must be off to the pier. We need to get young Jack here to the Salem Tide without delay, lest he be stuck ashore."

Matthew's shoulders slumped, though his face betrayed no sign of disappointment. From the reaction, Jack thought this must not have been the first time he prepared something for a guest only to have them fly right back out the front door. The coffee smelled bold and rich, it made Jack's mouth water and his stomach tighten with the realization that it had been more than a day since his last proper meal. He braced himself against the cold as Mr. Hancock and Sam led the way out of the office and back onto Merchant Lane. The wind had picked up, and on it fat flakes of snow drifted in meandering paths toward the ground. The cold was bitter, as bitter as it had been the night before, though somehow Jack didn't seem to feel its bite quite as potently.

A Bloody Beginning

"There is talk of the governor requesting more troops, Sam, that is counterproductive to our goals," Mr. Hancock said as he shielded his face from the wind with the lapel of his fine woolen coat.

"All in due time, sir. We will weather the storm. There is talk circulating, the events of last night are being called 'the bloody massacre' and 'the Boston Massacre'. People won't stand for these sorts of injustices. Not in Boston." Sam replied before cupping his hands around each other and blowing warm air into his fingers. "There are already calls for the militia to stand up and keep the peace between the king's soldiers and our citizens."

Jack watched Mr. Hancock regard Sam with a doubtful glare.

"Keep the peace, Sam? Adding more armed men into the mix will only invite further discord. No, we need to consider other measures," Mr. Hancock said with a stern shake of his head. "Our primary focus should be on legislative representation. We should have a voice in our governance if we are to be taxed at such exorbitant rates."

"I agree, sir. But, I would say that the only path that guarantees that outcome is total independence from the crown. Liberty for the colonies."

Jack listened while the two men debated what would come next for Boston. Their words drowned in the wind and the sound of washing surf beneath the pier as their footfalls crossed from

A Bloody Beginning

the cobbled road and onto wooden planks. The smell of the sea overpowered his senses, it washed over him and left a lingering salty taste on the back of his tongue.

"Jack?" a familiar voice shouted.

Jack looked around for the source of the greeting and found his friend Tom clattering his way up the pier behind them through a torrent of slanting snowflakes. Vapor trailed from his mouth as he hurried behind Jack on the pier.

"What are you doing?" Tom asked breathlessly, "Did you hear about what happened last night? My father is furious! He says he will refuse to work on any ship sailing for the crown, merchantman or man of war alike."

Jack offered his friend a sullen nod. "Is that so?"

"It is, my father was furious when he heard. That hull model in his office, the one that you liked, he slammed it against the wall and made it no more than a pile of kindling. He is still fuming!" Tom's reply was cut by the wind as he gasped to get out his words after his shuffle up the pier in the frigid wind. He paused for a long moment while Jack continued his march behind Sam and Mr. Hancock. "Wait, Jack, what are you doing?"

Jack took in a deep breath of sea air and let it out in a long sigh. "My parents were killed last night by the volley. I am going now with Sam and Mr. Hancock, they are going to introduce me to my new home."

A Bloody Beginning

Tom's steps came to an abrupt halt. "Jack, I'm sorry for your losses, but, you are going to sea? For him?" He pointed at Mr. Hancock.

Jack nodded his head and continued to pace his way behind the two men leading him. "Yes. I am." He looked over his shoulder and caught a shocked expression on the face of his friend. There was a glimmer of jealousy in the boy's eye, but it faded in the light of realizing why Jack was taking such a drastic leap in life.

"I must be getting back to the yard, Jack. My father will want to hear this. But, I wish you all the best. Good luck on your voyage." Tom said while stuffing his hands deep into his coat pockets.

"Thank you, Tom," Jack replied over his shoulder as the tender ship loomed high in front of him at the end of the pier.

"Wait," Tom cried as the distance grew between them. "Are you coming back to Boston?"

Jack shrugged his shoulders. "I don't know." As he said it, a heaviness tugged at his heart. The corner of his eye scanned the gray banked skyline of the city. It had been his home for all of his life. He turned and faced the tall masts and crossing yards of the Salem Tide. "I have to be a man now."

CHAPTER 6

'Salem Tide'
6th March 1770
Boston Harbor

"It's a right honor to 'ave ye aboard, Mr. Hancock," said a gruff, scruffy faced sailor as Sam, Jack and Mr. Hancock crossed the gangplank onto the deck of the Salem Tide. "I'll see about fetching up the captain, sir. He can't be far, just came aboard a few minutes before ye's all arrived."

"That will do," Mr. Hancock replied, his chin held high as he panned the deck of the ship with an inspecting gaze.

Jack was awash in the activity of the ship's deck. Sailors were up in the rigging calling back and forth with hands on the deck as they worked lines and ran up blocks. It seemed everywhere that Jack turned there was a new form of activity. Tools clattered as carpenters worked at various projects on deck and over the side, lines hummed through

A Bloody Beginning

pulleys, footfalls drummed on wooden planks, bells pealed, calls echoed, all while sailors grumbled and cursed. It was an inundation that flooded Jack and caused his head to spin while he tried to take it all in.

"Two days in port, and still they are not ready to put to sea. Their last visit ashore being not even a month ago, it is enough to drive a man to tears, if not into a debtor's prison. This damned captain, he must mean to see me to my very brink," Mr. Hancock muttered under his breath.

"Mr. Hancock? I just departed your office, sir. As you can see, we are preparing to sail with all haste," the flushed face captain said as he appeared on deck from the aft ladder well.

Jack turned and found the captain, the same portly man who he had just seen in the front office of Mr. Hancock's building. He appeared disheveled, if not a little irritated, by the unannounced visit from the ship's owner.

"I can see you are preparing to sail, as I said earlier it would have been prudent for you to have already been in transit, but that is not what I have come for now." Mr. Hancock turned slightly, angling his shoulders while looking back at Jack with a cocked brow. He turned back to the captain and offered a stern nod. "I have brought you a newly hired sailor. He is a strong lad, by the look of him, and with an intelligent manner about him. He will serve well as a deckhand until he learns the rigging and sail handling. I expect you to bring him under your tutelage as soon as you see it

A Bloody Beginning

prudent to teach him navigation and ship handling as well. He is also the son of a blacksmith, so he may have the added benefit of some knowledge of the trade."

Both men looked at Jack with stern glares, and for a moment he felt as if he would melt into the deck planks and slip beneath the ship into the frigid water of the harbor. A powerful hand clasped his shoulder and Jack turned to find Sam, giving him an encouraging nod.

"I'm not half the smith my father was," he stammered, choking on a rush of rising emotions for a heartbeat before continuing, "but I know my way around a forge and anvil."

Mr. Hancock and the captain exchanged glances before the captain looked Jack over with an inspecting glare. "Have you any time aboard a ship, boy? Any seafaring experience?"

Jack shook his head. "No, sir. But, I am a hard worker, and a quick learner."

While the tension inside of his chest had risen, Jack had failed to notice that activity on deck and in the rigging had come to a complete halt. The chatter had ceased, as had the clatter of mallets and hauling of lines. It became apparent to Jack as the scruffy-faced sailor leaned in toward the captain and whispered something into his ear. The captain's eyes went wide with surprise. He shot the scruffy faced sailor a look before narrowing his eyes at Jack.

"The first mate tells me that it was your father who sold us those harpoons. They fetch a right

A Bloody Beginning

pretty price from the whalers. Why would you forsake your father's trade to come to sea, boy? I imagine he has himself a thriving profit with the quality of his work." The captain asked with a weathered voice. Mr. Hancock leaned down and said something quietly into the captain's ear before turning back toward Jack with a tight expression. "I apologize, son. I didn't mean any offense by it. We will gladly take you on and have you right fit to sail in no time. My condolences for your loss."

Jack fought the tears welling in his eyes. Grief stabbed at him, cutting deep into his every thought. But, he didn't want to show these men any sign of weakness. His new shipmates would surely not want the likes of a sniveling boy aboard their vessel as they set out to brave the Atlantic. He pulled in a deep breath of frigid salty air through his nose. It stung his nostrils, but the cold helped him hold his emotions at bay. Everything was happening so fast. His life seemed to be spinning out of control, and he was powerless to stop it. He hardly noticed as the captain issued his first mate an order and motioned toward Jack.

"Aye, sir," the scruffy sailor replied before taking a lumbering step toward Jack. He planted a firm hand on his shoulder and offered him a grin and a nod. "I'll see to it that yer situated and supplied. Rain slicks, a bedroll fer yer hammock, and maybe a few more odds and ends."

A Bloody Beginning

Jack felt Sam's hand slip off of his other shoulder. He turned and found Sam and Mr. Hancock both looking at him with long stares.

"Best of luck to you, Jack," Sam said with a sullen smile, "do come and call on me when you make Boston next. My cousin's law office is a good place to start, as is Mr. Hancock's office."

Jack nodded, feeling a warmth for the kindness Sam had shown him. "Thank you, sir. I surely will." He extended his hand which Sam took and gripped in a firm but brief shake. Jack looked to Mr. Hancock, "I will do my best to earn my keep, sir."

Mr. Hancock nodded, his stony demeanor breaking into a full smile for the first time that Jack had seen. "Of that I am sure, young man. Keep your legs about you, on deck, but especially when you go aloft. Remember, one hand for the ship, one hand for yourself. Move one limb at a time and you will weather the foulest seas."

"Thank you, sir, I will remember that." Jack replied with a nod as he felt a tug from the hand on his shoulder.

"Come on there, young man. We 'aven't got all day. The captain will want to be making sail soon and I won't be able to lolly about showing ye around. Now, let's get ye down to the purser and see ye outfitted," the scruffy first mate growled.

"Whatever he needs," Mr. Hancock interjected, "it is on the company."

As the words passed, the first mate froze in his steps for a heartbeat. Jack thought he saw the

A Bloody Beginning

man's jaw slacken slightly. "I'll be a son of a…" he grumbled toward the deck before looking back up at Mr. Hancock. "Aye, sir, I'll see that he is outfitted, best aboard, all at your expense of course. Best set of riggins we got will be his, and he'll be dandied up right for the weather, never mind there's sailors been aboard two years that haven't got themselves a decent pair of shoes. I'll see him rightly squared, I will."

He felt the tug at his shoulder grow stronger as the first mate urged him along, prodding him to an opening in the deck that looked similar to the one he had passed through to go below deck on the warship.

"I'll show you to the purser to get outfitted, and then to your watch, and mess. They will show you where to hang your bunk tonight and where you can sit for breakfast and supper. Two meals a day on this ship, breakfast is usually boiled oats thick as paste, sometimes when we are in warmer climates, we get enough fruit aboard to have fruit with our oats, but that is rare. Supper always consists of a meat, beans or rice depending on what we've got, and your bread. It'll be baked bread, when we are recent out of a port, hard ship's bread the rest of the time. Sometimes we get lucky and get some cheese aboard, like today, we have half a dozen round wheels of cheese down in the hold. I'm hopeful the captain will keep one of them to feed the crew." He ducked down below the weather deck and gestured for Jack to do the same. Jack followed, taking careful steps down the stairs until his shoes clattered onto the next deck. "My name is Pete, Peter Winthrow, but most of the crew calls me by Petey, to my face at least. I'm sure there are far fouler names they have uttered."

They made their way through a throng of sailors that were stacking coils of heavy rope in piles along the curved hull of the ship. The smells that invaded Jack's senses aboard the warship were also found on this vessel in abundance. Coffee, tobacco, tea, leather, tarred timbers and smoke all combined with the smell of sweat soaked bodies packed into tight quarters. Jack could feel his eyes bulging as he tried to take everything in under the dim yellow of warm lantern light. Petey expertly wove his way in between passing sailors while offering greetings or giving direction as he went. Jack tried to keep up and stay out of the way where he could. The entire space felt crammed, like he was underfoot and in the way of every man with a heavy load on his shoulder or trying to get somewhere else in the ship.

"We'll get you set with a tarpaulin slicker and a hat, it's only oiled sailcloth, but it will keep you drier than if you had none," Petey said over his shoulder without looking back. He ducked beneath a timber that spanned the width of the ship while digging into the inside of his winter coat. "The purser is a prickly son of a bitch. Mr. Hancock hired him for it. He won't like that he has to front you gear without docking your pay, but I will let him know. The damned owner says, and what the ship owner says goes, even for the

A Bloody Beginning

captain." His hand produced a wooden pipe from the inside of his coat and he stuck the stem into his mouth. "I'll say you probably ought to be fitted with a pair of gloves for the cold. I'm guessing you don't have any of the such tucked away in that paper thin coat of yours."

Jack shook his head as he ducked beneath the wooden beam. "No, sir. No gloves."

Petey shrugged and opened a cabin door at the end of a narrow corridor. "A hammock, too. We'll need a hammock and bedroll for you. A hat and slicker, gloves, and mess gear."

Inside the cabin door sat a pinched face puff of a man wearing a shirt and vest that Jack judged to be sized for a man of lesser girth. His cheeks were as red as ripened apples and his hair was a wisp of thinning white. He wore wire frame spectacles which sat in a precarious manner near the end of a bulbous round nose. He looked perpetually miserable in his cramped space and snapped his neck toward Jack and Petey to shoot a scowl of disapproval.

"No knock, eh? There must be some kind of fiscal emergency, surely. Why else would I be so rudely disturbed without even the courtesy of a knock?" The heavy-set man snarled.

"My apologies, Mr. Ricketts," Petey said as he ran a hand over his scraggle of beard. "But, Mr. Hancock has hired this young man on as a deckhand. He is to be outfitted at cost to the company, on his orders."

A Bloody Beginning

Mr. Ricketts leaned forward and inspected Jack over the top of his spectacles. His frown deepened as he drew noisy breaths through his nose. "At the expense of the company? That sounds off, Mr. Winthrow. Very unlike Mr. Hancock, in fact I don't ever recall him bringing on a sailor and fronting the cost of the necessities. Not once."

Petey lifted a candle from the purser's desk and brought its flame to the bowl of his pipe. "This young man isn't just any sailor. He is of special interest to Mr. Hancock, and to the captain." He drew in a breath through the pipe and exhaled a bluish cloud of tobacco smoke. "He'll have the necessary goods, and a quarter pound of tobacco to boot, or there'll be hell to pay next time we make port."

Jack watched as Mr. Ricketts' face grew a deeper shade of red and his beady eyes locked onto the ship's first mate. Petey's casual manner reminded Jack of the crowd of sailors he had encountered on Mirk Street. Mr. Ricketts reached up and snapped the candle out of Petey's hand and sent a splatter of wax onto the floor.

"Now you've gone and done it, look at the mess you've made," Mr. Ricketts snapped.

Petey shrugged, "Needed to light me pipe." He drew in another breath and released more smoke into the cramped cabin. "Can we get the young man outfitted, or not?"

Mr. Ricketts seethed for a moment and shot Petey a poisonous glance as he tried to resettle the candle onto a holder on his minuscule desk. "Mess

A Bloody Beginning

gear we have. He'll have a cup, plate, fork and spoon. But, as for a slicker, hat and gloves, he will have to do with what he has for now. I was not able to make arrangements for procuring such items during this visit to Boston."

Jack watched the exchange between the two men as tension thrummed in the air of the small cabin. Petey's casual swagger seemed only to further infuriate Mr. Ricketts.

"We've only had two days, I know how difficult it can be to get anything done in such a short visit. Especially since you had so many other duties to attend," Petey quipped.

Jack waited for Mr. Ricketts to react. He wasn't disappointed. The sarcasm dripping from Petey's tone illustrated his disdain for the purser, while the evident frustration on Mr. Ricketts' face let Jack know the feeling was mutual.

"I had provisions to purchase and goods to sell. That is how we make a profit for our proprietor, and we need to remain profitable, Mr. Winthrow. I am sure I don't need to remind you that we are the last tender ship in his fleet. If he deems it prudent, you could find yourself slogging along on a regular merchantman, for far less pay," Mr. Ricketts sneered as he looked over both Jack and Petey past the top edge of his spectacle lenses. "Now, draw the young man's necessities. Hammock, bedroll, plate, cup and spoon. A quarter pound of tobacco, and not a pinch more. As soon as we have oiled sailcloth for a slicker, I will ensure that he gets one."

A Bloody Beginning

Jack started to reply to the purser, "I don't even smo-"

"That'll do well enough, Mr. Ricketts. Just be sure to put the stores down to the ship's expense. I know yer tricks, and if the boy's wages are docked, ye be getting a visit from me," Petey interrupted. His voice bordered on hostile as he turned and slammed the purser's cabin door shut. He pulled another breath of smoke from his pipe and looked at Jack with narrowed eyes. "My apologies, lad. Mr. Ricketts can be a son of a bitch even on his good days. Today isn't one of his best days, but I'm afraid to say, it isn't one of his worst either. Miserable bastard belongs in a lubber storefront, and he knows it. He's no sailorman." He stepped down the corridor in long, sure strides leaving a trail of pipe smoke.

"Petey, he said I get a quarter pound of tobacco," Jack said with a frown. "I don't even smoke. I have no use for tobacco."

"Aye," Petey replied with a chuckle, "Ye don't, lad, but I do. I'll take yer tobacco."

Jack smiled at the little con the first mate had plied against the purser. It wasn't going to be counted against his wages, so there seemed to be no harm in the ploy. He tried to match Petey's gait as they crossed from the corridor and into the open area of the first deck.

"Ye'll hang your hammock with first starboard watch," He said and pointed to a quarter of the open deck with the stem of his pipe. "They aren't a bad lot, and they can teach ye a thing or two about

A Bloody Beginning

deck life before we take ye aloft." He clamped the pipe back into his bite and motioned toward the stairs they had just descended to come below and see the purser. "Come with me and I will take ye up and make some introductions. We'll be underway soon and there won't be much time for niceties."

Jack frowned. "Shouldn't we do as Mr. Ricketts said and get my things?"

Petey cocked a crooked smile. "Don't worry, lad. I'll see ye down to the hold to get your gear before its time for supper and for you to turn down for the night. But, you need to meet your messmates before we set to sailing. Once we are underway, I won't have much time for making proper niceties or holding yer hand about the deck. Yer'll need to learn from your watch and your messmates." He lurched up the stairs and stepped up onto the ship's exposed main deck, a trail of sweet tobacco smoke left to swirl in his wake.

As Jack stepped back up onto the main deck of Salem Tide, a wave of cold wrapped its icy fingers around him. Snowflakes fluttered down from the heavens while Atlantic winds blustered in from the east. It gripped his skin and made the stitches above his eyebrow feel as tight as a drum. Despite the overcast sky, it took his eyes a moment to adjust to the flood of light above deck. He squinted for a moment and scanned the deck for Petey. The first mate had disappeared into a bustle of activity that seemed to be intensifying with every passing heartbeat.

A Bloody Beginning

"Water stores are loaded and secured, fifty-four casks, Mr. Winthrow," a sailor reported from somewhere behind Jack.

"Very well, enough water for a good while," Petey's gravelly voice replied.

Jack searched in the direction he heard Petey's voice and found the first mate at the base of a broad mast, holding a burning wick to the bowl of his pipe.

"See to it that the guns are all secured, and double check their rigging. March in the Atlantic can get nautical, last thing we need is a damned cannon getting loose and battering holes in the hull." Petey's orders were intermixed with a fresh cloud of pipe smoke. He extinguished the wick and casually closed the lantern which had supplied his flame.

"Hands, to the braces! Hands, to the braces!" a loud voice cried out. Jack turned to find a tall, thin man under a large brimmed tricorne and wearing a long gray coat. He was standing a double step away from the ship's great wheel with a metal cone held up near his mouth. "Lay off those mooring lines and pay out topsail and gallants, fore and main."

Jack searched out Petey in the flurry of activity stirred by the shouted orders. He found the first mate pacing toward the side of the ship nearest the docks, intermittent clouds of pipe smoke spilling over his shoulder as he redirected hands to their task. It seemed to Jack like chaos. Sailors moved about the deck like bees within their hive

A Bloody Beginning

while others took to the steep rope woven ladders leading aloft.

"Pay out windward clew, take in the lee," the amplified voice called over the deck.

Jack felt like a glass bottle lost over the side of a great ship, bobbing along as the ocean swept all about him. High overhead, the luff of sails unfurling sounded. Ropes whined and blocks squeaked. Voices called back and forth to each other as the crew worked through their tasks. Footfalls pattered on the deck. Jack watched, his heart thrumming within his chest as if it were going to beat its way right out of his ribcage. His eyes were locked on the hands aloft as they worked their sail while snowflakes swirled in the wind around them. Not a single man seemed anxious about working the heights in the cold or the wind, they each walked their course with the same casual swagger he had noted from the crew of navy men on Mirk Street. Ropes criss crossed in an intricate web of rigging high overhead. Canvas spread and filled with the force of the wind. Jack felt the deck shift beneath his feet. It was a strange sensation, one he had never known before. His heart pulsed harder while snowflakes dropped into his eyes and on his cheeks. The snowfall seemed to be intensifying. Still wanting to watch the sailors aloft, Jack exchanged his glances between the deck beneath him and the tops high above. He hardly noticed the sailors on deck, until a rough shoulder collided with his.

A Bloody Beginning

"Watch where you're going, lub, there's workin to be done," snapped a weathered face old sailor as he brushed past Jack on his way to the next task.

"Apologies, sir," Jack replied while sidestepping to move out of the sailor's path.

"Don't 'pologize to me none, just stay yer ass out the way, boy. There's sailorin to do, and leave it to the sailormen. This isn't your nursery and I'm not your cunny nursemaid, damn ye," the sailor spat with a sneer.

A shock traced through Jack's blood. Anger welled inside of him as he looked back at the wind and sun gnarled face of the testy sailor. He choked the urge to renounce the man and throw his fists into his throat as he felt the hot well of tears beginning to form behind his eyes. He clenched his jaw tight to prevent angry words from spilling out. The sailor stared at him with hard eyes, almost daring him to lash out in anger before swiping his hand through empty air in a dismissive gesture and turning to go about his tasks.

"That old gripe?" Petey's voice interrupted Jack's livid thoughts, "We call him Bitter End Bill, or just Bill. Depends on his mood. Today seems to be a bitter end day."

Jack turned and found Petey standing with his hands on his hips and his pipe clenched tight between his teeth. "Why is he so foul? I've never met the man before and he acted like I had cheated him out of wages."

A Bloody Beginning

Petey pulled a big drag of pipe smoke before snapping his pipe from his bite and knocking the wooden bowl against the ship's rail. "There's no rhyme or reason to it, lad. Don't give him a second thought. He's a Brit sailorman. Twice pressed in his youth. He is one hell of a top man, knows rigging part near as good as any hand I've ever seen. But, he is a damned pissy old gripe. Never happy. Not even when there is ale or rum to be had aboard. In fact, once he gets a slog or two in him, I would be sure to steer a wide berth, if ye catch my drift."

Jack looked back toward the part of the deck where Bitter End Bill had gone. "I'll remember that. Thank you."

"Now that we're sheeted and running out, let me show ye about the deck, eh?" Petey said while packing his pipe bowl with a pinch of tobacco.

"I would like that," Jack replied. His gaze fell from the rear of the ship to the wooden structure of Long Wharf and then traced the great vertical timbers and crossbeams back to where they met the shore. His entire life he had dreamed of watching Boston fade away behind him from the deck of a ship. Now, it was happening.

Petey stepped from the wooden rail that lined the border of the ship's deck and strutted his way to the broad base of the towering mast in the center of the deck. He opened the door of the same lantern he had used earlier and inserted a wick to steal some flame to light his freshly packed pipe. With a puff of success and a quick wink and a nod

A Bloody Beginning

to Jack he shook the wick to extinguish it before slapping his calloused hand against the thick timber trunk of the mast. "This here is the mainmast, she's our bread and butter. She gives the old girl her press against the seas. We can aid the ship in steering course with sails on the mainmast to a point, but thrust is nine-tenths of her job." He took a drag and cast a long look up the towering structure toward the platform that seemed so high and away it made Jack's neck ache when he followed the stare. "The main yard hangs our mainsail, the top yard hangs the topsail all the same, and above that we have top gallants higher still. Each level is supported by a set of stay lines and braces, and their canvas can be bent to favor the wind at angle if need be. She is a full rigged sea bird, so we can sail at damn near any point of wind except dead head-on into it." He paused and glanced at Jack with a mischievous grin. "That's not to say we can't make our way upwind, neither. It just takes some sailorin, and that we have no shortage of." He stabbed his pipe toward the rear of the ship. "Aft there we have the mizzenmast, an her with her jib, top and topgallant. But, there is no top-gallant to be fixed there right now, lest the cap'n orders it special like, then we get the carpenters aloft and they gets to shakin' in their damned shoes fixing the old girl with a mizzen top-gallant. Can't say I've ever seen it done, but that's not to say it couldn't be neither." He repeated the gesture toward the front of the ship. "Up there we have the foremast, she has her own

A Bloody Beginning

main and top, and top-gallant as well. We get some push from her, for sure, but steerage is the bulk of her work. Oft times you'll hear the quarter shout for tops fore and main. Now, for a lubber, that'll sometimes send 'em scurrying to rig the topsail and the mainsail on the foremast."

"But it is meant for topsails on the foremast and mainmast," Jack interrupted.

Petey's face spread with a grin so broad that his eyes seemed to smile. "Aye, it does. Ye catch on quick, young man."

The Salem Tide shifted with a slight rock as her sails caught the wind at angle. She pulled further away from Long Wharf and edged toward the mouth of the harbor. The wind was bitter cold, and Jack's face felt its stinging kiss as he looked over the ship's side and toward the shore side sprawl of Boston. The buildings seemed small from his distant perspective out in the harbor.

"Last chance to change 'yer mind and swim ashore. It'll be a cold swim, for sure, but a stout lad like you should make it," Petey chided with a grin and a puff of bluish smoke.

Jack shook his head. "There is nothing left for me in Boston."

The smile faded from Petey's face, and Jack noted a sadness in his eyes. "Come with me, lad. The foc'sle is calling my name and there is something ye ought to see."

Jack tugged the edges of his knit hat lower over his ears. Salem Tide angled away from Boston and cleared the sheltering fingers of land that

A Bloody Beginning

protected the harbor from the open ocean. The horizon spread wide under a sky of low hanging gray clouds while torrents of snow flurried down and disappeared on contact with the briny water. Petey clambered forward to the bow and stood at the base of a mast jutting forward over the sea. He tossed a look over his shoulder and motioned for Jack to come forward.

"Here she is boy! Yer new home," He said with his arms outstretched in a grand gesture. "She stretches so far it will bend your mind. A month sailing east and we may see Europe on the horizon, if we steered her south by east we could visit the African coast. Three weeks south and we could be in the Caribbean, a month after that and we could be battling the swells around the horn. It's all at our fingertips. The possibilities are endless."

Jack stepped forward and let his hands come to rest on the wooden bulwark of the bow. The horizon stretched out for as far as he could see to the north, the east, and the south. Despite the grand sight, Jack closed his eyes. He breathed in the smell of the frigid sea and the salty spray that flecked his cheeks as waves broke along the hull. He was going to sea.

CHAPTER 7

'Salem Tide'
7 March 1770
42 Degrees 39' N, 70 Degrees 15' W

The Atlantic swells had built during the night. They left the short, choppy ribbons of water Jack was used to seeing in the harbor a distant memory. When Salem Tide had first cleared the mouth of the harbor, the waves had been between two and three feet in size. Nothing more than water lapping against the hull of the tender ship as she angled her way out to sea amid a torrent of falling snow. But as Boston faded away in the distance, the seas grew progressively larger and the wind blew stouter and colder. Not long after clearing the bay, Jack had shuffled his way below deck to retreat from the cold spray of seawater and blustering winds. Petey, Salem Tide's first mate, had shown him where to hang his hammock

A Bloody Beginning

and how to climb into it. It was a delicate operation, but Jack managed to wriggle himself in on the first attempt.

Despite his hunger, Jack had forgone supper when the mess bell was sounded. Sailors crowded the deck and flopped makeshift tables in nearly every available space. A hefty wooden keg was tapped and ale flowed into cups of tin and wood. The food seemed reasonable enough fare, a thick stew of some type. The smell of it penetrated every corner of the ship. Salt and meat and cooked vegetables. The rest of the crew seemed well pleased with the meal and the deck of Salem Tide brimmed with chatter and laughter as the men regaled each other with tales from their brief stint ashore.

"Saw the whole thing with my own eyes, I did. Those redcoats leveled their weapons and plugged that crowd like they was slaughterin' sheep for supper. It was a mess of a sight. Blood runnin' through the streets, bodies everywhere," a sailor ranted over his cup as the cook wandered through the mess slopping spoonfuls of supper onto waiting wooden plates. "There were a few that walked away. But, it was a massacre like you've never seen."

Jack waited out the meal and mostly kept to himself despite several of the crew offering to fill his cup or load his plate. His heart felt heavy, and his empty stomach was unsettled from the constant motion of the ship. The deck was crowded and soon became almost stifling with the

A Bloody Beginning

heat of so many hands crammed so close together. But, despite the large gathering, Jack felt a loneliness welling in his chest. His thoughts drifted to his mother, the image of her face as life slipped out of her. His father's grip on his hand. He closed his eyes and he could almost feel it. Jack fought back tears, but he knew he would not be able to hold them off forever. Mercifully, the hands finished their supper and soon started clearing their tables and stowing away their mess gear.

Jack kept a wary distance from Bitter End Bill and carried on like everyone else when the time came to sling their hammocks for the night. Sleep came in fits amid the constant pitching and swaying of the ship and the throaty snores of her sailors. At several points during the night, Jack was jarred from his delicate hold on slumber by the penetrating peal of the ship's bell. The first such instance set his blood on fire. Was there a fire? Had they come across some foreign vessel that meant them harm? Jack placed one hand on the edge of his hammock and craned his neck to see if there was a scurry of action indicating danger. Nothing. After a few moments of tense waiting in the darkness, a lone sailor made his way through the maze of hammocks with a lantern in hand. He appeared to be looking for someone in particular as he lifted the light and inspected faces along his path.

When the sailor came near, Jack raised a whisper, "What is going on? Is something amiss?"

A Bloody Beginning

The sailor's lip curled and his brows furrowed into a frown. "What you mean?"

"The bell, is something wrong?"

A smile of stained, crooked teeth spread across the sailor's face and he broke into a hushed, dry chuckle. "No, ye lubber. Two bells in the midwatch. Ye still have time fer yer sleepin." He lifted the lantern a little higher and let the light shine into Jack's face. "If there be an alarm, yer will know it when ye hears it. That bell be ringing faster than ye think it can and there be sailormen all in a frenzy to get topside. Fear not, lad. If there be an alarm, yer'll know."

Jack sunk back into his hammock, embarrassed by his ignorance and exhausted from days of turmoil. His hammock swayed with the roll of Salem Tide while his eyes slowly succumbed to the warmth and darkness within the ship. Slumber finally took hold, and Jack was greeted by familiar feelings. The smell of his mother jarring stewed apples in the fall, her soft look and warm smile. His father coming into their small home after a day of labor at the forge and anvil, his hands calloused and covered in sooty stains. A sort of happiness rested on him, as he rocked gently within the confines of the ship and his mind drifted to days past when his parents were more than just a memory. It was fleeting, though, and soon his dreams soured. The warmth of home was replaced by a cold wind and the smell of stewed apples morphed into the acrid smell of spent gunpowder. His mother's face, wracked by pain,

A Bloody Beginning

filled his mind. The sound of his father's voice filled his ears. "You have to be a man now." Blood oozed between cobblestones. It soaked into the gathered bits of snow, turning them crimson red. His father's voice sounded, "Jacky, get up. Its time to get up." He felt the cold now. It pierced the warmth that had surrounded him. Bells sounded, footfalls began all around him.

Jack opened his eyes. The darkness of the upper deck was being flooded with lantern light.

"Time to rise, you dogs, rise and earn your damned wages," Petey's voice boomed through the cavernous deck cabin. "The seas run high and there is distance to cover. Sails need be sheeted home and they aren't going to sheet them damned selves."

Jack grabbed the edge of his hammock and pulled it down. All around him sailors hurried out of their suspension to drop their feet to the deck. He followed suit by wrapping one leg over the side of his hammock and stretched to plant his toes on the deck. With a slight twist and a pitch of the deck, Jack found himself slamming onto hard planks. Pain shot through his jaw and up into his forehead. His knees had hit hard as well, and they both throbbed from the impact. A rough hand grabbed at his shoulder and pulled him to his feet.

"That was a nasty spill ye took, boy. Are ye alright?" a voice growled.

Jack reeled from the blinding pain in his jaw and head while standing on wobbly knees. He nodded and managed to muster a feeble voice, "Yes, sir."

A Bloody Beginning

"No sirs here, lad. Just sailormen," the voice replied. "Let's get yer bunk down and stowed. There's work needs doing from the sound of Petey's hollerin an we best not be dawdling away the watch."

Jack fought through the pain and blinked the blur of sleep from his eyes. The sailor who was speaking to him looked as old as time itself. His face was weathered from too many days in the sun and the wind. His jaw was covered in an unkempt beard that looked like it had never seen a washing nor a brush or comb. The old man reached up and unhitched Jack's hammock on one end before rolling it toward the opposite end and looping a rope around to hitch it into a bundle.

"On a navy ship, they stows these in net rigging along the ships rail. Supposed to catch splinters and shot when they gets in a scrap. I suppose it works for them, buts here in a merchant ship, we just stows them here below deck," the sailor said with his growl. "There'll be breakfast, but we'll have to get sails set like the quarter wants them first. We earns our vittles, that's a surety."

Jack watched carefully while the sailor threaded the rope through itself before giving it a twist and then threading it back on itself. "Thank you," he said.

"No needs thankin' me, I'm just doing my part. New blood on the crews is good for everyone, lest they aren't proper trained. I'll see ye proper trained. That way I won't have to worry 'bout ye dropping a spar down on me in a gale," the sailor

A Bloody Beginning

growled before finishing with a floppy grin. He gestured towards the stairs that led up to the weather deck. "Up we go. Ye can't learn sailorin' down here, now can ye?"

Jack slipped on his shoes and pulled his arms through the sleeves of his wool coat. He hurried to keep up with the sailor while others headed in the same direction. "What is yer name?"

The sailor mounted the steps up to the weather hatch and shot a look back at Jack. His eyebrows drooped in a tight frown and his nose scrunched. "Ye mean the crews hasn't already told ye? That's a first, boy. First time they ever kept their yaps shut about me! My name is Robert, but I go by Bob. The crew calls me Bowline Bob, fer I'm the sailorinest sailor ye'll ever meet. I was born at sea, and haven't slept a single night on land me whole life. I've been a king's navy sailor and a whalin' fleet hand, and crossed the old 'quator more times than I could count."

Jack felt a rough bump on his shoulder that caused him to lose his balance as someone shoved his way past. "Get out of the way, Bob, ye damned smelly Irish goon. Filling this boy's head with lies and grand shite isn't going to sheet up those damned sails any faster." As he recovered his footing, Jack turned to find himself face to face with Bitter End Bill. "Well? Are ye two going up on deck or are ye going to stand here lollying all damned day like a pair of useless lubs?"

Jack clenched his jaw. He wanted to rebuke the ornery sailor with a withering reply, something

A Bloody Beginning

about his intelligence or appearance. But, nothing came to mind as he stared back into those penetrating beady eyes. Bob snorted a laugh and reached up for the weather hatch. "He's got a point, boy. Sooner we get these bastards sheeted, sooner we can have us our vittles."

The hatch opened, but instead of a rush of daylight pouring in, Jack's eyes were stunned to see the very faint yellow glow of lamplight surrounded in darkness. Cold rushed down the steps. It fell on Jack like an invisible hand that reached down and wrapped him in its icy clutch. Deep inside, he felt the urge to retreat into the warmth of cabin. He wanted to restring his hammock and steal away until the sun came up with its warmth. But, there would be no retreat. He heard his father's voice in his head. "You have to be a man now." Jack plunged himself forward and attacked the stairs one at a time, cold be damned. He rose out of the weather hatch to find the deck of Salem Tide caked in a thin layer of wet snow lit only by a pair of lanterns on either side of each mast and a pair flanking the portion of the deck where the ship's wheel stood.

"Hands to the braces," a voice rang through the cold.

Jack found the deck a frenzy of sailors moving to their stations and realized that he had not yet been assigned a job. Men slipped and slid their way to the rope webbing on the sides of the ship and began their harrowing climb upward or skittered their way to the base of the mainmast.

A Bloody Beginning

"Here, boy. Ye follow me," Bob growled from somewhere near the main.

Jack turned and made his way with unsteady footing toward the base of the main mast. The collection of snow caused his steps to slip with each landing, a problem that was only compounded by the steady pitching of the ship. He felt an uneasy knot working its way up from his intestines and into his stomach, like he had swallowed a rock that was being rejected by his innards. When he reached the mainmast, a collection of grizzled looking faces greeted him with stony glares and looks of dismissal.

"Every hand starts out here, at least aboard'n the Salem Tide they do. Ye heave on the line they tell ye to heave on, and pay out hand over hand when it time fer a payin' out," Bob said in his throaty growl of a voice. "Cap'n wants tops and gallants, fore and main. Topsail and jib on the mizzen. That's six sails to sheet home, boy. We ought be done with this in a half a turn, if nothing goes amiss. Then its vittles and keepin warm until the next sail change." He pointed towards the hands gathered around the mast. "Ye'll be working with this lot. Waisters, we call em. In the waist of the old girl." He swatted his hand against the chest of a tall, square shouldered hand. "This here is John Long, we picked him up down Virgina way sometime last year. He knows his way around the waist well enough, but he isn't fond of heights. So a deck hand he'll be." He pointed to the next man, a younger looking squat fellow with rounded features and a belly that protruded from beneath his ill-fitting coat. "This is Wally, most of the crew calls him Slop. If ye can't tell by his appearance, I don't know how else to explain it." He pointed at the next in line, a younger man who Jack judged to be around his own age. "Here we have our Joseph. He is supposedly the cap'n's bastard son, though I will admit, there is a bit of a resemblance in the face, he couldn't be further from the mark in the noggin. He's as smart as a whip, this one." Jack could hear the sarcasm dripping from Bob's tone. "His mother brought him down to the pier and left him there last time we made port in New York." He paused and looked at the last of the assembled sailors. "This young man comes to us from Japan, by way of London. It's a long story, and not one we have time for at the moment. His rightful name is hard for me to get proper like. Matsumoko, something." He shook his head in exasperation. "We just calls him Mat, and he doesn't seems to mind so much. But I'll warn you, boy. He's handy with his hands and damned lightning quick on his feet." He held one hand up to shield his mouth from Matsumoko's hearing, "There are names he doesn't like so much, and don't refer to him as a Chinaman. He hates that."

Jack looked the young man up and down. He was slight of frame and already shivering from the cold, but there was a strength there that Jack couldn't quite define, and something in his eyes that spoke to intelligence he kept hidden away from others.

A Bloody Beginning

Bob craned his neck and looked aloft. "I've got to be up into the riggings, boy. This lot will get ye squared away for deckhand work. Let's see to the canvas so we can all get out of this damned cold."

Without another word, Bob took up to the web of ropes that led high up into the rigging. He climbed hand over hand and step by step until his figure disappeared over the edge of the wooden platform high overhead. Jack was awed by the casual grace of the foul-mouthed old sailor, he had climbed higher than Jack had ever been in his life, and appeared as relaxed as if he were pulling on his trousers for the day.

"Hands at the ready!" A voice boomed over the deck with a tinny ring, "Main gallants, heads and clew."

A burst of activity took hold of the men surrounding Jack. He didn't know what to do or where to stand until he felt the slight hand of Matsumoko grab a hold of his shirt lapel. He spoke with urgency in his voice. "Hurry, come help me with this line." He directed Jack to a thick-looking rope that was twisted in an elaborate knot over a heavy wooden stake protruding from the ship's rail. With a deft movement, Matsumoko unhitched the thick line and took it in both hands. He peered over one shoulder at Jack. "Take the line in your hands, get ready, we are going to pull and take it in until it's tight.

"Heave!" came the tinny shout that echoed over the deck. Jack grabbed a hold on the thick line that trailed out from Matsumoko's grip. The lithe

A Bloody Beginning

young man began hauling at the line, hand over hand in great stretches so fast that they seemed barely visible to Jack's eyes. High above, canvas stretched out and instantly filled with wind. Salem Tide lurched forward from the added sail and Jack nearly lost his footing.

"Coil the line," Matsumoko said as he came to the end of the haul. "Hurry. You are going to set the next one."

The voice with the tinny ring boomed out over the deck and rang high up into the rigging, "Main topsail, unfurl and sheet her home. Hands, ready!"

Matsumoko pointed to the next line twisted around a wooden peg on the ship's side rail. "That one, get a good hold of her once you unhitch, there's going to be tension on it with this wind."

Jack was impressed by the young man's command of English. He took the thick rope that Matsumoko had pointed out in hand and lifted the top coil away from the peg before relieving the twist that had kept it in place. "Heave!" the tinny shout came. With all of his strength, Jack fetched in arm length after arm length of rope while the coarse fibers bit at the flesh of his palms and fingers. Each arm length became stouter than the last until Jack strained to pull the rope for the full length of his arm. The tension of the line increased, and Jack struggled against it until he could no longer gain any purchase.

"Secure lines and make ready at the foremast!" the tinny voice rang out through the cold wind.

A Bloody Beginning

The process was repeated at the foremast, where the men not only had to contend with the arduous labor and the frigid wind, but also the icy spray of seawater as waves broke against Salem Tide's bow. Jack's hands went from being painfully cold to frozen and numb. He deemed it a good thing, his palms and fingers had been chewed raw by the rough bite of rope. Within minutes of working near the foremast, his coat was sodden from the spray of the sea. Shivers started somewhere deep inside of him and began to work their way out in an uncontrollable tremble that seemed to shake his arms and legs uncontrollably. Jack fought against the cold as they finished at the foremast and moved their way back to the mizzen. His arms, shoulders and chest were completely soaked. Every gust of wind that hit him seemed to cut straight through to his bones. His muscles tensed, aching against the cold that penetrated every fiber of his being.

By the time they had finished the last of the sail changes, Jack felt colder than he had ever been in his life. Icy winds continued to blast Salem Tide while rising seas sent thick sprays of frigid water tracing back over her decks. The snow that had gathered during the night turned to a slush that made keeping his footing nearly impossible. His shoes slipped and slid with every step and several times Jack stumbled to his knees on the hard wooden planks. With each fall, his spirits dropped lower. A feeling of utter hopelessness took hold of him and clenched its icy fingers until he felt like he could not breathe. He was on a storm-tossed ship, miles out on the Atlantic Ocean. His parents were gone. His home was likely already occupied by some other tenant Mr. Albright had already waiting. His fingers locked around the grating roughness of rope. He hauled at it with all of his strength while a hot feeling welled just behind his eyes. Everything became a blur of white and gray as the form of fresh fallen snow and the dismal brine of the ocean became shapeless through his tears. He pulled at the rope, every movement an exercise in agony. His arms burned from the strain. His hands ached from the penetrating cold and raw flesh on his palms and fingers.

"Secure those lines and turn to," the tinny voice rang out again. "Mr. Winthrow, see to it those crates in the hold get secured, they shifted in the night and I won't have any loose cargo on my ship!"

Jack heard vaguely, but his mind didn't process what was being said. He was wrapped in grief, mourning the loss of his parents, his home, everything he had ever known. Salem Tide pitched up as her bow met a rolling wave. A wash of seawater showered the front of the ship and sent a spray all along her deck before her hull slid through the crest of the sea and dipped to meet the falling pitch. Jack trembled violently. What little heat he had left in his body had just been carried away in a wash of frigid water. His tears flowed, unchecked by any effort to stop them. Jack could no longer contain his sorrow, and as his

A Bloody Beginning

arms dripped with seawater, his face flooded with tears. He heard his father's voice again. "You have to be a man now, Jacky."

A hand landed on his shoulder. Jack spun to face the owner and found Matsumoko's lean features staring back at him.

"You have to get below, you are shivering harder than I am," he said. His expression looked like it was built of stone, impervious to the elements around him or anything he was seeing. "Come with me," he said with a tug on Jack's coat. "I'll take you down to the cook's galley where you can warm up and dry out."

Jack followed while Matsumoko guided him along the deck with a tight grip remaining on his sodden sea sodden coat. His thoughts were drowning in a sea of misery while his shoes slipped and slid on Salem Tide's slushy, sea soaked deck.

"Rogue wave!" a terrified voice screamed from somewhere high aloft.

Jack looked up, over the railing along the ship's side, and found a wall of dark gray sea was barreling toward the ship.

"Hold on, boys! She's going to take us on our beam!" Petey's voice echoed across the deck.

It hit like the hand of God had reached down from the heavens to smite Salem Tide. A wall of seawater came crashing over the side and for a heartbeat, Jack's world went silent. Frigid cold wrapped his entire being and forced the air from his lungs. He felt his feet being swept from under

A Bloody Beginning

him. Matsumoko's grip left the shoulder of his coat. He felt his back slam into the deck before being lifted by the rush of seawater. His vision was a blur of deck planks, frothing seawater, gray sky, white canvas, the myriad of ropes in the rigging. Something slammed against his shins and sent bolts of pain racing through his legs before radiating through his knees and up his thighs. Voices screamed in alarm. They were met by others shouting orders.

"Grab hold of something!" Petey's graveled voice shouted

"They are going over!" another voice called.

Petey shouted louder, "Get to them, someone, quickly!"

Another impact rocked through Jack's body. It slammed on his ribs just beneath his right arm. Jack knew he had to hold on, whatever he had slammed into could well be his last chance to stay aboard the ship. The press of the wave intensified, prying at his grip. He fought through the force being plied against him until his vision cleared. Roiling gray and white sea was beneath his dangling legs with nothing in between to arrest his fall should his grip fail. Fear flooded his veins, it sent lightning through his muscles and lit a fire deep in his belly. More seawater washed over him, but the chill had lost its sting. He looked inboard over the pitching deck of Salem Tide just in time to see a slight figure clad in soaked a soaked through tarpaulin jacket wash across the ship. Jack reached with his free hand. It was instinct more than

A Bloody Beginning

decision, somewhere inside he knew the figure would not be stopped by the railing the way he had. He stretched as the bundle of tarpaulin slid near him and was rewarded by a fistful of oiled canvas. His grip was tested immediately as seawater rushed over him and dragged the tarpaulin clad sailor's weight down toward the frothing sea. Jack heaved with every bit of strength he had. He clamped his right arm around the ship's railing and fought against the rush of the sea with every ounce of his defiant spirit.

The onslaught of water disappeared. Jack found himself clinging to a wooden railing under his arm and desperately holding onto canvas with his other hand. His strength was slipping away, receding just like the rush of the sea. Cold saturated every part of him and his mind centered around a single thought. *I'm going to die.*

"Hold on Jack! Hold on, we're coming!" the voice that shouted was recently familiar to him, though Jack couldn't name it. "Here, I've got you. I've got you now, lad. Up and over, up and over."

Rough hands grabbed hold of Jack by his shoulders, his arms. More hands grabbed his legs while still others wrapped around his midsection. Jack held his grip on the canvas.

"You can let go laddy, we've got him too," the voice said as Jack could feel himself being hoisted over the ship's rail and lowered to the wave-soaked deck. "You done a damn fine bit of work there, Jack."

A Bloody Beginning

Jack looked and found that the voice belonged to Petey. He tried to reply but could only manage a sputtering cough of seawater and spittle. His stomach twisted in a painful knot. Sailors crowded all around him and he writhed from his back onto his side. The knot in his stomach pulsed and worked its way up through his chest. He wretched, spewing seawater and bile onto the deck while his body convulsed with uncontrollable shivers.

"The poor sod is flopping like a damned fish," Petey's voice growled through the middle of the group. "Get him below, and Mat too. We're damn fortunate they didn't both go overboard."

Another voice chimed into the gathered group. "Luck had not a damned thing to do with it. Haul that young man to his feet."

Jack felt hands curl beneath both of his arms and lift him to stand on his shaking legs. He came face to face with the captain.

"It's a wonder, lad. I've seen some bravery in my day. Some acts that made me scratch my head and wonder what stuff I am truly made of. That was pure selfless valor, son. Matsumoko would be frozen solid, sinking his way into the abyss, if it weren't for you. But, he could have dragged you right along when you reached out to grab your hold on him." The captain looked him up and down before shooting a challenging glare at Petey. "Where are his damned tarpaulins? Mr. Hancock ordered him to be outfitted on the company's expense."

Petey offered a resigned shrug. "The purser has no stores of tarpaulins, Cap'n. Nor gloves, or half of the other items the boy needs."

The captain's face shot red with a flush of anger. "Take him below and get him stripped and dried out. Outfit him from my personal locker if needs be, but by God see to it he lacks nothing. And send that cursed Mr. Ricketts to my cabin, smartly, Mr. Winthrow."

"Aye, Cap'n. I'll see to it that the lad gets what he needs, and I will make sure Mr. Ricketts makes his way to your cabin. Kicking and screaming, if necessary," Petey growled in reply.

CHAPTER 8

'Salem Tide'
7 March 1770
42 Degrees 43' N, 70 Degrees 12' W

"It's a ripe old gale out there, laddy. The kind that's been known to toss a seasoned hand overboard. Not to mention rogue waves," Petey said in his customary growl. He drew a wick from his vest and inserted it into the front door of the iron wood stove to steal a bit of flame for his pipe. "The Cap'n was right. That was a brave stroke ye made out on deck. Proved your mettle, boy." He paused to light his pipe, sucking in puffs of smoke in short choppy little breaths that soon filled the cramped galley with a rich aroma and a haze of bluish smoke that stung Jack's eyes. "There isn't a soul on this tub that can claim he has the grit ye do. In fact, I've seen a few of them in the same

A Bloody Beginning

predicament ye just encountered. Hold your head high, laddy. That was the stuff tavern tales are woven of." Petey pulled a big draw on his pipe before pointing the stem of the implement toward Matsumoko. "He owes ye drinks until the day he dies, or until he returns the favor."

Jack was utterly failing at fighting his shivers. Though he had stripped away all his sodden clothing and now sat bundled in a wool blanket next to a piping hot stove, there was a chill in his bones that just refused to fade. Sitting across from him, similarly wrapped in a thick blanket of wool, was Matsumoko. His jet black hair was still dripping icy seawater as he trembled from his own chills. Jack looked at him. In the dull glimmer that emanated from the open wood stove, he caught the slightest hint of a shining drop working its way down Matsumoko's face.

"I've heard it said, a storm will flesh the sailors out in any crew," Petey continued his high-spirited rant. "It proves true, time and time again. It proves true." He nudged Jack on the shoulder. "There were experienced men that didn't budge a step when Mats lost his footing. Didn't budge for ye neither. Piss on 'em. I'd take one of ye for ten 'o the others. Least I know who'll chance it all on the yardarm in a gale for me, if'n needs be." He drew a big pull of smoke from his pipe and examined both Jack and Matsumoko with a deep frown. "I'll give ye both some time to gather yourselves. Warm up a bit. I'll be back." He let a puff of smoke escape as he stepped out of the galley while

A Bloody Beginning

shouting to nobody in particular, "I'll have Mr. Ricketts to the Cap'n's cabin! Never mind his objections or his current state. An extra tot if ye haul him in off of his feet!"

Jack let the warmth of the stove soak into him. He stared into the belly of the cast iron, where coals glowed orange hot and waves of heat rippled out like surf washing ashore. His eyes were transfixed by the glow. His thoughts drifted not to the extraordinary circumstances of his hypothermic caper, but to the courtyard in Boston. Again, his mind went to the face of his mother and the words of his father. Jack wondered for a moment if his father would have been proud to see him now.

"You didn't have to do that," Matsumoko's voice was low and soft.

Jack turned and faced him, his eyes narrowed involuntarily. "What do you mean?"

Matsumoko replied, "You didn't have to do that. None aboard would have faulted you for not reaching out for me. Some would probably have clapped you on the back for it. You could have lost your own grip on the railing, and you would have followed me right into the sea." He drew a breath, his face still directed toward the floor and mostly obscured by an unruly mop of black hair. "Thank you."

Jack shook his head. "You would do the same for me, Matsumoko."

A Bloody Beginning

"You don't even know me," Matsumoko lifted his face to look Jack in the eye. "You risked your life to save mine, you use my actual name. Why?"

Jack felt his face flush. He couldn't quite tell if Matsumoko was embarrassed or angry. "I, well, I just... it seemed..." Jack searched for the right words, but struggled as his mind was still sluggish from the cold. "It was the right thing to do, and I couldn't call you Mat, your name is Matsumoko. I had a classmate in my schoolhouse named Matthew and everyone called him Matt. He made the worst jokes about my family, for being poor and for being Irish. I couldn't call you Mat, not unless I hated you."

"It's a good thing for me that you don't," Matsumoko said, a smile breaking his stony reserve for the first time in Jack's witness.

Jack returned the smile as a shiver worked its way up his spine. He pulled his hands inside of the wool blanket and flexed his fingers. The heat of the stove was finally beginning to penetrate his chills and as his hands thawed the pain of raw flesh radiated through his fingertips, palms and knuckles.

"They will get better," Matsumoko said with a nod toward Jack's hands. "It takes a few weeks at sea, but your hands will harden to working the lines."

Jack opened his palms and examined them. They looked like he had slid them along raw timbers, the flesh was red and swollen, blisters had formed along the base of his fingers where

A Bloody Beginning

they met his palms. "I sure hope so. They feel miserable right now."

"They didn't stop you from holding my weight," Matsumoko observed.

Jack lifted his eyebrows. He was still surprised by the feat of strength he had somehow accomplished. "I'm not sure how." He smiled at Matsumoko. "It's a good thing you aren't very heavy."

Both of the young men laughed, and both laughs were cut short from bouts of pain in their ribs, shoulders, hands and heads. Matsumoko ran a hand through his thick, black hair while droplets fell to the galley deck. Salem Tide shifted from her rhythm of pitching and swaying. "The turn north," he said. "The seas will settle when we get closer to the whaling grounds.

Jack shifted his gaze and stared into the fire. "I've never seen a whale before. Not up close, like. I've seen drawings of them, in school."

Matsumoko shook his head. "We aren't likely to see any whales ourselves. If the fleet is successful, we may see some carcasses. Have you ever had whale meat before? It is good, if it's well prepared."

"No," Jack answered. "I've never had whale meat before. At least, not that I know of."

"It is a treat after our steady diet of beans and salt pork," Matsumoko said with raised eyebrows. "Roasted, or in a soup. There are few things better."

A Bloody Beginning

Jack grumbled. "I will settle for warm and dry for now. Beans and bread, pork, it makes no matter to me as long as I am still aboard the ship," He grimaced and flexed his hands as the sensation continued to return to his fingers and palms. "That water was so cold. It stole the breath from my lungs."

Matsumoko's face returned to its typical stony reserve. He drew a long breath and leaned back against the galley wall. "On our last voyage, there was a sailor who fell from the rigging in a gale. The captain ordered the ship around straight away. We turned her hard over, got to him as fast as fast could be. But, in the end it made no difference. The icy water killed him before we had a chance to fish him aboard. He was frozen stiff, with his eyes open and everything. It was horrid."

Jack imagined the desperation he would have felt. It was bad enough having a wave of the frigid sea wash over him and carry him off of his feet. The sight of the ship sailing away while cold invaded every fiber of the body. Just the thought inspired a well of hopelessness deep in his chest. "I can only imagine."

Matsumoko reached over and placed a hand on Jack's shoulder. "You saved me from that terrible fate. I would be dead right now, if not for you. Every breath I draw testifies to your courage," He drew a deep breath and squeezed at Jack's shoulder. "I owe you my life."

A Bloody Beginning

Jack, uncomfortable with the heartfelt words, could only manage a slight nod. "You would have done the same for me, Matsumoko."

Matsumoko smiled. "You keep saying that, but I am not so sure. I do know this, though. If I can ever return the favor, I will. In my home country, there is a concept called Giri. It is a responsibility we all have, a debt that we all must pay. I am in your debt, Jack, and you are stuck with me."

Jack smiled, determined to change the subject. "How is it that your English is so good?"

Matsumoko released Jack's shoulder. He withdrew his hands inside the wool blanket wrapped over his shoulders and tipped his head forward. "I've spent the last seven years aboard ships. A trade cog in the eastern seas, an East India Company ship, fishing vessels. My mother sent me away from home when I was only six or seven. To be honest, I think my English may be better than my Japanese."

Jack frowned and gave his new friend a hard look. "Why would your mother send you away? I don't understand."

Matsumoko fidgeted beneath his wool blanket and chewed at his lower lip for a long moment. "Things are not the same in the east." He drew a deep breath and released a reluctant sigh. "There are similarities of course, everywhere there are classes dividing people, but in Japan it is a rigid structure and controlled by the warrior class. Samurai serve the Daimyo, who reward them with land and wealth. The competition between these

A Bloody Beginning

samurai is never ending, there are power struggles and plots, schemes and betrayals. My father was a samurai, and loyal to the Tokugawa regime. He discovered a plot by a neighboring power to rise against the Daimyo, and was murdered. My mother sent me on a trade cog to China. If she hadn't I would have been killed within a year, if not sooner."

Jack shook his head. "Why? I don't understand. They killed your father. They would kill you too?"

Matsumoko nodded. "It is a very different world in Japan, Jack. My father's enemies would have killed me to ensure that I did not avenge his death later in life."

Jack stared at Matsumoko's face as he spoke. His expression remained solid, unchanged by emotion as if he felt nothing at all, though through his voice, Jack knew his friend struggled to recount the telling.

"It is a harsh place, but there is a beauty to it. Hopefully, someday I can return. Maybe you could join me. I would love for you to see it, Jack. It is a beautiful country."

Jack offered his new friend a smile. "I would love to. Someday."

Footfalls and a cloud of tobacco smoke announced the return of Petey. His face was plastered by a smile that Jack hadn't seen since they had first left Boston. He tossed a stack of neatly folded tarpaulins onto the galley floor at Jack's feet. "I got you your foul weather gear, boy," he growled and let fly with a breath of pipe

A Bloody Beginning

smoke. "Cap'n wants to see both of ye's in his cabin. I figures he's goin' to invites ye to supper with him. Enjoy it. There isn't often he does such, and when he does it's never deck hands or top men."

Jack looked underneath his wool blanket and then back at Petey. "Unless the captain wishes to see me as god made me, I will need clothes. Mine are still soaked through."

Petey smiled and chuckled with a puff of smoke. "Aye, I thought of that," He swung an arm laden with a stack of fresh sailor's attire into the tight confines of the galley. "It seems the purser has been holding out on the crew. A conspiracy that reaches deeper than yer withheld tarpaulins, I'm afraid. He has been docking wages for half the crew and withholding their goods. My guess is that he sells the wares in port, or never purchases them in the first place. Either way, the captain has ordered him to outfit yer both and at Mr. Rickett's personal expense. Inadequate recompense, if ye were to ask me, but it benefits the both of yers." He dropped the stack on top of Jack's tarpaulins and departed with a grunt. "Dress yerselves and report to the cap'n. He'll be wanting a word with ye both."

Jack and Matsumoko hurried to dress in their newly issued clothes. Jack found the heavy sailcloth trousers rough and ill fitting, but they were preferable to sitting in his sodden wool britches. The shirt was similarly baggy, and made from the same material. Once dressed, both of the

A Bloody Beginning

summoned sailors made their way from the galley and through the main corridor to the captain's cabin. Jack noted nods of approval from several sailors he passed on their way, though he only managed a sheepish nod in return. He wasn't used to this sort of recognition, and it was odd being among a crew of strangers who now recognized him as a hero. It was as unfamiliar to him as being on the ship.

When they reached the captain's door, Matsumoko gave it three stout knocks. A muffled voice growled from inside, "Enter." Matsumoko pushed open the cabin door and revealed the captain, sitting at a small desk along the cabin's side wall. He pushed back from the desk, his chair legs squealing against the deck planks. "Ah, lads. Just the fellows I wanted to see!" His ruddy face seemed to light up at the sight of Jack and Matsumoko. The captain folded his arms across his midsection and he leaned back in his chair in a precarious fashion. "The seas seem to be slacking, and Mr. Winthrow seems to think we will be out of this gale by evening. I always like to follow a healthy storm with a hearty supper. What say you lads? Would you care to join me this evening for a meal fit for a pair of sea hands such as you are?"

Jack nodded, his knit hat held in both hands before him. "Yes, sir. I would like that very much." He looked at Matsumoko, who nodded his assent.

"Good, good," the captain replied with a broad smile. "I am having the cook put on a beef roast. I have fresh beef in my personal stores, potatoes,

A Bloody Beginning

stewed apples, and beans of course, it wouldn't be a supper at sea without beans." He paused and looked hard at Jack. "Before we set out, Mr. Hancock relayed to me the unfortunate business about your parents. I am sorry for your troubles, young man, I truly am. He also instructed me to give your tutelage special care. It struck me odd at first, but I see it now. He clearly recognizes, as I do now, that there is something to you, boy. You are cut from a hardy cloth, indeed." He paused and looked Jack over as if inspecting him. "I have given the first mate, Mr. Winthrow, clear instructions. You are to be trained by the finest Salem Tide has to offer. We'll have Bowline Bob take you aloft and teach you the rigging, that will take some time, mind you, but be patient and learn as much as you can. He is the best hand we have for it. Once you have a thorough understanding of the world aloft, Mr. Winthrow will see to it that you get trained at the helm. That will make a sailor of you." He paused and dug a cigar from the drawer in his desk. He held the rolled tobacco to his nose and appeared to savor the smell for a moment before continuing. "Once you have been instructed in matters thusly, I will personally see to your training in navigation. You must prove yourself capable through each course along the way, but given the mettle you have already displayed, I doubt you will have any trouble."

Jack, unsure of how to respond, offered the captain a nod. "Thank you, sir."

A Bloody Beginning

The captain clamped his cigar between his teeth and leaned over to the lit candle on his desk. He puffed pulled three puffs of smoke from the cigar until the end was a bright red glow. "It is you who deserve thanks, lad. You saved our Mats here from a terrible fate." He gestured to the desk along the wall. "Either of you care for a smoke?"

Jack shook his head. He had never smoked, but always enjoyed the aroma. "No, thank you, sir." He looked at Matsumoko who repeated the gesture.

"Your loss," the captain growled through a cloud of rich smoke. "I picked these up in Boston from a friend of mine who had just returned from Hispaniola. They are the best I have ever tasted." He pulled at the cigar and blew a long stream of bluish smoke toward the cabin ceiling. He gestured toward the chart unrolled across his small desk. "The northern seas aren't for the faint of heart, as you have both have very recently seen. But, I expect that we will be on the whaling fleet within a week's sail." He drew another long puff off of his cigar and savored the smoke while holding it clenched between his teeth. "From there, it will take us a few weeks to make our rendezvous with Mr. Hancock's connection."

A pang of inquiry sunk into Jack's mind. A rendezvous? He wasn't aware of anything like that when they had set sail. But, then again, he hadn't been paying close attention to much other than the fact that his entire life had been capsized

A Bloody Beginning

overnight. His thoughts were interrupted by a knock at the cabin door.

"Enter," the captain said in a gruff croak of smoke.

"Pardon, sir," a fresh faced man wearing a flour and grease stained linen apron over his sailor's attire poked his head into the cabin. "But your supper is ready. I took the liberty of putting on coffee as well, some of what we got from Mr. Hancock hisself. It smells enough to put the mouth to water, I'm sure you will enjoy it, sir."

"Thank you Reginald, see to it that my guests are treated to some as well," the captain motioned Jack and Matsumoko further into the cabin. "Here, lads. We'll need to set up the table. Reginald will handle the rest." He moved to the corner of the cabin and pulled out a pair of folding a-frame table supports that looked to Jack suspiciously like saw horses. Along the wall of the cabin opposite the captain's desk sat a cross-work slab of planks. Jack and Matsumoko lifted the slab from either end and placed it on top of the supports after the captain had set them. Jack mused at how the table supports sat in grooves notched into the cabin floor. He hadn't noticed the grooves before, but in high swells, he imagined the table would be most impractical if it were not restrained from movement in some manner.

With the table set up, the captain scooted his chair from behind his desk to the far end and seated himself. Reginald spread a white linen tablecloth over the plank slab and disappeared to retrieve the food.

"You boys will eat well tonight. One thing to be said for Mr. Hancock, he ensures his captains are always well provisioned," He paused for a moment and looked at Matsumoko with a penetrating stare. "You fellows before the mast are being fed well enough I would assume, not fresh beef and baked bread, but you are getting regular rations. Are you not?"

Matsumoko nodded with arched eyebrows. "Yes, sir. I eat as well as I have on any ship and better than most."

"Good, good. I won't have starving hands," He replied with a hearty growl as he pulled the edge of the linen table cloth into his collar in preparation for the meal. "Bad enough that damned Mr. Ricketts was holding back clothing issue to the men. Pursers and the games they play. I've heard it is far worse aboard a man of war. Pursers buying spoiled meat and rotten vegetables, ale that has turned, even cutting corners with water rations. Greedy bastards that they are, if you ask me they should be strung by the neck. Depriving a man of decent rations at sea is a damned good way to spark a mutiny. But, it isn't the purser who gets gutted in a mutiny, its the captain!"

The cabin door opened and Reginald entered carrying a tray so large he had to hold it lengthwise in front of himself to fit it through the cabin doorway. The tray was loaded with lidded

A Bloody Beginning

platters and a stack of plates and flatware that Jack would have thought to fine to survive aboard a ship. Jack's nose filled with the pleasant aromas of well seasoned food. Reginald deposited the large tray onto the table before distributing the polished plates and flatware to each of the three seated around the captain's table.

"In addition to the beef roast, sir, I took the liberty of boiling crab legs that were procured in Boston," Reginald said in a drolling tone indicating no particular excitement.

The captain clapped his hands and rubbed them together. "Excellent, Reginald. Well done, my man. It smells divine."

"Shall I pull a bottle for your supper, sir?" Reginald asked after he had placed dining ware in front of each eager appetite.

The captain shook his head. "No, no liquor tonight. But, some ale would do well for this. The darkest we have aboard."

Reginald offered a nod. "We have porter from Boston, also a dark brown nut ale purchased from Mr. Hancock's friend."

"The nut ale would do nicely, thank you," the captain replied while lifting one of the platter lids.

Jack's eyes lit as he watched a cloud of steam escape from beneath the lid of the beef roast. The smell of seasoned meat, salt, pepper, and rendered fat mixed into the lingering aroma of the captain's extinguished cigar. The roast glistened under dim lantern light as it sat in a pool of gravy and cooked potatoes, onions and carrots. The captain lifted a

A Bloody Beginning

thin cloth to reveal a small loaf of freshly baked bread laden with nuts and dried berries. Another lid was lifted to reveal a heap of red and white crab legs hearkened by a thick cloud of steam.

Th captain offered both Jack and Matsumoko a broad smile before nodding down at the feast laid before them. "Eat your fill, lads."

Jack exchanged a glance with his new friend and together they both stood to fill their plates with generous helpings from each of the dishes served. A slice of beef roast dressed in gravy and chunks of potatoes, carrots and onions. Steaming crab legs with their flaky white meat protruding from the knuckles of the legs. Stewed apples laden with cinnamon and nutmeg in a sauce so thick it stuck to the spoon when Jack dished a portion for himself. The bread was crisp on the outside and soft on the inside, it produced tendrils of steam when Jack sliced into the loaf and brought his mouth to water.

All three in company delved into their supper with reckless abandon. The roast beef was well seasoned and perfectly accompanied by its entourage of gravy, onions, potatoes and carrots. It would have been a supper all to itself, except there was so much more. The crab legs were a treat like Jack had never experienced. Growing up in Boston, he had enjoyed crab before, but not like this. These crab legs were robust, and their meat was so tender it broke apart as it was being pulled from the white and red shells. The ale that accompanied their meal was full bodied and rich,

A Bloody Beginning

almost sweet on the tongue, it was an experience unlike anything he had ever had the privilege to enjoy. Jack's stomach felt full long before he had cleared the remnants of his serving from the plate before him. He savored the last dregs of his ale and sat back into his chair as a satisfied lethargy took hold.

The captain smacked his lips as he sucked crab meat from a section of shell. He eyed both of his supper guests and cracked a smile. "You are both well pleased now, I hope. Don't hold it against me if it goes hard for you later. A rich meal like this can either stop you up for a time or run straight through you."

Matsumoko and Jack shared a long look between each other while the captain stood from his seat to rummage through a desk drawer. He produced a cigar and held out a pair of the same in offering to his guests. Jack and Matsumoko both shook their heads in polite denial while the captain shrugged and returned the offered smokes back to their resting place in his desk drawer. He bent to the lantern resting between the ravaged dishes on the supper table and puffed until he brought forth a great cloud of rich smoke. Jack noted that the pitch and sway of Salem Tide had lessened during the course of their meal and he stole a glance out of the after array of windows lining the back of the captain's cabin. The captain noticed his look and turned for a look of his own. A winter's sunset traced along the edge of the

A Bloody Beginning

southern view just as stars were beginning to make their evening appearance.

"Fresh air will do us all wonders, and with slacking seas, it will be good for you both to make yourselves seen on deck. Give heart to the fellows who witnessed your spill earlier and show that the captain takes care after lads who brave the storm." The captain took a long draw from his cigar before gesturing toward the cabin door. "Care to take in the evening air with me?"

Jack rose from his seat and felt the sudden onset of the ale he had consumed. He knew it had been a stronger brew than anything he had ever sampled before, and he was used to nipping a sip or two from his father's draft, when their meager fortunes allowed it. This was an entirely new sensation. Jack felt his head swim for a moment as he stood on his feet. The pains that had plagued him when he sat down to supper had all but vanished and a feeling of warmth and contentedness washed over him. Matsumoko led the way to the cabin door, a stagger interrupted his gate as the deck rose with the meeting of a wave. Jack smiled in amusement, but the smile faded as he staggered when the deck pitched forward. The captain broke out in a deep roll of laughter at both of the young men. "Your first tot at sea?"

Jack laughed as the captain made his way out of the cabin leaving a trail of cigar smoke in his wake. "Yes, sir. I've only ever had sips at my father's cups, and nothing as strong as that."

A Bloody Beginning

The captain climbed his way up the steep steps to the weather deck, with his cigar clamped between his teeth. He bellowed over one shoulder, "Reginald, we'll take our coffee up on deck, thank you."

Jack followed behind the captain and Matsumoko as they made their way up on deck. The cold, crisp air was refreshing after being in the closeness of the captain's cabin. It brought a chill back to Jack's skin, but he dared not complain while in the company of Matsumoko and the captain.

"A fine night at sea," the captain growled as he made his way across the quarterdeck with his cigar in hand. "We'll have our first lesson, young Jack. What say you?"

Jack wished for his wool coat as the wind bit at his skin through the fabric of his new sailor's clothes. "Yes, sir."

The captain nodded and puffed at his cigar causing the end to glow bright red. "Good, good. Eager to learn is a good thing, my boy." He pointed his cigar out toward the sea. "This is what we call a following sea, meaning the waves are moving with the ship. There is a danger in a following sea, if she isn't handled as she ought to be. But, generally speaking, that could be applied to about anything." He paused to release a hearty breath of rich smoke into the cold night. "We stand on the quarterdeck, or as some of the hands refer to it, the quarter. When you get your sea legs, and learn the rigging, we'll have you on to learn

A Bloody Beginning

handling the helm. It is a big responsibility, in the naval service only able seamen have a chance to learn the helm, and most of them only in passing. It's a skill set in its own right, and it takes a special touch." He motioned toward the front of the ship. "Forward there, stands the foremast, and before it the foc'sle. That's where the hands do most of their assembly, but I will warn ye, it can get a might bitter up there during a gale when we are head on into the sea. Waves break along the bow and send up a spray that will soak you to the bone."

Jack nodded in the dim light of the deck lamps. "That much I have learned, sir."

The captain offered a hearty laugh ripe with the pungent smell of his cigar. "I imagine so, boy."

Over the course of the next hour, the captain led Jack through an intricate description of the various lines of rigging and their uses. Head lines, clew lines, bunt lines and their corresponding blocks. He elaborated on the system of sails in use aboard Salem Tide and described how it varied from ship to ship depending on their size and the number of masts they had. The captain covered points of sail in relation to the wind, and briefly enumerated a few of the maneuvers that sailors would make in order to change direction at various points of sail. It all made Jack's head swim as the shivers began to take hold of him once again. The fourth bell of the night watch sounded, and it seemed to shake the captain out of his thoughts. He gave Jack a stern look.

A Bloody Beginning

"You've let me drone on until you caught the shakes again," he said with a wink. "Why don't you head below and crawl into your hammock, lad? Your lot has the morning watch, and those bells have a way of slipping by too quickly while a man slumbers."

CHAPTER 9

'Salem Tide'
8 March 1770
44 Degrees 13' N, 62 Degrees 12' W

Dawn came in a manner Jack had never witnessed before in his life. He'd been woken from a dead sleep in the wee hours of the morning while the sun was still hours away from making its appearance. Bowline Bob had done him the courtesy of aiding him out of his hammock, and even been kind enough to walk him through the preferred way to stow the hammock again. Before he was able to fully shake the effects of deep slumber from his mind, Jack was hurried out on deck and then up into the rigging for his first watch aloft. Bob led him to the slanted web of ropes that Jack had seen bear sailors high up into the tops.

A Bloody Beginning

"These is the fore shrouds, named such because they is on the foremast, see. It's hand over hand on these, mate," Bowline Bob grunted. "Keep three limbs in contact wit' the riggins. Two fer the ship, and one fer yerself. Grip yer meat hooks onto the shroud lines, not the thin ratlines in between. Those is for yer feet."

Jack watched as the sailor's gnarled hands clamped onto the thick shroud lines and he launched himself aloft. He reached up and took hold of the shroud lines with both hands. They were thick and coarse, and Jack felt the sensation of burning pain return to the raw flesh of his fingers and palms. He craned his neck to look at Bob who was already close to the halfway point and still making his way to the fore top. With his heart in his throat, Jack raised one foot and stepped onto one of the thin ratlines. He raised himself up and took another step before moving one hand further up the shrouds. Darkness surrounded Salem Tide in the early morning hours while the ship pitched over gentle swells. The winds were cold, but not nearly as strong as they had been the day before. Jack continued up the shroud with a procession of slow but steady progress into the dark world aloft while the yellow glow of lantern light faded below him. He felt as though he were crossing into another world entirely, away from the warm light and relatively solid footing on deck and into a realm of swaying rope and whipping winds.

A Bloody Beginning

His palms cried out with every grasp, but Jack continued upward toward the fore tops in stubborn defiance of the fear grasping his guts. Wind whistled in his ears and nipped at his skin. Every step and every handhold was a battle. He fought against the paralyzing grasp of fear that threatened to seize his mind and plunge him back to the deck in defeat. Somewhere deep inside, he longed for the warmth and safety of his hammock below deck. The rest and comfort of warmth and deep slumber, the gentle sway of hammocks amid the intermittent snort of snores and lap of the waves against the hull. Jack's hands ached anew as the shroud lines bit into the already raw flesh of his palms. Every handhold sent a fresh wave of aches through his fingers. The pain radiated in his knuckles and was soon climbing through his wrists and into his forearms where his muscles burned from exertion. It seemed like an eternity, but finally Jack reached the wooden platform of the fore top.

"Just climb through the lubber hole, lad. No need for acrobatics this morning," Bowline Bob said as Jack approached the platform.

"Lubber hole?" Jack asked while fighting the tremble threatening to invade his voice. He looked up at the shadowy outline of the tops platform, barely visible through the darkness.

"By the mast, ye'll see yer shroud lines lead ye right to it," Bowline Bob's growl came through the darkness even though Jack couldn't see him. "It's a source of pride for sailormen, to climb around the

A Bloody Beginning

edge and mount the tops over the railing. We leave the hole to the lubbers, but that is a worry for a different day, let's just get ye aloft to start."

Jack felt the pang of fear wrapping around his ribs. His hands ached grievously, his arms were exhausted and his legs felt shaky on the thin cords of ratlines. He examined the tops platform in the darkness, a dim glow emanated from an opening close to the mast and Jack could see that the shrouds led him straight for it. His thoughts centered on planting his feet onto a solid platform. He reached up and grabbed at the shroud line, his fingers screamed in protest as rough fibers bit into their flesh. The top platform hung right over his head. He could reach out and touch it with his free hand if he wished. Salem Tide pitched as she crested a wave and Jack felt the exaggerated rock and sway from his elevated position in the rigging. He looked down. Little orbs of warm lantern light radiated their soft glow far below him. The haze of the cold morning shrouded their light in small halos. This far above the deck, Jack could not hear the footfalls of shoes on wooden deck planks, nor the wash of the sea against the hull, only the whistle and whisper of the wind in his ears and the pulsing, pounding tremor of his heartbeat. A wave of panic seized his mind, it froze his grip on the shrouds and stubbornly refused to let his feet move. Jack closed his eyes, he wondered if his friend Tom had ever climbed into the rigging of a ship. The thought was replaced by the voice of his father. "You have to be

A Bloody Beginning

a man now." He felt a sudden urge. As if a gauntlet had been laid down before him. Jack looked across the underside of the fore top platform. There were two thick lines that stretched from the narrow lubber hole out to the end of the timbers. He drew a ragged breath and forced the fear from his mind. Fire raced through his veins. He reached upward and took one of the lines in hand. It was just as rough as the shrouds and sent the same waves of protest through his palms and fingers. With his other hand he took hold of the opposite line, a feeling crept into his gut and he could tell he was reaching a point of no return. Doubt threatened to creep into his thoughts, and for a moment he questioned his decision. Could he manage this? Would he fall to his death? Silently he suffocated his fears and lifted his feet off of the ratlines below him. He threaded one foot around the bowing line he held in the hand of the same side before repeating the movement with the next foot. Footsteps on the platform above indicated that Bowline Bob was moving to the lubber's hole.

"Jack, my boy? Are ye going to make 'er?" Bob growled from atop the platform.

Jack shuffled his legs along and moved one hand at a time across the underside of the top. He could feel fatigue compounding in his forearms, his palms and fingers agonized under the sudden increase in strain. He inched forward, his world now upside down. One hand, then the other, one foot, then the other. A soft yellow glow stretched out into the icy morning haze from the lantern above the fore top. It cut into the darkness of the night like a beacon of safety reaching out into the dark world high above the main deck. One hand, then the other. On foot, then the other. His heartbeat reverberated through him, thrumming through every fiber of muscle and pulsing the fire that now ran in his veins. He reached the edge and clasped one hand on the outside of the plank's edge.

"What in hell happened?" Bob muttered into the cold dark, "He was just below me. I didn't scurry up that damned fast."

Jack took hold of the platform edge with his other hand. He could feel warm blood oozing from his palm as the coarse grain of wood met his grip. Another set of shrouds wrapped from the edge of the platform and angled their course upward to the higher masts. Jack shuffled his feet along the lines and stretched for a grasp on the upper shrouds. He pulled his weight up and seized a higher grip on the shrouds with one hand, then the other. His arms quaked in protest of the strain but he forced himself onward and upward.

"Jack? What sort of madness is in yer head, boy?" Bowline Bob raced from the edge of the lubber's hole to the shroud lines. "Are ye trying to fall to yer death?"

Jack heaved in a final effort. He stretched to grab a higher hold on the shrouds and was rewarded with the ragged bite of rope into his hand. In a swinging arc, he unlaced his legs from

A Bloody Beginning

the lines below and pulled his weight with only the strength left in his arms. One knee, then the other set to rest on the platform of the fore top. Jack raised himself up to stand on his feet. His limbs throbbed from exhaustion, but his heart raced with the glory of triumph. A flood of pride swelled inside of his chest to the point he felt he could not contain, it threatened to beat its way outward in a shout of triumphant fury. Jack drew a deep breath of the freezing night air. He quelled the urge to shout his victory and channeled the energy back to his limbs so he could stagger his way toward the foremast.

"Well, damn my soul to the depths," Bob mused in a growling mutter. "Yer'll do, lad. Ye'll be a sailorman yet. Shunned the lubber hole 'is first time up in the tops, 'e did. God damn me back to land, I've never seen it in all me years at sea. Ye must have a damned marlin spike fer a prick, eh?"

Jack cracked a smile and laughed at the crude jest. He rested his thrashed palms on the tops of his knees and doubled over to recover his wind from the rush of his climb. "I'm not sure why. I just couldn't bring myself to crawl through the lubber hole."

"That's a cause yer a sailorman, Jack. Yer born fer it," He paused and withdrew a pipe from within his thick wool coat. He packed in a pinch of tobacco and opened the fore top lantern to steal a bit of flame. "Ye gots nothin left to prove ter me, Jack. Whatever cloth yer cut from makes for good

A Bloody Beginning

sailorin. I'll bet yer old man was as hard as a damned iron spike in white oak."

Jack felt a jab of grief in his chest. The image of his father, lying on the ground in that Boston courtyard flashed into his mind. "You have to be a man now." Jack forced himself to stand upright. "This is the fore top," he said while heaving in gasping breaths of frigid sea air. "But, the shrouds lead higher."

Bowline Bob broke out in a crackling chuckle. "Fore t'gallant mast, but there's no top up there, Jack. Nowhere for ye to double over and breath like a bellows. A might scant for space up on the yard, but, it be up there awaitin' fer us, iff'n yer stout enough to make the haul."

Jack flexed his hands. They were still wrought with an ache like he had never known. He looked at Bob. "Lead on."

Bowline Bob shook his head and arched his eyebrows. He blew out a cloud of smoke in a thin trailing wisp. "Probly a fool's errand, but 'e says lead on, so 'ere we go."

Bowline Bob paced to the edge of the foretop and seized the shroud lines in his fists. His pipe spilled clouds of smoke as he hoisted himself further aloft. Jack marveled at Bob's swagger as he moved skyward. He seemed to glide almost effortlessly up the lines, his motions were as smooth as silk. Jack grabbed hold of the shroud lines and began his own ascent. Hand over hand and step by step he climbed as wind whipped at his face. He dared not look down now. This was

A Bloody Beginning

higher than he had ever been. Every movement of the ship, even the slightest pitch of the deck, sent Jack and Bob swaying through the cold night. Jack noted how much higher this second tier of shrouds was than the first. The form of the ship became a small dark spot far below him, with the tiniest blobs of light from the lanterns on deck. Words from a conversation drifted downwind from the mainmast rigging. Jack strained his ears to hear what was being said, but he could only pick up bits and pieces. Griping about the cold, bits about their short visit to Boston and curses for what the Brits had recently done. Hand over hand, Jack continued up the shroud, his legs growing shaky and his grip feeling more strained with every gain in elevation. He reached the top-gallant yard and swung a leg over at the direction of Bowline Bob, thankful for the bit of respite high above the deck.

"A mite farther than I thought we would climb on such a cold morn, Jack. But, ye'll be glad of it soon. It's something ye'll remember for as long as your mind is still working. Your first sunrise in the rigging. Judging by the stars, the skies are clear. It should be quite a sight."

Jack braced his hands on the mast and craned his neck to look up into the night sky. In Boston, there were always streetlamps lit, or the light of fires burning nearby. He had seen the stars at night, but nothing like what was on display above him now. Twinkling brightness from a million stars shone down. They littered the sky so thick

A Bloody Beginning

that in some places he couldn't tell where one ended and the next began. There was almost a color to it, a celestial ribbon of stars running through the night.

"Spectacular," He muttered, "I never knew there were so many. Just look at it!" He realized what a childlike lubber he must sound in front of Bowline Bob, a man who had surely gazed at the brilliance more times than he could count before Jack was even born.

"It is something, eh?" Bowline Bob said with a furious puff at his pipe. "And by night, they're all a true sailorman needs to navigate. He leaned in toward the mast and craned his neck to look over his shoulder. "See there, shaped like a big damned ladle? The big dipper, always in the north." He drew at his pipe, which threw up a ghostly red glow against his weather-beaten face. "Ye see it? Looks like a soup ladle Reginald would use to spoon out the cap'n his damned dinner."

Jack searched the glimmers in the night sky in the area Bob had pointed to with the stem of his pipe. He found a set of three in the form of an arc that connected to an off shape rectangular pattern with three more. "Yes, I think I see it." He pointed into the northern sky, a few hand widths above the horizon. "There, a big soup ladle. I can see it."

Bowline Bob chuckled and took a drag from his pipe. "Aye, a big, damned soup ladle. They call her Big Dipper, that is most sailormen do. Schooled folks have a different name for her. But I just remember that she looks like a big soup ladle."

A Bloody Beginning

He paused for a moment and blew out a cloud of rich smoke into the freezing wind as it whipped around them. "If ye look at the far edge of the ladle cup, away from the handle, and follow the line of those two stars, it will point to the little soup ladle, and that will show ye the North Star."

Jack tried to follow Bob's directions. He drew an imaginary line between the two stars at the far edge of the constellation and followed it across a small expanse of night sky littered with stars. "I guess, I don't see it."

Bob leaned into the mast opposite Jack. "If yer just looking for the North Star, ye'll miss her. Look for the small soup ladle. She'll be upside down, like she's pouring her goodness into the big one nearabouts." He leaned back and drew from his pipe again, the red glow flared across his face and showed his eyebrows arcing in encouragement.

Jack traced his imaginary line again, but this time he studied the pattern of stars for an upside-down soup ladle. "There!" He nearly shouted. "I found it!"

"Right, see, I knew ye would, Jack. Sometimes it just takes the sailorinest sailor to teach a fellow," Bob drew at his pipe again before withdrawing it from his bite and using the stem to point. "Now, ye see the little soup ladle. Follow the handle, the last star in that arc will be the North Star. Schooled folk have another name for that one too. But, if ye can find her, ye have no more need of a compass at night. If ye can find north, then ye know which way is which. Leave the rest to dead reckoning and making yer next landfall. There's other'n too, Southern Cross, Orion and the damned bull he is trying to kill. I can teach you some of them, too. But, it looks like our night sky might be a fading away on us. Nows for the proper show to begin."

Bob poked his pipe stem toward the horizon over Jack's shoulder. Jack twisted and leaned as far as he dared to look over to the east. The horizon was visible, a crisp line of gray sea bordered by a subtle glow of growing gold and orange that invaded the night sky like the steady advance of the tide onto a sandy beach. The stars gave way to the brilliance of the sun in a steady retreat while columns of light stretched upward and displayed a range of color from crimson and violet to the deepest shades of orange and gold. It reminded Jack of the turning colors of autumn in Boston, only this was a far more awe-striking sight. Light stretched out over the cresting waves between Salem Tide and the horizon while thin white wisps of cloud striated high overhead in the icy wind. It was more than an image, it was an experience. How could he ever describe what he was seeing? He wished for a moment that he could show his mother, how she would love a sight like this! The thought fleeted away as soon as it struck, and Jack scanned over the sea, watching the waves far below and far away crest in little caps of white as they were pressed by the wind. It was more brilliant than he could ever have imagined during those long afternoons of loitering near the harbor. The chill of the wind seemed to

A Bloody Beginning

lose its bite on his skin. His hands seemed to cease in their dull throbbing ache, and his limbs felt rejuvenated from their taxing climb.

"It's a sight, for sure," Bob growled and tapped the wooden bowl of his pipe against the mast to knock out the ash. "It makes fouled rations and cramped quarters seem worth it, at times."

Jack nodded in silent agreement as the sun finally peeked its face over the edge of the horizon. Its brilliant rays shone in columns of bright golden light and threw new hues of pink and radiant orange across the sea as a renewed breeze shifted slightly off of Salem Tide's aft quarter. Jack looked below and found the sunlight had yet to reach the deck of the ship. It struck him, that the deckhands would be deprived of the sun's warmth for a while longer. He smiled and soaked in the direct sunshine. It felt good on his wind whipped face. With his heart in his throat, he raised one hand away from the mast to shield his eyes from the direct shine of the sun. The sea stretched out as far as he could see in every direction. Jack looked around in every direction, taking in the enormity of it all, until something caught his attention against the sprawl of gray waves crested with small caps of foaming white. At first, he thought his mind had played a trick on him. But, there was something off to the north and east that kept drawing his eye. A break in the pattern of waves, an anomaly that he couldn't quite place and for a moment, couldn't quite locate. Jack scoured the area where he thought he

A Bloody Beginning

saw something. He narrowed his eyes against the glare of the sun as its rays grew brighter and more of its golden orb revealed itself over the horizon.

"Shift in the wind, Jacky," Bob grunted as he packed a fresh pinch of tobacco into his pipe. "Dawn always brings a change in the wind, sometimes small, but there is always some change. The quarter will want a sail adjustment soon."

Jack continued searching the area of sea that caught his eye, unable to locate exactly what it was. "I thought I saw something, Bob," He said while squinting his eyes in a struggled focus on the waves.

"Where away?" Bob growled from his side of the mast.

Jack pointed toward the northeast. "Just shy of the horizon. I'm not even sure what it was, but something caught my eye."

Bob lifted himself up and stood on the yard with one arm wrapped around the column of the mast. With his off hand, he shielded his eyes from the brightness of dawn in the same fashion Jack had. "We call thataway three points of the starboard bow, but I can explains all that to yer later," He said with a grunt. For a long moment, Bob stood as still as a statue, unmoving even as Salem Tide pitched and swayed. Jack began to wonder if he had raised a false alarm until Bob stuck his pipe into his teeth and clenched its stem in his bite. "I'll be damned straight back to land, Jacky."

A Bloody Beginning

A ribbon of fire traced through Jack's blood. The fear of his mind playing tricks on him vanished. "What is it? What's out there?"

"Plumes, Jacky. Seems yer found a school of whales out there in the open sea," Bob said before breaking into a chuckle, "ye never ceases amazing me, Jacky. That's a lucky omen, too, being the first to sight a whale on a voyage. I'd curse for a scoundrel, sighting them while I'm sitting right here next to ye. Could have been my good luck ye just hoarded up fer yourself. But, I can't say I knows of anyone more deserving." He paused and stared out into the vast stretches of the sea. "There, see. There goes another!" He said in his throaty growl of a voice, "and look! A tail! That's lucky indeed, Jack."

Jack found the plume right as Bob pointed it out, and sighted the large whale tail arcing over the water's surface not far from the blown mist of the plume. "I see it!" He replied, "That is something. I don't think I have ever seen anything like that before!"

Bob nodded his head, "Quite a morning for ye, Jack. Quite a morn indeed." He gestured down toward the deck. "Ye spotted 'em, I'll let ye do the honors."

Jack frowned and cocked his head. "Honors?"

"Aye, lad." Bob smiled broad. "Call it out to the deck, let them know what ye see and where away, once they ask."

"Oh, right," Jack said, feeling thick for missing the point at first. He turned his face down toward

A Bloody Beginning

the deck, it seemed miles away below them.
"Deck! Whales spotted!"

Jack watched as a figure ambled forward into view around the billowing sail obscuring most of the ship from his view. He cupped his hands and called aloft, "Where away?"

Jack smiled as he realized he had daydreamed about holding this conversation, in various forms, all through his boyhood years. "Three points off starboard bow, about two miles distant!"

Jack turned and looked back toward Bowline Bob who met his gaze with an approving nod. "We'll make a sailorman out of ye Jacky. Ye stick with old Bowline Bob and we'll have the crew ranting about ye being the sailorinest sailor there ever was, mark me words Jack." Bob lowered himself to sit on the yard and took one more long survey of the surrounding sea.

"Haaaands to braaaaaces!" the shout came from Petey somewhere aft of the mainmast.

Jack looked at Bob while the old sailor's brow furrowed tight down over his nose. "Something amiss, Bob?"

"Aye," Bob answered, with an edge of concern in his voice. "Iffn thars whales, then there ought to be the whalin fleet in tow. But, I can't says I see a single sign of sail, nor of small boats. Not unheard of, mind ye, but it is odd. Especially when the fleet was so close to these seas just a week ago."

Jack twisted again to steal one last look toward the whales. Beneath him, he could feel Salem Tide shifting in her course. The quarterdeck was

A Bloody Beginning

striking toward the whale sighting in hopes of catching the fleet in their pursuit of the sea beasts. Bob was right, a sail change would be coming any moment now.

"Hands aloft, t'gallents fore and main, stun'sls fore and main smartly after," Petey's voice bellowed over the deck with a tinny ring to it.

Bob nudged Jack on his shoulder and arched his eyebrows high. "Well, since yer on hand anyway, ye might as well help us unfurl the top-gallant and get her sheeted home. We'll need the hand booming out the stun'sls too."

Jack felt a rush in his blood. "Won't I be missed on deck? I don't want to get into trouble."

Bob swung his leg over the yard and slipped onto the tightrope strung just beneath it. "Yer messmates will be green with envy. But, from what I've heard, Mr. Hancock doesn't much care to see you idling on deck neither. He 'structed the cap'n to have you trained up in sailorin'. That's just what we'll do."

Jack did his best to mimic Bob's maneuver, though not with the same smooth swagger that Bowline Bob managed. "We'll loose this sail ourselves?"

Bob shook his head, "Nay," he said with a throaty laugh. "Look below. The fore top men are on their way up already. Make yer way on the tightrope. They won't be as patient ad old Bowline Bob iffn' they have to wait on you when they gets here."

A Bloody Beginning

Steadying himself on the topgallant yard, Jack edged his way along the tightrope until he was a mere three feet from the end. He could tell the other sailors had made their way onto the tightrope behind him without looking over his shoulder, their feet stepping and sliding along it sent little tugs on the line that made his heart race with each one. When he reached the furthest point he dared, Jack turned and wrapped both arms over the top of the yard just as he saw the other sailors do. He looked up and felt a massive wave of relief when he saw the stony face of Matsumoko on the line next to him.

"Matsumoko! Bob told me to help loose the topgallant," he paused for a second before lowering his voice to avoid being overheard by the hands behind his friend. "What do I do?"

Laughter broke out among the sailors on the line and Jack felt his face flush as he realized he hadn't lowered his voice enough. Matsumoko did not partake in their amusement. "Keep your torso leaned over the yard, just like you are. Whatever you do, don't lean back. There is nothing to catch you if you spill." He ran a hand over the yard and indicated a taut knot of cordage bundling the sail to the wooden beam. "When you here the signal, unfasten your knot and let the canvas pull as smooth as you can. The deckhands will take in the lines below and she'll sheet home nicely in this breeze. But be ready, when the wind fills her and the ship answers, she'll shift under our feet. Make

A Bloody Beginning

sure you keep a good hold and don't let the movement carry you off your balance."

Jack tried to digest the cascade of instructions all at once. He felt his head spin. He looked down. It was hard to tell from the height he was at where he would land if he happened to fall. One moment it looked as if he would splash down into the icy sea, a fate he had narrowly avoided once but from a much lower height. The next moment it looked as if a fall would land him directly on the weather deck, that he imagined, would somehow be a more wicked end than being thrust into frigid waters and drowning.

"Ready on the line!" Bowline Bob's voice roared from somewhere near the mast. The sailors stood ready and all shouted so in reply. "Loose!" Bob growled loudly.

Matsumoko turned to Jack. "Now. Unfasten your hitch and let it out while they pull it taut."

Jack nodded and he worked the cordage until it freed from itself. Below he could hear the deckhands reply their order to heave and canvas began to run out in a steady flow that filled with wind before it even sheeted home. He craned his neck and caught the main top men loosing their own top-gallant. Just as Matsumoko had warned, he could feel a definite shift in the motion of the ship. Far below, the bow of Salem Tide began throwing off a wake from the front of her hull.

"She's alive and moving now boys! Nine knots or I'm a blind bloody fool, wait until we get those stun'sls out, we'll be pushing twelve!" a cheer rose

A Bloody Beginning

up from the sailors on line and all together they began making their way inboard toward the shrouds to work their way down.

CHAPTER 10

'Salem Tide'
8 March 1770
44 Degrees 13' N, 62 Degrees 12' W

The deck was alive with excitement. Once the sail changes had been made, Petey called for idle hands to breakfast. Jack joined his messmates in the warmth below deck for a quick meal of boiled oats with bits of ham and small beer. It was far from the decadent fare he had partaken in with Matsumoko and the captain, but it was hearty enough to dull away the ache of his muscles from their morning trials. Chatter centered around Jack spotting the whales and how close the whaling fleet must be. Jack felt the urge to relay Bob's concern about not sighting a sail or a small boat, but held his tongue for reasons he couldn't quite pinpoint. Bob had grown concerned quickly after

A Bloody Beginning

the sighting and Jack had thought it was a little odd that he should be so worried. The whalers would be chasing after the whales, after all, Salem Tide just had to shadow the pod for a spell and the whalers would surely turn up. It made him wonder if there was something to the exchange he did not understand, and for some reason, he wasn't quite sure why, it made him think of the captain's mention of a rendezvous they must make. It felt connected, how, Jack didn't quite understand. But, he felt that there was something there.

"Boiled oats? Again! We were just in port and that damned purser has us eating slop we'd see after three months to sea!" Bitter End Bill shouted as he made his way past Jack and his mess mates. "If'fn my wages are docked for these vittles, I should be 'avin a bit of fruit this near making port. That filching bastard is like to cut our rations and pocket the difference he is. Nothin in it for 'im not to."

Jack kept his eyes straight away as the salty sea hand snatched his portions from the cook and stomped toward the foc'sle where he squatted to eat alone.

"Never mind 'im, Jack," said John Long from his seat next to one of Salem Tide's small six pounder cannons. "He is always griping and complaining about near everything. It's hard to swallow, but easier that than to actually have to deal with him."

Jack ate a spoonful of his boiled oats. The taste of ham was barely present, but it was something.

A Bloody Beginning

"Petey told me that Bill has been a pressed man on three different occasions. I imagine if that happened to me, I would be angry too."

"Not just a pressed man," Slop, the heavyset deckhand added with wide eyes. "Wait 'til you see him strip off his shirt! He's had his back striped a half dozen times at least, its enough to make your blood run cold just thinkin about it!"

Jack stole a side eyed glance at Bitter End Bill as he sat in the mess corner and stared into his bowl of boiled oats and ham. "What would cause a man to get flogged aboard a navy ship?" He asked.

"Any number of things, lad," interrupted Bowline Bob with a gesture for Matsumoko and Jack to make room for him to sit among them. He laid his bowl and cup down onto the rough pair of planks they were using as a table. "A man can get flogged for stealing, or falling asleep on watch. He can get flogged for fighting, or if the officers decide they don't like the cut 'o your jib as yer taking yer orders from them. They can flog a man fer near anything 'cording to their articles of war. But, what get most folks, is usually one they call insubordinate. Being insubordinate, least that's how I thinks it's called. Refusing to give the proper respects, or do your duties. When I was aboard the navy frigate, that's what I seen, floggings for insubordinate, more times ' I could count. Couple of fellers got flogged one week, and then was back at the capstan a week later fer some other infraction. They got numb to it, almost. Like they just didn't care anymore."

A Bloody Beginning

"Numb? To a kiss from the cat?" John Long shriveled his face as if he were about to spit. "That's hogwash if I've ever heard. I've seen a boatswain rip flesh with his cat strikes, every swing drew blood. More 'n three dozen left a sailor flirting with the grave, and four dozen would do the job sure as the sunset." He shook his head. "No. Nobody is that thick, to not care for a lashing. Not a chance."

Bowline Bob spooned some oats and ham into his mouth and smiled at John with a mouthful of crooked, smoke-stained teeth. "How long 'ave you been at sea, again? A year? Two? I've spent more time climbing rigging than you have drawing breath you little bilge rat. In fact, Salem Tide has more men who've been at sea longer than you've been alive then don't." He ate another spoonful of his breakfast and set his bowl down. "I said what I said, and I'll stand by it. I've had my brushes with a boatswain's swing, drunkenness, thievin' liquor. Can't say the thought of another stripin' doesn't make my blood run cold. But, I can't say it was enough to stop me either. When a man has the itch to get a good drunk on, and he thinks he can get to it without getting caught, he will. Cat or no." He dug into his ragged waistcoat and pulled out his pipe. "There's few things in this world fouler than being pressed into the king's navy, but, it's part of life at sea. I'll say, I'd rather chance the press for a life at sea than live me whole damned life on land."

A Bloody Beginning

Jack took in all the chattering sailors. The men near him were discussing the hardships of British impressment, while the table next to theirs discussed the good luck that had befallen crews who had sighted whales so near the start of their journey. One man piped in to suggest that it was best to see whales near the end of a journey, for proper good luck, which was met with grunts of disagreement. The talk soon shifted to poor omens rather than good ones, and Jack's ears perked up at a mention of the Bermuda Triangle. He ceased listening to his own messmates as Slop was telling of how his second cousin's husband or some such was pressed right out of a fishing vessel.

"Their captain and crew, the whole lot of them, couldn't get a fix on their navigation. It was like they was cursed. One of the officers would get a reading and do his calculations while the next did 'em at the same time. Every bloody one of them comes up with a different reading, including their skipper. They sailed 'round for weeks not knowing where they was, or where they was going. I heard the hours was all mixed up too. The watch would turn the glass and men were dying of boredom before it would run out of sand, next turn, they barely feels like it's turned over before it needs turnin' again," one sailor said in a foreboding tone. "They run out of food, run out 'o water. Ship run aground on a reef, it did. Not a soul lived."

Another sailor shriveled his face and shook his head. "None left alive, eh?"

A Bloody Beginning

The first sailor looked at the man next to him and nodded. "That's what I said, innit?"

The second man lifted his cup of small beer and took a deep drink before setting it down again. "Then where do the tales from their doomed voyage come from? Ghosts?" A roll of laughter engulfed their table and the sailor who had told the grim tale went beet red in the face.

"I heard it true, from a sailor I met in Baltimore. No reason to doubt it's a true telling," he objected.

"Just relax Scott, ye old blister. It's all in sport. It wouldn't be the first time we did!" another sailor chimed.

A third chipped in, "Or the first time you've lied!" Another roll of laughter tore through the wide cabin, and Jack caught himself smiling at their jests.

More conversations drifted across the deck and Jack couldn't help but overhear another sailor telling a tall tale. He had his messmates leaning over their bowls, with wide eyes and expectant expressions as he regaled them with a telling Jack suspected was mostly fabrication.

"We saw it off the Nova Scotia coast, as terrifying a thing as anyone has ever seen. Arms forty fathoms in length, thrice as big around as the mainmast. We never saw its body, but with appendages like that, could you imagine?" The sailor said over his empty bowl and half-drunk cup. "It brushed against our hull, but I guess it didn't have the appetite for a man 'o war, cause it slipped out to sea and wrapped its deadly grasp

A Bloody Beginning

around a fishing cog. Pulled her right under, masts and all. Wasn't a bit of scrap or flotsam left afterwards, just trickles of little bubbles trailing up from the deep. Coldest damn thing I've ever seen. Must've been a hundred souls aboard that ship, and it took 'em all under in less time than it takes ye to blow yer honker. She didn't stand a chance."

"Bullocks! I've heard the last time you sang this song and it was a trade galleon from Spain, except that time you were off the coast of Jamaica." A resounding wave of laughter drowned the angry objections of the sailor defending his tall tale and Jack looked around to find his own messmates joining in with the revelries. Bob shrugged before upending the last of his beer in a long drink while Slop, Matsumoko and John Long all laughed along with the rest of the crew. It was warm, there was food, and for the first time since that cold night in the courtyard in Boston, Jack felt a glimmer of happiness. He looked around at smiling faces, red with laughter, and wondered if he had found his way to where he was supposed to be.

The ship's bell pealed in a rapid pattern, one ring blending into the next in a stream of ear-piercing sound that made Jack's hair stand on end. He looked around and found concern spreading to the faces of his messmates. All except Bowline Bob, who held up one hand as if he were waiting on something.

"Sails sighted!" A voice announced down the aft ladder.

A Bloody Beginning

Bob smiled. "Easy, lads. As I suspected, that'll be the whaling fleet!" He packed a pinch of tobacco into the bowl of his pipe and clamped the stem into his bite. "Cap'n will want to stand off from them for a bit, make sure they aren't in the midst of bringing in one of the old beasts. Once they are ready to offload and take on fresh goods, they'll signal us over. For now, we wait." He leaned back and stole a look around the room for a nearby lantern or candle.

Despite his tired limbs and sore hands, Jack felt a crushing desire to go back on deck and take in the sight of the spotted vessel. He looked toward Matsumoko and then John Long. "I'm sure it's a sight, to watch them chase down their quarry."

Bowline Bob eased up from his seat into a crouch to avoid hitting his head on a beam while he stole some flame from a lantern hanging on a nearby bulkhead beam. "Not as glorious a sight as you might think, young Jack." He drew in a deep breath and released a cloud of bluish smoke over their makeshift table. "See, the mind conjures images of a brave whaler standing on the prow of their mighty ship with harpoons in hand as they chase down the great beast. Which is great if you are a whaler telling stories in a pub to a gaggle of ladies and landsmen. But, in reality, they sends out small boats to do their spearing. It's dangerous, cold, miserable and wet. The small boats end up getting dragged forever, sometimes pulled under, or broke up entirely. In waters this cold, that's a death sentence, as you well know.

A Bloody Beginning

You are welcome to go on up and have a look-see, but don't say old Bob didn't warn ye. Yer best use of time would be practicin' some knots with me or getting a bit of rest while ye can. Unloading those greasy buggers will take the better part of a day and a night, and that's before we load any fresh goods over to them. Then we will have three or four more ships to do the same with. Tending the whaling fleet earns good coin, sure, but it is a hold full of hard work when we finally sets upon them."

The ship's bell pealed again in rapid succession. Jack looked around, confusion digging into his mind while the faces surrounding him appeared to be struck with the same malady.

"Hands to make sail!" Petey's voice ripped through the cabin from the ladder well. "Deck hands, to the guns!"

Jack looked at Bowline Bob and saw confusion bleed across his face, followed shortly by a wide eyed grimace of apprehension. "Son of a bitch," He growled.

"What?" Jack asked in a growing panic, "What is it?"

Bowline Bob tamped the bowl of his pipe onto the table and swept the ash and embers onto the deck. "Calling hands to the guns can only mean one of two things. Pirates, or a Brit navy ship."

Jack's head spun. "There are pirates in these waters?"

A Bloody Beginning

Bowline Bob met his eyes with an intense glare. "Not this far north, Jacky. Odds are it's a Brit man 'o war cruising to press men off the fleet."

Jack's mind raced with the possibilities of this encounter. Would they fire on a merchant ship? Would they take a brand-new sailor and press him into the king's service? He wondered if he should make for the highest hold in the rigging. Surely, they wouldn't bother to climb aloft to drag a skinny kid down from the highest heights of the mast. Or, perhaps, a hiding hole in the hold, or the captain's cabin? Indecision plagued him. It paralyzed his limbs and froze his thoughts. He drifted back to the courtyard in Boston as snow fluttered down from the darkened sky and soaked into the ooze of blood weaving its way in between cobblestones. "You have to be a man now."

Sailors hurried to clear the deck from breakfast. Tables were put away in a hasty and haphazard fashion, and everyone raced to the weather deck to see the sighted vessel for themselves.

"Hull is up, sir. She looks like a man of war, a frigate, most like." A lookout called down to the captain as Jack stepped from the aft weather hatch up onto the deck.

The captain grimaced and squinted toward the horizon. He stared for a long moment before turning aloft and shouting up to the lookout, "Do you see any colors? Is she a Brit?"

A long moment elapsed before any answer was called back. Jack's ears filled with the wash of the sea against Salem Tide's hull and the creak of her

A Bloody Beginning

rigging in the wind. "Can't make out any colors, sir. But, she's Brit made, I'd bet a bottle on it."

The captain turned and let his eyes fall to the deck, not noticing that his every move held the attention of the entire crew. "God damn them to hell and back," He growled under his breath before pacing from behind the helm to the quarterdeck bulwark and then back again. "Pompous bastards, bulling their way around the world as if they own it." He looked up across the expanse of sea separating his ship from the mysterious man of war. "Well, you don't own us, you damn king's toadies!" He shouted out over the waves. "I will be damned for a raving mad man, but I won't let a single man from this crew be pressed. Not one!" With that he turned defiantly on one heel and stormed below deck without issuing a single order or acknowledging anyone along his path.

The tension on deck escalated further when the helmsman turned toward Petey with a helpless stare and asked. "Now what do we do?"

Petey growled under his breath for a moment, gnawing at the stem of his wooden pipe. No smoke emanated from the object, it merely rocked and swayed while Petey's lips moved, uttering silent curses against malign forces that had stacked against them on this day. He finally took one long look aloft and then stared hard out over the sea before issuing a low-voiced command. "Bring her about, lar'bd, hard lar'bd. Put the wind at our stern quarter and head us north by

A Bloody Beginning

northwest." The young man at the wheel of the ship hesitated for a moment, his eyes darted around for some confirmation that what Petey was ordering was indeed correct. He got none. Petey turned on the helmsman and rapped his knuckles on the hard wood of the ship's wheel. "Aye, lad. I said bring her hard to lar'bd, north by northwest. Now snap to, or I'll put someone else on the damned helm!"

Pale faced, the helmsman turned the ships wheel over to steer the vessel over north by northwest. It took a moment, and some fast work by the deckhands and men aloft, but Salem Tide's sails fluttered and filled taut with the wind on her new course. Jack could feel the ship picking up speed, as her deck began to pitch and heave with the gentle rise of swells. They were sailing cross wise to the seas, and soon Salem Tide began a nauseating rock in synchrony with her steady rising and lowering. All hands lined the starboard railing, eyes locked on the triple hung sails plowing their way over the seas just below the horizon. Either the mystery ship had not yet made sight of their sail, or their course change had gone unnoticed. Jack hoped for the former, but knew the futility of it. As surely as they had spotted the warship, the warship had spotted them. The course change would be noted in due time, and the question of the warship's intent would be immediately answered by their response. Seconds dragged into minutes. The slosh of waves breaking along the bow filled Jack's ears. Ropes

A Bloody Beginning

creaked and groaned under the strain of wind filled sails.

"Deck!" a voice in the rigging called out. "Deck! She's coming about, she turning toward us!"

"Damn!" Petey said in a seething growl. He turned to the gathered sailors on deck. "Every stitch of canvas we have to fly, fly it. We have to make for the inlets of the coast if we have any hope of evasion, and even then it may not be enough." He ran a hand across his scruffy beard and then around his head to the back of his neck before turning toward the starboard rail and staring hard as squares of white canvas turned to face them.

The warship was stacking on more sail, even while the winds were stout and already in their favor. Jack watched helplessly from the waist as Petey paced the quarterdeck. Occasionally he would look aloft and give the helmsman a minor adjustment. He ordered every idle hand to stand at the weather railing, and then ordered other deck hands to go below and start throwing their sparse supply of shot for the cannons overboard. Anything and everything Salem Tide could do to increase her speed, Petey ordered. She gained a knot here, and a knot there and for a while her increase seemed like it would be enough. Hours slipped through the glass and with every watch bell the crew looked on in horror as the warship slipped closer on an intercept course. There could be no denying it, they were being pursued.

A Bloody Beginning

Jack watched with a sinking heart as the warship came into full view of the deck, waves crested and broke along the underside of her bow, her masts stood tall in the distance and Jack was beginning to make out the forms of sailors in her rigging.

"We'll 'ave some explaining to do, when they catch us," Bowline Bob growled through a cloud of rich pipe smoke. "It might have been better to just reef sail and await our fate."

Jack frowned and turned to the sailor who had taken to mentoring him. "How could you say that? You don't think we could lose them in darkness along the coast?"

Bob shook his head. "No, Jack. Any sailorman could see, they'll be a-catching us long before sunset. Even at that, if we lost them in the dark, they're faster than us by a good measure. It'll take a miracle for 'em not to be pulling us alongside now."

Jack felt a rush of indignant defiance. He pictured the red coats of the soldiers that had lined up on King's Street. He remembered the demeaning attitude of the soldier he had blundered into on his way to the pier. Anger welled inside of him, boiling just beneath the surface. "The captain said he won't let a single man be pressed," Jack replied.

Bob blew a stream of smoke out the side of his mouth and gave Jack a grim look and a tight grin. "It's not up to him, Jack. If anything, he may be able to spare a man by putting another in his

A Bloody Beginning

place, but that would be the extent of it. The Brits look at ships from the colonies as within their dominion. They'll board us, search our hold if they please, take whatever pleases them and a grip full of hands to do their hard laborin'. Best thing to do if yer grabbed for the press is to do as yer told. Sailoring in the king's navy isn't the worst of fates, despite what ye have heard. They eat fair enough, and as long as ye tend to yer duties and keep yerself free of mischief, yer've no need to fear the cat."

Jack felt a welling ache in his stomach. The warship pitched and rolled with a course correction that brought her in line with Salem Tide's stern. She was fast. Her sleek lines seemed to cut the waves rather than plowing through them. Jack scanned the faces of the crew around him on deck, he wasn't the only one feeling a sense of helpless dread. Even Bowline Bob seemed to lack the usual luster of his crooked smile and the spring from his step had all but faded away. The cloud formations overhead thickened and the wind seemed to blow a little colder. The sunrise that had awed Jack so thoroughly had slipped behind a dense ceiling of gray while fluttering white flakes of snow dropped from the clouds in tumultuous swirls.

A thunderous boom echoed out over the gap of sea between Salem Tide and her pursuer. Jack's heart seized in his chest. They were being fired upon! Everyone on deck froze. A shriek followed the report. It grew in intensity until Jack could feel

A Bloody Beginning

as much as hear the cannonball fly past the starboard side. It could not have been far from the side of the ship. All eyes locked onto the pursuing warship.

"Colonial vessel! In the name of King George the third, I order you to furl your sails and prepare to be boarded for inspection of your holds and your crew!" a voice with a tinny ring floated in across the wind.

Petey paced to the taff rail along Salem Tide's fantail. "These bastards have us by the hip. There's no way we can hold them back until sunset, and they know it."

"What do we do?" a sailor from the deck shouted.

Petey's shoulders slumped in defeat. He tapped the wooden bowl of his pipe on the railing. "Heave to, reef sails and prepare to be boarded," He said while staring back at the British warship. He turned and faced the crew on deck. "They mean to search our holds for any goods in violation of the king's taxes, and I'm sure, to press some of ye into their crew. Don't fight them, we'll not give the vicious bastards any excuses to further violate the ship," he said in a rough but calm tone.

Aloft, the top men went straight to work taking in sail. Jack wondered again in silence if he should excuse himself from the deck and take up a high perch among the rigging. His question was answered as the last of the sails was finally taken in and secured as all the top hands made their way through rigging and down the shrouds to the

A Bloody Beginning

main deck. Their assembly was less than orderly. A messy group gathered in between the mainmast and the quarterdeck before filing along the lee railing to watch as the warship slid next to Salem Tide and coasted to an easy saunter. Lines with grapple hooks were thrown onto Salem Tide's deck and within a few heartbeats the ships were being pulled close together in a manner that would allow for boarding parties to cross. Drums rattled in a formal militant tattoo while a broad gangplank clattered down in between the vessels.

A storm of redcoats flooded Salem Tide's deck, each holding a musket vertically as they fanned out and surrounded the crew on deck. Jack's heart thrummed in his throat, he found there was a knot at the top of his windpipe that made it impossible to swallow. His mind raced with the fears of a repeat of that night in Boston. Were they going to open fire? Who would they kill? The captain? Petey? Everyone aboard? The attempted flight had been a mistake, Jack could see that clearly in the temperament of the warship's marines as they encircled the crew and then collectively lowered their weapons to a firing position.

Part Two

CHAPTER 11

'Salem Tide'
8 March 1770
44 Degrees 26' N, 61 Degrees 07' W

"My name is Captain Harold Williams, commanding officer of His Majesty's Frigate Allegiance," The officer's voice carried over Salem Tide's crew. He was a thin set man, with deep-set eyes, dark hair and a sharp, almost gaunt face. He paused a moment, seeming to size up the lot of them. "It is the privilege of His Majesty the King to compel certain numbers of his subjects into service when necessary. It is also his privilege, and the duty of those in his service, to ensure that taxes levied in his name are being complied with." The officer nodded to a group of waiting sailors aboard his own vessel. They stormed across the

A Bloody Beginning

gangplank and made a direct path for the weather hatch leading below. "The Royal Navy is severely under-manned, I will take aboard a score of able-bodied men from your crew for a term of service not to exceed one year. I would advise compliance. I have already been merciful, considering your pathetic attempt to flee, I would have been within my rights to sink your ship outright and leave you all to the frigid water and the crushing depths."

Jack felt the lump in his throat seize. He couldn't breathe, he couldn't speak. Even if he had the use of his voice, he wasn't sure of what he would say. It seemed the impressment was a foregone conclusion. The Royal Navy had boarded and would take their desired number of men and that was all there was to it. It burned Jack's mind with a rage he could barely contain. He felt his face flushing and his hands go cold.

"Twenty men?" Petey protested, "And how are we supposed to get this girl back to port? Twenty men leaves me with naught but a single watch."

The officer turned and faced Petey with a wry smile. "If you hadn't tried to evade us, I was only planning to take a half dozen, and landsmen at that. As it stands, I will have a full score, and I want at least half that number to be capable hands. Men with two or more years at sea. Times are perilous, the king needs his most experienced subjects to ensure the safety and longevity of the empire." He scanned Salem Tide's deck with a inspecting stare. His facial expression shriveled as

A Bloody Beginning

he surveyed the results, displaying a look of disgust. "Hands, capable or otherwise. We need strong backs at the capstan too." He turned on one heel and departed across the gangplank while navy sailors plunged into Salem Tide's hold and the marines closed in around her crew.

Jack felt like a lamb being led to slaughter. He was shuffled by the press of sailors behind him and then pushed back as marines on the opposite side forced several hands over toward the lee rail where the gangplank extended between ships. It was a mix of anger and anxiety among the sailors. Jack's vision became obstructed by striped sailor's shirts and wool coats as they were herded toward the railing like livestock.

"You there, old man," a marine shouted and pointed across the deck with the muzzle of his musket. "What's your name?"

Silence fell over the deck as the crew realized the marine was talking to Petey. The first mate stood proudly on the quarterdeck, his arms folded in tight formation across his chest. "My name is Pete Winthrow, I be the first mate aboard the Salem Tide, and out of your grasp. You cannot press a crew to the point of endangering their voyage home."

"We'll let the captain be the judge of that," The marine snapped and gestured toward the rail where the other sailors had gathered. "Over there, with the rest."

"Nay, let your cap'n come over here and tell me that. I'm not moving for the likes of you, or any of

A Bloody Beginning

ye others. Ye hear?" Petey remained as still as a marble column, his pipe barely shifting in his bite as he spoke. "You Brits prowl about the sea and stalk ashore in the colonies, but there is a reckoning coming, and it won't be long, boy."

The marine looked around at the faces of his company, his own face flushed as red as his coat. "You'll be marching to the rail, or we will drag you there and stow you below deck in irons." He clicked the brass hammer of his musket to emphasize his threat.

Petey laughed, letting a cloud of pipe smoke roll out over his bulky figure. "Not sure you brought enough men for that."

"Enough!" the shout came from the deck of the navy ship. Jack and the crew of Salem Tide looked over and saw the navy officer staring back at the detachment of marines. "Leave the first mate, find a seasoned hand in his stead."

Petey Let a cloud of smoke escape through a half smile and nodded triumphantly at the marine detachment. Jack wasn't sure how he felt about the first mate staying aboard Salem Tide. He liked the grizzled old sailor who had welcomed him aboard so warmly. The hand of a marine stretched through the crowd and shoved Jack toward the periphery of the gathered sailors. His feet shuffled until he regained his balance and he found himself on the far edge of the group staring at a pair of armed marines, a sailor, and what appeared to be another officer. The officer was holding a thick log of paper bound in leather, in his other hand was a

A Bloody Beginning

rudimentary quill that looked as if it had seen better days.

"Name?" the officer said without looking up.

Jack's mind stumbled, he looked over one shoulder, then the other, wondering if the officer was talking to him. He hesitated and stared at the officer until the man looked up at him with a look of disdainful annoyance painted on his pinched features.

"Name?" He said again.

Jack drew a breath and swallowed the lump that had persisted in his throat for the better part of the last hour. "Jack," he said.

The officer rolled his eyes and flourished his worn quill in Jack's face. "Well, have you a last name, Jack? Jack what? Or are you another bastard Irish pup from the colonies?"

Jack felt his face flush as a rush of anger boiled up into his chest. "Jack Horner, sir. If you please."

The officer waved his quill as he scribbled something onto his tablet of paper. "Very well, Jack Horner. You are rated landsman and will be assigned to the lar'bd mess. Cross deck and remain amidships until we have assembled the rest of the press."

A heartbeat passed. Jack felt detached from everything occurring around him, as if he was a spectator unable to influence the outcome of his situation. He looked over his shoulder, hoping to find Bowline Bob or Matsumoko, John Long, Slop, or any of his other messmates. He saw faces he recognized, but didn't know by name yet. A slash

A Bloody Beginning

of pain crossed his shoulder and Jack recoiled from it before stumbling to his knees.

"Are you hard of hearing?" a voice crackled in a hostile growl. "The lieutenant said cross deck and wait amidships!"

Another lance of pain struck Jack across his back, followed quickly by a third and then a fourth. Jack fought his way to his feet, stunned by the slashing strikes that had been inflicted on him. He turned and saw that the sailor who had been standing next to the officer with the paper and quill was holding a short length of thin rope balled in one fist. The sailor's face was beet red and set with a look of seething contempt.

"Well?" He shouted, winding his arm up for another slash. "What are ye waiting for? Cross deck, boy!"

With a stutter step and then a scurry, Jack hurried his way across the gangplank between vessels while a ripple of laughter spread through the waiting sailors on the warship. As his feet touched down onto the deck, he looked around and saw a gathering of hard faces. Men who had seen strenuous duty in sun and wind. Calloused stares and hard set brows.

"Amidships, boy! In between the main and the foremast!" a sailor in the crowd shouted.

Jack hurried forward while taking in the look of the crew all around him. He felt strangely alone in the thick press of navy men.

"Next!" shouted the navy officer still aboard Salem Tide.

A Bloody Beginning

Jack strained his hearing in an effort to find out who would be following him across next, but the chatter of the navy crew drowned away any chance of hearing.

"Look at this one," a sailor said, "He's already caught hisself a beating from the boatswain's mate!" Jack found the sailor making the observation, a scowl faced man with a patchwork of scars across his forehead and a ragged circlet of leather covering one eye. "You'll fit in with this lot, boy. So long as you don't do nothin' to get me a flogging!"

The welcome felt anything but. Jack fought against the hot feeling in the back of his eyes, he grappled with the knot in his stomach and the taunting voice in the back of his mind that told him he was all alone. The looks cast upon him by the crew on the deck of the warship ranged from dismissive to utter contempt. He felt a weight of defeat crushing down on his shoulders. Everywhere he looked there was a scowl or a look of predatory intent. He wondered how long it would be until it wasn't just the boatswain raising a hand to strike out at him for his ignorance.

"Where you from, lubby?" the one-eyed navy sailor asked in a throaty, crackling voice.

Jack returned the one-eyed man's look and gave his response, which came out in a feeble voice betraying the hopelessness in his belly. "B-Boston," he stuttered.

A Bloody Beginning

"Boston, aye. I thought so," the one-eyed sailor growled. "I could tell just by looking at you. From the colonies. Ye 'aven't been at sea long, 'ave ye?"

Jack shook his head, and drew in a sharp breath through his nose. He was still fighting away tears that threatened to come pouring out of his eyes at any moment. "No. Just a few days, sir."

The one eyed man broke into a crackling laugh before looking over both of his shoulders and then flashing a smile of gnarled teeth back at Jack. "There be no sirs hereabouts, boy. But, ye best keep it close on yer lips. The officers on this barky will 'ave you flogged fer failing to render their respects proper like." He scrunched his nose at Jack and leaned close. "What's yer name, boy?"

Jack found it easier to speak, and it seemed that this particular navy sailor had no ill will toward him. "Jack Horner," he replied.

The one-eyed sailor nodded before giving Jack a nod while seeming to take his measure with an inspecting glare. "Seems you're outfitted well enough. Ye 'ave shoes, which is more 'n most of us." He leaned even closer to Jack and spoke in a low voice that reeked of alcohol, "Be watching fer some of these tars, they will try and take those from you whether they fit 'em or not. Shoes is a luxury most of us don't 'ave." The sailor returned to a more comfortable distance and Jack was thankful for the absence of his breath. "My name is Kenny, least that's what the crew all calls me. I don't even recall what me true name given by me mother was, but she isn't here to correct nobody,

A Bloody Beginning

so the 'ell with 'er," he broke into another crackling chuckle. "You probably feel about like a doomed man walking to the gallows, judging by the look in yer eyes. But, take heart, laddy. It isn't so bad as it seems, being a pressed man. Most of the crew here is pressed men, 'cepting fer the officers and a few of the mates." He thumbed at his nose and cast a look toward the quarterdeck. "Cap'n's not so bad once yer've been aboard fer a bit. He's free with the grog ration, but he's a hard son-of-a bitch when it comes to dealings with the cat. I've seen 'im sentence more'n a few to six dozen lashes, 'nuff to kill a man," He said. A throaty crackling cough interrupted his impromptu introduction for a moment before he continued. "But, if ye does yer duties, and keeps ter yerself, hands and all, yer'll 'ave no needs fearing the cat. The boatswain and his like use their starters freely, so yer'll 'ave to get used to them. But, we all do. It seems they swing them on all of us about the same. If we displeases them."

A commotion erupted further aft, and Jack's attention was commandeered away from the one eyed sailor named Kenny. Shouts rose and Jack sensed a scuffle at the frigate's larboard rail.

"William Perrin! I seem to remember another name for you," the officer next to the gangplank said loud enough for all to hear. A hush settled over the crowded decks of both vessels. "Bitter End Bill, wasn't it? At one time you were an able seaman aboard H.M.S Resolute. That is, until we made port in the Virginia colony. Decided you

A Bloody Beginning

would try for fortune aboard a merchant vessel, eh? Deserter."

Jack wormed his way through the press of sailors until he reached the larboard railing and had a clear view of what was taking place.

"Mr. Donovan, please see this man below and clap him in irons," the officer announced loudly. He turned back toward Bitter End Bill and said something that Jack couldn't hear before a pair of red coats snatched Bill up under each arm and hurried him across the gangplank and then down the aft ladder way.

Jack muttered out loud, "Where are they taking him?"

"Below deck," Kenny rasped over Jack's shoulder. "He'll be locked up tight in irons until he sees the cap'n."

Jack's stare remained locked on Bitter End Bill. "What will happen to him then?"

Kenny's reply waited until Jack turned and met the old sailor's one-eyed gaze. "He'll be flogged, more'n likely. Or maybe hanged. It depends on the cap'n's mood. But the old sailor disappeared in the night, he'll get whatever comes to him and rightful so. It takes a special kind of coward to abandon yer crew mates, 'specially once the cap'n's gone and trusted a man with shore leave." He paused and glared in the direction of Bitter End Bill. "Those poor souls probably didn't see another shore leave fer half a damned year, all because of that sour grape. Selfish bastard."

A Bloody Beginning

Jack turned back and looked at the gangplank. The crowd of sailors aboard Salem Tide seemed to have thinned considerably. He scoured them looking for his messmates, but only found faces he couldn't place a name on. He shifted side to side on his feet in a straining effort to see around the crowd of Allegiance sailors gathered in the way. Guilt gnawed at him for hoping that some of his messmates had been pressed aboard with him, but he searched the crowd of sailors amidships in the hope of finding someone he knew. The mix of sailors thinned before opening up to reveal a small gathering of pressed men from Salem Tide.

"Hands to make sail!" a tinny voice rang out from the quarterdeck, "Haul away that gangplank and cast-off lines fore and aft, topsails and courses fore and main. Prepare to tack over star'bd."

A cascade of following orders ricocheted around the ship as the midshipmen and petty officers issued commands to their respective areas of responsibility. Jack made his way through the mix to where his fellow pressed men had gathered. At first, he was dismayed to see faces that looked familiar, but that he didn't know well. Upon further inspection, and getting close in to the group, he was relieved to find Slop standing next to Matsumoko.

"There he is!" Slop pointed and nudged Matsumoko on the arm. "I told you he was the first man pressed."

Matsumoko turned and looked equally relieved to see Jack. A rare half smile crossed his face. "I was worried that I had been pressed without you, though it would have been better off for you to stay aboard Salem Tide."

Jack felt guilty for the relief having his messmates pressed along with him brought. He grimaced. "I was thinking the same, Matsumoko. I'm afraid I've already gotten on the wrong side of the mast with one of the lieutenants and apparently a boatswain's mate. I've already been well introduced to his starter."

"I saw," said a gravelly voice that was accompanied by a cloud of pipe smoke. Jack looked past Matsumoko and found Bowline Bob. "You would think the bastard would know a green hand when he saw one. Both of them ought to be tossed from a yardarm into a cold, wet splash so we can watch 'em fade into the distance after the wake washes off their Brit sensibilities."

Jack couldn't help but smile. A strange relief flooded his veins almost rinsing away the foreboding sense of dread that had accumulated throughout the day. "Bob. Thank God you are here," he said.

Bob puffed at his pipe and returned the smile. "Things were getting a little too routine for old Bowline Bob aboard Salem Tide. A good time ter shake things up a bit. Plus, I couldn't let a promising good hand like ye get ruint by these king's men. Don't ye worry, lad. Ye've got the sailorinest sailorman on the whole of the Atlantic ter show ye the ropes. We'll see to it that this tub is

A Bloody Beginning

right fer a storm and ship shape by sunrise, if ye catch my drift."

Jack exchanged a glance with Matsumoko, who shrugged his shoulders along with his brows. "Can't say I do, Bob. But I'm still glad you are here."

Bob drew deep from his pipe and turned toward the quarterdeck. "I've already run into an old mate of mine from back in my navy days. This lot isn't so bad, 'ceptin fer that boatswain's mate yer already was introduced to, and a few of the officers. But, yer can expect that on any damned king's ship."

A flutter of canvas sounded overhead, and the frigate lurched as her sails were sheeted home and filled with the icy breeze. The ship shifted in a sweeping starboard turn and soon Salem's Tide was passing by the stern and then baring her own sails to continue her search for the whaling fleet. Jack remained at the rail, both hands braced against it as the frigate began to pitch and sway with the roll of the waves and the force of her sails. He watched as the ship that had been his first home away from Boston faded into the gray haze of falling sleet and waves.

"There'll be a mess call soon, 'pipe the hands to supper' they call it aboard a navy ship," Bob muttered low for the group of young sailors to hear. "Ye lot stick close with old Bob. There's some different practices aboard a king's ship, and yer'll not want to be getting into the wrong lot." He paused and looked over the deck of the frigate

A Bloody Beginning

before turning his gaze back onto the group. "Were any of ye's rated ordinary or able hands?" His question was met with a turn of shaking heads. Bob let his stare fall onto Matsumoko. "Mats, they rated you a landsman?"

Matsumoko nodded. "Fine by me. I'll stick with Jacky."

Bob smiled and nodded. "I'll bet ye will." He cast another quick glance around the deck before turning back to the group, "Alright, lads. I've got to go see one of the mates about a favor. Yer lot stick around and keep handy about anything yer ordered to do. Mats knows how to handle hisself aboard a navy ship, stick with him. Keep quiet and snap to whatever yer told. I'll be back."

Jack watched as Bowline Bob disappeared below deck through the forward ladder well. He wondered what the weathered old sea hand was up to when a gentle hand grabbed at his upper arm. He was relieved to find the hand belonged to Matsumoko.

"I am glad you are here with me," Matsumoko said in a low voice. "But, this is not a good situation. Pressed men aren't well treated until they have proved themselves capable, and the British treat everyone who is not British like they are a lesser life form."

Jack drew a deep breath. When he had envisioned a life at sea, it had certainly not been aboard a British Navy warship. "A year," he grumbled while looking out over the Atlantic swells.

A Bloody Beginning

"A year at least," Matsumoko replied. "The Royal Navy has a habit of understating that term of service. They are also only supposed to be able to press a man into the service once. Bitter End Bill is living proof on the contrary. There are a number of schemes they use to keep men aboard longer, staying put to sea, denying shore leave to crews, transferring pressed men between vessels before making port. If they truly want to keep hands, they will."

Jack felt like a weight was being slowly loaded onto his shoulders. A year of service to the Royal Navy seemed like an insurmountable obstacle. A mountain sitting squarely in front of his path forward in life. He released a long sigh and thought of his father's never ending efforts to spark his interest in the blacksmith trade. It would have been warmer, and drier. But, Jack pushed those thoughts from his mind. He had chosen his course, and there was certainly no turning back now.

"Haaaaands to the braaaaaaaces!" the tinny voice sounded from the quarterdeck. "Lar'bd mess, landsmen to the capstan! Starb'd mess, Foretops and Maintops standby to haul up royal masts and hang canvas!"

Jack looked around the deck as sailors began hurrying to their designated stations. The shrouds filled with hands climbing aloft like a troop of spiders shimmying their way up a web. The deck of the frigate became a flurry of activity. Hands made their way in short order, hurrying across the

A Bloody Beginning

deck. At one point a sailor nearly knocked Jack from his feet while he was looking high into the rigging where the foretop men and maintop men were working their way higher and then out onto the top-gallant yards of each respective mast.

"Watch where yer standin, lubber!" the sailor snapped before heaving himself up onto the lee railing and scurrying his way aloft.

Jack watched his expert hand placement, and footwork that seemed to land precisely with every step.

"You there, landsman from the press!" a coarse voice howled. Jack turned and found the sour scowl of a petty officer focused squarely on him. "Didn't you hear the order? Or are you just that thick?" the petty officer growled while letting his starter line sway freely from one hand, a not-so-subtle reminder for Jack.

Jack went rigid. "Yes, larb'd mess landsmen to the capstan."

The petty officer flashed a malicious smile. "So, it's a willful disobedience, is it?"

Jack began to shake his head when a hand grabbed him up by the collar. "I've got him, off to the capstan, lads. Here we go. No need fer any more beatings Mr. Jays, we'll 'ave them both at their stations proper in snap-to fashion from now on, they just don't know their way around quite yet, that's all," a crackling voice said while pulling at Jack's coat collar. He could tell Matsumoko was being dragged along with him and looked to find that the one doing the dragging was the one-eyed

A Bloody Beginning

sailor Kenny. He grumbled in a lower tone, "You two 'ave a death wish? Or do you just like beatings? That Tolley is about the nastiest bit of ornery aboard this tub. You'd do well to avoid 'im and you'd do better to make sure when the boatswain blows his damned whistle, ye's snap to and get to it lively. The quarterdeck don't take kindly to lollygaggers or layabouts, and so the mates, they are always a-lookin' fer it. Best to keep moving or outta sight."

"Where are we going?" Jack asked as Kenny led them down the forward ladder way and below deck.

Kenny gave him a twisted frown. "Maybe you are as thick as Mr. Jays says. We're going to the lower capstan, boy. Yer going to learn to heave on the bloody bugger, around and around, until ye's can't walk a straight line no more."

Jack exchanged a look with Matsumoko. His friend's stony disposition confirmed what he feared. They were in for an exercise in excruciating labor. Kenny led them through the forward berth and then the larger opening of the gun deck where they descended another steep set of steps to a cramped deck just above the hold. These decks were different from the ones aboard Salem Tide. They were neat and orderly, everything in its particular place. The gun deck doubled as berthing for the crew, and along the hull, every few feet, sat a large twelve pounder cannon in its respective carriage. These were nothing like the small six pounders aboard Salem Tide. There were

A Bloody Beginning

more of them for starters, and the lot of them looked to be maintained in meticulous fashion. The cold metal of their iron barrels gleamed black in the dimness of the gun deck and the mere sight of them gave Jack a bit of a shiver. Once they had descended from the gun deck, near darkness swallowed them. There were no gun ports letting slim columns of the gray day inside down here, only a soot-stained old lantern at the far end of a clammy and cramped corridor lit their way.

"We'll be hoisting on the foremast first, so you will be heaving at the fore capstan. Allegiance has two, fore and aft," Kenny growled as he led them to a small cabin at the end of the corridor. He extended one hand and gestured to the sailors already in place between thick wooden beams protruding from a round column of shaped timbers in the center. "Best way is to give evr'thing you've got into her, heave fer all yer worth evr'time. Lest the Boatswain notices yer slackin, he's not like to get into yer with 'is starter."

A dim light trickled down through the grating two decks overhead. It offered just enough visibility for Jack to see where he was going as he slipped beneath one of the capstan bars and found his way to an open gap where he settled in and prepared to throw his weight into the labor. Matsumoko slid next to him and without a word the two stood ready for their work to begin.

"Alright you dogs," a raspy voiced mate crowed from the opening where Kenny had just led Jack and Matsumoko into the narrow space. "They're

A Bloody Beginning

going to be hoisting a pair of royal masts up into the rigging. That means, if you lubs can't make a pawl, there'll be a fifty-foot section of timber up there takes a fathom or more drop right above evr'body's heads. So keep 'em steady, but for God's sake don't you dare lose a pawl or I'll flog your backside bloody before the cap'n even has a chance to deal with ye's."

Jack felt a lump work its way into his throat again. He didn't want to fail, not only to avoid the menacing kiss of the mate's starter, but because he didn't want to be the cause of any calamity, injuries, or deaths up on deck. A whistle chimed in a high pitch and the mate standing by the lower capstan bellowed out the order to heave. Jack pushed with all his weight onto the capstan bar in front of him and found that it was stiff, but not impossible to push. The pawls clunked rhythmically while the laboring deckhands continued to push in their circuitous route, around and around, until a high pitched whistle sounded and the mate shouted out a command to hold. Jack and the others held their position. They were just before the point where the pawls would drop into their place to lock the capstan against backward motion.

"Hold there you lubbers," the mate hissed in his scratchy crackling voice. He stepped forward toward the capstan and shouted upward toward the main deck through the gratings, "Can you take another two feet to catch a pawl?"

A Bloody Beginning

A long pause elapsed. Jack could feel the weight of the capstan bar pressing against his arms. He thought of the late night walk he had endured with his father's harpoons slung over one shoulder. He could do this, he was strong enough.

"No. Hold there," a voice echoed back down from the main deck.

"Aye, holding," the mate shouted back. He turned toward the men at the capstan with a poisonous glare. "Ye'll hold there until they relieve the weight or until we can take another couple feet to get the pawl. Hold steady, now, no slacking and no luffing off. Remember what I said, if that mast drops to the next pawl, I'll bloody yer damned backs, every last one of ye scurvy lubber's sons!"

Jack's arms began to shake from the strain of held tension. The narrow capstan chamber was near silent but for the sound of heavy breathing and the wash of the sea against the hull. A burning sensation worked its way up Jack's forearms and into his shoulders. He felt his elbows trembling harder with every heartbeat that passed.

"Not like that, Jack," Matsumoko whispered.

Jack looked over at his friend who was laboring at the same capstan bar as he. The slab of wood was held against his chest, and his lithe figure leaned into his with his body weight. With a smooth a motion as he could muster, Jack eased his chest against the worn woodgrain of the capstan bar. He leaned into it and let his back and legs bear more of the load. The doubt that had been working into his mind eased. Visions of the suspended royal mast plummeting four or six feet on account of his unconditioned arms faded and a realization that he would not fail rose up from his belly and into his chest. He felt taller in that moment, taller and somewhat stronger. The form of Matsumoko's face remained as stony and unchanged as ever, but inside Jack could tell that his friend was beaming with a sailor's pride.

CHAPTER 12

'H.M.S Allegiance'
14 March 1770
40 Degrees 46' N, 72 Degrees 01' W

"Land on the horizon!" the voice drifted down from high in the foretop. Jack ceased his work on deck and stole a glance aloft. His hands were raw from the holystone he had been working back and forth along a section of the main deck that the third lieutenant had found in need. At first, Jack hadn't understood why. The portion of deck in question looked the same as the rest of the deck he could see. After the first day however, it became quite clear to him. Lining the landsmen along the deck, on their knees, and placing the abrasive stone in their hands for each to work for hours on end was a torture. It was punishment for the heinous crime of drawing rations and breath

A Bloody Beginning

among Royal Navy men, while he and his mates were still deemed unworthy.

"Where away?" shouted back the watch officer from his place on the quarterdeck.

"Two points for'ard of starb'd beam!" the lookout replied in a shout that betrayed neither excitement nor dread. He was announcing the sight of land with as much enthusiasm as the marines took in ringing the watch bells. Just another day at sea. But, for Jack, it was anything but routine. They had been aboard the British warship for nearly a week and he had been tormented by the monotonous scenery of a thick sandstone block, woodgrain, and an infrequent splash of seawater to wash away the debris of the deck. The sight of land was too tantalizing to pass up, especially when he had heard rumors of their intended port being New York.

Curiosity overrode his sensible caution and Jack lifted his head to peer over the starboard rail in hopes of seeing land. Pale blue sky met small gray waves in an unremarkable yet familiar scene that had surrounded Allegiance for the last six days. Jack felt a sharp jab in his side.

"Are you mad?" John Long hissed in a angry whisper. "Get your eyes back on your work before you draw the boatswain's mate over here." His face was drawn into a tight frown as he nearly spit his words between lips rigid with frustration.

Jack grunted, "I only want a look. I've never seen New York before."

A Bloody Beginning

"Yes, we know," another voice hissed in disapproval. "You've never seen anything but Boston. But, now is not the time for gawking." The voice belonged to Slop, the only soul among the pressed men to have drawn more ire among the crew than Jack. He had been ridden incessantly about his size, even to the point of having his rations taken and divided up amongst a few of the more seasoned hands. Jack pitied him, even to the point of letting it rouse his anger when one of the boatswain's mates had decided to compare Slop to a hog of a ripe age for slaughter. The malicious petty officer had threatened to jam an apple in his mouth and slice off a side of bacon for the crew to enjoy. Only by Matsumoko's timely placed hand on Jack's shoulder had he restrained himself from saying something horribly unwise in Slop's defense.

Disappointed, Jack leaned back down and took the holystone in hand. He worked the gritty block back and forth with the woodgrain in a never ending pattern of torturous monotony. The torment of hearing the top men make their well timed adjustments burned him. Physically, Jack was grinding away with his detested holy stone, but in his mind he was aloft. He remembered the stark colors of the dawn he had witness. It had been like the first dawn of his life. Brilliant violets and oranges, the glimmer of the first rays shining on cresting waves. He pushed the holy stone out in a deep lunge across the deck and thought of the brilliant dawn. He dragged the stone back with a

A Bloody Beginning

swipe and his mind traveled to the courtyard in Boston and that horrid night that had changed his life so drastically. The stone reminded him of his father's anvil, the same repetition over and over again, the same burning exertion in his forearms and shoulders. Jack pushed and dragged, back and forth. His back ached with a deep pain like nothing he had ever felt before. It radiated from the base of his spine up and into his neck. It sent throbs into his head as the stone ground this way and then that, over and over.

A high pitch from the boatswain's whistle was the sweetest sound Jack could have hoped to hear. Over the course of six days, he had learned when the mates were calling off deck work and preparing to let the hands 'lay aft' as they called it.

"Haaaands to make sail!" a tinny voice thundered over the deck. "Mr. Swaley, see to it those lubbers get below deck and make ready cables for the anchor."

One of the boatswain's mates, Mr. Swaley, stormed past Jack with a discontented grumble under his breath. "Lay off those stones, lads. Stow away the cleaning gear, we'll 'ave some real laboring to do."

Jack pulled himself up onto his feet with the aid of one hand on the ship's starboard railing. His knees ached grudgingly and his elbows and shoulders were exhausted and sore from days of the monotonous work." He turned toward Matsumoko and shook his head. "Does this ever get better?"

A Bloody Beginning

Matsumoko frowned as he considered the question. "Holy stoning the deck isn't usually all day every day." He pointed toward the bow. "My guess is that the captain expects to have someone important come aboard. New York is somewhat of a stronghold of British forces in the colonies. Lots of navy ships come and go from there."

Jack shriveled his nose. "Matsumoko. Have you been to New York before?"

Matsumoko nodded with his unchanging matter of fact disposition. "I have. When the East India Company took me into their service as a ship's boy, the captain of the vessel that had me assumed I spoke Chinese. When he learned I am in fact from Japan, he bartered me off at the first opportunity. That happened in London. I was passed to a British Royal Navy ship, a battleship named duke of something, I forget. We sailed from London with a governor, an admiral, and two generals and three colonels, I think, all bound for New York."

Jack suddenly felt a tinge of embarrassment. His whole life had been spent within the confines of Boston. His father's blacksmith shop, the tailor shop his mother worked at, the schoolhouse, and the harbor had been the extent of his world. On occasion he had ventured outside of town. Several times he had gone with his father to retrieve firewood. The more Jack thought of it, the more he felt like clamming up and keeping his questions to himself. Here his friend had seen Japan, China,

A Bloody Beginning

London, and those were just the ones he had mentioned in Jack's presence.

Mr. Swaley motioned for the deck hands to follow him below and they all descended in a staggered column down the forward ladder way. Jack lamented leaving the main deck. He longed to see New York as they approached, but instead he was following Matumoko as the group of pressed men worked their way through the gun deck and then further below into the narrow corridor just above the ship's hold.

"Three cables ought to do, I'm thinking," Mr. Swaley crowed over his shoulder as he worked his way to an small cabin door with rough wear around its frame. "The quarterdeck may ask for 'nother, But by my reckoning three ought to do." He opened the cabin and stepped into a cramped space lined with massively thick ropes coiled in every space. He swatted his hand down onto the nearest coil. "Up and onto the main deck with three of them, then we'll show you lubbers how we rig anchor in the King's Navy. Make sailors out of some of you yet," he said before glancing up the column and spotting Slop. "Don't get excited you tub of lard, I said some of you." Mr. Swaley nodded his head toward Jack and Matsumoko. "Meaning them, not you. The king and all his riches can't afford rations for the likes of you." He chuckled at his own menace and lumbered off down the corridor, leaving them to their task.

"That Mr. Swaley, blighter that he is. A bloody arseling, if you ask me. I swear if I got my hands on him, I'd tear him in two!" Slop exclaimed while Jack and Matsumoko began digging at the coils of rope in the small cabin.

"Ye'd piss yer pants and run for the railing if Swaley ever turned on ye with his starter," John Long said with a chuckle. "They're ragging on you to make you better, Slop. To toughen you up so you can be like them. A proper King's man!" The tall youth doubled over and laughed when Slop turned an evil red and shot him a sour look.

"I'll knock you one too, if you don't shut it. They pick on me for being fat, but I am big, and strong too. Watch, you'll see," Slop hissed before reaching into the cabin and pulling on the rope Jack and Matsumoko had worked loose. He took the thick course braid and looped it over his shoulder twice, then thrice, until the load nearly made him stagger. "I'll haul up this end, the rest of ye's just try and haul this much!"

With the massive line shouldered, the small band of pressed men made their way up on deck. It was no small effort, and along their path, Jack noticed several of the experienced sailors stopped with mouth agape at Slop. The husky young man was carrying three times the load as any of them and doing so as if it were a summer stroll through a park. With the first line laid out in the exact fashion prescribed by the boatswain's mates, Jack again noticed that their effort had drawn the attention of onlookers from the rest of the crew. Slop took up as just much of the line for their second trip up on deck and did so with what

A Bloody Beginning

seemed like a cocksure ease. The mess moved through the narrow corridor, and across the gun deck before emerging up on the forecastle to lay out the line just as they had the first. Their third and last trip was finally upon them and Jack was excited to complete the work in hopes of being on deck when sighting of New York was made. He followed Slop and Matsumoko to the cable stowage and nearly lost his footing when he entered the close margin of the cabin door as a thick fingered hand reached out and grabbed the front of his shirt, hauling him inward. It was Slop, doubled over at the waist and breathing as hard as a man on the run.

"Did you see them? The looks on their faces?" He asked in between ragged breaths.

Jack smiled and nodded. "Yes, Slop. We all saw them. They are awe struck."

The portly young man heaved in a few more breaths and leaned against a stack of coiled ropes. "Good. Now maybe those bastard boatswain's mates will shove their insults and pick on somebody else. I meant it when I said, I'd knock that Mr. Swaley right off the ship. He wouldn't know what to do with hisself."

Matsumoko broke his typical reserve. "Swim probably."

Jack fought the urge for a moment. He stared hard at Matsumoko, trying to channel his friend's stony disposition for himself. But, it was no good. A chuckle worked its way upward into his ribs until he broke forth in uncontrollable laughter.

A Bloody Beginning

Slop started in much the same manner, his belly rolling with deep laughs until he was again wheezing for breath. Jack thought he even caught Matsumoko's shoulders heaving with humor while he faced away from both of them. The last trip up on deck with the heavy length of rope felt like the easiest, even though they were exhausted, the gang of pressed men threw their backs into the work with happy hearts and high spirits. It wasn't such a bad life at sea, Jack thought, if a man can find spots of joy.

For several hours a sense of excitement and expectation hung over the deck of Allegiance. Occasional course changes brought them ever closer to New York as the sun began to beat its own course west toward the horizon. With her anchor rigged and ready, she slipped through low seas on a gentle breeze while her crew grew ever more anxious for port. Jack imagined what New York would look like. It was not as populated as Boston, he knew that. But, I recent years, New York had become a more frequented port town, drawing in bigger ships from their cross-Atlantic voyages from distant shores and exotic ports. Long before he could make out the peaks of rooftops, Jack's eyes were drawn to the seeming forest of ship masts. Rows and rows of mast tops protruded from the close stretches of the harbor.

"Haaands to the braces," bellowed the voice of the sailing master through a brass speaking trumpet. "Reef the mains!"

A Bloody Beginning

Aloft, the top men sprang into action. It awed Jack. What had first looked to him like pure pandemonium was now beginning to strike him more like a rugged grace. A dance of sorts, where the men knew each step and could perform them in near synchrony with a minimum of shouts or calls. Their foot placement was precise, their hands always moving. If sailing was an art, these men were the brush that enabled the master to paint his scene.

"Ready salute," called the quartermaster. "Captain Ballamy, have your marines take post on the weather rail."

In quick fashion, a cluster of red coated Royal Marines made their way to the starboard railing where they stood in a line of rigid discipline from the just forward of the foremast extending back toward the quarterdeck, just forward of the mizzen.

"Drums!" shouted the marine captain.

From just in front of the mainmast, a rapid rattle of snare drum tattoo rapped to life and continued as Allegiance slipped her way closer to a cluster of large warships sitting at anchor. Jack couldn't open his eyes wide enough. The drumbeat, the formation of marines, a massive three deck warship just two cable lengths off Allegiance's starboard bow, not to mention a litany of smaller vessels. Sloops, cutters, brigs, gunboats and other frigates were scattered through the harbor in a broad array of the king's firepower. Not being as tall as most of the marines, Jack had to settle for

A Bloody Beginning

peering in between their shoulders as Allegiance slipped past the behemoth.

"That's the king's pride, there. H.M.S Queen Charlotte. A hundred guns, if I remember correctly," one of the marines muttered to another. "Can you imagine who they have aboard? There has to be an admiral."

"More than one I would reckon," replied the marine standing next to him.

Jack slunk away behind the formation in search of some way to get a better view. Suddenly a pair of thundering roars sounded from Allegiance's larboard side. A cloud of thick gun smoke bloomed from the gun deck and washed over the calm water of the harbor. With lightning in his veins, Jack raced to the larboard rail in search of the source of the action. His eyes were wide, his heart pounding and as he gripped the railing in trembling hands he searched for some sign of action.

"Jus' a salute, Jacky. Don' go getting yer blood up. The navy way of renderin' respects as we pass a senior ship." Said a familiar voice.

Jack turned to face the speaker and found Bowline Bob drawing at his pipe from the corner of his mouth. "Where in the hell have you been?"

Bob smiled and let out a stream of bluish tobacco smoke. "I told ye lad. I went to visit with the master's mate. He was an old shipmate 'o mine from years ago. He helped me with a little task, and got me re-rated as an able seaman."

A Bloody Beginning

The last bit gave Jack a bit of let down in his spirit. He had hoped to find Bob on his watch at some point. But, with him rated able and Jack only a landsman, even if they were on the same watch, Jack wouldn't be able to converse with the old sailor. "Don't look so down about it, Jacky. Yer'll come along fine. Ye just have to keep that mettle ye showed us all aboard Salem Tide."

Jack shook his head. "It's not the same, Bob. I know most of the boatswain's mates already don't care for me, and I doubt I'll be afforded the chance to go aloft. Not for a long time anyway."

Bowline Bob narrowed his eyes and drew at his pipe. He stared at Jack as if he were disappointed before letting a puff of smoke go. "That doesn't sound like the lad who refused the lubber hole his first time up in the rigging. Or the sodden wet bastard who cared so little for hisself that he grabbed hold of a fellow sailor right before he was about washed overboard in a storm. Not at all." Bob pulled from his pipe again and let the smoke dribble from his mouth as he spoke. "I'm counting on ye, Jacky. I put in word with the master's mate, and he's told me first chance he gets he is going to get yer and Mats aloft. Yer both got it in ye to be great sailormen. I see it, and they will too. Yer just can't go forgettin' it yerself."

A pang of guilt struck Jack as the quarterdeck broke into a flurry of activity. He wanted to answer Bowline Bob with something that would reassure the old sailor he still had it in him to be a good sea hand, but he struggled for words.

A Bloody Beginning

"Ye've nothing to fear Jacky," Bob said with his trademark grin between his thick chop sideburns. "I knows just what yer fearin' and I'll tell ye, it isn't what ye say, it's what yer do. Deeds, Jacky, deeds, not words."

Jack felt his blood light on fire. It was as if Bowline Bob had read his mind.

"Signal from the admiral," a tight voice called out on the quarterdeck.

"Aye, what's it say?" the captain's voice replied.

Jack looked past the mainmast to the quarterdeck. Captain Williams was standing two great paces aft and one to windward from the helm. He was in a sharp uniform, one Jack suspected did not see daylight except for very special occasions.

"It says, heave to, captain to come aboard," the tight voice replied. Jack could not tell which midshipman or lieutenant was relaying the signal to the captain through the cluster of officers on the quarterdeck.

"Very well," the captain said before turning to the group of finely dressed officers. "Heave to and drop anchor. Have the longboats readied."

"Aye, aye, captain," replied another voice Jack couldn't distinguish.

"Clear away, clear away for the anchor line," a red-faced Boatswain's mate crowed as he walked the length of the ship. He waved one arm and cleared the larboard side of the ship for the path of the anchor cable. "Clear back you lubber! You

A Bloody Beginning

know what that line will do if it hits you? Snap you right in half like a piece of straw, that's what!"

Jack wandered back toward the starboard side of the ship. He gazed over the rigid discipline of the marines while they still stood firm amongst all the activity. Their red coats brought back images of the courtyard in Boston, and the soldiers who murdered his parents.

"Captain's been called over to the flagship," Bowline Bob said over Jack's shoulder. "It will probably be a short holdover here in New York. But, all the same. We wouldn't be allowed to step foot off the ship anyhow."

Jack scrunched his face and turned to Bob. "What? Why not?"

Bob shrugged and tapped out the bowl of his pipe into one hand. "We're pressed men. The fear is that we would all desert, take flight for home or seek some better arrangements with another ship." He fussed over his pipe for a moment before scraping one finger in the bowl and then turned it over and began packing in a fresh pinch of tobacco. "It's a valid concern too. Many a pressed man has taken their ungranted leave at the first sight of land. Some without even going ashore. Poor bastards most often get caught and flogged near enough to death to make no difference with a hangman's noose. I've even heard of lads jumping ship when close enough to shore. They try to swim for land. Misguided at best. That water is cold, even summers, its close enough to freezing to kill ye. But, what most of them don't reckon on, is the

A Bloody Beginning

lookouts. Watch on ship will raise the alarm," he said, then he pointed over at the line of marines. "Then that lot will plug 'im full of holes before he can even gather 'is wits and get to swimming."

The anchor splashed down and sent a geyser of water shooting into the air. Sails were reefed and secured and the longboat was hoisted over the side and lowered for Captain Williams' departure. Boatswain's whistles piped the customary pitch as the captain stepped off ship and hands were promptly turned to for the evening. Jack remained on deck long after the formation of marines had departed. He outlasted even Bowline Bob, who made his way below deck when supper was called. The New York harbor was abuzz with activity long after the sun had gone down. Across the gently lapping waters of the port, Jack could see lights and people on shore. The smell of cooking fires, spices and herbs, rum, wine and roasting meat all floated on the cold wind. Sounds of laughter and music trickled into his ears while small jolly boats rowed between the waterfront and ships at anchor. After gazing out longingly at the scene, Jack felt his eyes begin to well with hot tears. He thought of his mother and father, their nights spent at home huddled in front of the stone hearth. The stories his parents would tell him of their childhoods and the extended family they had left in Ireland. Jack longed to sit at his father's feet as a fire slowly crackled away and lit their faces with its warm glow. His tears began to flow. Warm streaks glistened on his face, and he didn't

A Bloody Beginning

even bother to wipe them away. Perhaps if he had just kept his focus on his studies, he wouldn't be in his current predicament. If he hadn't been walking back from the shipyard that afternoon, he would not have struck his head trying to retrieve his mother. The sailors had saved her, he hadn't even accomplished that to his account. But, if they hadn't been returning from that cursed warship where he had his forehead stitched, his parents would surely be alive. The tears continued and New York became a blur of hazy yellow lights mixed into the inky blackness of night.

"Taking in the night air, Jack?" Matsumoko asked, giving Jack a start that almost made him jump out of his skin.

"Wha-" Jack cried, rising to his feet. "Damn, you gave me a scare! Where did you come from?"

Matsumoko's face broke into a slight grin. "I missed you at supper. Our mess was asking where you were."

Jack shrugged and looked back out over the water of the harbor. "I'm not hungry."

"That isn't possible," Matsumoko said while leaning against the ship's rail next to Jack. "We were hard at it all day."

Jack drew a breath and released it in a sigh. "It was the Brits that killed my parents, Matsumoko. Or, maybe the crowd that drew their ire. But, in a way, it's also my fault." He fought back another wave of tears, barely managing to control himself while forcing in another deep breath. "But, it was red coat soldiers who fired their muskets into the crowd, and it was their musket balls that killed them."

Matsumoko gripped Jack's shoulder and faced the harbor alongside him. "What happened to you is horrible, and you have my condolences, Jack. But, you cannot blame yourself, and you cannot live in the past. If you do, it will consume you, it will poison your future." He squeezed Jack's shoulder, prompting their gaze to meet. "Do you remember the Japanese concept I told you about? The debt that we all have?"

Jack thought for a moment, trying to recall the word. "Giri?" he asked.

Matsumoko nodded. "Giri. It's an obligation we have, to everyone around us. You saved my life, and I owe it to you to live up to that, and to do so in return if I ever can."

Jack nodded his understanding, but he struggled to connect what Matsumoko was saying with how he was feeling.

"The same way that I owe you a debt," Matsumoko continued, "you owe a debt to your parents. Or, to their memory at least. You owe it to them to live the best life you possibly can. You owe it to them to conduct yourself in a way that they would look at and be proud of, and you owe it to them to make something of the name and life that they gave you."

Jack felt a rush of emotion boiling inside of him. He knew that his friend was right. He knew that stewing on the past would only drive him to be bitter and resentful. But, in the deepest parts of his

A Bloody Beginning

soul, he could not rectify serving the same forces responsible for the death of his parents. He looked back out over the harbor and took in the chill of the night air. Without averting his stare, he said out loud, "I will make the best of this, for now. But, mark my words, Matsumoko, I will not serve the king or his navy for a second longer than I must. At the first opportunity, I will depart this ship and never look back."

Matsumoko nodded in agreement. "You can count me with you, Jack."

The two young men spent the next hour talking about the possibilities of their departure and Matsumoko relayed what he knew of life aboard a king's navy ship. It wasn't until the watch bell was sounded that they saw the longboat with their returning captain slicing its way through the calm blackness of the harbor. He was standing forward in the prow of the boat and struck a proud figure in his fine fitting uniform. Boatswain's whistles piped their customary signal as he came aboard and the lieutenants and midshipmen snapped to rigid attention as he ascended the last ladder steps up onto the ship and crossed to the quarter deck. He carried a thick packet beneath one arm and seemed to be driven by a sense of urgency.

"Have the hands stand to and raise the signal for sea orders," the captain said. "We will be taking on new hands from the press as well as supplies for our voyage."

A Bloody Beginning

One of the lieutenants standing near the helm spoke up, "I will arrange for a detail in the morning, sir."

The captain shook his head. "No, that will not serve. We are taking on hands before the midwatch and supplies thereafter, the admiral wants us to sail with the morning tide. We have actionable intelligence that demands haste. There will be no shore leave or liberty granted and we will have to make do without refit for the time being." He turned to another of the assembled officers. "You had mentioned need of a replacement for the yard on the mizzen tops'l. Can we press on without it?"

"Aye, she'll hold for now. As long as we aren't straining her too hard in foul weather," a voice replied among the gathered officers. "I suppose we could brace her up, just to be sure."

"Good," Captain Williams replied. "Let's do that. Is there anything else that would become an issue from our early departure?"

"Sir," a midshipman spoke up. "The deserter. Are we to put him ashore or to the flagship?"

A moment of tense silence crossed the quarterdeck and Jack strained to hear while the officers held a private exchange in low voices. Together the officers seemed to reach a consensus on something and parted for their respective tasks.

"That doesn't look good," Matsumoko uttered while he and Jack both looked on toward the quarterdeck. "I would wager that Allegiance has been put on the hunt."

A Bloody Beginning

Jack shriveled his nose. "The hunt?"

"For an enemy ship," Matsumoko answered. "We make port and sail again in less than a day. After they just crossed the whole of the Atlantic, that is a tall order. Every man aboard, except those of us recently pressed, is expecting some form of respite. A shore leave, liberty call, just a taste of land life. The officers know it, they too would be looking forward to it. That's the only thing I can think of that would have them in such an urgent state. There is a ship out there the navy's higher command wants Allegiance to find and confront. To whatever end."

Jack thought of the possibilities that presented. It made his skin crawl and tightened his stomach to the point that it was painful to draw breath. "It's possible they won't find the ship."

Matsumoko shrugged and nodded. "It is. But, Captain Williams isn't the captain of a frigate for no reason. He is a man of combat, and I wouldn't bet against him finding his quarry."

CHAPTER 13

'H.M.S Allegiance'
15 March 1770
40 Degrees 31' N, 74 Degrees 03' W

    The morning tide saw H.M.S Allegiance slipping out of New York Harbor just as dawn was beginning to touch the eastern horizon. It had been a sleepless night for all aboard, a night of manic rushing followed by lengthy waits and then snapping to the next task. Jack had endured it along with the rest of the crew, but it seemed to him that everyone was on edge. The officers all seemed to be operating under a sense of urgent haste, rushing as if their lives depended on it. The midshipmen, warrant officers and petty officers all seemed especially hostile as the new sailing orders had begrudged them a night, or several nights, spent ashore. The rated sailors seemed to tolerate

A Bloody Beginning

it, some even cracking jokes about their collective misfortune while others pondered the prize that awaited them for such a mission that required them to sail so quickly. It was enough to make Jack's head spin. He was rushed from one part of the ship to the next to help unload some cargo or heave on a line. With the completion of each task he would take the opportunity to rest while they waited on the next task to arise. Jolly boats brought supplies, and it seemed to Jack as if he would spend the rest of his life handling crates and bags. Then he was rushed up on deck and a line of men formed to pass assorted items from one to the next all the way down to the ship's hold. The next task saw them on the gun deck where they passed casks of powder and ammunition through an emptied gun port all the way to the magazine. There were canisters, chains, bar shot, and finally heavy round cannon balls. He had so many questions about the different types of ammunition, but none of his friends were close and the sailors around him were not of the mind to converse with a landsmen about such things.

Pressed men from New York arrived throughout the night. They were seen aboard and shuffled away in just as hostile a manner as those from Salem Tide. Jack felt for them, but he had to keep his mind on his labor as the petty officers remained close and with starters in hand. At one point during the night, Jack had heard the figure that forty men had been brought onto the ship. Word traveled amongst the crew that there had

A Bloody Beginning

been a press gang sent through New York for the express purpose of fully outfitting Allegiance for her mission. It brought the tension level on deck to new heights. They were as varied in age and appearance as Jack's friends from Salem Tide, he guessed one was as young as thirteen and the oldest looked to be on the other side of forty. It wasn't long before the chatter began about them and soon it was decided amongst the crew that there wasn't a sailor among them. They were landsmen all, and landsmen in the truest sense. They had not been pressed from a ship, but right off the streets of New York. Jack heard the older sailors griping about how they would have to explain everything from the simplest tasks to teaching the new crop how to speak in sailorly fashion.

The fitful night culminated in Allegiance's anchor being hoisted, which saw Jack back at the capstan. This time however, turning the massive wooden column was not as easy as when they were lifting the relatively light load of a royal mast. This time it took Jack and every other man at the bars every fiber of their muscle and every ounce of their resolve to see the task through. The anchor found itself stubborn in the harbor mud, and the men laboring to free it found no mercy from the foul tempered boatswain's mate who had just lost his chance at a shore leave. The starter flew in relentless swings that landed on their backs and shoulders. Curses and threats reverberated through the small space below deck

A Bloody Beginning

as they fought against impossibly stiff resistance. The first few attempts resulted in a pawl dropping, and then another, but the mate cursed their souls and informed them that they had only taken up slack on the anchor cable. They had yet to free the iron behemoth from the mud, and thus Allegiance could not yet sail. Jack, along with Matsumoko and the others redoubled their efforts which resulted in the pawls dropping twice before they found themselves stuck yet again. After a stream of threats and insults, the mate crowed up to the deck for bars to be slid through on the main deck and more hands to take up the fight. Jack could feel the impacts reverberate through the wooden column and after only a moment of respite the mate was howling at them to heave again. This time, with the added force of more men applying their strength, the capstan finally began to turn. Another pawl drop, then another and a third. Two more saw Jack and his comrades finally feel a slack in resistance and after a moment they were freely turning the capstan around in circles until the mate shouted for them to hold.

With the anchor freed, Allegiance was finally able to set sail. She slid with ease through the harbor under a slight wind from the northwest just as the eastern horizon was beginning to show signs of life. The frigate rounded past a shore battery before the quarterdeck ordered more sail and began to turn easterly out to sea. No sooner had the bowsprit aimed for the open ocean than

A Bloody Beginning

the call went up for more sail. Allegiance piled on canvas, spreading sails that Jack hadn't even heard of until her mast tops were barely visible. Mainsails, topsails, top gallants, royals, stunsels, staysails, mizzen tops, foretops, fore top gallants, all manner of billowing white canvas bent to the wind above the deck. Allegiance lurched forward and spread a wake like Jack had never seen. She was moving fast and meeting the seas with her proud bow in great pitches that threw sprays of sea up with each rush. After the long night of hard work and frenzied preparations, and despite his misgivings about serving aboard a king's ship, Jack felt an exhilarating rush as they plunged away from New York and out into open water. He followed several sailors as they made their way forward and ignored the frigid spray. The wind tore at his clothing, and droplets of seawater landed on his face, but the beauty of the sunrise reminded him of his venture up the rigging of Salem Tide and Jack held hope for the possibility that Bowline Bob had promised was coming. He would be given his chance and soon he would be aloft with the others.

"It's a sight, isn't it?" a familiar voice growled over Jack's shoulder.

"It is," Jack replied after turning to find Bob struggling with his pipe in the wind.

"Jus' keep it in mind, we're all about to witness something we would rather forget," he said without further explanation.

A Bloody Beginning

Jack puzzled over it for a moment before finally asking, "What do you mean by that?"

Bob succeeded with his pipe and drew a deep pull of sweet smoke before a bell pealed and a boatswain's whistle piped. "You'll see in a minute, lad. Best we lay aft and fall in with the others."

"Haaands, lay aft to witness punishment!" a voice shouted from the fore-edge of Allegiance's quarterdeck. "Fall in and form up, hats off!"

Bob shook his head and tapped out the bowl of his pipe. He nodded toward the quarterdeck. "Come on Jack, we better go. Just keep yer words to yerself and try not to be sick."

He followed the old sea hand toward the rear of the ship until they were in the midst of of a crowd gathered amidships. Sailors milled about quietly in search of their mess in the tight press of men on deck.

"Landsmen to the front!" the same voice that had beckoned all hands shouted.

Jack wove his way in between sailors until he was past the mainmast. He found Matsumoko, Slop and John Long near the lee rail and fell in with them. The quarterdeck was lined with marines in their bright red uniform coats with officers in rank right behind them. Another bell peal sounded, and around the periphery of the ship more marines fell into formation facing inboard. They marched into position with rigid uniformity before snapping in turn and holding their muskets vertically in front of their chests. Jack's heart thundered. Ha saw the image of a line

A Bloody Beginning

of soldiers in the streets of Boston, smoke rising from the bores of their weapons.

"Bring the prisoner forward," Captain Williams' voice beckoned from the quarterdeck. Every eye aboard shifted to the aft main hatch, where two marines escorted Bitter End Bill up on deck. With brisk steps they forcibly dragged him before the captain and then took their posts next to the brothers in arms. Captain Williams produced a parchment scroll and unrolled it. He held the document at arms length and began a lengthy recitation of the Articles of War. Each infraction listed seemed to end in a prescribed sentence that far outweighed any just measure of the accused crime. When Captain Williams read off the article concerning desertion, he paused and gave emphasis to particular sentences and phrases, levying a greater impact upon the crew. As he finished, he read the prescribed sentence, and Jack felt his stomach twist into knots and turn to water.

"Its called a flog around the fleet," one sailor said to another over Jack's shoulder. "He is fortunate we aren't still at anchor in New York, else he'd be getting every lash he 'as coming to 'im."

"Bitter End Bill, or so I am told you are called. What is your given name?" Captain Williams asked in a demanding voice.

Bill shook his head. "Long forgot, cap'n. Bitter End serves me fine."

Captain Williams drew a slow breath through flared nostrils and continued, "Have you anything to say for yourself man? Some reason you departed the king's navy before your term of service was completed?"

Bitter End Bill lifted his shackled hands and shook the irons attached to his wrists. "This is me third time bein' pressed by yer king's navy, and not the first time to 'ave me back striped open bloody," he growled defiantly. "I'll not be 'splaining myself to you or any other jack what licks the king's ass. Go on, lick his ass, lay me open if if yer wish." His voice raised loud and he spit on the deck at the captain's feet. "Better 'ope you 'ave a boatswain with some mettle, boy, and some strength in his arm. Me back is oak, and me will is hard as iron."

Captain Williams face flared crimson. His eyes locked onto the defiant sailor and his lips pursed tight for a long moment of silent tension while everyone awaited his sentencing.

"Were we among the fleet, I would sentence you to a dozen from every vessel in sight. A sentence as sure as death, even for a man who claims to be made of oak. But, we are not among the fleet. It prevails to me that death may be a stroke of mercy to such a soul, and for your part, I would not dream of relieving you for the remainder of your term of service." He paused and let his gaze fall over the gathered crew. "Three dozen, and you will be rated as landsman, in perpetuity, ineligible for advancement. You will also forgo wages for the next three, no, six months." He paused again and focused back onto Bitter End Bill. "This, Bill, is

A Bloody Beginning

a mercy. By rights you should be strung from the yardarm and left to swing in the breeze."

"That'd be me preference," Bill said, spitting on the deck again.

"Secure the prisoner to the capstan," Captain Williams ordered before turning to a nearby boatswain who was standing ready with a canvas bag containing the instrument of punishment. "Boatswain, to your work. Please ensure the doctor has a chance to check on the prisoner after every few."

"Aye, cap'n," the boatswain growled in a voice that cracked from overuse.

The marines who had escorted Bill up on deck took him forcefully by his arms and secured him to the aft capstan before unceremoniously grabbing the collar of his shirt and ripping the fabric away to reveal the flesh of his back. Despite the hardened appearance of Allegiance's crew, Jack heard a gasp escape from an unknown sailor's throat, while another grunted in revulsion. Bill's back was indeed a latticework of scars and for a moment Jack was beginning to contemplate if the salted old sailor would feel the effects of the cat at all. Those notions slipped from his mind, however, when the boatswain pulled the wicked looking whip from its canvas cover and threaded his fingers through its knotted strands of thick leather.

"You'll be glad we 'aven't been piped to breakfast yet, lad. I've seen this more than a few times, and it never gets any better," Bob's voice

A Bloody Beginning

crackled over Jack's shoulder. "Brace yerself, lad. And try not to let yer stomach turn. It'll be a bad look in front 'o the rest 'o the crew."

A sharp snap cut through the tense silence and the boatswain crowed out in his weathered voice, "One!" Without so much as a pause, the boatswain cocked his arm back and swung the cat of nine tails again. "Two!" The impact sounded like the sharpest slap Jack had ever heard. He grimaced as the third stroke landed against the scarred flesh of Bill's leathery back. "Three!" The lash strokes continued in a slow but unrelenting fury. One by one the boatswain counted them in his roaring shouts while the crew looked on. By the eighth stroke, blood could be seen oozing from opened flesh. By the twelfth, Bill's back had become a patch of raw red flesh striped by open wounds. The flogging continued without pause. Three more strikes and Bill's arms and legs were shaking uncontrollably, the iron shackles around his wrists chattered like teeth in the cold. He lost his footing after eighteen, and at twenty two he seemed to lose consciousness. A pause was called by the ship's doctor, who inspected Bill's wounds and checked him for signs of life. A marine doused Bill with a bucket of seawater and the barbaric punishment continued.

The skin on Jack's back tingled and stung as he witnessed the horror inflicted on Bitter End Bill. With each lash a stream of blood trailed across Allegiance's deck. Bill's defiant grunts had faded to whimpers before escalating to a crescendo of

A Bloody Beginning

agonized screams that reached the upper limits of the rigging and rang in between the taffrail and the bowsprit. It seemed as though it would never end. And then, with only four lashes left to apply, the boatswain swung the cat and struck Bill's back to no reaction whatsoever. He hung limp, suspended only by his contorted arms draped over the squat drum column of the aft capstan and the iron shackles tied to the capstan bars of the opposing side. Without ceremony or emotion, the boatswain swung the last of Bill's punishment and retired from his position on deck.

A silent gesture from the captain sent the ship's doctor hurrying to Bill's side. He crouched to inspect the prisoner while a profound silence hung over the deck of the ship. Jack found it hard to swallow, as he watched in anticipation of what was to follow. His breath came in halting pants as if he had received a stroke of the cat himself. He tried to imagine the pain Bill had just endured. It made his skin crawl and turned his stomach. He felt the urge to retch, but fought it when he remembered the warning uttered by his friend Bowline Bob. The doctor felt at Bill's neck with one hand, lingered there for the span of a heartbeat and then stood to face the captain. He offered only a solemn nod.

"Good God, how can that be?" Bob growled over Jack's shoulder.

Jack shriveled his nose at the remark. "What do you mean?"

A Bloody Beginning

"Looks like the sawbones is saying he's alive. Three dozen lashes is more'n enough to kill a man. Makes the heart seize up from what I've been told, can't deals with the stresses and whatnot. But he nodded at the cap'n, like Bill might be livin' and breathin'."

The marines who had secured Bill to the capstan moved in at a signal from the ship's doctor.

"Loose his hands and take him below to my cabin. I will treat him there, but you will need to help him to sick bay when I am finished. It will be some time before he is fit for duty, if he recovers," the doctor said with an ominous disposition.

The group of four men made their way below deck with Bill's shoes dragging on the planks and leaving a bloody smear behind them. They left only silence on deck, the sound of waves lapping against the hull and a whistle of lonely wind whipping over the ship. Jack focused on Captain Williams and thought of what other atrocities he may be responsible for. He was clean, sharp and polished in his uniform coat and fine three cornered hat, but in Jack's mind his hands were dripping with blood. The blood of his parents, the blood just lost through the flesh of Bill's back, and countless others who had surely paid the cost of his arrogant station.

"Now that we are through with that unpleasantness," Captain Williams announced, raising his hands and gesturing the sailors on deck to come closer. "We come to a more pleasant, and pressing matter." He paused while the press of

A Bloody Beginning

sailors closed in closer, every hand wanting to know what was coming next. "As you all know, we very unfortunately had to depart from New York Harbor in some haste. It was unavoidable, as you will soon understand, and the needs of the service do come before our own. I will see to it that this crew receives an extended shore leave in a suitable port at the first possible opportunity," he paused as several of the sailors on deck raised their voices in grunts and shouts of approval. "We were hurried from New York on a special set of sailing orders directly from Admiral Collier. This is a time sensitive endeavor, and thus the haste from New York could not be avoided." He looked over the gathering of sailors on deck, his eyes focusing on Jack for a moment before moving on to others. "There has been a sighting of a French employed privateer named Saber just off the shores of Bermuda. She is said to be a fast warship, manned by a full crew of hard, capable hands. The admiral also tells me that she was built on the design of a well known shipwright in Boston. She is said to have forty-four guns, and the bulk of those will be eighteen pounders. Currently, no state of war exists with France. However, this particular ship has been preying on merchant shipping under the protection of King George."

Jack looked around to the faces of the sailors on deck. He found expressions ranging from bemused surrender to the inevitable, to eager joy of the new assignment. Bob looked on with

A Bloody Beginning

narrowed eyes, a grimace pulling his face tight as he took in word of what was to come.

"We are to sail for Bermuda, where we will rendezvous with a squadron being formed to hunt this rogue French menace. From there we will sail for all points in search of our enemy, sink, burn, or..." he paused for dramatic effect, "take her a'prize!"

A cheer rushed up from the crew on deck and took Jack off guard. He nearly toppled over as the sailors behind him shouted and stomped their feet. So exuberant was their joy that it was almost a full two minutes before the captain could resume speaking.

"Now, now, don't count your prize money just yet. We still have to find her, and finding her, we have to take her. Our crew is full of fresh pressed men. Not many of them will be experienced in the art of naval combat, so we will begin training with full vigor, today. Gun drills will occur twice a day, every day, with live fire every third until we can get two broadsides per minute. That is what we will need to overwhelm the enemy. Further, we will begin close order training on the main deck everyday after breakfast. Boarding pikes, boarding axes, muskets, pistols and cutlass will be the order of the hour. We will train daily until the master at arms is satisfied that all hands are proficient with each class of weapon," the captain announced. "Sailing maneuvers will also be conducted during the forenoon and afternoon watches. When we arrive in Bermuda, I expect that this ship will be in

A Bloody Beginning

the finest fitness to fight. Only then, will we be up to the task of taking Saber. Give me what I ask, men, and I will deliver you to your prize, with shore leave thereafter."

Another round of cheers rose from the deck. Captain Williams nodded his approval before swiftly making his way below deck and presumably to his cabin. Jack remained quiet while the sailors around him cheered and shouted for the glory of the promises laid before them. He searched through the crowd and found Bowline Bob fussing over his pipe near the foremast.

"Damn empty-headed fools, promise them a prize and watch them sacrifice everything they have to get to her," Bob grumbled under his breath as he inserted a wick into the hanging lantern on the foremast. "Oldest trick spit out from the quarterdeck, and it works on a crew like a damned magic spell." He held the flaming wick to his pipe and pulled in a draw before blowing a couple of rapid puffs into the wind. "A forty-four gun frigate is nothing to toy about with, Jack. These dogs are ignoring the fact that they are being sent against an enemy who has them outgunned. And if she's built to design, from that fellow in Boston, she'll probably sail circles around this Brit box of a tub. Their, well damn me to land, our only hope of taking her is to surprise her and board her, and before she can run away, or plug this barkey full of holes and watch us all drown. It's a fool's errand," He pointed the stem of his pipe toward

A Bloody Beginning

the quarterdeck. "And that admiral found his fool to do it."

Jack hesitated for a moment. He looked over the decks of Allegiance. Her crew had begun to disperse and carry on with their tasks, laden with the new information they had all just been presented with a general mood of excitement hung in the air. "Bob, didn't the captain say Allegiance would be sailing with a squadron? Wouldn't that even the odds some? Maybe even stack them in our favor?"

"Aye, that it would, Jacky. The problem is, when these captains gets together, they is all in it for the prize, for themselves. They don't want to be sharin' no spoils with the other captains nor the other crews. You mark me words. We'll start our sailing looking all together in formation like, but after a few days, maybe a week, they'll all start finding reasons to drift away from the others. That's when it'll happen. That French privateer will find her an opportunity and before yer know it we'll be missing a ship from our consort. I've seen these things before, my boy. Yer watch, it'll be just like old Bowline says."

Jack wondered at the possible hardships that lay before them as Allegiance slid through a set of waves and sent a shower of mist tracing back along her deck. The image of Bill's punishment still weighed heavy on his mind. He knew he would not fare through three dozen lashes, but, deep down he could not come to terms with spending a year of his life in service to the king's

A Bloody Beginning

navy. From the quarterdeck, a drum beat rattled its penetrating tattoo before the hoarse voice of a midshipman cried out, "Quarters!" In an instant, the deck became a frenzy of activity. Men hurried to their stations and prepared their part of ship for action.

"Jacky, get below to your gun, lad! Hurry!" Bowline Bob said as he made his way toward the main shrouds. "Get below and do exactly as they tell you. You'll be fine, just keep yer wits about ye!"

Jack found the fore ladder way and descended to the gun deck amid a crowd of sailors doing the same. Below deck, Allegiance was in chaos. Men hurried away their makeshift mess tables, mallets knocked at wedges meant to chock gun carriages in place and gun ports were opened to the brunt of the sea spray and wind. Jack moved to the gun he had been assigned. Number seven, larboard battery. His gun crew was already assembled and the gun captain gave him a weary look of disapproval as he rushed to his place alongside the length of the iron weapon.

"Dawdling, is it?" the gun captain asked with a snort.

Jack shook his head. "First time to quarters. Won't happen again." He looked and found the side eyed stares of Matsumoko and Slop, both waiting to see what would develop from Jack's late arrival.

"Bet your eye it won't or I'll beat yer bloody, hear?" the gun captain growled. His breath had

A Bloody Beginning

the tangy edge of alcohol on it. He turned and looked up the line toward the bow, and then aft toward the lieutenant standing dutifully at the threshold of the officer's wardroom.

"Dry fire, run them out and back for three rounds. Best time gets to knock off while the rest try to beat it, might be an extra tot in it for the gun crew that meets the captain's time. Two full cycles in under one minute!" the lieutenant's voice roared through the gun deck. "Starting, now!"

Jack's gun crew captain turned toward his gun. "Load!"

Opposite Jack, Matsumoko hoisted an imaginary bag of powder. He mimed placing the bag into the muzzle of the iron cannon and then slapping a leather wad on top of it. Jack took up the ramrod, a double ended device with a spongy swab on one end and a small circle of brass on the other. He plunged the ramrod down the cannon's bore and tapped it twice before pulling the rod out and clearing away for Slop to place an imaginary ball of shot into the gun. Jack repeated his process again once the gun was shotted and Matsumoko had placed another imaginary leather wad into the bore. With the gun loaded, the gun captain bellowed over them to run it out. Jack took up one end of a tackle line with John Long falling in behind him, while Slop and Matsumoko took up the opposite side. Together, they heaved on the thick braid of coarse rope until the gun carriage's wheels rumbled their weapon into its firing position.

A Bloody Beginning

At the rear of the iron behemoth, the gun captain stepped forward and huddled over the breech. He mimicked piercing the fabric of the powder charge and priming the pan before cocking back the brass hammer and inspecting the flint. With a nod of satisfaction to Jack and the rest of the gun crew he turned toward the lieutenant at the end of the deck and called out, "Gun seven, ready!" A storm of activity had enveloped the gun deck, and Jack noted how many gun crews were still fussing at running their pieces out.

"Fire when ready!" the lieutenant shouted back.

The captain of gun seven on the larboard battery pulled at his lanyard and sent the small hammer of the firing mechanism down with a metallic clink. A bright spark traced off of the flint and smoldered for a moment in the pan before dying away to darkness. "On the training tackle, yer dogs, run her back in!" the gun captain shouted. Jack and the others scrambled to the heavy rope that traced through a block attached to an overhead beam. They took up the line and began heaving. At first, the cannon sat stubbornly in its place while the force applied was not yet great enough to overcome its weight and the relative angle of the deck. Jack pulled with everything he had and felt only the slightest give. "Pull, boys! Run her in, damn you!" the gun captain roared, "And you!" he said leaning in to where Slop was struggling at the heavy line. "Ye haul up three coils of anchor cable but ye can't run in a twelve pounder? I knew it was a fluke. Or maybe ye are

A Bloody Beginning

just lollying off ter make me look shite, eh?" Slop grunted deep and redoubled his efforts. Jack felt more give in the rope, and then slowly the carriage wheels began turning. "That's it boys, haul her back!" the gun captain crowed.

With the gun resting in its rear position, the gun captain called for it to be reloaded. Matsumoko, Slop, and Jack all went through the same process as they had been taught. Imaginary powder was loaded, and a wad applied, Jack rammed them down and tapped them twice. Around shot was hefted into the gun and then rammed down to ensure it was seated correctly. Finally, a last wad was applied and then rammed in next to the ammunition. The gun captain called for his crew to run out their gun and the lot all took up the tackle, heaving until their cannon was run forward to its firing position. As the gun captain went through his motions of priming and inspecting the flint, he grumbled in a low tone, "Ye blokes may just have it. We missed being finished first, but that wasn't bad by any stretch." He stood and gave the firing lanyard a tug.

CHAPTER 14

'H.M.S Allegiance'
19 March 1770
37 Degrees 54' N, 68 Degrees 45' W

"Scoot over there youngin" Kenny said with a rasp and cough. "The tars in my mess are being enough to drive a man to drink, figured I'd haul me carcass over here and 'ave me vittles with you lot."

"Have a seat, shipmate," Jack edged over on the crude bench he and his messmates had rigged with a pair of empty barrels and a plank. The rest of the mess adjusted their seats accordingly and Kenny took his place amongst them.

"Much appreciated, yer very kind, all of yers," Kenny growled and plopped his bowl of boiled oats and pork bits onto the rough table set in

A Bloody Beginning

between gun seven and gun six on the larboard battery. "Seems we're a ship on the hunt, eh?"

Jack looked around at his messmates and saw their eyes widen, all except for Matsumoko. He swallowed his mouthful of boiled oats and took a drink from his cup of small beer to clear his throat. "You've been in combat at sea Kenny?"

Kenny took a spoonful of his breakfast and nodded his head. He answered with a mouthful of food, "Aye, of course I have! You think I lost me eye in a tavern duster? Old Kenny here has been yardarm to yardarm with the Frenchies a time or two, let me tell yer. The last was a Frog sloop they slipped out of Brest. We chased her down for three days, firing bow chasers the whole time. When she finally turned to, the cap'n came about alongside an' we lit into her, full broadside. She managed a return volley 'bouts the same time we fired an I caught a splinter in me peeper!" He flipped up the crude leather patch to show the men gathered around the mess table. Jack suddenly felt his appetite wane. "Lucky it didn't burrow in there further, might have lost some of me gray matter, and that old Kenny just can't afford to lose!" The old sailor broke out in a raucous laughter at his own jest.

"But, the ship we're after isn't a sloop. The captain said we're hunting a privateer frigate, a forty-four gunner!" Slop replied in between spoonfuls. His own appetite unaffected by Kenny's grotesque eye socket.

A Bloody Beginning

Kenny nodded and fed himself another bite of his oats. "It's going to be a fight fer sure, lad. That's why the cap'n's going to press so hard at training you lads. We have to be squared with the wind and rigged tight, top-notch gunnery, quick at the helm and lightning aloft. Its seamanship and fighting the ship that will carry the day, and there's no other nation afloat on the high seas that can hold a candle to the king's navy in these respects. Not even frog privateers."

Kenny's bravado seemed to lift the spirits of the mess, but Jack noticed Matsumoko's expression remained unchanged. There was something his friend knew that he was not sharing with the group, and Jack determined to ask him later in private company.

"Kenny," Jack said with a halting tone. He hesitated before continuing, hoping he wouldn't be berated for his ignorance. "The captain mentioned something about taking the privateer as a prize. Forgive me for my ignorance. But, what exactly does that mean?"

Kenny's lone eye glittered as he answered, "Aye, it's all for the prize, lads. Means the cap'n intends to come alongside her and we all go aboard. We slug it out with the frog crew until they surrender or until they're all fish food. Then the cap'n assigns a prize crew to take her to the nearest friendly port. Any valuable cargo she has aboard gets sold, and if the navy decides to purchase her into the service all the money gets split amongst the crew. It's the perks of naval service. Those poor sods in

A Bloody Beginning

the king's army don't get a chance at prize money, nor regular vittles like we do, makes a sailors life the life fer me, boy." He drained his cup of small beer and slammed the vessel onto the mess table. "Twice at sea I've come away with decent prize money, it's a thing to experience, yer'll never hear me say otherwise. But, it never lasts. A few weeks ashore an the coin all fritters away on drink an women, hot meals and warm soft beds. Some lads take to spending their coin on loved ones, and better off fer it, but not me. I spent me coin in the pubs and taverns at Portsmouth."

"Boarding a ship," Slop said over a mouth of oats and pork bits, "can't be an easy go."

Kenny shook his head. "No, lad. In that yer right. Most often a ship gets boarded it turns into a fight to the death, to the last man. Especially where navies and privateers are concerned, they'll fight until there's no fight left in 'em, or until everyone is dead. Officers get to court martial by surrenderin' too easy like, and privateers will lose their letter of marque. No, it's no easy sail. But, the rewards is great fer them that can."

Jack looked across the table at the rest of his mess. "Sounds to me like we would be well served by taking to our training."

"Well served is an understatement," interrupted Bob in a throaty growl over Jack's shoulder. He walked around the makeshift mess table, ducking for an overhead beam, before nudging John Long to make some room. "I was just talking to my old shipmate aft. He says the close order training will

A Bloody Beginning

begin today. That's where ye lads needs to be paying close attention. Training to fight fer yer own sake. Dangerous bit, going over the bulwark and boarding another ship. Yer best served if ye knows yer way round a pistol and a cutlass." He folded his arms across his chest and leaned back to fuss over his pipe. "A combat at sea isn't what yer thinking it is. Most of it is boredom and tension. Hours and hours, sometimes days, spent watching the other bastards on the horizon." He succeeded in lighting his pipe and took a few moments to spread a cloud of bluish tobacco smoke over the mess table. "When the cap'n finally gets us within striking distance, then it starts in earnest. Cannon fire to start, usually round shot while we are at a distance. Once we get in closer, gunner's mates will order ammunition change to grapeshot or chain. This is so we can cripple the ship and kill her men, keeps her from running away but doesn't damage the prize as much as a twelve pounder ball. Then muskets and pistols be a firin' back and forth while each crew is trying to kill the other before a boarding happens. But, finally, when the ships are near close enough to reach out and touch, we toss grapple lines and secure them to us, we drops a plank down in between ships and then it's over the side and onto the enemy ship we goes."

"You've done this as well?" Slop asked with wide eyed disbelief.

"Aye, of course I have," Bob said through a cloud of pipe smoke. "I wouldn't be the sailorinest

A Bloody Beginning

sailorman you've ever met without havin' tasted a bit 'o combat at sea! They don't call me Bowline fer nothing!"

Kenny added his raspy voice to the mix. "I can tell ye one thing, and that is the cap'n has no quit in him when it comes to hunting a ship. Outclassed, outgunned, it won't matter. He's done it before. He's a mind fer it, the strategy and seamanship of it all. But, he won't hesitate to pull us alongside pistol range and slug it out to splinters. Don't yer doubt it fer a second."

Jack felt his stomach tighten. The idea of floating next to an enemy ship and blasting cannons at them, all while they blasted their own back, seemed like madness. He looked around at the crowded gun deck and imagined a cannonball smashing its way through the thick hull timbers. The wooden debris alone would be enough to maim or kill a half dozen men, and that was just from a single round. The enemy would be firing their full broadside, just as Allegiance would be firing theirs.

"Hands on deck and make ready for close order training!" a voice bellowed down the aft ladder way.

Jack stood from his seat and began to help his messmates stow away their makeshift table and seating. His mind was already consumed by the challenges lying in wait ahead of him. Training for hand-to-hand combat was not part of his idyllic dream of a life at sea. With the table and benches stowed, he pulled on his thin wool coat over the

A Bloody Beginning

striped sailor's shirt he had been issued. He fished his knit cap from the pocket of the coat and started to put it on when one eyed Kenny stopped him with a rough growl.

"Ye'll not be needing the cap, nor the coat, lad." He poked at Jack's ribs and tugged on his wool sleeve. "Yer'll be sweating buckets if yer wear 'em, that I promise."

Jack removed his coat and stripped the knit hat from his head. He stacked them on top of the larboard number seven carriage and braced himself for the hours of cold he would have to endure topside. The gun deck went from teeming with sailors, to nearly deserted within the span of only a few moments and Jack found himself arriving at the top of the aft ladder just as Mr. Finnick, the ship's master-at-arms, was beginning his instruction.

"A dawdler, eh?" Mr. Finnick's voice snapped as Jack stepped on deck. "Very well, you will be our first volunteer." He leaned over to an open top barrel with a score of training swords protruding upward like a bouquet of lethal arrangement. "Here, boy. You take this one." He handed one of the wooden blades to Jack and then nodded to a marine standing near the quarterdeck. "Sergeant Bremmer will be your opponent this morning. I imagine he will impress the importance of not dawdling about when it comes to matters of combat."

The marine smiled maliciously and began to strip his uniform coat and hat before taking up a

A Bloody Beginning

training sword from the barrel. Jack felt his stomach tighten and his legs go loose at the knees. The marine stood a few paces from him, broad in the shoulders and thick in the arms. His chest looked as stout and round as the barrel holding training weapons and his knuckles and forearms bore the scars of what must have been a hundred fights. He held the wooden cutlass as if it were made of paper, while in Jack's hand his training blade felt as if it had a lead core.

"Hoist your weapon lad," Mr. Finnick scolded, "you won't be killing any frogs with the tip pointed down at the deck."

Sergeant Bremmer held his training sword up and pointed it toward Jack in a menacing gesture. "Go ahead, boy. Try and strike me."

Jack hefted the wooden sword and tried to get a sense of balance with it. The marine facing him seemed to be in his natural element with a weapon in hand. His movements were measured and smooth, his sword seemed to float in the grip of his meaty hands. Jack narrowed his eyes and drew a breath, he tried to attack with a lunge, but the result was a clumsy stab that found his wooden blade in empty space while Sergeant Bremmer pivoted and swung his own weapon into a high arc that connected with Jack's forearms on its downward swing. Bolts of pain ran through Jack's arms and wrists. He dropped his weapon onto the deck half a heartbeat before Sergeant Bremmer doubled his attack by slamming his training blade across the back of Jack's shoulders.

A Bloody Beginning

"Pick up that weapon and fight, damn you!" Mr. Finnick roared. "This lad will be the first casualty when we take Saber, mark my words!"

A red flush blossomed on Jack's face while a boil of rage erupted somewhere deep in his belly. He scrambled to retrieve the wooden weapon from the deck only to have Mr. Finnick kick it away. Jack doubled his effort and ran for the training blade. His shoes skidded to a halt and he fetched the weapon just as the marine sergeant pressed his attack. With shaking hands, Jack lifted his sword in just barely enough time to absorb the blow of Sergeant Bremmer's overhand strike. The blow nearly knocked the weapon from Jack's hand again and sent him reeling backward three paces. Another swing from the marine landed on Jack's shoulder and caused him to buckle under its force. Inadvertently, Jack lost his grip on his weapon yet again and the wooden sword clattered to the deck. Sergeant Bremmer unleashed a series of three strikes on Jack's neck and arms, each landing with more force than the last. He was on his knees, holding his hands up to shield his head and face from the next blow when the onslaught suddenly stopped as a ripple of laughter broke out among the gathered sailors on deck. Slowly, Jack lowered his hands and looked around to find Sergeant Bremmer mocking him to the amusement of Mr. Finnick and the rest of the crew.

"Well, that certainly won't inspire any fear in our enemies," Mr. Finnick shouted as the laughter died away. "Maybe you'd be better off being used

A Bloody Beginning

as a shield." He turned and faced the crowd of sailors. "Do we have any other brave volunteers who think they'll fare any better against the sergeant here?"

Jack looked over the faces of the sailors and found that it hadn't been all of them laughing at his misfortune. In fact, by his estimate, it hadn't even been most. There were quite a number of men toward the front of the group with hard pressed expressions, stony with disapproval. Pressed men. The hardest look among them was Matsumoko. All the rage Jack felt within his belly seemed to be teeming from his friend's eyes. Even though there was no noticeable change in his facial expression, Jack could see there was something different with his friend. A sort of grave seriousness, a determined look that spoke volumes to Jack.

"I will face him," Matsumoko said and lifted his hand.

A brief exchange took place between him and Bowline Bob, who happened to be standing just behind the young man's shoulder. Bob was shaking his head and trying to repress Matsumoko's arm back down before it was seen, but it was already too late.

"Another volunteer," Mr. Finnick said. "And the Chinaman, no less. This should be interesting to watch. Maybe Sergeant Bremmer will actually get to draw blood today."

Matsumoko strode forward from the crowd as Bowline Bob's protests withered under the

A Bloody Beginning

collective attention of the crew and officers on deck. Without a heartbeat's hesitation, Matsumoko stalked to the weapons barrel and selected a training sword. He hefted the weapon a few times in one hand before pacing across the deck to face down Sergeant Bremmer. Jack retreated from the scene, unable to take his eyes off of Matsumoko. He knew his friend had accepted the Master-at-arms' challenge because of the thrashing he had just taken. Guilt crept through his blood as he passed by on his way to the gathering of sailors by the mainmast.

"Matsumoko, you shouldn't have…" Jack began to say.

"Silence on deck!" Mr. Finnick roared. He faced Matsumoko and Sergeant Bremmer. "Well. Get on with it, we haven't got all day!"

Jack hurried his way next to Bowline Bob, his neck, arms and back still throbbing with pain from the savage blows landed by the superior swordsman. He was received with a few nods of approval from Slop, John Long and Bowline Bob before he turned back to watch the inevitable pummeling of his friend.

"It's alright, Jacky. You haven't been trained up yet, there was no other way that could have gone, the bastards," Bob growled.

Matsumoko faced Sergeant Bremmer, his face stone cold and focused. He showed absolutely no fear as he tested the weight of the training sword before taking the handle in both hands and spreading his feet out into a wide stance. He held

A Bloody Beginning

the hilt of the weapon close to his torso, just above his waistline, and let the tip of the sword lean forward just slightly.

"That's not how it's done, lad," Mr. Finnick scolded with a demeaning edge in his voice. He looked to the sergeant. "Show the Chinaman the deck so we can get on with training."

"Aye aye, sir," Sergeant Bremmer replied with a grin.

With his sword in one hand, the sergeant approached Matsumoko in an overconfident stride and attempted a swinging side strike. With lightning reflex, Matsumoko blocked the strike and wheeled his sword around to its original position with the hilt right in front of his torso. Sergeant Bremmer seemed amused by the first exchange and began another attack with a slashing overhead. Matsumoko shuffled his footing to the side while simultaneously blocking the sergeant's attack as if it were a mere nuisance. The block forced Sergeant Bremmer off his balance, and Matsumoko exploited the gap in his defense by slashing down onto the marine's leg with his training sword. The impact sent a fleshy slapping sound echoing over Allegiance's deck and several of the crew groaned in sympathy for the pain it must have invoked.

Sergeant Bremmer recovered his balance and shook away the blow. "Quick little bastard, aren't you?" he said with a sneer. He checked the weight of his sword and wheeled it in one hand before

A Bloody Beginning

setting his footing in a more deliberate fighting stance.

"Matsumoko has gone and pissed him off now," Jack mumbled.

Bob pulled his pipe from out of his bite. "Jacky, I think our friend has a few surprises in store for this big Brit."

A heartbeat of silent tension passed on deck as the two opponents faced each other. Sergeant Bremmer launched himself in a plunging thrust aimed at Matsumoko's chest. With a flash of movement, Matsumoko swung his training sword, blocked the sergeant's thrust and sidestepped. He countered with a series of wicked strikes that landed on Sergeant Bremmer's arms, shoulders and back. He pressed his advantage by landing a snapping kick to the back of the marine's knee and then another sword strike to the side of his neck. The marine doubled over onto the deck, his wooden weapon clattered out of his hands as his knees thudded down onto the hard planks. Jack's breath caught in his chest as he watched a shimmer of rage boil up over the sergeant's face. He swallowed hard as the marine picked himself up and retrieved his weapon to face Matsumoko, who had assumed the same stance he had originally been in.

"Master-at-arms didn't kick away his weapon, now did he? Bloody, buggering bastards," Bob grumbled.

Sergeant Bremmer hefted his wooden sword and flexed his neck from side to side. He held the

A Bloody Beginning

blade up and pointed its tip toward Matsumoko before plunging himself in for another attack. He swung hard, in a vicious cross swing that was met with Matsumoko's timely block. The sergeant pressed his attack by doubling over into another cross swing in the opposite direction that was again met with a block from Matsumoko's wooden blade. A third swing found empty space as Matsumoko shifted his footing with cat like quickness before countering with a strike that landed on the sergeant's ribs. Matsumoko shifted his footing again and slashed his training sword on the marine's chest and then again across his abdomen before launching himself upward and driving his knee directly into the stunned marine's stomach. With one hand, Matsumoko seized the sleeve of the sergeant's blouse and side stepped while simultaneously slapping him in the face with his wooden sword. With a lightening quick swoop, Matsumoko plunged himself forward while locking Sergeant Bremmer's sword arm under one shoulder. He lifted his training blade to the marine's throat and pressed it forward, forcing the now humbled swordsman to his knees.

"I yield, I yield," Sergeant Bremmer said through the choking force of Matsumoko's blade. He was defeated.

A lone round of applause sounded from the far side of the quarterdeck. Jack looked and found Captain Willaims smiling broad and clapping his hands at the result of the duel.

A Bloody Beginning

"Well done, lad. Well done!" the captain exclaimed. "I don't recognize you at all, and it seems that I should. What is your name?"

Matsumoko stood sharp and offered a rigid half bow. "Matsumoko Tadaaki, sir. From Japan, originally. Not China."

Captain Williams offered a slight nod of his head in return for Matsumoko's bow and looked briefly at a lieutenant standing at his shoulder.

"One of the pressed men, sir. I believe from Salem Tide, the whaling tender," the lieutenant said.

"Very well," Captain Williams continued, "that was a fine display of swordplay. On both parts." He looked back to Matsumoko. "I hope you will help instruct your shipmates and bring them up to be as deadly with a cutlass as you are."

Matsumoko offered only a silent nod before departing to resume his place with the crew. His eyes were distant as he strode across the deck, his face betrayed no emotion at his victory. He took up a spot next to Jack and gave him a slight pat on the shoulder.

"I think the word for that, is humbled," Matsumoko said in a voice soft enough for only Jack to hear.

Jack nodded. "It is. Thank you, friend."

A general sense of excitement had gripped the crew. Jack heard a mix of grumblings and praise about Matsumoko defeating Sergeant Bremmer so thoroughly. It seemed as if there was a distinct division through the crew, and it ran along the

A Bloody Beginning

same lines as the distinction of pressed men from the colonies and the sailors who had been aboard Allegiance for some time.

"Alright, you dogs, get some space and pair off," Mr. Finnick shouted over the assembled sailors. "We'll start with swords and boarding axes. Some of you may know your way around them," he said while shooting a glare toward Matsumoko. "But, for most of you, there is some work needs doing. Pair off and take up a training sword. We'll start with the basics."

Jack paired up with Matsumoko and they moved to a space along the larboard side of the deck near the foremast.

"Where did you learn to handle a sword so well Matsumoko?" Jack asked as soon as they were out of earshot from the bulk of the crew.

Matsumoko met his gaze as others pairs lined up on either side of them, forward and aft. "I told you, in Japan, my father was a samurai. He was a very skilled fighter, not just with a sword, he was skilled in many disciplines, and he insisted that I start training from a very early age. I was training with wooden swords from the time I was four or five."

"You made that sergeant look like an amateur," Jack said while imitating Matsumoko's grip on the training sword.

Matsumoko lifted his own training weapon. "He is," he said with a half grin flirting at the edges of his mouth. "I've seen Brits at swordplay before, the French too. They are crude, clumsy and unskilled.

A Bloody Beginning

They rely on brute force. There is no soul in western swordsmanship." He held his wooden blade out toward Jack and ran one hand along it's flat side. "In Japan, sword fighting is an art form. Everything from drawing the blade, to foot placement. It is something I trained at since before I can remember. It is poetry in motion, grace and skill over strength, like a dance."

Jack wasn't sure what to say. He was awed at his friend's skill and wondered what other surprises Matsumoko had in store for him. For the next several hours, the deck was filled with the sounds of wooden cutlasses clacking together interspersed by slaps of wood against flesh. The difference to Jack was astounding. Matsumoko showed him how to deflect an opponent's strike and move in fluid steps to exploit the natural position of an attacker. He noticed that the Master-at-arms had taken particular interest in the two of them as he made his way up and down the line offering curt corrections and instruction where he saw fit. He stopped dead in his steps when he came to Jack and Matsumoko, his eyes locked on them both and he waited until their attention turned toward him before speaking.

"I've never seen anyone best Sergeant Bremmer like you just did," he said to Matsumoko. "Usually anyone who meets him with a sword in hand looks more like your friend here did."

Matsumoko offered his typical stony look. "That is why it was so easy for me," he replied.

A Bloody Beginning

The Master-at-arms shook his head and shifted his feet. "You are an arrogant little bastard, aren't you? But damn it all if you aren't the best I've ever seen with a blade." He paused for a long beat as if he were summoning something from within himself. "Would you help, with instruction, that is. For the sake of the crew. I think you could do us a service with your, style, as it were."

Matsumoko looked the Master-at-arms dead in the eye and answered, "As well as you could teach hogs to pour tea. But, I will try."

Mr. Finnick looked taken back for a moment as he processed Matsumoko's answer. A flash of offense crossed his face until he realized the young man had agreed to help, or at least attempt. He nodded with satisfaction and gestured for both him and Jack to move their practice aft near the quarterdeck where many of the ship's officers, including the captain, took particular interest in Matsumoko's techniques. Jack did his best, and tried to replicate the fluid smooth movements his friend made as he wove in and out from his opponents with as much ease as it took to draw breath. Close order training lasted until the last bell of the afternoon watch, at which time Captain Williams granted the boatswain to have all hands piped to supper.

During a standard meal of beans, salted pork, and hard ship's biscuit, Matsumoko was the talk of the gun deck. Every sailor that saw the action retold the tale, each swearing he had a better view than the rest of the crew. By the end of the meal

A Bloody Beginning

and with the last dregs of grog, Matsumoko had become a legend who could challenge any swordsman in history and prevail with ease.

"Those frogs will be shaking in their boots when they see our Mats carve up his first Frenchy. When word gets around, they'll be running up white flags from Brest all the way to Paris!" a sailor ranted over the last of his grog.

Another sailor lifted his can and shouted, "Now every navy ship will be wanting fer a Chinaman to come aboard! We'll be the envy of the whole fleet!"

Jack immediately fixed his eyes on Matsumoko. He knew his friend would be disturbed by the term, and he wasn't wrong. Matsumoko's face blossomed red. His brows set into a hard furrow and his lips drew tight together. He drew a slow breath and stood from the makeshift mess table as the entire gun deck fell silent.

"I am from Japan!" Matsumoko said in a measured voice that punctuated with each word. "The next one of you who calls me a Chinaman will find out how gentle I was to Sergeant Bremmer!"

A heartbeat of silence elapsed, followed by another. Matsumoko looked over the deck of sailors in various stages of their supper and grog before finally sinking back down to his seat across from Jack.

A sailor on the far side of the gun deck stood and lifted his grog high in salute. "Here's to Mats, our Japanese!" A roar of cheers tore through the crowd and shook the deck of Allegiance.

A Bloody Beginning

Jack looked to his friend, who appeared to be more annoyed at this point than angry. "You alright?" He asked.

Matsumoko nodded before letting out a deep sigh. "Sailors, Jack. There's no help for them."

CHAPTER 15

'H.M.S Allegiance'
24 March 1770
34 Degrees 26' N, 65 Degrees 26' W

    Winds blew hard from the northwest while the seas ran high. Allegiance pitched and heaved over the swells under topsails and partially reefed mainsails while the bow of the ship endured a near constant deluge of freezing spray. Ambient temperatures had warmed slightly, but the chill of the wind had yet to depart and with every wave breaking at the bow a mist of frigid water reminded the crew of the dangerously cold sea. Amidships in the waist, Jack took to his duties on deck with diligence and earnest interest. The complex web of lines that crossed through blocks overhead corresponded with many of the lines tied around cleats at the railing in the waist. Every

A Bloody Beginning

sail adjustment required a measure of action from the waisters, and resulted in another lesson for Jack and his messmates. Leeward lines would be taken in while windward lines paid out as the ship turned from running before the wind to taking it at her quarter and then beam reach before tacking back over to hold the wind on the opposite quarter. Solid skies of gray broke as they traveled south and east to let columns of golden sunlight peer through the gaps of overhead cover and illuminate spots here and there on the sea surface. Each day at sea blended to the next and Jack became accustomed to the routine of living his life by the peal of the watch bell and the call of the boatswain's whistle. He lived from meal to meal, with a mix of watch, labor and sleep in between. Boiled oats with bits of salt pork and small beer in the morning, and beans, salt pork or beef with ship's biscuit and grog for supper.

Jack learned all he could of his trade on deck while still looking aloft every chance he could steal. In his mind, the top men had to be the pinnacle of sailoring. They climbed the rigging as if they were born to it, springing from handhold to handhold up the shrouds and shimmying across the yards with the same casual swagger that carried them on the deck. Their shouts and calls echoed through the air, repeating each order and relaying for the men higher or lower. It was more than craft in Jack's eye, it was an art form, an elaborate dance that harnessed the wind to conquer the waves. Their skilled handling

A Bloody Beginning

propelled Allegiance over heaving swells through a never ending world of deep blue. While the main deck consumed his time, Jack could not help himself but to look aloft in longing anticipation of the day he would again be able to ascend the shrouds and view the world from the highest perches.

Working lines in the waist afforded Jack the opportunity to learn rigging from the deck upward, and how the various lines being hauled in or paid out coincided with sail changes. His hands toughened from near constant contact with the grating fibers of thick, coarse ropes. His arms and shoulders, which were in a near constant state of fatigue, grew stronger by the day. The pitch and roll of the deck became more natural to him, and traversing the ship while she was in constant motion was soon second nature. Watch in the waist became less of a burden and while he still despised holy stoning the deck and regarded it as an oppressive torture, a near constant state of training and exercise had lessened the frequency of the laborious practice.

Jack's stint in the waist began in the same manner everyday at the sounding of the last bell for the forenoon watch. Close order training was conducted in the mornings right after all hands concluded their breakfast. They trained with cutlass and boarding axes, or practiced the repetitious process of firing and reloading muskets, pistols or the swivel guns on deck. The training brought warmth to his bones and stretched his muscles, which made his turn at the waist not quite as taxing. He spent his time in the waist practicing the different knots Bowline Bob had been teaching him and either heaving or paying out lines according to the croaked orders of the boatswain's mate on watch. When the last bell of the first afternoon watch sounded, Jack would retreat from the deck to escape the wind and sea spray for a time before the drums rattled out a tattoo and sent every hand to quarters for gunnery drills, where they would remain until they were piped to supper.

It was during gun drills when Jack's fate aboard Allegiance shifted. It was a rare live fire, with both batteries competing against one another for the chance at an extra tot in their evening grog. The first two rounds had been the usual fare of dry firing, where the gun crews were required to heave their pieces back with the use of the training tackle when Captain Williams appeared on the gun deck.

"Lieutenant Sifton, let's make this evening's training a little more interesting. I want two rounds of successive fire from each battery in order, stem to stern. The battery with the fastest time will receive a neat tot with their evening grog ration." Captain Williams announced loud enough for the entire deck to hear.

"Aye, sir," Lieutenant Sifton replied before turning forward and shouting, "make ready with powder and shot! Two rounds, successive fire forward to aft!"

A Bloody Beginning

Jack's blood lit with fire as he realized the larboard battery would be in direct competition with their starboard counterparts. Their gun was ready to load, and he shared a quick glance with Matsumoko before the gun seven captain began barking his orders.

"Alright, boys. Load her!" he shouted.

Jack started the process by dousing the swab end of his ramrod in a bucket holding a mixture of vinegar and fresh water. He quickly punched the rod through the muzzle and swabbed the length of the bore. Matsumoko stood ready with a cartridge of powder sewn in thin cotton fabric and a leather wad immediately after. Jack reversed his ramrod and forced the powder charge down to the breech of the cannon in one uniform push. Matsumoko was ready with a twelve pound ball of iron shot as soon as Jack cleared the ramrod from the cannon and lifted the projectile into the muzzle of the gun. Jack pushed the iron ball down into the cannon and retrieved his ramrod just as Matsumoko hoisted another leather wad and inserted it into the bore. One final push of the ramrod seated the wad against the ammunition and as soon as Jack cleared away from the cannon's end he took up the tackle rope at his feet. Together, the gun crew heaved at the heavy line and ran their cannon into its firing position. Even with the added strength from the weeks they had spent before the mast, they still strained against the heavy rope with every ounce of strength they possessed. With the gun run out, the gun crew captain set to his task of

A Bloody Beginning

pointing and priming. He drove a sharpened steel spike into the breech of the cannon to pierce the powder bag before pouring a small amount of fine powder into the brass pan beneath the flint striker. When the gun was primed, and the gun captain had cocked the flint striker, he took up the firing lanyard in one hand before stepping back and checking both sides of the carriage. When he was satisfied that his crew was clear from the path of travel the gun would take on recoil he turned aft and called out his gun's readiness.

The first round went down the line without event. Each gun thundered out in turn billowing smoke and embers into the Atlantic evening and washing back through the gun ports and into the faces of sweating sailors. At the end of the first volley, the starboard battery finished their fire two guns ahead of their larboard brethren. Gun captains all along the larboard battery shouted encouragement and admonished their crews to double their efforts.

"Come on, lads," the gun seven captain bellowed, "put your backs into it! The whole of the battery is counting on us! The whole of the ship is counting on us! For king and for country boys! Let's haul away!"

Jack raced through each task in the process with lethal urgency nipping at his mind as he imagined a French privateer lined up across from his gun, yardarm to yardarm with Allegiance. He swabbed, Matsumoko loaded, he drove the ramrod, Matsumoko wadded, he punched yet

A Bloody Beginning

again, and they all heaved for everything that they were worth. Their gun crew worked so fast that as the succession of fire worked its way down the line of the larboard battery gun seven was ready to fire a full half minute before the gun forward of them.

"Well done, boys! Well done!" the gun captain crowed triumphantly as the first cannons began to fire. "That's fine gunnery, that is!"

Gun one of the larboard battery fired, just before the first gun on starboard. The race was on, and each battery too close to call with its counterpart. The cannon blasts fired within a heartbeat of one another as turns to fire worked their way down the line until the shots were near simultaneous. By the time it was gun seven's turn, the larboard battery was one gun ahead of starboard. Boom, boom, boom. Ear piercing reports filled the gun deck just as thick as the acrid smoke washing back into the gun ports until a blood chilling scream erupted a few guns aft.

"Aghhhh! Aghhh! Me leg! Oh God in heaven, me foot!" the scream wailed.

All eyes departed their tasks and drifted in search for the source of the agony. Captain Williams stormed across the gun deck, his voice booming, "Cease fire! Cease fire!" He hurried past the readied crews who had yet to fire their guns and halted at the larboard gun nine. "Mr. Sifton, the ship's doctor if you please. Tell him to bring a pair of his mates and do it smartly!"

A Bloody Beginning

Jack edged his way into the narrow passage in the center of the gun deck to steal a look at the commotion that had halted their training. Captain Williams had dropped to one knee next to the larboard gun nine carriage, and the gun crew crowded around him in a tight formation as they looked on at the screaming sailor.

"Me leg, oh damn! I'm sorry, sir, it's ruint, I know it. I can feel the bones are broken, my God I can feel them!" the sailor screamed a shriek that could curdle the hardest sailor's blood. "Help me, please. Some rum, laudanum, anything!"

Captain Williams took the stricken sailor's hand and held it tight. "Quiet, now man. The doctor is coming and he will do what he can for you. It isn't fatal, sailor, you'll live. You'll live."

The sailor's screams died away and Jack took another step toward the gun nine carriage. Whoever had been screaming, his face had been obscured by the barrel of the iron cannon separating him from Jack's curious gaze. There was blood on the deck. It seeped along the tight spaces between deck planks and followed the grain of the wood. Much like blood flowing between cobblestones. Another reluctant step forward revealed the wounded sailor's face and Jack guts tied into knots as he recognized one-eyed Kenny, his face twisted in agony as he looked upward at the captain.

"Make way, make way," the ship's doctor groaned on his way forward from the officer's mess. He paused as he came upon the scene with

A Bloody Beginning

Kenny and Captain Williams. "Oh, my." He surveyed the injury with a twisted scorn. "I am afraid, the foot will almost certainly be lost." The doctor hunched over to examine further. "As will part of the lower leg." He turned to one of his surgeon's mates and said, "Laudanum, two, eh, three doses. Prep the table and instruments for an amputation and be sure to sand the floor."

The surgeon's mate hurried away through the crowd of sailors who had pressed in around the scene of larboard gun nine with a morbid curiosity. A brief exchange occurred between the doctor and Captain Williams, though most of it was lost on Jack as he fixated on one-eyed Kenny's agonized grimace. The old sailor hadn't completely cleared the recoil path of the gun carriage and the resulting impact had seized his foot and ankle, smashing both to a pulp of their former form. The doctor stood abruptly and pointed to Jack and then another sailor.

"You, and you," he snapped. "Carry this man below, gingerly if you please. Bring him to my quarters and see to it that you stick around. I will need extra hands to hold him down."

A touch of lightning traced through Jack's blood. His feet felt frozen to the deck as the ship's doctor and Captain Williams continued their exchange. A nudge at his shoulder stirred him from his paralysis, he turned and saw that his gun captain was the one urging him onward.

"Go ahead, lad," the petty officer said with a grunt. "Don't make him tell you twice."

A Bloody Beginning

Jack stepped his way through the crowd of sailors surrounding one-eyed Kenny, he passed the captain and the ship's doctor before reaching Kenny's side and seeing the effects of the carriage wheel. Blood and bone fragments were splattered on the deck. Everything below Kenny's mid shin seemed to be a mess of torn flesh with no form or structure to it. Unsure of how to best lift the old sailor, Jack hooked his hands behind both of Kenny's knees while the man assisting him looped his forearms under the wounded sailor's arms and clasped his hands around his chest. Kenny howled in pain as they lifted him from the deck and began to carry him off toward the doctor's quarters.

"Did you not check to see that the recoil path was clear before you fired?" Captain Williams pressed the gun nine captain in a hard voice.

The gun captain stuttered back to the commander of the ship, "I-I-I did, sir. I swear it. I checked both sides, God's truth, sir. Honest. He must have stepped forward before I fired. I checked the c-c-carriage, sir, the r—recoil path."

As they carried Kenny away Jack heard the captain admonish the gun captain. He threatened to relieve him of his charge of gun nine and re-rate him as an ordinary seaman to fill the vacancy his carelessness had just created. The voice were soon lost to Kenny's growling and grunting as Jack and the other sailor carrying him made their way through the last quarter of the gun deck and below deck to the officer's wardroom which adjoined the doctor's quarters. With each step

A Bloody Beginning

down the narrow, steep stairs, Jack felt a pang of sympathetic pain for Kenny. Try as he did, he could not keep from jostling the wounded limb with each step down. The grunts turned into shouts and curses. Kenny called Jack a range of foul names and insisted that he had been sent by the devil with the express purpose of torturing him. At the base of the stairs, Kenny went completely limp and gave no more mutterings, foul or otherwise.

The doctor's quarters were little more than what would pass for a broom closet on land. A cramped space with wooden shelving along the fore and aft bulkheads and a flattop table in the center barely large enough to support Kenny's torso. The surgeon's mates had done as they were bid, sand was spread on the floor and on one of the shelves Jack could see three small tin cups had been laid out in the warm yellow light of an oil lantern. He and the other sailor hoisted Kenny onto the table and did their best to situate him somewhat comfortably. The doctor followed a moment later and gave the room an approving nod.

"Nasty bit of business we have before us, but, best not to put it off," he said as he wormed his way into the tight quarters and alongside the table holding Kenny. He took notice that the sailor was no longer conscious and lifted one of the tin cups from the nearby shelf. "Wake him, he needs to get at least one of these down the hatch. Preferably all three, but I'll take whatever I can get at this point."

A Bloody Beginning

Jack reached out and tapped on Kenny's chest, gently at first, but as he got no response he tried with slightly more force. It was no use. The sailor laid as still as the dead. Jack feared he had passed from more than just consciousness until the doctor grew impatient and slapped the wounded sailor's cheek several times.

"Is he, is he dead?" Jack asked.

The doctor shook his head scornfully. "No, he isn't dead. He's lost some blood, but not that much. The pain probably caused him to pass out, that is all." He continued swatting at Kenny's cheek until the one-eyed sailor roused.

"Wha-what? What in hell? Oh, me leg. Give me some rum fer God's sakes. Damn yer all ter hell and damn yer wives and children too. Bloody bludgeoning bastards bumped every bloody pillar and post in the ship. Poxy lubbers, damn yer souls." Kenny growled as he came to.

The doctor ignored the admonishments and held a small tin cup in front of Kenny's good eye. "Get this into you, sailor. I have two more after that. You'll need all three of them, and this is still going to be rough on you. Drink up."

Jack's stomach turned as Kenny slurped at the laudanum. The pungent aroma of the rum and opium solution filled his nose and burned his throat as Kenny finished the first cup and began on the second. Allegiance's movements seemed to be magnified in the cramped cabin, the air felt close and he couldn't escape the stinging laudanum smell, or the tinny taste of blood in the

A Bloody Beginning

back of his throat. His head swooned. He felt his legs going loose.

"There, that's it. That'll nip the pain a little," the doctor said with a nod. He looked up at Jack and gestured toward Kenny. "You two each take and arm and hold him. Once I start there's no stopping, I have to get through flesh and bone, which will take a few minutes. I need him as still as you can manage." The doctor extolled both sailors with bouts of piercing eye contact before turning to his patient with a thick leather strap in hand. He wrapped the leather around Kenny's leg just above the knee and inserted a metal rod which he then turned end over end several times. Kenny grunted as the strap was wound tight over his leg and grasped at the edges of the table he was propped on.

"I don't think the laudanum is working, doctor. Better give me some more," He growled with wide eyes and beads of sweat rolling down his face.

"You will feel the effects momentarily, sailor," the doctor replied in a sympathetic tone. "The fact that you are sweating as you are is already a very good sign." He turned to Jack and the other sailor and gestured to Kenny's arms. "Let's get on with this, lads."

The doctor's knife made a wet sound as he worked it through Kenny's flesh. For his part, Kenny held it together fairly well. He struggled against Jack and the other sailor when the doctor first began to cut, but after a few moments of hard struggling, he seemed to lose his strength and slumped back onto the table. Without pause, the doctor put his knife up and retrieved a fine toothed saw about the width of Jack's hand. The rasping saw sound was grating on Jack's ears and it turned his stomach over and then over again with each stroke the doctor made. Jack felt the small cabin beginning to spin. His throat burned and a horrid, acrid taste rose into the back of his throat. Kenny was no longer conscious, so there was no need to restrain his arms any longer. A wet slop plodded into the doctor's wooden bucket at the foot of the table.

"There, lads," the doctor said with a sigh, "almost done."

It was too much. Jack felt the remnants of his breakfast returning to him all at once. He leaned toward the bucket and retched for all he was worth. The first heave produced nothing, but as he drew breath, the sticky sweet smell of blood mixed with the pungent tang of laudanum and caused a second bout that emptied his stomach contents into the bucket and onto the floor.

After the terrors of the doctor's cabin, Jack found that the fresh air on deck wasn't quite as purifying as he had hoped. The smell of blood and laudanum lingered in his nose and on his tongue. His throat stung with the bitter acid from being sick, and his nerves felt shaky, like he couldn't

A Bloody Beginning

summon his full strength just yet. The skies remained marbled by ribbons of thick gray clouds and the sun was setting fast over the western horizon. His eyes stretched their gaze out to the east where rolling waves seemed to repeat themselves for eternity. The great ocean seemed so broad and vast, and Allegiance was just a spot of wood and sails on its surface, a pathetic gesture of man to conquer the waves. The pitch and roll of the deck had dulled since his bout with the bucket below deck. Jack took in a deep breath of salty sea air. It was not unlike the smell of the harbor in Boston, but larger somehow, wide open. The wind had warmed in the weeks since departing. Allegiance was pressing her way into warmer climes, and that meant that the captain's quarry would be nearer by the day.

"Landsman Horner, Jack Horner," petty officer crowed from the fore rail of the quarterdeck. "Report! Horner, or it'll be scuppers and the capstan fer ye fer the life of ye."

Jack's heart leapt in his chest. He felt a bolt of lightning trace through his blood as he stepped from the leeward rail and walked past the mainmast toward the quarterdeck. A group of three mates were gathered before the fore rail and a lieutenant stood in between them with a rolled paper in one hand.

"Y-yes," he knuckled his forehead to the lieutenant. "I'm Jack Horner." Jack recognized the officer as the man who had read off his name the day he had been forced from Salem Tide. He hoped the man had forgotten his mindless babbling from that day.

"Ah, yes," the lieutenant said with an arrogantly bemused smirk. "Jack Horner. It is good to see that you have finally figured out your name." He turned to the group of mates standing close by. "Our unfortunate mishap on the gun deck has created a bit of hardship for the maintop captain, and he wishes for you to fill his empty position."

Jack nodded his understanding, though he couldn't believe what was taking place. "Do m' best, sir."

The lieutenant smirked again and pointed forward and aloft. "To work the maintops, you must be rated as an ordinary seaman. Prove to me that you are capable and I will grant you this, to rate as such from the day of your impressment." He paused and looked at Jack, one finger still pointing up into the rigging. "Run aloft and touch the lee clew block on the t'gallant yard. Then, come down the after stayline." He paused for a moment, letting his gaze linger on Jack. "Well? Get to it."

A rich aroma crept into Jack's nose as he turned forward and made his way to the foremast shrouds. He found Bowline Bob leaning against the foremast, his pipe clenched in his bite and puffing furiously.

"Up and after it, Jacky," Bob called as Jack took the shrouds in hand. "Now's yer chance, mate. Up and after it. Shun that lubber hole just like ye did aboard Salem Tide. I been yapping me gums

A Bloody Beginning

abouts it since we was pressed, now don't let me down!"

The shrouds stood before Jack like a gauntlet. He had climbed a similar set aboard Salem Tide, but these seemed more daunting. The angle looked steeper, the masts were taller, and the ship was pitching and swaying with the action of waves that were twice the size of the seas when he had previously climbed aloft. His heart hammered at the inside of his chest. He felt as though it would beat its way out and go flopping on the deck like a freshly caught fish. He reached high and grasped one hand onto the thick shroud lines. With a leap and a heave, he pulled himself up onto the bulwark and began his ascent.

"Thar ye go, lad. One hand after t' other, steady as she goes boy!" Bob shouted through a cloud of smoke.

Jack focused on his hands and tried to mimic the steady action he had seen the other sailors use in their climbs aloft. One hand, then the other, then a foot, then the other. He pressed onward; his eyes set on the wooden platform of the foretop. It seemed easier than the first time he had climbed the shrouds, though this time he was climbing in daylight. The slant of shrouds angled back as he reached the underside of the foretop, and just as Bob suggested, he grabbed hold on the reversing angle of webbed lines and climbed over the edge of the wooden platform. Some cheers erupted from down on the deck but Jack was of a single mind. He gripped the next level of shrouds and

A Bloody Beginning

continued his climb while Allegiance pitched and swayed over a steady set of waves. Upward he climbed, he had passed the foretop with ease, his arms not even wanting for a break. As he reached the gap between topsail and top-gallant, Jack stole a glimpse along the yard and between the sails. The sea stretched out for miles and miles further than he could see from on deck, briny gray waves capped in white frothing white seemed to him like wrinkles in a carpet far below. From up here the world was a different place, all his problems, all the pressures of life aboard ship withered away in comparison with the exuberant thrill in his chest. He continued his climb until he reached the end of the foretop shroud where it buckled to the top-gallant mast. Here there was no wooden platform, only a diamond-shaped web of ropes that formed a small footing beneath the cross between the mast and the yards. Jack took a tentative step out onto the tightrope and worked his way along the yard until he came to the lee side clew block. Just as he was instructed, he leaned down and touched the wooden block. Victory pulsed through his muscles, it rang in his ears and lent strength to his arms. He worked his way back to the after stays and took hold of one that stretched down to the deck just forward of the mainmast. With a heave, he lifted his legs and wrapped them around the thick stay line and then descended hand over hand while sliding his legs along the coarse rope. The stay had very little give and it was difficult for Jack to control his speed downward. Several times

A Bloody Beginning

he had to force his arms to move slower so that he didn't out pace them and lose his grip.

As his feet touched down onto the deck, Jack was met with several greetings and congratulations from his fellow pressed men. John Long, Slop and Matsumoko all offered stout jabs onto his shoulders while Bowline Bob offered a hearty handshake accompanied by a burst of smoke that stung Jack's eyes.

"That's the way, Jacky," Bob said with another puff at his pipe. "I knew you could do it, lad. Now, go see the lieutenant and get your new watch and mess sorted."

Jack walked back to the quarterdeck fore rail and knuckled his brow to the waiting lieutenant. "Touched the lee clew block atop the t'gallant yard, sir, and returned by the after brace. Skipped the lubber's hole on the way up too," he reported.

The lieutenant looked him over for a long moment while waves washed along Allegiance's hull and her rigging groaned in the wind. "I suppose that is what will have to pass as an ordinary seaman. Truth be told, I thought you would either shy from the task or fall to your death. But, one of your fellow pressed men has been lobbying the master's mate on your behalf, so it stands, Ordinary Seaman Jack Horner. It's the maintop for you, main topman. You will report to Mr. Skagg for duty, he will be the petty officer in charge of the main top on your watch. You may remain with your current mess, it will be the same watch as you had before, just different part-of-ship. Do you understand?"

"Yes sir," Jack nodded and knuckled his forehead. He paused for a moment and frowned.

"Is there a problem, Horner?" the lieutenant asked with a scowl.

"Just one thing, sir. Does this change quarters for me? If we beat to quarters, like?" Jack asked.

"No. You will report to Mr. Skagg for your watch. If we happen to beat to quarters while you are on watch, then you will have a bit of a climb to get back to your station once we have finished blowing holes in the enemy, that is all," the lieutenant gave Jack a tight-lipped nod and then turned back to the company of the quarter deck as if he wasn't even there.

CHAPTER 16

'H.M.S Allegiance'
27 March 1770
32 Degrees 26' N, 64 Degrees 21' W

 Sea air whipped at Jack's face as he looked out over the gray blue seas. He was climbing the main shrouds among a line of sailors to set the top gallants and then run out the topmast studding sails. The previous evening had seen strong gales from the west and sails had been reefed to avoid damaging the masts, now that dawn was breaking over the sea, it was time to bare more canvas. Jack felt like a proper sailorman, in Bowline Bob's terms. He was climbing the shrouds on his way to let out sail. The wind kissed his skin with a warmth he had only felt in the late part of spring or early summers in Boston. The eastern horizon was as glorious a sunrise as he had ever seen with orange and pink hues blending into brilliant golden rays of sunshine that reached forward into the retreating night sky. A waxing moon was beating its course to the west in a similar retreat from its fiery bright counterpart.

As Jack worked his way out along the top-gallant yard, the wind pulled at his loose sailor's rig. In line with the others, he slid his feet along the tightrope until the men in front of them halted in their place.

"Unhitch and loose sail!" shouted Mr. Skagg, captain of the maintop.

Jack repeated with the others, "Unhitch and loose, aye!" As quick as his fingers could, he untied the two tidy cordage knots that were within arm's reach and gripped at the canvas with whichever hand was not engaged in work. The canvas sails billowed with wind as they were loosed and quickly sheeted home. Allegiance lurched with a burst of speed from the additional sail. Her wake intensified from a gentle roll to a breaking wave that slid away from where the bow parted the sea. As the hands made their way to their next task a sailor began to sing in a voice loud enough to carry all the way back to Boston.

"Farewell and adieu, to you Spanish ladies. Farewell and adieu, to you ladies of Spain," He sang loudly.

The rest of the top men in the rigging nearby joined in, "For we've received orders, for to sail for old England. We hope in a short time to see you again."

A Bloody Beginning

More voices joined for the chorus, "We'll rant and we'll roar, like true British sailors. We'll rant and we'll roar all on the salt seas. Until we strike sounding, in the channel of old England, from Ushant to Scilly, tis thirty-five leagues."

Jack had never heard sailors bellow out with such merriment. It reverberated through him as his shipmates raised their voices together in harmony as they worked. He dared not lift his own voice, as he concentrated his focus on the tightrope beneath his feet. But, part of him wished he knew the words so he could join in their song.

"We hove our ship to, with a wind from sou'west, boys. We hove our ship to, for to strike soundings clear. It's forty fathoms, with a white sandy bottom, we squared our main yard and up channel did steer," the voices rang clear and true as the hands of the maintop made their way below to run out studding sails from the topsail yard.

"We'll rant and we'll roar, like true British sailors. We'll rant and we'll roar all on the salt seas. Until we strike sounding, in the channel of old England, from Ushant to Scilly, tis thirty-five leagues."

As the final sail changes were completed, the captain of the maintop picked a pair of men to stay aloft as lookouts. To Jack's immediate joy, he was chosen to sit aloft atop the rigging above the topgallant. Not only did this afford him some precious time alone to his thoughts, but it allowed him to stay high above the ship with an unobstructed view of the progressing morning.

A Bloody Beginning

Spending his watch as a lookout was fast becoming one of his favorite details. He hauled himself aloft and took in deep breaths of pure sea air, untainted by the smell of the deck or of his shipmates. As he settled in on the top-gallant yard, Jack marveled at the expanse of sea stretching forth in all directions. As far as the eye could see, rolling gray blue waves capped by little white crowns where the wind tousled the tops of the briny rises. He looked on for over an hour with nothing but the vastness to catch his eye until a small dark spot arose on the southern horizon.

"Mr. Skagg, Mr. Skagg!" Jack shouted from his post on the top-gallant mast.

"What is it, Horner?" Mr. Skagg called back.

"Land sighted, two points off larboard bow!" Jack replied with one hand cupped around the side of his mouth in a makeshift speaking trumpet. He watched as a shuffle of activity broke out on maintop and the foretop. Shouts echoed between the top platforms and the deck. Sailors flooded up from below to catch a glimpse of the landfall. It gave Jack an immense feeling of satisfaction to have been the first one to report the sighting. He almost felt like a part of the crew, a sentiment that he grappled with on a daily basis. He still had no desire to serve the king's navy, nor to play host to soldiers wearing the same uniform as the men who had killed his parents. But, he was living the life he had once dreamed of.

Allegiance shifted her course and the bow slipped over toward the spit of land Jack had

A Bloody Beginning

sighted. He felt ten feet tall up in the rigging as they crept toward the long finger of green that grew on the horizon with every passing watch bell. Trees and foliage dominated the southern stretch of what was visible, while a collection of masts rose up between Allegiance and the sandy shoreline. It was Bermuda. The crew had been talking about it since Jack had been risen from the decks to work aloft. Bermuda being an important hub for both merchant and military vessels coming and going between the Caribbean and England, it was an important milestone in their search for their French privateer. Jack thought over the stories he had heard the previous night about the Devil's Triangle. Ships lost, seasoned navigators suddenly befuddled, krakens, cthulhu and other sea monsters were said to prowl those waters. Jack scoured the southern horizon with his gaze. Clear skies marked by feathery wisps of white clouds, brilliant sunshine and regular sets of rolling waves were all he could see for miles to the south. Not even a storm cloud on the horizon would mark their entrance into the most feared waters in the world. Peals from the last watch bell rang out and Jack reluctantly took to the shrouds to climb his way back to the deck. The climb down was long and arduous, Jack often felt that sliding down the stay lines would be faster. But, he had been warned off of this by his friend Bowline Bob. Sliding the stays was often the cause of sailors falling to the deck, Bob had cautioned him. Jack could think of few worse fates, so he endured the

A Bloody Beginning

shrouds even while experienced sailors took to the fore and after stays to quickly make their way down.

"That'll be Bermuda, by my reckon," Bob said as he met Jack at the weather railing.

Jack slung himself down from his last step on the shrouds and nodded triumphantly. "That's what I was thinking. It's a long island, crescent-shaped like you said, and there is a collection of ships moored just inside of a cove."

Bob furrowed his brow and leaned close to Jack, pipe smoke poured from his nose as he asked, "You didn't happen to catch the banners on the signal stand? Did ye?"

Jack thought for a moment before shaking his head. "I couldn't make out the signal stand. But the captain didn't sound the gun, how would they know what signals to give?"

A puff of smoke escaped from Bob's mouth, then another. He nodded his head and looked over each of his shoulders in turn. "That signal mast is going to run up flags sending Allegiance on her way toward the Frenchy privateer. Then you'll see Jacky, see what horrors await us when we join another ship in battle at sea. If'n you thought Kenny's leg was awful, you've just scratched the surface. It'll be hell aboard, Jack. Mark my words."

"The captain is going to port at Bermuda," Jack said. "Isn't he?"

"Nay, me boy," Bob answered in a growl. "Even if the signal mast is barren and remains that way,

A Bloody Beginning

we'll be standin' offshore from Bermuda. Bet on it. The cap'n wouldn't even let his true crew ashore in New York, afraid fer he'd lose 'em to desertions and such. He won't be lettin' a single soul ashore in Bermuda neither. We'll either get our signals from the mast, or he'll be taking a jolly boat ashore fer naught but an hour. Sightings of the privateer, that's what he's after." Bob pulled a draft from his pipe and blew a thin line of smoke skyward. "It doesn't take a scholar to figurin' where they went either. Cap'n already said they was harassing ships just to the south o' here, means they either made fer the straights south of the keys, or they'll have sailed southerly fer latitudes more friendly fer a Frenchy. Hispaniola, Martinique, Guyana coast, maybe even Spanish waters. They won't linger in these parts long, not with word getting around about a Brit frigate prowling about in search of them."

"Word about a frigate," Jack said with a deepening frown. "Bob, we just arrived in these waters."

Bob nodded and smiled as he let a dribble of smoke pour from his nostrils. "Aye, but word we were on our way proceeded us by at least two days. You mark my words. And word will reach wherever we are headed long before we get there. Could be anyone, a tavern wench, a merchant sailor who don't much like the king, or any number of spies scattered all through the new world." He leaned against the bulwark and plucked his pipe out from his bite. "England has

A Bloody Beginning

their spies, as do the other nations of the world. Naught is kept secret for long anymore, Jacky. Not the sailing of ships, or the moving of troops. Nor even that bloody business in Boston. Word gets around."

The mention of Boston and the bloody business set Jack's mind to racing. "What is it that you have heard, Bob? And while we have both been aboard this ship this entire time."

Bob jutted his chin toward a deserted part of the foc'sl and departed his resting place against the bulwark. Jack followed him over to the base of the foremast, where the two could have a moment of privy conversation.

"I've spoken with several of our fellow pressed men, those boys brought on board in New York. They say news has gotten around about what happened in Boston, and folks in the colonies are none too happy about it neither. They've taken to calling it 'The Boston Massacre'. One of the blokes below deck, that angry looking sod that swears he's never been to sea a day in his life, he told me there is a silversmith in Boston did an engraving of it. Folks are riled about it Jack, riled enough they've all but forgotten the business of taxes and such."

Jack's gaze fell to the deck. He wasn't sure how he felt about this new revelation, but it didn't ease his qualms about serving aboard a king's ship. If anything, it inflamed his desire to depart.

A Bloody Beginning

"What's more, Jacky," Bob continued in a low voice, "there's some of them that's got plans to try and take the ship."

Jack couldn't believe what he was hearing. He looked at Bob as a ribbon of fire ran through his blood. "What? When?" he asked.

Bob shook his head. "No time too soon, lad. There's too many goings on that need happen first, and the stakes are too high to let anything fall amiss. But, these boys is serious Jacky. Something we ought to make sure we are on the right side of."

Jack narrowed his eyes, trying to discern what Bob was hinting at. "You aren't saying we would fall on the side of the captain, are you?"

Bob shook his head and stuck his pipe back into his mouth. "Nay, not a chance, Jacky. I'm pressed here against me will jus' same as you. Don't much care fer partin' with a year of me life in the king's name anyhow. But, this has to be done careful, like. Can't be any stone left unturned, or them that's a party to it will be swinging by their neck from the yards." He drew a pull from his pipe and quieted while a sailor passed them on his way to the forward hatch leading below. "But, Jacky. You and I, we're the only pressed men working aloft. Figured I would let you in on details so you weren't left in the dark."

Jack shriveled his nose, he tried to work out just how he felt about a mutiny. On one hand, he would love to be free from the king's navy to press his own dreams on the high seas. On the other,

A Bloody Beginning

being a party to a mutiny would more than likely leave him a wanted man everywhere the empire of Britain held sway. That didn't sound like a promising future. "I don't know, Bob. It sounds dangerous, it sounds like a good way to get strung up like you said."

"It be happening with or without us, Jacky," Bob said in his usual growl of a voice. "Something the cap'n and his admiral didn't take into account when they shuttled aboard all these pressed men. If'n you count the souls from Salem Tide, and those from New York, we make up almost half the crew. That's a fair shot at taking the ship if the plan holds water. It's not a question of if. Only question is when."

"But, when do they plan to do this?" Jack asked.

Bob shook his head and frowned deep. "The two lubbers I spoke with thinks they already should have. By all accounts, that's an awful idea. This sort of thing has to be organized, planned out so the lobsterbacks don't have a chance to squash it. It'll take some doing, but I think its smartest to get her done before we wind up lining yardarms across from a French privateer and getting half the souls aboard blown to bits and pieces."

"That makes sense," Jack replied with a cautious look over his shoulder. "Bob, if this happens and fails, they won't distinguish one from another. They will hang us all. Every pressed man aboard from the colonies."

"Aye, Jack," Bob said with a knowing look and a long drag on his pipe. "That be true. That's why I

A Bloody Beginning

want to make sure they aren't too hasty about things."

"Haaaands to the braces!" a shout from the quarterdeck interrupted their covert conversation and the foremast suddenly became thick with sailors swarming to their tasks.

Jack followed Bowline Bob aft, his head filled with the notions of mutiny. As they made their way past the mainmast, while waisters prepared to haul on lines for a sail change, marines formed on the deck in preparation of a formal salute to a senior vessel should one be in port. Their muskets and bayonets glinted in the sunlight and gave Jack a menacing chill that penetrated his ribs right down to his core. He had seen the damage a volley of fire could do at close range, and there were more marines aboard Allegiance than had been in the streets of Boston that night.

"Deck! Deck! Signal flags!" a lookout called down from high in the foremast rigging.

Jack saw the quarterdeck come to life before his eyes. Officer hurried to the railing to catch a glimpse while a collection of expanding telescopes were aimed toward Bermuda. It was an exciting time. The ship was approaching land for the first time since they had sailed from New York. But, Jack felt numbed to the excitement. His inside felt as if they were being torn in a tug of war. Part of him wanted to carry on with the new life he had found himself in, but part of him was disgusted by the notion and still laid blame for what happened

A Bloody Beginning

to his parents on every man wearing the king's colors.

"Captain! Signal flags," a midshipman shouted out excitedly while exchanging his gaze between his telescope and a book held by his companion.

"Well, what do they say?" the captain asked.

"Enemy sighted. French frigate, southbound. Less than twelve hours," the midshipman's voice trailed away as he answered the captain's demand.

"Are you certain?" Captain Williams asked. He stepped forward toward the helm and began to examine the sails aloft with narrowed eyes.

"Yes, sir. Yes I am certain. Enemy sighted, French frigate, southbound, less than twelve hours," the midshipman repeated his previous reading.

"I have the ship!" Captain Williams snapped over the quarterdeck. "Hard over starboard, bring the wind to our starboard quarter. I want every damned scrap of infernal sail flying, now. Royals, t'gallants, tops, mains, studding sails, stay sails, everything we have." He looked to the lieutenants and midshipmen assembled on the quarterdeck. "Coax every knot of speed we can from her. Twelve hours could place her within our reach, but only if we sail hellbent for broke. I want extra lookouts fore and aft, marines to accompany the watch. See it done." The captain paced to the taff rail and back again, his hands clutched together behind his back and his chin tucked down in a posture of deep thought.

A Bloody Beginning

"He means to pursue her," Bob growled over Jack's shoulder. "Might mean a precious few days left to organize ourselves. Not enough time. Not by half."

Jack swallowed a lump threatening to form in his throat. "The ship passed by here a mere twelve hours ago?"

"Aye, that's what it sounds like," Bob grunted as he packed a fresh pinch of tobacco into his pipe. "Twelve hours at sea sounds like a lot, and it can be, but when you consider that the Frenchy is probably scouting around looking for merchant vessels to raid, she could be just over that horizon."

Allegiance lurched forward as canvas was piled onto every yard on every mast. Booms were run out, studding sails filled with wind and the ship picked up even more speed. The officers on the quarter deck seemed to be consumed with working out some problem and a midshipman stood dutifully by Captain Williams with a section of rolled charts in hand.

"The western passage around Hispaniola is the obvious choice. There are friendly port nearby where they can restock their supplies and sell the good they have pilfered," one of the officers said over the captain's shoulder. "I propose that is the course we should plot. If we cannot catch them there, then we can patrol those waters, they will surely turn up at some point."

Captain Williams grimaced and turned toward the other officer. "Do you seriously believe they

A Bloody Beginning

would make sail for the western passage? Are you mad? The most frequented seas between Bermuda and the Jamaican Colony. Not to mention Nassau being a stone's throw to the north. No, Mr. Harrison, they will not have sailed for the western passage. East of Hispaniola," he paused and pointed to a spot on the chart in the midshipman's shaking hand. "East of Hispaniola, where they are within reach of San Juan and a dozen other ports friendly to their monarch. We will plot our course in that direction and sail with all haste. Am I understood?"

The gathering of officers and midshipmen snapped to rigid attention. Several of them touched their hat brims and a few offered their verbal assent to the captain's unwavering commands. Without another parting word, the captain glowered over them and stormed off the quarterdeck to retire to his cabin. Jack watched from amidships while Bowline Bob fiddled with his pipe.

"It's sound reasonin' the cap'n has," Bob grunted as he got flame to take to his pipe bowl. "Whoever the frogs got skipperin' their frigate isn't like to be a green landsman. They got themselves a prime privateer. Thin line that is between privateer and pirate, a thin line indeed. A time or two through history that line has gotten so thin that privateer crews find themselves standing gallows for their final moments. But, they don't take lubbers to sea. Only prime sailormen and seasoned officers. That cap'n will give this one a fair challenge, I'd wager."

A Bloody Beginning

"Then, it is too late for our pressed friends from New York to spring their plan?" Jack asked swatting away a puff of Bob's pipe smoke before it stung his eyes.

"Aye, you heard 'im. He wants extra lookouts fore and aft, marines on every watch. This tub will be locked down tighter than the king's coin purse. It's no use fer now, lad," Bob grumbled with a wink. "But, that doesn't mean we can't use our time to visit with a few more 'o them pressed lads, get 'em to see things our way, eh?"

A rush of sailors crowded the foc'sle in preparation for a sail change and Jack wound his way through the crowd to avoid interfering in their work. He slipped through the fore hatch and found himself on the gun deck amid a group of lingering sailors off watch. The air was warm and close in the tight quarters and a conversation about the Bermuda triangle was in full swing. Jack tried to clear his thoughts from what Bowline Bob had just discussed with him, but the images of a bloody war on deck amongst the crew refused to lose their grip on his mind.

"The triangle, many a ship 'as lost its way down 'ere. It 'as to do with the ancients and their sea gods. The triangle is the abode of old Neptune 'isself, 'is watery throne lays fathoms below the surface on the sea bottom. That's where 'e summons 'is creatures. Krakens, cthulhu, giant squids and octopuses, sharks and whales as big as a damned first rate. That's not to mention the hidden reefs and shoals, many a ship 'as lost her

A Bloody Beginning

bottom in the dead 'o night down 'ere. There's fingers 'o rock out in the sea that's not marked on any charts. Rip a hull right open and bare the crew to the briny abyss," a salted old sea hand ranted to a gathering of wide-eyed landsmen. Jack lingered on the edge of the crowd, still considering the horrors that would await them should a mutiny kick off and fail. "The watch 'as to be particular sharp in the triangle. Lest the ole girl winds herself up on a reef or a rock in the dead 'o night, or maybe that frog privateer springs a trap on us all."

Solemn looks dominated the faces of the sailors in attendance. Jack found himself drawn from the thoughts of one horrid outcome to the possibilities of dozens. Visions of sea beasts, raging storms and hidden rocks ran through his mind. As if to confirm his fears, the old sea hand continued.

"Last time I sails south of Bermuda, we come into a storm like nothing I'd ever seen before. I been at sea me whole life, an' I never seen anything like it. Winds were so strong they ripped able seaman right outta the riggin'. The rains felt like daggers, an aloft there was naught me could do but take the abuse. Ship heeled over like she was a goin' t' turn keel up," the weathered old sailor said. He produced a wooden pipe similar to Bowline Bob's and clamped it between his teeth. "We lost more'n a score 'o good hands that night, an' spent the better part of a week getting our bearings after that. Rigging was all a mess, sails were torn all to hell. We had to replace to sections of the mast at sea. But the strangest part, was in

A Bloody Beginning

the middle 'o the blusterin' gale, everything settled dead calm. Winds stopped. Sky cleared. Strangest damned thing I ever saw."

"That's called a hurricane, you dolt," another rough voice cut in from the fringe of the crowd. All eyes turned and found the pinched scowl of Bitter End Bill, his back still covered in bandages from the flogging he had received just a day out of New York. "You been at sea yer whole life an' only seen one hurricane? Must not 'ave spent much time Caribbean side. Probably a deckhand scrubbing yer life away, ye lubber."

Tension electrified the deck as if Allegiance had been struck by lightning. The gathered sailors switched their gazes between the tale teller and Bitter End Bill. Both of the experienced sailors locked their stares. Neither of them showed any signs of altering course.

"What're ye sayin'? Ye saying I dern't know what I'm talking about? Ye poxy, bastard?" the tale teller snapped in a throaty growl.

Bitter End Bill glowered and chuffed a breath out through his nose. "Aye, ye lubber. I'm saying, this'n lot of landsmen probably has more sea skills than yer whole damned crew had. 'Cluding yer cap'n."

The tale teller rose to his feet and folded his stout sailor's arms over his chest. "I suppose yer just a born johnny tar then, eh? What makes you lord 'o the sea, can name a sailorman worthy er not?"

A Bloody Beginning

Bill scoffed and then spit on the deck in front of him. "Nothing, I just know a damned lubber when I see one. Ye shouldn't be passin' off yer yarns as fact to these green hands. They'll get the wrong ideas."

Jack couldn't work out what Bitter End Bill was up to. The tale teller hadn't done anything to him, as far as Jack knew. It almost seemed as if Bill was trying to provoke a scrap, for the sake of a scrap. He certainly wasn't mincing his words, and he showed no signs of altering from his chosen course.

"Yer should be fer choosin' yer words more carefully. But, I suppose we should all expect as much from a cowardly dog of a deserter like yerself," the tale teller hissed. His hand drifted dangerously close to the sailor's blade stowed in a sheath at his belt. He lowered his voice and sneered, "Maybe someone ought t' open yer up, so we can all see what yer yellow guts looks like."

Jack's guts tensed into knots as the two old sailors stared each other down. It seemed there was no diverting either party from an inevitable confrontation. Both men locked stares. The tale teller finally let his hand come to rest on the wooden handle of his seaman's knife.

"What's going on here?" howled an angry petty officer as he plowed his way into the crowd. "Make way you dogs!" He bulled past the fringe of the group and came to where Bill and the tale teller were staring one another down. "Ah. You two scally scrubs fancy a duster, do ye? Enough!

A Bloody Beginning

Go yer separate ways or I'll have the skin from yer backs! All of you! Disperse or I'll have yer holy stoning the decks until yer knees are black and bloody!" He fished a length of thin rope from his thick leather belt and dangled it in an open challenge. "Lay aft! Gun drills will be starting soon and that deck needs ter see a swab and squared away or the cap'n will have you lot running 'em through the paces until ye puke!"

CHAPTER 17

'H.M.S Allegiance'
30 March 1770
28 Degrees 54' N, 65 Degrees 34' W

  The bright peal of the watch bell sounding made its way through Jack's slumber and roused him into a groggy state of consciousness somewhere in between sleep and alert. He fought against the urge to remain in his hammock until one of his messmates roused him. Slop had to be roused almost every morning, but Jack didn't like to be thought of as a sluggard, so he forced himself to sit upright and crawl down from the precarious swinging sling of canvas. Allegiance's motion was gentle compared to the heavy pitch and sway they had endured further north. The deck was quiet. Only the hands going on watch were rousing from sleep to climb and stumble out

A Bloody Beginning

of their hammocks as a boatswain's mate stalked his way through the near total darkness with a shrouded lantern to light his path. He checked the gun carriages along his route, ensuring they were secured against the motion of the ship, and carefully threaded his way through a myriad of slung hammocks.

"Morning watch, up and on yer feet. Stow those hammocks and be on the deck smartly," the boatswain's mate rasped in a throaty whisper.

Jack rubbed the sleep from his eyes and unhitched both ends of his hanging bed. Aside from the few clothes that he owned, a square wooden plate and bent fork, the hammock was the only thing he could call his own. Even his grog cup was shared with Matsumoko since his friend's had been pilfered by some unknown party amongst the crew. He stowed away the rope and canvas hammock before tugging his knit watch cap over his head and down around his ears. The climate they were in was considerably warmer than the northern seas, but morning watch always had an edge of chill to it, and aloft, the winds could still get bitter. He made his way topside and mustered before the quarterdeck to receive any additional instructions for the beginning of their watch. A moment of private joy and celebration chased the fog of sleep from Jack's mind when the watch petty officer called on him for the mainmast lookout. The urge to smile overwhelmed his sensibilities and he looked forward to another glorious dawn high in the rigging. The sky was

A Bloody Beginning

still dark, with only the faintest glow along the eastern horizon. Glimmering stars littered the inky blackness above and Jack looked forward to picking out the constellations that he knew. Mornings at sea were his favorite time, the precious span of hours between the start of his watch and when the rest of the crew were summoned from slumber to begin the day's labors. The skies were dark, the winds were cold, but there was a peace about everything, a quiet solitude aloft in the rigging that Jack savored more fervently than a palatable meal or an extra tot in his grog ration.

The solitude of being a lookout had become a place of solace for Jack. Allegiance was an oaken fortress of hostility and tension floating on a sea of malice. With every passing day, a new grudge or malcontent was revealed. It seemed for every one of the pressed sailors from the colonies, there was a Brit sailor who took particular interest in tormenting them. With a crew split nearly down the middle between colonial pressed men and Brits pressed or otherwise, there was a near endless source of division and discontent aboard the frigate. Adding to the ever-rising tensions was the fact that Allegiance was stalking through the infamous Bermuda Triangle in search of a ship that almost every experienced had aboard agreed would be a deadly opponent in a confrontation. But, aloft, high above the deck with only the wind and the sail and his thoughts, Jack found time to think away from the scuffle and tyranny of life

A Bloody Beginning

aboard a Royal Navy ship. For most of his trick as a lookout, the closest sailor would be far enough away to require a shout. For two hours, his watch would consist of staring out over the ocean, searching for any sign of land or vessel and basking in the solitude and scenery. Sunrises were a treasured event, and marked the end of his peaceful vigil. Captain Williams had issued standing orders for all hands to be roused before full daylight, to ensure their readiness in the event of an enemy sighting. The crew would roust from their hammocks and prepare the ship to clear for action while Jack descended the shrouds to the maintop and spent the rest of his watch either making adjustments to sails with the rest of the maintop men, or practicing knots under the watchful eye of Mr. Skagg.

Jack watched the eastern horizon brighten. Long before the sun actually peered above the edge of the world a glow would begin to chase away the night. The stars would recede from their nighttime glory and hide as the sun's radiance beat its way higher into the sky. The black void of night retreated to a spectrum of colors while the seas grew more visible with every heartbeat. It was more than the break of day, to Jack dawn at sea was an event to behold, the moment of time he lived for, and looked forward to.

When the fourth bell of the morning watch sounded, Jack descended grudgingly to the maintop. He was met by Mr. Skagg who sized up the set and trim of the sails and judged them

A Bloody Beginning

fitting for the time being. He handed Jack a length of rope and set him to his training.

"A bowline fer starters, young Horner. Ye can't practice it enough. I want ye ter be able t' tie a bowline in yer sleep," said Mr. Skagg in his throaty rasp. "Tie it seven times and then practice yer clove hitch to the maintop railing. Tie those seven times, and then we'll see about teaching ye the rolling hitch."

Jack worked at the coarse length of rope, he tied a bowline and tested its hold before untying and then re-tying the knot over again. Mr. Skagg had him practice with knots, hitches and splicing every day when there was no sail changes to make. It was repetitive, but Jack found that learning the knots was satisfying. He was learning the craft of sailoring, and the more he could do with lines and cables, the better he would be. He was halfway through his fourth iteration of tying the clove hitch when the call came down from the foretop watchman up on the top-gallant mast.

"Sail ho!" the lookout bellowed loud for all to hear.

Sailors hurried to the rails, bumping and knocking each other for the better view. Jack tried to see what the lookout had spotted, but his view was obscured by the taut form of foremast sails flying full of wind in front of him.

"Where away?" shouted back the officer of the watch as he stormed forward of the quarterdeck with a telescope in hand.

A Bloody Beginning

"Single point off the bow! Barely visible, maybe just her t'gallants, but it looks like three masts," the lookout shouted back toward the deck.

A flutter entered Jack's chest. It sped his heartbeat and caused his head to go swimming with thoughts in rapid fire. There was a palpable excitement from the crew, but in the whole vastness of the great ocean, had they really found their French privateer? He untied his clove hitch and handed back the length of rope to Mr. Skagg, knowing that the orders for more sail were coming soon. A tinny ring of orders confirmed his prediction and the watch officer ordered studding sails to be boomed out on the main and topsail yards. Allegiance sprung into action. The rigging became alive with sailors move up and down the shrouds, the tightropes of both main yards and topsail yards filled with shuffling feet as they moved into position to fly more canvas. The captain's prize was on the horizon and no man dared be the one who dawdled and risk robbing him of it.

With the booms extended and all sails stretched and sheeted home, Jack finally chanced a glance toward the quarterdeck. A line of officers and midshipmen packed the space between helm and lee rail while only a pair of men in officer coats, the captain being one of them, occupied the space toward the windward side of the ship. Captain Williams looked every bit as sharp as the day he had departed Allegiance for the admiral's flagship in New York Harbor. His eyes scanned aloft,

A Bloody Beginning

presumably taking in the state of their sails and looking for any shortfalls. He nodded, almost imperceptibly and uttered something to the lieutenant standing nearby before departing the quarter deck. He marched forward at a brisk pace with a collapsible telescope in hand and his three-cornered hat canted nearly to the tops of his eyebrows. The last bell of Jack's watch tolled its call to relieve the hands, but his focus remained locked onto Captain Williams.

"Fancy a look?" Mr. Skagg asked over Jack's shoulder.

Jack turned and found the petty officer grasping the shrouds leading up to the top-gallant mast. "Aye, but I haven't a telescope."

Mr. Skagg smiled, revealing a set of rotten, crooked teeth. "Of course, ye don't, yer a pressed man. The greenest ordinary seaman aboard. I have one. I'll let yer look through it from aloft. Maybe we can see somethin' the cap'n can't."

The appeal of being the first to discover something outstretched Jack's desire to go below and seek out the company of his friend Matsumoko. Together, they would most likely spend the rest of the morning staring from the foc'sl before getting cornered into doing some laborious task or another. But, sailors in the tops almost never got pulled for the back breaking details. It stung Jack a little, to shun his friend on deck for a view from on high, but he figured Matsumoko would understand. It would only be for a little while.

A Bloody Beginning

Jack followed Mr. Skagg up the shrouds to where the top-gallant yard intersected with the mast. The sun was now beating its way higher into the sky, having left the horizon for its march toward its lofty noon perch. The winds were steady from the northwest and much warmer than Jack had felt before. His hands were used to the coarse ropes, and his arms had been toned by weeks of hard use. The climb felt as casual as if he were walking a set of stairs, or strolling the length of the pier in Boston. It struck Jack as he reached the top end of the shrouds, that to a sailor on deck, he might almost appear as if he belonged in the rigging, like a real sailor.

"There," Mr. Skagg noted as he situated himself across from Jack next to the thickness of the mast. "There she is, hull up too. Looks like we are gaining on her."

Jack frowned deep at Mr. Skagg as he settled himself on the yard. "Hull up?" he asked.

Another smile broke across the petty officer's face. "You are green as the pine, aren't ye lad? Hull up, meaning we can see the bulk of the ship, not just her masts. Lookouts call her hull down when the horizon obstructs the view. Her sails are showing, but not the ship itself," he said while pointing out over the bow of Allegiance. "See there, we can see the ship. She's hull up."

"Ah, I see," Jack said with a sheepish voice. He felt a flush of embarrassment creeping up his neck and turning his face red. "How long do you think before we have her in range?"

A Bloody Beginning

Mr. Skagg nodded and stared pensively toward the vessel out ahead of them. "I'd imagine that's just what the cap'n is figuring right now." He scratched at his patchy beard and glowered for a moment. "I'd say we should be drawing up on them in a matter of hours, if they don't turn back at us. But, the more likely course is that their cap'n will fly all sail and make a run fer it."

Jack kept his stare locked across the sea gap to the ship they were sailing toward. "Why would he do that? Everyone has been carrying on about being outmatched."

"Aye, and if he is a forty-four, they are right. But only in a manner. What they means to say is we are outgunned, least by count of the cannons, and we are. But, outmatched? Never. Allegiance is a frigate, fast, maneuverable, and we carry a few cannons ourselves, Jack. Cap'n Williams will have them by the belt buckle. They may have more guns than we do, but he has our gun crews doing firing times that give the best crews I've served with a run. It's not always the number of guns ye have, but how fast ye can keep firing the bloody things," Mr. Skagg said with his raspy voice carrying in the wind. "And as far as being outmatched? I've yet to see a finer mind than the cap'n's fer seamanship. He'll whip them frogs with pure seamanship. Ye watch, young Horner. It's cunning, he'll whip 'em with cunning."

Mr. Skagg withdrew a conical brass telescope and expanded the instrument to its full length. He held it up and awkwardly gazed through the lens while Jack looked on in anticipation. To the naked eye, he could see the form of the ship, but there was no fine detail to be revealed through the distance, just the form of a ship roughly the same in size as Allegiance.

"She's a frigate alright," Mr. Skagg growled. "Looks like they are flying the French colors too. Damned easy to confuse with a white flag iff'n ye ask me."

"Is it Saber?" Jack asked as he squinted his eyes to try and get a better look.

Mr. Skaggs remained silent for a long pause while he struggled to keep the telescope steady. "Hard sayin' this far out, Horner. But, a frigate, flying a French flag, and after the sighting reported by Bermuda. I'd say that is our French lady."

Jack received the telescope as Mr. Skaggs handed it over to him and mimicked the posture the petty officer had assumed to look through it. His first look revealed nothing but sun sparkles on bluish gray sea. He adjusted his hold slightly and looked back through the instrument. The image was like nothing Jack had seen before, he marveled at the closeness with which he was looking at a ship that was sailing miles in front of them.

"It looks only half the distance it truly is with this," Jack said.

"Aye, that's the point, Horner," Mr. Skagg replied. "Ye should get a chance to look with the cap'n's glass. His is far finer than this. He can

A Bloody Beginning

probably pick out how many men they have in their rigging right now. In fact, I wouldn't be surprised if he already had a count in the time it took us to climb aloft."

"So, you think the French captain will run, despite his ship's advantage in number of guns?" Jack pressed his question as he examined the slightly distorted image of the ship through the telescope.

"That's my guess," Mr. Skagg answered. "We have the weather gauge, for now at least. Things may change if he runs for warmer latitudes. The westerlies will be the predominate winds down there and he may chance running upwind under the cover of dark. Cap'n Williams has the upper hand right as we sail, but that can change."

Jack lowered the telescope. "Weather gauge?"

Mr. Skagg shook his head. "I ought have you tie up a special knot just fer yerself, Horner. Rid us all of yer infernal lubberly questions. The weather gauge, the wind, we have the advantage of wind on them. Means we can sail and maneuver while remaining upwind of her. That's important when it comes to close battle with an enemy ship."

Jack clenched his teeth and focused through the telescope onto the French ship. He could see movement at the lee rail, and some movement in the rigging. A spread of canvas became visible to her windward side as studding sails were boomed out to starboard.

"They're flying more canvas. Looks like their captain wants to run for it," Jack said before lowering the telescope and handing it back to Mr. Skagg.

The petty officer peered through for a long moment. "So it does," he paused and lowered the scope, "another look?"

Jack shook his head. He'd seen enough. The figure of the ship, while distorted, had revealed a long row of dark squares on the side of her hull, squares that could only be gun ports. He hadn't counted them, but by his figuring, the rumors of her being a forty-four gun ship had to be true. "I think I'll head down, it's probably going to be a long day," he said.

Mr. Skagg nodded. "Aye, a long day indeed, and an even longer night."

"Have one of the long nine-pounder guns hauled up and rigged on the bow for a chase gun. We should be close enough to range them in three to four hours if the wind holds," Captain Williams rattled off orders to a midshipman as he passed the main shrouds on his way back to the quarterdeck. "Check the aft braces on the mizzen, they look slack to my eye, and get some idle hands to stand the weather rail. She has more speed to offer, and I won't be bested by a Frenchman. Not today!"

"Aye aye, sir," the midshipman snapped to rigid attention and replied as Captain Williams paced

A Bloody Beginning

by at urgent speed. "Long nine to the bow, after braces on the mizzen and idle hands to the weather rail."

Jack eased himself to the deck from the main shrouds after the captain had passed. He knuckled his forehead and gave way to the ship's commander. "Good morning, sir," he said in his best approximation of formality.

"A good morning indeed," Captain Williams replied with a rare smile crossing his tight drawn features. "Perhaps you and your swordsman friend will get a chance to see the enemy up close today, eh?"

Jack nodded at the sentiment, not sure just how he should respond. The moment passed as the captain strutted back to the quarterdeck and he was left with a midshipman he did not know, and Mr. Skagg.

"Well, you two will do," the midshipman turned and addressed Jack and the petty officer. "Rig up a hoist line to the foremast head blocks so we can transfer one of the long nines on deck to the bow. Take idle hands from the off watches, don't use any of the men on watch at this time." He turned and paced off to aft weather hatch with a flush on his face.

Mr. Skagg growled and shot Jack an unsettling look. "That ninny, I was hoping to visit the mate's berthing fer a quick nip at a bottle I've got tucked away," he growled and then scratched at the back of his head. "Nerves could certainly stand fer a taste, if just a taste. Oh well, there's nothing fer it.

A Bloody Beginning

Let's get to it, Horner. Fetch us a hoist line from the locker, get your messmates to help. That fat one seemed to be pretty handy hauling heavy line, make sure he lends a hand."

Jack found his messmates below deck settling into their after-watch routine. He knew that they were waiting for the morning meal and he was hesitant to break the news that they were being called for a work detail on his account. Slop took it the hardest, his shoulders slumped forward and his head rode low like the bow of a ship that had taken on too much in its hold. Matsumoko and John Long offered no resistance, but Jack could tell they weren't overjoyed at delaying their vittles either.

"We need to fetch a heavy tackle line from the locker and heave it up on deck, the captain wants a nine-pounder moved up to the bow to serve as a chase gun," he said.

"This bodes ill, Jack. You heard what Bob said. A forty-four gun ship. We'll be outgunned from the drop, and that's before we even pull alongside. We're pressed men, half of us, do you think we'll stack up against a privateer crew? They make their living doing this sort of thing," Slop said with a groan. "That captain will line us up as shields for his Brit sailors sooner than see us go as free men. He'd like to watch us all die. I'm sure of it. I'd rather not march right behind him until he steps to the side and lets us be blown to bits."

Jack felt his temper flare. Not that what Slop was saying wasn't true, some of it was, but that he

A Bloody Beginning

was putting Jack in the position of insisting they follow the orders of Mr. Skagg. "Fine, Slop. We will haul the line up ourselves, and when the mate asks where our fat messmate is, we'll tell him you refused work."

"You wouldn't," Slop snapped. His face went white at first, then flushed an angry red.

Jack drew in a deliberate breath through his nostrils and tensed his arms. "Is that not what you are doing?"

The large young man dipped his brow and shook his head. "I knew you'd act different to us, since they made you an ordinary seaman and you're up in the riggings and all. It's almost like you think you're better. You tell the mate what you want. But, you'll look a fool when I carry up twice the tackle line you can."

Jack led the group down to the cable stowage and picked the heaviest line he could. The cannon barrels weighed hundreds of pounds, not to mention the carriage they sat on, it would take a hefty line and all the strength they could muster to move the piece. When they finally struggled to the deck with the massive rope, all hands involved were working through a thin layer of sweat. The breeze on deck felt good and the sun was rising still higher toward the noon position. Jack looked and figured it to be ten in the morning. His estimation was soon proved by the sounding of the watch bell.

Mr. Skagg rigged the tackle line while a pair of top men hoisted the other end up and through a

A Bloody Beginning

head block on the foremast. A pair of secondary lines were rigged to prevent the payload from falling in the case that the main hoist should fail, and a guide line was attached to the gun carriage to control the heavy load from spinning as it was lifted. Jack eased into place by his messmates around the capstan and prepared to throw his back in the work.

"Aye, Jack," Mr. Skagg said with a crooked grin, "ye can do hard laboring if ye wants, but I was going to have ye man the guide line."

Jack shook his head and cuffed the sleeves of his loose-fitting seaman's shirt. "Nay, Mr. Skagg. My messmates are laboring, I'll heave alongside them."

"Suit yerself young Horner," Mr. Skagg rasped as the wind kicked up in a gust. He turned and checked over the scene of their work to ensure the deck was clear before barking out commands. "Alright, put yer backs into it, Give me twelve drops on the pawls and we'll see where we're at!"

It took everything Jack and his messmates had, but by the time the capstan pawls had clunked down for the twelfth time the cannon was suspended just over a foot above the deck. Another crew set to dragging the heavy gun forward with use of another set of rope and tackle, which necessitated Jack and his mates to lower the capstan in order to give slack. It was twice as arduous as the lift. The men had to heave themselves against the capstan bars just enough to free the pressure off the pawl, then back off slowly

A Bloody Beginning

to give slack to the hoisting cable. When the gun was finally set in place, every soul who had been laboring at the capstan looked ready to collapse.

"Mr. Jacobs, if you please. Assemble a gun crew and get this piece ready for firing," Captain Williams' voice struck a pang of lightning into Jack's blood. He turned from where he had been recovering his breath at the capstan bars and found the hard features of the captain staring directly at him. "This lot should do. See to the gunnery yourself, your mates will be busy below preparing the gun deck."

Mr. Jacobs, a fleshy cheeked man with pasty complexion and chop sideburns as thick as some of the petty officer's knuckled the brim of his hat and nodded his assent. "Aye, sir. We'll have her ready to range inside of three minutes, sir."

"Very well," the captain replied. "I'll leave you to it then." He strutted aft toward the quarterdeck without another word.

Jack felt a crushing weight of despair creeping into his chest as he stole a glance over the bow rail where the cannon had been laid. The enemy ship was much closer now, and the sun had passed its noon position to begin its course down to the western horizon. They would be within reach of the captain's quarry by nightfall.

CHAPTER 18

'H.M.S Allegiance'
30 March 1770
27 Degrees 54' N, 65 Degrees 13' W

"Fire!" Captain Williams snarled in the wind as Allegiance's bow rose from the break of a wave. Mr. Jacobs pulled the gun's firing lanyard himself and the long-barreled nine-pounder cannon roared its report and shuddered violently with recoil. Jack, Matsumoko, Slop and John Long sprang into action to reload the chase gun. They followed the same process they would below on the gun deck, except here they had the ship's gunner standing over their shoulders and the ship's captain looming large over all. Jack swabbed the bore just before Matsumoko loaded the powder charge, he had to fight against the

A Bloody Beginning

urge to look up and see if the shot had any effect on the enemy.

"Just shy of their stern, sir," Mr. Jacobs reported. "And that's with the added elevation from the pitch of the ship."

Captain Williams sucked at his teeth for a long moment as Jack was ramming down the shot Matsumoko had loaded. "Quite shorter than I had hoped. I have to say, I estimated them closer than that," he said.

Jack heard his footsteps begin to pace rail to rail on the foc'sl as he rammed the top wad down over the shot. He promptly stowed the ramrod and all hands on the gun crew set to heaving the piece forward for the next shot. His heart pounded in his chest from the combination of fear, exhilaration and exertion. His ears rang from the thunderous boom of the cannon, and his chest swelled with pride at the nod of approval from the ship's gunner as the crew finished heaving the piece forward.

"Well done, lads," Mr. Jacobs said under his breath as he inspected the firing pan and looked down the side of the gun's long barrel.

"Either they are opening the gap on us, or we had a short charge in the cannon," Captain Williams said as he paced between rails with his arms folded tight in front of his chest. "We will try another ranging shot in an hour." He turned and examined the sails aloft with a critical eye. "We are losing wind from the foretop, see to it that it is trimmed, Mr. Higgsby."

A Bloody Beginning

"Aye, sir," a nearby midshipman knuckled the brim of his hat before turning aft to relay the order.

"And idle hands to the weather rail, I believe I had already given that command, did I not?" the captain hissed.

"You did, sir. I will see to it, straight away, sir," Mr. Higgsby replied with a pitch to his voice. He bolted aft in as fast a pace as a dignified midshipman could carry without being chastised by a senior officer for running.

Captain Williams turned his gaze from the sails toward the sun and then forward to the ship that was somehow slipping further away. "Damn. Damn it all. I should have them by the hip! Every stitch of canvas flying..." His voice trailed away as he extended his telescope and leaned next to the base of the bowsprit. He looked through the instrument for a long moment, as still as a statue despite the pitching of the bow. "Cheeky bastard. He's flying royals and boomed out studding sails from his top gallants. Can't say I have ever seen that. But, he is running hell bent for broke, and risking every mast he has to outrun us." He collapsed the telescope and looked directly at Jack. "Because he knows in a straight away fight we will batter him with superior gunnery. I'll bet we can fire three broadsides to a single of theirs. They're running scared, lad, and they should be. The king's colors rule the waves of this world, and I don't speak of that pompous fool from France."

A Bloody Beginning

Unsure of how to respond, Jack nodded and knuckled his forehead. Secretly, he hoped that the French ship would evade them and slip away into the night, never to be seen again. But, somewhere deep down he knew it couldn't work that way. If they lost the ship, it could easily ambush them later. Hopelessness crept into the corners of his mind. Every scenario he imagined seemed to end with him and all his friends being blown into shards or drowned in the sea.

The captain resumed his pacing with a glowering expression on his face. He stalked from one side of the bow to the other, casting intense glares toward the French ship every few steps and grumbling under his breath. He came to a sudden stop and turned to a nearby petty officer. "Give my compliments to Mr. Sifton, and let him know I would like for him to report to the foc'sl. Smartly, if you please," he said in a voice edged by resolve.

Jack sensed a decision had been made. He could almost feel them drawing closer to the enemy ship as the captain resumed his pacing. He chanced a look back at the captain as the gaunt faced officer paced behind their bow chaser.

"Sixty casks of water, twenty-eight barrels of rum, thirty-two barrels of ale. An anchor we can part with, half a dozen useless other items of considerable weight…" his voice trailed into the wind. Whatever he was planning, Jack had a feeling that his ruminating meant that it would be an unpopular decision.

A Bloody Beginning

Footfalls announced the arrival of Lieutenant Sifton. Jack looked over his shoulder and saw the two officers come face to face, the lieutenant briskly touched the brim of his hat as he reported to the captain.

"Reporting as ordered, sir," Lieutenant Sifton said.

Captain Williams nodded brusquely. "Mr. Sifton, by my figures, we should have approximately fifteen casks of fresh water, eighteen barrels of rum, ten barrels of ale, and one anchor that we can part with to lighten our burden."

"Sir?" the lieutenant's face narrowed in a tight frown of confusion.

"Did I stutter, Mr. Sifton? Fifteen casks of water, eighteen barrels of rum, ten of ale and one anchor. See to it that they are jettisoned over the side, and be quick about it. I would say we could stand to lose a few of the cannons, but seeing as how we are already outnumbered in guns I will part with any more. If there are any other items of considerable weight that you deem unnecessary, see that they are also thrown overboard. Furniture, wood stoves, whatever we can do to gain a few more knots." He paused for a moment while spray from a breaking wave settled over the bow of Allegiance. "I say, if we cannot coax a little more speed from her, I fear what sunset will bring. I don't want to lose sight of her."

Lieutenant Sifton nodded, a tight, grim look on his face. "Aye, sir. I'll see it done."

A Bloody Beginning

Jack turned forward as the captain resumed his pacing, not wanting to be found paying attention to the officer's exchange. He traded concerned looks with Matsumoko before looking out over the barrel of the bow chaser. The French ship did seem to be shrinking in size as it continued to open the gap of sea separating the two ships.

"Tossing off rum, that won't settle well with the crew if we run short of grog rations later," John Long muttered.

"Shut it," Jack snapped with a hiss. "If he hears you griping it'll be irons and the cat for you!"

"He's right," Mr. Jacobs growled.

Jack and Matsumoko exchanged another look, this one wide eyed and fearful for their friend John.

"Tipping the rum, the water, and some other such may buy us more speed, but the consequences may be dire," the ship's gunner muttered. He lowered his voice down to a whisper, "But, your friend is right too, young man. Don't let the captain hear your gripes or it will be the cat for you."

Jack's stomach knotted. Hearing the confirmation from an experienced sailor solidified his suspicions. The captain would have his confrontation, consequence be damned. Even through the distance, the French ship loomed a little larger. The prospect of sailing for days or weeks with a short supply of water crossed through Jack's thoughts. He cared less about the rum than most of the other sailors, and naught for

A Bloody Beginning

the anchor, the ship had two anyway and he had never understood exactly why. But fresh water running low could lead to desperate circumstances whether they bested the French privateer or not.

"Mr. Jacobs, another ranging round, if you please. Maximum elevation," Captain Williams said without so much as a look in the gun crew's direction.

"Aye, sir," Mr. Jacobs replied, "Maximum elevation." He glanced over the sides of the chase gun carriage to ensure all limbs and digits were clear before giving the firing lanyard a stout tug and sending a thunderous roar booming out over the sea. A cloud of smoke and embers belched from the cannon's muzzle as the gun carriage recoiled against the tackles restraining it. Without hesitation, or a wasted second looking for the effect of the shot, Jack and his messmates set to work on reloading the spent cannon as fast as they could. Swab, powder, ram, wad, ram, shot, ram, wad, ram, every step was met with the next motion timed so well that it almost felt to Jack like a dance. There was no wasted movements, no wasted effort. They worked in near perfect synchrony until Mr. Jacobs hunched over the gun as it seated forward in its firing position and inspected the firing pan. With a long metal spike, he pierced the powder bag and pulled some of the coarse powder onto the brass firing pan.

He poured a small amount of fine powder into the pan from a fist sized leather case kept in his belt

A Bloody Beginning

and cocked the firing mechanism. "Gun ready, captain," he reported.

Captain Williams ceased his pacing and looked over the chase gun crew. His features were as hard as iron, gaunt from years of abstention and stress, and they focused right onto Jack. "That was an admirable reload time for a long-barreled nine-pounder gun," he said. His gaze shifted over each man of the gun crew. "Pressed men, all of you, am I correct?"

Jack held his tongue for a long moment until he realized that the captain was staring a hole into him. He expected an answer. "Aye, sir. Matsumoko and I are from Salem Tide, the uh, whaling fleet tender, sir," Jack said in as steady a voice as he could muster.

"You are Allegiance men now, son, and I couldn't be prouder. Fine work at the gun, a fine job indeed. But, don't be too hasty with your swab when you douse the barrel. Take care with it, you don't want a stubborn ember to ignite that powder charge prematurely," He paused and leaned forward. "I believe you were present for the incident on the gun deck, were you not?"

Jack nodded and swallowed hard as he remembered the carnage that had resulted from the recoil of the gun carriage. "I was, sir. We were."

Captain Williams nodded and grimaced. "Nasty bit of business that was, and so completely unnecessary. It would be a shame to repeat it on account of a rushed swab. Take your time and do it right, you lads have the process down. All that is

A Bloody Beginning

left is to maintain your heads under fire and keep that gun firing as quickly as you can load and run it out."

The sound of a splash broke into their conversation. Jack thought of asking the captain why he would jettison so much valuable cargo, but decided better of it. He seemed to be on good standing with the man, and desired to keep it that way.

"Hurry up, you rotten dogs! Cap'n wants this here off so we can catch that Frenchy. Get to it!" one of the boatswain's mates croaked in a crackled gravelly voice. "Hand over hand, make a chain and get this old girl lean for the chase!"

Another splash sounded, and shouts echoed around the main deck as the hands took up the main deck's gratings to expose the decks below. A hoist was rigged and the aft capstan manned with a half dozen seamen to lift a net with casks of fresh water and barrels of rum and ale. Another working party had set to hoisting the longboats over the side in preparation for their engagement with the French privateer. Jack watched the preparations being made in a series of stolen glances over his shoulder. He dared not stare while they worked, lest a, angry mate catch his wandering eyes and replace him on the gun crew with a man from the working details. In addition to the casks and barrels the captain had ordered the crew threw over two iron wood stoves, a mess of pots and a large vat from the galley, two slab tables from the officer's mess, and a desk from

A Bloody Beginning

their wardroom. Captain Williams abandoned his pacing on the foc'sl to return to the quarterdeck while the crew mercilessly jettisoned everything they could get their hands on. Foodstuffs, the remaining water, powder and ammunition seemed to be the only items safe from their efforts as the makeshift tables the crew used for mess and all manner of other items were thrown overboard. The soundings continued, with every hand listening keenly for the leadsman's readings.

"Fourteen knots!" a quartermaster's mate shouted over the deck as the leadsman seized his line for the measurement. A cheer erupted all across the deck. Allegiance wasn't just sailing, she was flying.

"Have the working parties turn to and stand along the weather rail," Captain Williams ordered as the cheers died away. "Mr. Tullsby, hands aloft to make sail. Rig the royals and t'gallant studding sails. Fourteen knots is good, but sixteen is what I want. Our adversary is flying every manner of canvas, with the shed weight, if we fly ours, she won't outrun us."

Allegiance's shrouds filled with sailors and soon her masts were loaded with even more canvas plying her forward under fair winds. The pitching action of the ship became more exaggerated, and with every surge forward a spray of sea drifted over the bow and misted the foc'sl. Jack watched with a heavy sense of dread as the ship on the horizon stopped shrinking into the distance and began to grow while they stalked nearer with

A Bloody Beginning

every passing moment. Captain Williams had pulled all the stops and demonstrated there were few lengths he would not go to in order to seize his objective. Conversation among the sailors on deck ranged from how quickly the French privateer would strike their colors, to how they intended to spend their share of the prize money.

"A privateer," one sailor fresh out of the shrouds ranted. "She'll be loaded with the spoils of merchantmen from the Caribbean and Mediterranean. Casks of dark rum, and bolts of silk and velvet, ivory, and spices! More'n a year's wages fer every man!"

"She's Boston built, according to the first l'tenant," another sailor chimed in, "navy won't let that one pass. They'll buy her up fer sure! Can you imagine? Our shares will probably be among the biggest the crown has paid out in decades."

"The pubs of Kingston won't know what hit them!" a third voice bellowed, ushering a roar of raucous laughter from every sailor nearby. The roar grew more intense when the sailor shouted louder, "The bawdy houses neither!"

Allegiance surged forward and crested over a wave. A fine mist of seawater settled over the deck forward of the foremast and Jack couldn't help but smile at the antics of the sailors. Their nerves were as tight as a fiddle string as they stalked ever closer to the French privateer. Nervous laughter, ribald jokes and bold statements of battle prowess simmered over the deck as they plunged forward toward sure combat. The French vessel had gone

A Bloody Beginning

from just out of cannon range to just within sight and was now steadily getting closer as Allegiance pressed on with a lightened burden and every sail they could fly bent to the wind. The nervous chatter continued among the idle hands who all stood at the weather side of the ship in an effort to coax more speed.

"Sixteen knots!" the leadsman cried out in stunned disbelief. His shout carried over the deck and ushered forth a new wave of cheers and insults hurled into the sea gap between them and their target.

"Silence on deck! Silence fore and aft!" Captain Williams voice bellowed out over the din of celebration. "We will close this gap and then I want every hand to quarters." He stormed off the quarterdeck and paced the weather rail forward as sailors brought knuckle to forehead at his passing. He crossed onto the foc'sl and extended his telescope in a smooth and deliberate stroke before leaning against the base of the bowsprit. He held the instrument up to one eye and looked through it for what felt like an eternity to Jack. It was a much nicer telescope than the one Mr. Skagg had let him gaze through. "Faster than she's ever sailed before and we will still be lucky to catch her by sunset. Damn the luck," Captain Williams cursed as he looked onward through his telescope. He withdrew his eye for a moment and shot a glance over to Jack and the rest of the chase gun crew. "You lads keep a sharp eye on her. She will no doubt douse her lights if we don't catch her by

A Bloody Beginning

nightfall and it will take keen eyes to keep tabs on her in the dark. We cannot lose her, not when we have her by the hip."

Jack felt the weight of what he knew was coming. He looked at each of his messmates. Matsumoko had become his closest friend in the world, closer by far than Tom in Boston. Jack solemnly hoped that he would make it through this trial unscathed. He hoped they all would, though he knew how far fetched those hopes were. Slop leaned over the barrel of the nine pounder chase cannon and looked down the slightly conical iron length. He was young too, almost as young as Jack. The crew aboard Allegiance had not gone easy on him, but over the course of their weeks at sea, he had proved himself to an extent that their harassment had waned. John Long stood at the rear of the gun carriage, his arms folded across his midsection as if to cradle some pain in his gut. The dark haired young man was quiet to a fault, but learned quickly and snapped to every task given to him. Jack wondered about his origins and decided that when he next got a chance, he would ask John about what his life was before being a pressed man in the king's navy.

The sun sank through the course of the afternoon watch and continued its downward fall to the western horizon through the beginning of the first dog-watch. Jack and his messmates remained huddled around the chase gun while Allegiance drew closer to the privateer at a

A Bloody Beginning

frustratingly slow rate despite the speed they had achieved. Captain Williams had resumed pacing the foc'sl and scowling over the bow at their enemy every few laps. It was apparent to all aboard that they would not catch their prey before nightfall. But, Jack could see the steely determination in the captain's glare. He would not relent. His eyes narrowed as he cast scowling looks forward at the fleeing enemy.

"Mr. Jacobs, fire a ranging shot, if you please," Captain Williams grumbled as he stalked behind the chase gun.

"Aye, sir. A single round for range," Mr. Jacobs replied before turning to Jack and the rest of the gun crew. "Clear away lads, and be at the ready to reload."

The ship's gunner squatted slightly to look directly over the top of the iron cannon. He squinted one eye closed and looked for a heartbeat longer before reaching under the breech of the gun and pivoting the elevation swivel to the maximum position. With a nod of satisfaction, he checked the sides of the gun carriage one more time and then tugged at the firing lanyard. Jack was prepared for the explosion of sound and spewing cloud of smoke, he tucked his chin to his chest and plugged his ears with his fingers. The concussion of the blast still ripped right through him, it pressed his baggy sailor's rig to his skin and seemed to pry some of the air from his lungs. As acrid smoke swill wafted through the salty sea breeze, Jack and his mates sprang into action.

A Bloody Beginning

"Damn!" Captain Williams growled, a note of exasperation creeping into the edges of his voice. "Still short by at least two cables. Confound it! They won't be in range before nightfall."

"Unless something slows them, sir," Lieutenant Sifton added over the captain's shoulder. "We can keep firing on them after darkness falls. I'll see to the first watch myself. We won't lose them."

Captain Williams paused and drew a long breath, releasing it in a slow sigh that gave Jack a chill to hear. "We'll keep as close a watch as we can on them. My fear is that they will come about on us in the night and let us sail right past them. I don't want to surrender the day today and wake up as their prey tomorrow." He clenched his fist around the body of his brass telescope. "If only we could gain some more speed on them."

"I'm afraid the only thing we could do to shed more weight, sir, is drop cannons," Lieutenant Sifton replied with a helpless shrug. "Or perhaps, crewmen."

"Now, there's an idea," the captain stated flatly. He looked down at Jack and his messmates before breaking his reserve with a broad smile. "Never fear, lads. I wouldn't abandon my men to the cold sea for any prize."

A streak of relief ran through Jack. For the last several hours he had been wondering if the captain would be maddened by the chase and do something so rash as set a crew of men into a longboat, or worse, jettison them like so much of the cargo already tossed adrift.

A Bloody Beginning

"A sharp watch, lieutenant. If they give any sign of coming about, match their turn and loose the guns as they bear. That should dissuade them. In the meantime, let's stand the men down and pipe them to their supper. I can't imagine any will rest soundly tonight, the least we can do is make sure that they are well fed," Captain Williams ordered.

"Aye, sir," Lieutenant Sifton answered, "sharp is the word."

"Have supper brought up for this lot," the captain motioned to Jack and his mates. "But they are not to turn to. I want these lads on the chase gun until such a time as we need them below on the gun deck."

Without thought, Jack spoke out of turn. "When will that be, sir?" he asked.

Captain Williams looked taken aback by the interruption, and Jack immediately cursed his quick tongue and slow mind. "If there is any doubt, lad, keep to the chase gun. But, I imagine there will be none if it comes to launching broadsides, eh?"

Jack nodded and knuckled his forehead, in an effort to somehow make up for his impropriety. "Aye, sir. We won't let ye down, sir."

"It never crossed my mind, lad," the captain replied before departing the foc'sl and heading for his cabin. He called over his shoulder to Lieutenant Sifton, "Send for me if there are any developments."

The lieutenant turned on Jack when the captain was out of earshot. "Are you mad, boy? Hands

A Bloody Beginning

don't address the captain unless they are directly spoken to! You ought know that!"

"Apologies, sir," Jack said with a humbled tone. "Don't know what came over me. I just don't want to let the crew or my shipmates down."

Bells signaling the mid point of the first dog-watch sounded. The sun was beginning to dip below the horizon, its fiery orb breaking the gray plane where the sea met the sky. Light blue was giving to golden hues of yellow and orange as if lit on fire. Posts changed throughout the watch, top men moved in between the yards and the deck to take up a different task for the last two hours of their watch. Supper was a bland affair, a mug of stale, warm small beer and two hunks of hard ship's biscuit. It would be a cold supper for all aboard, officers included. Jack wondered how long that would continue, as he remembered the sight of iron stoves being thrown overboard. He sipped at the bitter beer in his cup and tried to break the hard bread into manageable chunks so he could eat without fear of breaking teeth.

"Cold vittles," Bowline Bob's voice broke Jack's vigil over his supper. "It's enough to dampen even the stoutest sailorman's spirits. Not to mention tossin' off all that rum, means we're like to get grog rations cut down soon. Maybe even go without."

Jack looked up and found his trusty mentor standing behind the chase gun, his own mug and a handful of ship's biscuit in his grasp. "What are

A Bloody Beginning

you doing? All the other idle hands turned to supper."

"Aye, gatherin' their supper they are, but eating on deck at the weather rail they'll be. Cap'n wants every bit 'o speed he can gain. Not sure if'n you noticed, but we had to toss off just about ever'thing that wasn't tied down. He's got a mad on fer this Frenchman. We'll be lining up across from them, yardarm ter yardarm, bet yer cold vittles and watered down grog on it." He turned and knuckled his forehead as Lieutenant Sifton brought back his own plate of cold food. "Evenin', sir."

The lieutenant nodded before sipping at his mug. "Finish your supper, lads. We will fire another ranging shot before we lose the daylight."

Jack noted how much of the sun had drifted below the horizon. Less than half of the bright sphere was now visible. He finished the last of his supper and exchanged looks with his messmates while Lieutenant Sifton hovered over them. The French ship was close now, closer than it had been all afternoon. Jack cast a look toward Bowline Bob. "Do you think she is within our reach?"

The salty old sea hand slogged down the last of his beer before staring out into the evening light with a furrowed brow. "Hard tellin' Jack. If she isn't, she's damn close."

Lieutenant Sifton interrupted the exchange by clearing his throat. "We'll do better than speculate," he said with a firm voice. He turned to Mr. Jacobs. "Point your guns, Mr. Jacobs and lay

A Bloody Beginning

us a shot. Let's see where we stand as the sun settles."

"Aye, sir," Mr. Jacobs wiped at his mouth with his sleeve and set the empty mug in his hand onto the deck. He went through the same process of checking the gun and timing the rise and fall of Allegiance's bow. Jack pushed the tips of his index fingers over his ears and waited for the rattling thunder of the shot to sound. A moment passed. The ship pitched forward with action from a wave before catching on the next and promptly rising again. At the crest of the next wave Mr. Jacobs tore at the firing lanyard and a roar erupted from the gun. Thick smoke blew forward and in the dying light of evening Jack could see a shower of embers fly out into the breeze as they sent a nine pound iron ball of fury whizzing through the wind. For the first time, Jack watched to see if their fire had any effect on the ship they had been pursuing for most of the day. His heart thumped, then thumped again. He relaxed his hands and unplugged his ears. The sun was now gone from the sky and the only light remaining was a dim glow. A plume of seawater gushed skyward just behind the privateer's stern. Jack's heart thrummed again, faster than before. Their target was almost in range.

"Almost within reach," the lieutenant grumbled before extending his telescope and peering through it. "And they know it too. Sorry sacks of moaning Frenchmen, they are probably cursing just as hard as we are." He collapsed the telescope

A Bloody Beginning

and tucked it smartly into the breast of his dark blue officer's coat. "If only we had more damned daylight. We'd have her dead to rights. With the weather at our back, we could land shots on her stern at will. Damn!" He turned to Mr. Jacobs a released a deep sigh. "Make ready for another. I won't part with the last sighting of her without reminded them we are here."

"Aye, sir," Mr. Jacobs rasped as Jack and his mates were already hard at making their gun ready to fire again.

The last notes of light faded fast from the sky while a tapestry of stars spread overhead. The moon wouldn't show itself for some time, and the seas surrounding Allegiance had turned from a bluish gray capped in white to waves of inky blackness rising and falling all around them. Lieutenant Sifton ordered another round to be fired from the chase gun, and the cannon spit a brilliant flash into the dark. Visibility was gone now, and the only means with which anyone had to judge if the shot had any effect were by sounds. They were too far to hear the iron ball splash into the sea, but if they scored a hit, Jack assumed that the sound of smashing timber would meet their ears. In between his tasks at the gun, he stole looks over the bow. A trio of dim yellow lights floated through the darkness, too low to be stars. Without warning, one of the lights disappeared, followed by another. Soon, all three lights were gone.

"Now is the time, lads," Lieutenant Sifton said in a low voice. "Keep your ears keen for any change, and your eyes peeled for any sign. If they try to come about on us, it will be between now and the rise of the moon."

CHAPTER 19

'H.M.S Allegiance'
30 March 1770
27 Degrees 2' N, 65 Degrees 7' W

Darkness had closed in around Allegiance. With moonlight still a few hours from revealing itself, the only aid to vision was a warm yellow glow from lanterns hung by the mast and a spill of light emanating from the hatchways fore and aft. The silence was eerie. Not a soul dared raise their voice beyond a whisper for fear of missing some audible indicator that the French privateer they were pursuing had heaved over to turn on them in darkness. But for the wind playing on her sails. and the sea breaking against her bow, the frigate plied her way through the night in near total silence. Jack waited, his heart beating in jaunts of rapid succession while Allegiance's bow rose and

A Bloody Beginning

fell with the waves. After the light of day had given out, Captain Williams had ordered a reduction in sail. It made sense in Jack's mind, plowing forward at a mad pace in total darkness when they could no longer see the enemy was a good way to wind up foundering on rocks.

Every hand remained quiet in the warmth of the evening. The footsteps of officers making their way in between the foc'sl and quarterdeck echoed over the ship as she slid through the dark sea. Ropes and timbers creaked and groaned under the strain of wind and waves, water lapped gently at the sides of the hull. At Lieutenant Sifton's order, there would be no bells until the moon was out and darkness had passed. Jack strained his ears to hear any out of place sound, any sign that the ship in front of them was making to turn, but he could hear nothing except for the sounds of Allegiance. Whispers passed among the crew. The idle hands lining the weather rail had been turned to and filed below to stand ready by the guns. It would be a long night of watchful waiting and listening, but until the moon rose to bathe the world in its silvery light, every hand waited with expectant vigilance.

"They're going to turn on us in this darkness," John Long whispered in a distressed voice. "We should still be firing at them."

"Into the darkness? What good would that do?" Slop whispered back in an annoyed hiss. "Stick ter what ye know, cully. Heaving gun tackle, that's what yer good for."

A Bloody Beginning

"Same as you, Slop, 'cept I eat less fer it!" John Long hissed back.

Jack's face flushed with anger at their petty squabble. "Both of you, can it! You want the mate to hear and come slash you both with his starter?" He whispered louder than both of them. "You both heard the captain. Keep your ears sharp for anything out of the ordinary!"

Footfalls clomped across the deck. Jack knew what was coming before he turned to see the tall hat of one mate making his way toward them. He swallowed hard as he realized he had been the last one speaking.

"Last orders I heard was silence fore n' aft, or didn't ye lubbers hear?" the petty officer hissed in a raspy whisper. His face was obscured by shadows cast by the lantern hanging on the foremast, but the silhouette clearly showed a length of rope with a frayed end dangling form his grip. "Keep yer mouths shut or I'll beat the four of ye's bloody."

Jack felt a flush build in his ears. The petty officer's shadow loomed over him and his messmates. He waited to feel the biting sting of the mate's starter, but it didn't come. The warmth in his ears continued to build, they felt hot to the point that they were tingling. He turned and looked at his messmates. Their stares had shifted away from the irritated mate and drifted to somewhere out in the darkness that surrounded Allegiance.

"Did you hear that?" Slop whispered in a rasp.

A Bloody Beginning

A heartbeat of silence elapsed. The sound of seawater parting under the bow rushed up to meet the soft brush of wind against canvas. Jack held his breath. Something was off. Out of place somehow, he just couldn't pinpoint it. He stared out into the dark as his stomach tightened into a knot that stole the breath from his lungs. A flash erupted, followed by another, and then a third and forth. Each flash bared the image of a ship in the distance for a split second.

"They've turned to and they're firing! Get down!" the petty officer screamed as a hollow shriek tore through the darkness, its pitch rising in tone and volume in a terror invoking crescendo.

Jack felt an impact against his side. An arm wrapped around his chest and tore him from his feet down to the deck planks. Allegiance shuddered as the shrieks of incoming fire culminated in a series of crashing impacts. Jack pressed himself hard into the deck until wood grain bit at his skin and he was sure that an imprint would be left on his flesh for the rest of his life. The sound of shattering wood filled his ears as wave after wave of concussive power rippled through every part of his body. He felt his innards tremble. Men screamed and cried out in vain attempts to warn their shipmates. More howls signaled a continuance of the barrage and Jack braced himself for the impact that would be his end. He imagined the iron ball that would slam into the bow railing just under the chase gun he and his friends were huddled around, the force

A Bloody Beginning

would shatter the oak timbers around them and send jagged shards of wood slicing into flesh. Allegiance trembled with another series of impacts while more shouts rose from her deck. Jack squeezed his eyes tight as if to shut out the reality of what was unfolding all around him.

Another shudder seized Allegiance and the sound of twisting and cracking wood fibers sliced up into the dark sky. Then, as quickly as they had begun, the horrid howls ceased. For a heartbeat, the ship was silent but for the patter of falling debris. Jack felt the falling of tiny fragments of their ship drop like rain. A scream boiled through the unsettling quiet. Moans rose from amidships, and Jack lifted himself from his sprawled position behind the bow chase gun to brave the scene of what had just occurred. As he opened his eyes, he could see that the arm which had dragged him to the safety of the deck belonged to his friend Matsumoko.

"Are you alright?" Jack asked helping his friend from the deck. "Are you injured?"

Matsumoko patted over his torso and checked his limbs in a quick survey. "Unscathed," he replied flatly before turning back to Jack, "and you?"

Jack hadn't even thought of his own wellbeing. He patted his torso and checked his arms and legs in the same manner Matsumoko had. There were no pains other than his knees which had hit the deck with the force of his weight and that of his

A Bloody Beginning

friend's. He had emerged unscathed. "I appear to be whole and no worse for the wear," Jack said.

The booming sound of Captain Williams' voice interrupted their exchange. He shouted from the quarterdeck as though he was trying to relay a message all the way back to New York Harbor. "Lieutenant Sifton, damage report if you please!" A pause settled over Allegiance and the sound of footfalls through the dark announced someone's arrival.

"On your feet sailors, on your feet and to your stations. This isn't over," the voice was thick and deep, though unrecognized to Jack. "Mr. Jacobs? Are you about?"

Jack chimed in after a heartbeat elapsed without an answer, "He was just here, sir."

"No need fer sirs, lad. I'm Mr. Sorel, Gunner's Mate," the voice growled back. "Was he 'ere when the incoming fire landed?"

Jack nodded in the dark and then replied in a shaky voice, "Aye, he was, Mr. Sorel."

"Get to your stations lads, I'll figure out what has become of the ship's gunner," Mr. Sorel replied. A sense of urgency cut into his voice as another pain wracked groan lifted on the air.

Jack looked to his messmates. Matsumoko was close at hand, but John Long and Slop were nowhere to be seen. "Where is Slop, and John?" Jack asked his friend.

Even through the darkness, Jack could see the change in Matsumoko's typically stony expression. He met his friend's stare at the deck right by

A Bloody Beginning

where they had both just been taking cover. John Long's tall, thin frame lay just out of arms reach from where they stood, his body disfigured and covered in blood. Jack stooped and pulled at John's shoulder in an effort to rouse him. "John we have to get below…" His voice trailed as John's body rolled with limp slackness and revealed a face and chest riddled with jagged shards of wood. Next to John, Matsumoko checked on Slop, who was sprawled in an awkward face down manner with his right arm twisted around behind his torso. Matsumoko stooped and lifted Slop's shoulder only to lower the heavy young man's upper arm back where it had come to rest. Matsumoko uttered no words, he only rose to his feet and offered a solemn shake of his head.

"Never mind them, lads," Mr. Sorel growled, "I will handle this. Get below and get your gun ready to fire. We aren't finished here, likely jus' gettin' started."

"Hands to the braces!" a booming voice cried out from the quarterdeck. "Bring her about larboard, hard over and beam reach to the wind! We'll be fer answerin' their volley!"

A lantern swung freely in the hand of someone coming forward on the starboard side of the ship. Orders snapped into the night with every few paces from the light bearer and soon he was standing in front of the foremast holding his light high and peering toward Jack, Mr. Sorel, and Matsumoko.

A Bloody Beginning

"What have we here?" the voice belonged to Lieutenant Sifton. "You lads get below deck and get your gun ready to fire. We're coming about to meet that privateer and we'll need every gun to pummel her."

Warm yellow light from the soot-stained globe of the lieutenant's lantern bathed the foc'sl and brought the carnage into stark focus. Jack lost his breath as the light touched John Long's remains. His lanky messmate had been killed in gruesome fashion with large shards of wood still protruding from his face, throat and chest. Blood matted his dark hair and still wept from a wound in the side of his neck. The grisly scene didn't end there, though. As light stretched from rail to rail on the bow, the mystery of Allegiance's missing gunner was solved as Lieutenant Sifton paced his way from the foremast to the chase gun. A huddle of bloody uniform heaped along the larboard rail had caught his eye and he hastened over to check on the disposition of his fellow officer. He lowered himself to one knee over the mass of bloodstained flesh and fabric. Jack watched as he extended one hand to check the motionless gunner for vitals.

"Mr. Sorel, get these men below. There is nothing more we can do here, he is dead," said the lieutenant as he stood and faced back toward Jack and Matsumoko. Allegiance began to groan as her hull shifted direction. She was coming about to bring her guns to bear on the enemy ship.

A Bloody Beginning

Below deck was a scene of chaos, as Jack reached the bottom of the ladderway he soon discovered that several of the impacts he had felt were direct hits that Allegiance had sustained on her starboard battery. He hurried forward toward the larboard gun number seven with Matsumoko following close behind. As they passed, he saw that starboard gun number eleven, nine and eight had all received direct hits. The gun carriages were splintered to shards, their cannons cracked, and their crews decimated. Bloodstains on the planks underfoot confirmed to Jack that Mr. Jacobs, John Long and Slop had not been the only casualties. Long faces met his gaze everywhere Jack looked.

"Larboard battery, run out!" Lieutenant Sifton's voice thundered through the gun deck.

Jack and Matsumoko hurried to their gun and quickly made ready to fire. Though there was only two of them, they were able to remove the gun's tompion and heave on the tackle lines until the iron cannon was in the firing position.

"Where is the gun captain?" Jack asked Matsumoko as they were both doubled over and recovering their breath. His friend could only shrug his shoulders and shake his head. Another look around the deck revealed to Jack that the blasts effecting the now disabled guns had not been the only hit Allegiance had suffered. In several places, the hull timbers were shattered in between guns, each visible hole had a similar gruesome scene on the deck in front of it. "I think

A Bloody Beginning

we're on our own, Matsumoko," Jack said through a panted breath. He forced himself upright and staggered to the rear of the gun in search of the gun captain's spike. Jack had seen the petty officer retrieve it from a small peg embedded into the wood of the carriage frame several times. He found the shiny steel instrument and proceeded to pierce the powder charge. With the end of the wire spike, he dragged a small amount of course powder in the same way he had seen done many times over. He cocked the striker and took the firing lanyard into a loose grip.

"Gun one ready!"

"Gun two ready!"

The gun captains shouted out their preparations in turn. Jack's blood lit with a burning fire as if set by a charge of burning powder. He squeezed his hand around the firing lanyard, careful not to pull until the moment arrived.

"Gun four ready!"

"Gun five, ready!"

Jack's hands went cold. His eyes locked back to Lieutenant Sifton who stood rigid near the aft ladder, a grave look on his face.

"Gun six ready!"

Jack shouted for all he was worth, "Gun seven, ready!"

Another shift in Allegiance's decks signaled that she had made her turn and would be coming to bear on the enemy ship. Jack's heart pounded in his chest. His mouth went dry and his tongue grew thick. He exchanged a knowing glance with

A Bloody Beginning

Matsumoko, both friends instantly understood that this moment may be among the last they shared together. Lantern light flickered through the gun deck, a dim, warm yellow light that caused long shadows to wobble and dance along the wooden world that contained them. The last of the battery reported their guns ready to fire. All eyes turned outboard through the narrow gaps between cannons and gun port frames. Inky black seas rolled alongside Allegiance as she plied her way toward the enemy. Glimmers of silvery moonlight became visible. It bathed the empty space of sea in a bluish silver glow and sparkled along the surface of washing waves and exposed the white foam that capped their crests. Jack stared out of the gun port in front of him, his eyes searched the moonlight for any sign of their target, in his heart he half hoped that the privateer had slipped from their reach.

The moonlight revealed her sleek lines and bluff stern. A battle ensign flew from her her after line as the rear of her frame slid into view. Jack tried to swallow but found that his throat was seized. Breaths came only in forced ragged jaunts. The privateer's gun ports were still open, the ugly snouts of cold iron protruded through the side of her hull with a dim glow of lantern light behind them. He heard shouted commands and the rattle of fast spoken French.

"Piss on you all, bunch of dandies!" a sailor from Allegiance's gun deck shouted. "Tell your king he can lick my ass!"

A Bloody Beginning

The lone insult that flew from Allegiance caught Jack off guard. Despite the tension, the overwhelming experience he had already been through, and the fact that it was not over, a smile spread across his face. A chuckle wriggled its way free from somewhere deep in his belly and, bewildered, Jack found himself stifling a laugh as he leaned close to the twelve pounder cannon next to him. The insult echoed in his mind and his laugh grew stronger. He tried to suppress it, but to no avail, it only came on all the stronger. His laugh boiled up and escaped in a raucous snort that refused to quit no matter how he fought against it.

"Jack?" Matsumoko asked in a hiss, "What is the matter with you?"

Jack fought his laugh down to a chuckle and chortled as he struggled to speak, "He told him… He yelled for them to lick… his ass!" Another wave rendered Jack unable to speak any further. His nerves were on fire. He knew that this was not the time, nor the place for such a ridiculous cut up, but the tension that had gripped him all day long had finally found an escape and he could not cease. To make matters worse, with a bleary, laugh induced tear filled eye, he spied Matsumoko smiling broad and fighting away a laughing fit of his own.

"Ready at the guns! Larboard battery!" Lieutenant Sifton's voice roared through the gun deck and brought a sobering wave of reality to Jack and Matsumoko. "Fire!"

A Bloody Beginning

Jack shifted his feet and checked to ensure Matsumoko was clear of the path of travel. He clenched the firing lanyard in his hand and gave it a tug sending gun number seven of the larboard battery into a violent stab of recoil. The rest of the battery fired alongside them and the bitter taste of gunpowder hung thick in the air as the deck filled with a near fog of smoke.

"Reload!" a voice shouted from near the fore end of the gun deck.

Jack sprang into action. The intensity of the battery firing had rung his bell somewhat and he felt more than a little woozy after the burst of action that interrupted him cutting up with Matsumoko. He swabbed the gun barrel, Matsumoko loaded a bag of powder. Jack rammed the bag. Matsumoko loaded a wad, Jack repeated the ramming, then a ball of round shot was loaded. A roll of thunder caused Jack to pause for half a heartbeat, except it wasn't thunder. In an instant, Allegiance's gun deck was thrown into mayhem. An explosion of wooden shards erupted aft. The sound of iron on iron rang like a monstrous church bell. Another impact send splinters of wood careening through the ship, then another. Jack forced himself back to his task, he plunged the ramrod down the cannon's bore and seated the final leather wad. Together, he and Matsumoko heaved at their tackle lines until able hands from nearby guns were able to lend the strength of their backs and arms to the two lone gunners.

A Bloody Beginning

"Fire when ready!" Lieutenant Sifton screamed forward through the bedlam of the gun deck. "Keep firing lads! Pour it to them!"

When the cannon seated forward Jack took a cursory look at each side of the gun carriage before pulling the firing lanyard in an unceremonious jerk. The cannon roared and belched sparks and floating embers in a cloud of smoke and fire. More guns aboard Allegiance fired in singles and pairs, their booming reports drowned the cries and wails of the wounded, but each for only a moment before the songs of agony returned. The gun deck had become seven fold the scene of carnage Jack had witnessed on the foc'sl. Sailors tore about the deck, going through the process of reloading their gun and firing. Muskets and swivel guns erupted from up on the main deck, their reports seeming like pathetic impressions of the big guns. Another impact tore into Allegiance's side, this one dangerously close to Jack and Matsumoko. The deck heaved under Jack's feet and threw him flat onto his back. His face felt hot and a stinging sensation radiated through his right ear. Panic laced through his veins. He fought to stand. Another vicious impact threw him from one side of the gun deck to the other. He pulled himself forcefully back to his feet, desperate to see if Matsumoko had been hurt by the blasts. Shouts and screams cut through the smoke and spent gunpowder hanging in the air. Embers floated on the air like dust motes. Jack

A Bloody Beginning

fought his way across the deck and ran face first into his friend.

"Jack! Are you hurt?" Matsumoko asked.

Jack was shaken by the sight of his friend, gunpowder and blood stained his face. "I'm fine, I think. But, what about you? There's blood…"

"Not mine," Matsumoko replied. He reached up and touched Jack's ear, withdrawing a hand covered in deep crimson. He grimaced at Jack. "Almost took it clean off."

Jack shook his head, they had no time to dawdle over a cut on his ear. "The gun! We have to keep firing!"

Panic had set its gnarled grip on Jack's mind and dulled his senses. He fumbled the ramrod in his effort to swab the cannon and had to take it up from the deck. Once Matsumoko loaded the powder charge, Jack rammed the bag down and prepared for the next step. A single gun roared from across the sea gap, it was followed by the now familiar sound of a careening cannonball that smashed into Allegiance somewhere above deck. Jack stuffed the ramrod into the cannon and tamped the twelve pounder shot twice before the deck heaved violently over to one side and he and Matsumoko both found themselves face down next to the heavy wooden gun carriage. All around them the sound of straining beams and creaking planks indicated a massive strain on the ship. It sent icy chills through Jack's blood. He fought his way to his feet and hoisted Matsumoko onto his. Through the gun port, all that could be seen was dark open ocean.

"Able bodies! I need able hands, now! The helm's been shot away! Get to the tiller in the officer's ward to brace it!" a thundering command came from somewhere aft, though Jack could not see the source, he heeded the call.

"Come on, they need help!" He shouted to Matsumoko. Together, the two friends made their way through the devastation of the gun deck and into the officer's wardroom where a pair of carpenter's mates were struggling to seize the tiller as it slammed against one side of its brace beam with the force of the entire ship and the sea bearing against it.

"I've got wooden blocks, we need to wedge one in place and then heave the tiller over so she is centered, or we won't be able to regain control of the ship!" One of the carpenter's mates shouted, "You two," he pointed at Jack and Matsumoko, "get hold of that tiller shaft and hang on for dear life! You need to steady it while we get blocks on place or one of us will be losing a hand in the trying."

Jack looked up at the overhead timber as it remained hard over to one side under the pressure of the ship's wild turn. He reached up and put his weight against it with both hands while Matsumoko did the same. At first, the timber seemed to be held over under its own force with nothing required from either Jack or Matsumoko to keep it in place, but with a tremor from the ship

A Bloody Beginning

the thick beam jumped into their weight and nearly threw them off of their feet.

"I said hold it steady you two!" the carpenter's mate howled. "Let us get the first block in place and then we'll help you heave her over to center!"

Jack doubled his effort and the next shudder of motion from the tiller beam was dampened by a heave of effort that tested Jack almost to the last of his strength. The clatter of a mallet filled the recesses of the wardroom's tight quarters and both carpenter's mates immediately moved to help Jack and Matsumoko heave over the tiller beam. The first attempt met with resounding failure. Jack strained against the wood until his vision started to darken until one of the carpenter's mates tapped him on the shoulder.

"Easy, lad," he said, "let's give it a minute and try to heave her over when she naturally gets a bump from the action of the waves." Just as the mate had predicted, with a sway of Allegiance's deck, the tiller beam slackened and separated from the sidewall of cabin. "Now!" he shouted. All four sailors three their full weight and strength against the hard oak beam until it clattered against the block already hammered into place. With three of the four remaining to hold pressure against the tiller, one of the mates slipped away and wedged a block into the brace beam before hammering it snug with a heavy mallet.

"That'll do, lads," the mate said. Small satisfaction was shown on his face, and Jack quickly understood why. They had put a

A Bloody Beginning

temporary fix in place for one of probably a hundred problems, and the rest still remained unattended. "Topside, all of us. We need to make sure the French haven't come about to press the fight."

On the main deck, Allegiance looked far different than the orderly military vessel that had become Jack's home over the last month. Rigging hung in tatters, tangled and criss crossed in an awful mess that spun Jack's mind as he tried to think of setting things square up in the tops. The main deck was in just as much disarray as the gun deck and the rigging. Sections of bulwark were blown to shatters, lengths of railing were splintered and missing. Sailors assisted their wounded brethren to places of relative safety while others were removing the bodies of the dead and placing them in a row along the starboard side of the ship. Jack searched outside the shattered remains of the deck for any sign of their enemy. He found only dark seas and glimmers of moonlight half obscured by a thin layer of cloud.

"Lieutenant Sifton, a damage report if you please, and see to a party aloft to sort the rigging. We need to get underway for the nearest friendly port." The captain's voice was tight and proper, giving no indication of sorrow over their defeat.

"Aye, sir," Lieutenant Sifton replied from amidships, close to where Jack and Matsumoko were surveying the ship. "Bermuda, by my

A Bloody Beginning

reckoning, but we will have to get our bearings to confirm."

The captain only nodded his assent and paced to the fantail. He stood alone in the moonlight. Jack assumed he would be brooding over the confrontation, but was shaken from his thoughts for Captain Williams by the first lieutenant's voice.

"You," he nodded the brim of his hat toward Jack, "get aloft and help the other top men sort out that mess. The captain wants us underway, and we need to be rigged to sail by daylight, lest the enemy turns on us again to resume the fight." He looked to Matsumoko for a moment and then continued, "Take your friend here with you. I don't know the casualty count yet, but I am sure we are shorthanded in the tops."

Jack knuckled his forehead. "At least four down on th' gun deck that didn't survive, sir. Prob'ly three times that is wounded."

The lieutenant shook his head and let a deep sigh escape. He looked over the side and then back at Jack. "You're one of the press from that whaling tender. I'm sure this was your first real confrontation at sea."

Jack nodded. "Aye, sir. It was."

The lieutenant let a hand come to rest on Jack's shoulder. "Well, you survived," he took notice of Jack's ear and grimaced, "not quite unscathed, but near enough. If it wasn't for Allegiance's gun deck, we would have really taken a hammering. You lads did a fine job below deck. Next time, we'll have the jump on them and you'll get to see how

A Bloody Beginning

Captain Williams intended for that fight to unfold."

Next time. The words hung in Jack's mind like the arm of a pendulum, swinging back and forth but refusing to leave its course of travel. The officers intended to press their pursuit. "N-next time, sir?" he asked in a cracking voice.

"Undoubtedly, lad. Next time the captain will be having his say, and we won't let those frogs get a word in edgewise. Wait and see." Lieutenant Sifton replied. He gave Jack's shoulder a squeeze before letting go to point aloft. "Alright, lads, up and after it. There is work to be done."

CHAPTER 20

'H.M.S Allegiance'
31 March 1770
27 Degrees 2' N, 65 Degrees 7' W

The early stretches of dawn found Jack high aloft above Allegiance. He straddled the yard atop the main top-gallant and fed the end of a line through the leeward head black. Below, a crew of men were preparing to raise a spare yard for the mainsail which had been battered beyond repair in the exchange with their enemy. Arm length over arm length he fed the line through until it stretched below to where the men in the maintop could grab hold and begin to haul the end to the capstan. When his part of the task was complete Jack took a moment to gaze outward to the open sea. The first notes of dawn were hearkening the day, gold and pink mixed with the last remnants

A Bloody Beginning

of night and chased stars from the sky. It was a welcome sight, after the night he had survived, Jack felt fortunate to gaze on the sunrise again. But, he longed for the quiet solitude of the mornings before their encounter. Shouted commands echoed through the rigging and out over the sea.

"Jacky!" Bowline Bob shouted from the maintop, "any sign of the frog?"

Jack panned the horizon in all directions and found nothing but lightening pink and gold bordered the gray blue of the sea. There was no sign of any other ship. They were again alone out on the swells. Jack turned and shouted below, "No sign of sail anywheres I can see."

Bowline Bob nodded his head and puffed at his pipe from the maintop. All around him sailors were working at un-fouling the tangled mess that had become of Allegiance's rigging. She was still under sail by tops and jib only, her rudder locked by the blocks in the officer's wardroom and her steerage was being accomplished only from manipulation of the jib. The main deck was another swarm of activity, mallets clattered, saws bit into timbers and men labored at every whim of the carpenter's mates in order to set the ship to rights. Jack had heard several of the men lament over Allegiance's condition, but none gave voice to any doubts of her seaworthiness. They would make port in Bermuda and refit their vessel in order to finish the task of finding and taking the captain's French prize.

A Bloody Beginning

Matsumoko climbed his way upward from the maintop, sure of foot and sure of grasp, just as Jack expected he would be. He joined Jack at the cross tree without a word of greeting, blood still splattered on his face. The two friends sat in silence for a long moment while Allegiance maneuvered her course northward in search of Bermuda.

"A refit and then back at it," Jack said with a sigh, "in a quest for a ship that has already defeated us once."

Matsumoko gave Jack a long look before averting his stare out over the sea. "The officers seem confident that we can take her, if they can manage to approach in advantageous circumstances. It is possible, strategically, for a smaller vessel with fewer guns to take a larger one. I've heard tales, and even seen it myself on one occasion. But, we were bested last night, there is no doubt of that."

"Did you hear the final tally?" Jack asked. "Of the dead and the wounded?"

"Eleven dead, three times that were wounded," Matsumoko replied. "Not a small figure by any stretch, but not enough to render the ship incapable."

"That was horrid, Matsumoko. Cannon balls smashing into every part of the ship, men wounded and screaming, blood everywhere," Jack said with a long breath. "I don't understand, why the captain would want to continue hunting that ship."

A Bloody Beginning

"It smacks of ego, yes," Matsumoko said in reply. "But, it is also his duty. He is honor bound to protect English shipping on the high seas. If that rogue privateer were to continue her tirade, how many more ships would they harass? He doesn't account the casualties as a greater cost than failing to fulfill his duty."

Jack thought it over for a long moment. Below them, the mainsail yard was being hung into place and secured with chain scantlings. They would make fast progress back to Bermuda, where their helm and many other fixtures could be repaired properly. Jack hoped the ship's stores would also be replenished, though he doubted the captain would sacrifice the speed he had gained by throwing much of the weight overboard. A brisk wind out of the south and west filled their sails and Allegiance plied her way forward. A mixture of emotion still played tug of war in Jack's soul. He despised the service of the king, but he had grown used to his shipmates. The loss of both Slop and John Long weighed on his mind. He had grown fond of them both, Slop, strong as an ox and overly fond of his vittles no matter how unpalatable, and John's reserved and often timid nature. He mourned the losses.

"Hey, yer two!" Bowline Bob shouted between hands cupped around his mouth. "L'tenant is callin' fer ye's ter report ter the quarterdeck. Better snap to! He seems ter be short of patience about now!"

A Bloody Beginning

The two young men exchanged an apprehensive glance before making their way below to the main deck. It was uncommon for the ship's first lieutenant to address crewmen on the quarterdeck. More oft if there was an order to be passed it would go through one of the warrant officers and then their mates would address the sailors directly. Jack wondered what the fuss could be about. Had his and Matsumoko's work aloft not been satisfactory? Did the lieutenant spy them high up and sitting idle? When the line had been run, and the hands below had been heaving the main yard into place, he had assumed there would be other tasks for them aloft, else one of the mates or Bowline Bob would have shouted for them to come down. His stomach twisted at the thought that he may be in some sort of trouble.

Jack and Matsumoko knuckled their foreheads as they reported to Lieutenant Sifton at the fore edge of the quarterdeck. An awkward silence hung over the three of them while the officer appeared to be sizing them both up and weighing what he wanted to say.

"Allegiance has need of capable hands, we lost more than reckoned in the exchange with that Frenchman and the ship's doctor has just informed me of the numbers of wounded he believes won't make it to port before they depart from the living world," the lieutenant said in a ragged voice that spoke to his exhaustion. "You both handled yourselves extremely well last night, both up at the foc'sl and below on the gun deck. I am told

A Bloody Beginning

that you two kept your gun firing, by yourselves, even after we received fire from the enemy. That is commendable. The king's service needs more men just like you two. Brave, strong lads who refuse to shirk their duty even in the face of death. I have a mind to rate you both able seamen, by necessity if not by virtue. Though I will say that both of you have earned it."

Jack couldn't believe what he was hearing. He had been at sea for less than a month and the lieutenant was making him and Matsumoko both able seamen! It was the mark of a sailor who knew their way around the ship, and could complete tasks that Jack hadn't even witnessed.

"We are in sore need of capable hands aloft, whatever skills you do not possess, I am certain you will make short work of learning. Now, back at it, men," the lieutenant said with a slight grin. "We have sea to cover before we gain Bermuda, and I need every hand available to get it done."

"Aye, sir," Jack said before knuckling at his brow. He dipped his head slightly and retreated to the waist with Matsumoko at his shoulder.

"Able seamen, that's a bump in wages from landsman for me, and a share for both of us if we take that prize the captain has his eye on," Matsumoko said as they worked their way up the shrouds. "The other thing is, as able hands, when we make port, we'll be considered for shore leave."

That thought stuck in Jack's mind from the time they began their ascent until they topped the shrouds. Shore leave. Perhaps even shore leave in

A Bloody Beginning

Bermuda. But, if he and Matsumoko slipped away from the ship's company, they would then be stuck on an island in the middle of the ocean. Unless they made port on the continent, and that was not likely until after the captain found his prize.

Allegiance shifted course northward, and Jack took to the main shrouds with the rest of his remaining messmates. There was still much to do, and Bermuda was days beyond the horizon. As promising as the thought of shore leave was, absconding in the middle of the Atlantic was a sure way to meet the same fate as Bitter End Bill. Flogged around the fleet. Sunshine, fresh wind and focused labor kept Jack's mind steady as they drummed a course for safer waters.

Promotion, and the promise of the horizon lifted his spirit. When the course sails were hung from their newly installed yard, and sheeted home with freshly threaded lines, Jack took a beat to pause and stare out at the horizon. It seemed to stretch on forever, blue skies and blue gray seas for as far as he could see.

"Dreamin' of home lad?" Bowline Bob asked as he hoisted himself to the topsail yard with a grunt.

Jack shook his head. "Yes," Jack answered with an absent-minded mutter as he took in the stunning sight of glittering waves surrounding the ship.

"It'll be awhile before ye lay eyes on Boston, lad. Best come ter terms with it, eh?" Bob grumbled as he settled himself onto the yard.

A Bloody Beginning

Jack shook his head. "Boston isn't the home I was talking about."

Bob met Jack's eyes and a broad grin spread across his bearded face. "Really, lad? Then pray, what home is ye referrin' ter?"

Jack spread his arms wide gesturing to the open expanse of sea surrounding them. "This, Bob. This is home now."

Bowline Bob, in his typical fashion, stuck the stem of his pipe into his bite and nodded with narrowed eyes. "Aye, laddy. A sailorman yer'll be."

Thank you for reading the first installment of

The Patriot Sailor

Keep a weather eye out for the next title in the series.

At the Mast

Find my other book series, sign up for newsletter announcements including special releases, sneak peeks, and giveaways. Just scan the QR code below.

Follow along on Facebook and Instagram for cover reveals and special announcements.

If you enjoyed this title, please be sure to leave a review on Amazon or Goodreads.

Made in the USA
Coppell, TX
18 November 2024